OUR THREADS SPAN LIFETIMES

OUR THREADS SPAN LIFETIMES

AMANDA PANAZZOLO

Amanda Steps Beyond

For
Adrian, Jessie, Dominic and Annika

First Printing, 2022

This book is a work of fiction set within true historical periods. Whilst a few
of the historical characters and events, are real, the majority are fiction and
any resemblance to actual people, or events, is purely coincidental.

Publishing Company: Amanda Steps Beyond

This book is a work of fiction set within true historical periods. Whilst a few
of the historical characters and events, are real, the majority are fiction and
any resemblance to actual people, or events, is purely coincidental.

.

I

Prologue

Of all the animals I've ever encountered, spiders intrigue me the most. Their magnificent talent is confidently displayed for the astute observer. I find them mysterious creatures, their power and ability to be self-sustaining greatly impresses me.

With mindfulness, spiders use their silk, generated from their spinnerets, making sure that the first placement of their precious thread is precise as it forms the foundation of their home and subsequently, supplies all of their nourishment. Perfectionism is a necessary requirement, because if the first placement of a silk thread is incorrect, then subsequent threads will be ill placed and the whole project becomes ineffective. The unproductive web may be abandoned by the builder, a waste of their precious energy and resources.

In the next incarnation, using careful and methodical skills, a beautiful network of threads are created, the hard work is done and the spider can relax, it waits for the spoils of her endeavour to arrive. Innately, she knows her web will provide all of her needs.

Phase 1: Chapter 1 Ailie

Roughly a thousand years ago

I sit Araignee, my rag doll, on the floor next to me. I'm on a carpet, contemplating what I want to do with my life, but at five years old, I don't know what my options are. My body has been sending me clues from the past. I have muscle memory of past occupations in my right hand. I can feel a stick, moving in and out through strings.

I'm a daydreamer, I want to travel the world. But up until now, the world has been my home in the village of Breteuil. What lies beyond the forests and lakes surrounding our village, I don't know, but I'm particularly fond of the animals that I have seen, especially the spiders, they are the most creative creatures in the animal kingdom.

According to my father the carpet I'm sitting on is a masterpiece. Our family crest was woven by skilled artisans using the most colourful silks. The carpet features two impressive lions, one crimson, one golden, surrounded by two intrepid knights. I imagine the knights existing harmoniously with the lions, nobody would be devoured. I've never seen an actual lion, they are few and far between in the French countryside. They look pretty ferocious though. The golden lion sits majestically on a royal blue background, appearing to swim in a bottomless azure ocean. That's what I imagine anyway, I've never seen an ocean, Papa has described them to me though. "I'm going to make a beautiful carpet like this one day." I announce to my father.

"Don't be stupid girl, you can't work in the village, with common people. You're destined to become a lady and you'll find your entertainment at Court, with the other ladies."

After Papa dismisses my artistic dreams, I inch closer to the fireplace to inspect a messy web that a Daddy Long Legs constructed near the log pile. It isn't as precise or as intricate as the webs I'd seen in the garden this morning. However, the Daddy Long Legs doesn't have to rely on a beautiful web to provide its food, it merely sets a trap. The gangly spider actually leaves its web and when a misguided fly wanders by, the Daddy Long Legs wraps its silk around the prey to keep it in place. When it's ready to eat, it delivers a lethal dose of poison to its victim, via its small fangs.

While I'm playing in the garden, I notice a magnificent and complex web built between the branches of a blue berry bush. As I tilt my head to the side I see droplets of dew on the strands of silk giving the illusion of rainbows encased in miniature glass cylinders. The shiny filaments sparkle like one of my mother's jewelled pins which she wears on special occasions. I observe the beautiful black creature resting in the middle of her web as she waits patiently for her prey. I marvel that such a small being is capable of creating something so lovely. I don't care what my father says, one day I'm going to create something just as beautiful.

My parents named me Ailie. They never let me forget that I was born of great privilege. I've never wanted for anything material. However, my mother and father are very busy attending to household business with the servants and answering to a special man who lives far away. Papa calls him the Duke. I will spend two years maturing before I'm considered a suitable candidate to become a lady of Court, like Mama. Well, I won't be a lady right away, but I will begin my training. For the time being I'm free to roam the vast grounds of the chateau when the weather is fine, or when the weather's inclement, I play in front of the giant hearth with my toys, mainly Araignee who is a natural confidant.

I share all the family gossip with Araignee, including Mama and Papa's daily business of course. Then we discuss what the maids have been up to in their free time, they don't have any free time, if I'm honest and I generally am. I can only reveal a level of certainty garnered from my own experiences which thus far isn't much and therefore my perspectives are quite narrow. But I often ponder, with Araignee's help, why the young village messenger rides to the chateau on a regular basis to visit my nurse, Florrie and doesn't have a message to pass on to Papa.

The way they look at each other, or don't as it happens is so peculiar. Mama has instructed me to always look people in the eye when speaking to another. Sometimes Florrie and the messenger make excuses to go into the garden, but I don't understand why she makes such a fuss about needing to go outside. It's her job to collect vegetables and herbs, isn't it? After the messenger has ridden away Florrie's face resembles the crimson lion on the hall carpet. Letting out a nervous giggle, she'll quickly smooth her skirts while resuming her duties in the kitchen.

Sometimes I wander into the immense kitchen to see if there are any scraps of food lying around on the preparation table. I'm always looking for food and a bit of company. The day has stretched out, it's a long time between meals for a little girl. Bietriz, an excellent cook and Florrie, are busy preparing the meals. When they're finished cooking, they'll clean the kitchen, attend to the mending, haul water from the creek which flows at the bottom of the garden, gather wood for the fires from the stack stored in the stables, clean the great hall, and the bedroom loft upstairs. There's barely any spare time for them to relax and enjoy themselves as I do.

Now and again, Bietriz suspends her activity, gathers me in her arms, I like that immensely as my parents don't embrace me much. I snuggle into the crook of her neck. You know, she smells of sweet onions. She hands me the large wooden spoon letting me stir the pot of stew which bubbles over the fire. All the while looking out for my parents, it isn't a suitable game for a noble child.

Amis, the page boy runs errands for Papa, sometimes for Mama. He helps in the gardens and the stables. He sleeps on a hessian sack in a small room next to the kitchen on the lower floor. It must be crowded in there, he shares the room with Bietriz, Florrie, and the hounds. I sometimes feel sorry for Amis, he doesn't get to see his mama and papa very often, but he never shares his feelings with me. Like a ghost boy he lives with us, at the same time his life is detached from mine. We barely speak to each other.

Papa, Roger Belanger the First, Lord of the Manor possesses vast tracts of farmland and by deed owns the serfs who farm the land and pay him taxes. He answers to the Duke of Normandy who in turn answers to the King of France. By law, Papa also owns Mama, Lady Isabea. However, within their marriage, Mama exercises more power than she is granted by the wider community. For several days at a time, she enjoys the role of Commander of the Chateau while Papa is absent for business at the Duke's chateau. Well, he mostly visits the Duke's chateau. At other times he lies to Mama of his exact whereabouts.

I'm an only child though not through lack of trying by my parents. They dearly want, no require a son, to carry on the Belanger name and since my birth, Mama has been pregnant three more times, yet all three babies have returned to God. The last infant, a boy, almost lived to full term. He was delivered stillborn by the local midwife. Besides the grief of losing another baby, Papa's hope to raise a potential knight, an inductee into the Duke's Inner Circle of Knights, shattered again. His dream is to sire an heir who will someday protect France, the local region, and our land, from invasion by the fierce and brutal North-men. He used to keep his true feelings hidden to himself until that is, he stumbled home from the tavern one evening, stinking of ale, he didn't mince words.

I'm on the stairs playing with Araignee, I hear Papa trying to talk to Mama.

"Try to understand woman, producing a girl preordains us to pay a dowry to prospective in-laws. We will lose out from such a transaction." I don't really know what he's talking about, his tone is not light. "Even though we're wealthy and can easily afford to pay an endowment, it will ease my mind when our sons become knights at Court. It will give us the prestige we deserve. You have to try harder to keep with child." He demanded as he hit the table with his fist, but his hand caught the edge of the table and although he was too drunk to feel it now, it was going to be throbbing blue in the morning.

"I'm sorry that I've let you down." I hear Mama apologise meekly. Papa doesn't spare her feelings, but continues her torture.

"Our sons will be dubbed knights and lords, we'll earn a sizeable income to help increase our coffers. We'll gain more importance in the region. I will be important at Court, damn it. What's not to understand." Mama weeps quietly as Papa strides away without consoling her.

It's amazing considering their relationship, but Mama fell pregnant yet again and we collectively held our breath in order that the pregnancy holds. However, conception is just the first of many hurdles that the embryo has to conquer, once to term the baby has to survive child-birth with little available medical intervention. There is only so much a midwife can do to help.

Papa and Mama marvel at my strength to endure. I've become a strong, inquisitive child and although I'm given many freedoms, I know I'm cherished and valued, though not through outward displays of affection. Perhaps I'm hoping that they do indeed love me, their only offspring. However, I'm merely a female child after all. When Papa realises yet again that there will be no son and heir, I feel the waves of his disappointment wash upon my soul. I always feel less than because of my gender.

Our chateau is located in the village of Breteuil, in Normandy, North Western France. The township recently engaged a clergyman to preach in the new church built from local timbers which kept many of the local carpenters employed for months. Father Jean relies on tithings from his parishioners to feed and clothe himself. He doesn't receive a wage from the Bishop. Luckily our parish is wealthy and he's able to live somewhat comfortably compared to the priests at poorer parishes. Visiting priests know straight away that Father Jean is residing in an affluent parish given his his robust frame and ruddy complexion. He really likes his food. When he's not presenting a sermon he eats and drinks heartily. As he gnaws on a bone at the end of his meal Mama complains to Papa about his atrocious eating habits.

"He's a greedy little man. Look at him, shovelling his food into his mouth like that. It's a wonder there's anything left for us to eat."

"That man really appreciates my cooking." Bietriz boasts to Florrie as they clear the table.

A jovial man, Father Jean, a farmer's son, isn't as educated as the city priests. He can't read well and when he refers to the church Bible which come to think of it, is seldom, he only recognises two, maybe three of the Latin words here and there. He is a good listener though. He remembers the Bible stories from his childhood and recounts them with enthusiasm at Sunday Mass. The story I like the most is the one about King David and the spider's web. It was definitely the spider who saved the day for David, it's web found intact over the entrance of the cave he was hiding in. The soldiers who were after David believed that he couldn't be in there as he would have had to tear the web in order to hide in the cave. There was obviously some kind of magic going on in there.

"When we require a more intellectual counsel, we ride to Rouen for an audience with the Bishop, a more learned fellow and more our rank in life." Papa says to a fellow parishioner after Mass. "You don't have to suffer through those silly spider stories with the Bishop."

"Yes indeed." The parishioner searches the throng for his wife.

The townsfolk consist of artisans, merchants, and craftsmen. A guild of weavers oversee the practice and administration of the main craft in the village creating exquisite tapestries and embroideries. However, the guild members rely heavily on grants and commissions from the royal houses to stay afloat and to provide a sustainable living. They also promote their products with the local gentry to encourage them to buy from the Breteuil weavers rather than their competitors in Paris. Our weavers are fast gaining in reputation for their beautiful fabrics, tapestries, and embroideries, and one day I hope to be one of them.

But these are dangerous times and the North-men have been able to penetrate areas not yet fortified by the knights. One man in particular, Guilliam the Conqueror, has begun to strengthen the area to lessen the impact the Vikings have on our region and even though I am a little young for such conversations, Papa once tried to explain the situation to me as we ate dinner.

"He's in denial that he has a little girl who isn't interested in the local politics." Mama whispers to Florrie as she brings in some stewed pears for dessert. Luckily Papa doesn't hear her, he continues his diatribe.

"Guilliam is a worthy competitor in battle. So much so, that he rules over the Duchy of Normandy under the Capet King of Paris. One day he'll do battle with the English Army across The Channel to become the King of England, mark my words on that. King Capet has little control over the lands outside of the capital and therefore Guilliam, for all intents and purposes, is the King of Normandy."

I pick at my food and try to understand what Papa has said. Out of the corner of my eye my attention is drawn to a black spider scuttling over the floor. I forget about the Duke and the King. I want to scurry over the floor and travel far away but the furthest I have ever been is to the village.

The village tavern is a bustling and noisy place especially on market days. On the posh side of the inn wealthy lords, counts, and barons, clutch their takings, as they discuss business and drink ale pomme. The market stall holders congregate on the other side of the tavern with farmers, peasants, and other merchants, who discuss their business, farming processes, and the unusually warm weather. The farmers grip their takings while another vessel of ale hops from one punter to the next. Vagabonds and vagrants scam townsfolk with games of chance as they lurk on the peripheries to determine which drunken man will temporarily forget to protect his earnings. Some of the women also find market day particularly lucrative as they make their entry in the evening, by then the men are well lubricated and merry from ale.

I overhear Bietriz and Florrie talking about Papa as they stir mutton stew in enormous iron pots. I know that I shouldn't be listening. I can't help myself.

"They say he pays extra for his favourite girl not to go with anyone else for the night. He can be so deluded sometimes. You know Florrie, he thinks that if he pays more for her she won't give him the pox which he could pass on to Lady Belanger."

"It isn't right for a nobleman of his standing, to be seen cavorting with strange women from the tavern a place of such intense gossip." Florrie and Bietriz both agree.

"But he slinks off with Sabine into the depths of the dark alley."

"Her dark alley don't you mean?" Florrie snorts.

"Have you seen that one Florrie?" Bietriz allows a smile to cross her lips as she continues.

"No, I don't think so which one is she?"

"She's the tall one, a big bosom, long ebony hair, and olive skin, unusual features for someone 'round here. Anyway, I hear he waits until his cronies are plastered and when they're making their way home he gives Sabine the signal, a scratch on his left ear lobe and she meets him outside the northern wall of the tavern where he roughly lifts her skirts and has his way with her."

"Oh yeah, I know her." I hear Florrie snort again from my sentry behind the door.

"Apparently, when life's good, he's gentle and caring, but when the Lady of the house has miscarried, there will be no male heir to bear his name, he's rough as guts. He fiercely yanks Sabine's long hair down her back and when he's done he gathers up his trousers. And get this, as he walks away he throws his coins at her and with super fast reflexes Sabine catches the purse expertly in her left hand, turns and walks away to her next customer."

"Is that so? How do you know all of that then?" Florrie is curious to know the truth as they continue their work.

"Sancta, from the Du Bois's Manor, she told me."

"Ah, figures. She's such a gossip."

I run to my room covering my mouth, with my hand. I don't understand much of what was said. I hope Araignee can fill me in.

Chapter 2 Allie

Over a thousand years later

I'm sitting in front of a chrome television set, upon a cream shag pile rug, constructed from man made fibres, purchased from the Loco Rug Emporium on the Golden Mile. As we drive into the small car park, we see a massive sign with a picture of an old guy, in a large floral print shirt, who by the way looks a little weird, typical messy hair and horrifically bugged out eyes. The marketers have employed the required stereotypes, to convince my parents, that this guy has no business running a successful enterprise and they need help urgently so that he can continue to remain open.

"Honey look, its closing down we should be able to get a good deal on a rug here don't you think?" Mum inspects the faded fluoro signs while Dad shakes his head in disbelief.

"Darling, don't be so stupid. This place has been closing down for almost a year now. Who knows what the real price of a rug is?"

We know that Mum makes all of the decor decisions, but to show some fairness, she still wants to hear Dad's hypothetical opinion.

"What about this cream one, it'll go well with the sofa, don't you think?

"Cream? With two kids? No, how about this red one with the gold and navy stripes?"

"God no. I think well get this cream one."

I slowly nibble fish fingers and avoid paying any attention to the steamed carrot sticks lined up like soldiers on my acrylic plate. I've been told off more than once for spilling tomato sauce on the rug. I sit on top of the pink stain so that I don't have to look at it and feel guilty, Mum does that for me. She gives me the evil eye every time she sees me sitting on the rug with my lunch. I wipe my finger around the edge of the plate, stopping the sauce from dripping again, then I lick my finger.

Wacky cartoon characters noisily enact outrageously dangerous scenarios while I absently munch on crumb shards surrounding the nameless fish species. To my left sits my favourite toy Arachne, a plush spider won by my dad on on the laughing clowns at a country show we went to once. I didn't look at them, I don't like clowns. Ever since that day Arachne has accompanied me on all of my adventures. She's a useful tool to scare my easily flappable mother which is hysterically funny to me, apparently not to Mum.

With stealth, I place Arachne on the seat next to her while she reads the latest copy of her favourite travel magazine. I crouch down below the arm of the chocolate brown sofa and gingerly move one of Arachne's limbs, ever so slightly to mobilise my mother's peripheral attention. Sensing movement, Mum turns slightly and sees a large hairy spider on the couch, she screams, jumps all the way over to the next cushion practically out of her skin.

"Oh my Goddess Allie! Stop doing that it scares Mummy."

I sprint to my bedroom giggling, the look on my mother's frightened face. Despite the commotion her glass of red wine manages to remain upright and the carpet continues to be cream in colour with only minor pink stains. Arachne lays inert on the floor her role complete.

I was born Allie Jane Bell. And no, not Alison, everyone thinks my name is shortened. My ancestors were predominantly Irish, my aunty has discovered that our lineage spans back to William the Conqueror in medieval France. However our family now lives in an outer suburb of Adelaide, on Kaurna Country. Our house is close enough to the coast to go for a swim, though not that far from the tree lined hills. If we want to go for a hike, or a picnic, its not that far either, we don't do any of these activities very often. Typical of our middle class suburb our house is a modest three bedroom brick dwelling in front of a small backyard lined with a few fruit trees, apricot, mandarin, and lemon. There's an area of lawn to play on and a large circular clothes hoist which holds all of our washing in fine and windy weather. The clothes line is an excellent swing for entertainment purposes when no-one is looking of course, I usually get caught having fun though.

"Get off that bloody clothes line Allie! You're stretching the wires. Get off now!"

My Mum Isabelle is an incessant traveller and often leaves home with little to no warning.

"Oh, didn't I tell you I'm going to Sydney next week to visit Helen?"

"Oh, didn't I tell you that I'm off to Costa Rica tomorrow with Sandy? We're doing a cacao ceremony, its going to be amazing. I thought Daddy would've complained again. Sorry, I thought you knew."

She doesn't really prepare for travel. If she's going to a health retreat for a week of relaxation, meditation, and yoga, she gives the same consideration to a three week trek across Peru. She doesn't have to give it much thought though, her luggage is always ready and waiting for departure. It winks at her from the top shelf of her walk-in wardrobe.

"Take me away from here." It says, she gladly obliges.

Mum doesn't have the usual type of escapist addictions that my friend's mothers have like alcohol, prescription pills, and other drugs like excessive shopping habits. She has though, escaped from her assigned reality since my younger brother Finn and I were out of nappies. With friends dotted around the world, she rarely stays in hotels alone not that that would worry her, she's happy by herself and also in a crowd. When she is by herself it's never for long, she attracts interesting people and they always want to hang out with her, she's so fun to be around. These people from around the world who I don't know get to see the best side of my mother. I get a bit jealous when I hear about these people. Although I don't name it jealousy, I just feel mad.

My Dad Rodger, most people call him Rod, not Rog which is weird, works in "financial development". He uses air quotes when people ask what he does.

"Basically I help people build wealth and find ways so they pay as little tax as possible." He explained to me when I had to do a class presentation about my family the next day. He's available to his clients at all hours of the day and night. He says he works hard to keep up with Mum's travelling expenses. Actually she has so many frequent flyer points and spare bed options, her expenses are minimal. Dad noisily protests her absences especially to their female friends, and his co-workers, he craves their sympathy, at the same time he also secretly enjoys the freedom an absent wife gives him. It's not just Dad who likes his freedom. We can all relax when Mum's away.

Mum has too much energy. Given it's the late 1970's she's not a stereotypical domestic wife and mother, her energy fills the house and beyond. She has way too much vitality to be sustained by one man and two small children, our suburban family, our mundane routines. We throw open the house and let the breeze carry her restless energy away. As much as she needs to get away, she travels to allow us a sigh of relief as well. We love her dearly but she can be too much for us. To stay sane she needs to constantly leave.

"Oh my Goddess, Peru was so amazing! It was great meeting new, and such interesting people. We had a really great time. Gael was hysterical, a real hoot. It's a shame she lives so far away. Oh well, I'll just have to visit Lima again soon." She mentions this just as the boom gate rises on our way out of the airport car park.

"But we've just picked you up. At least wait until you've walked through the front door before you start planning your next trip, hey?" Dad's a bit angry. I can tell by the way he's gripping the steering wheel, his knuckles are white. Mum is still talking about Gael, a raw fish salad, and a drink called Pisco Sour, both of which don't sound tasty to me.

When we were small Mum employed a housekeeper to look after us while she was gone. She understands that she leaves a domestic hole in the family so to appease her guilt she filled the mothering gap with an older lady from down the street. Flo is a fair bit older than Mum and Dad. She cherishes her time with us because her own children have grown up and left home. A widow of ten years, her husband died in a car crash which has obviously left a massive hole in her life, and her heart. Sometimes to sooth herself, she imagines Dad is her husband, and Finn and I, are her new children. This doesn't help though it just makes her sadder. Filling the space our mother leaves fills a space in her own heart.

Flo stays with us until Dad returns from work in the evenings, sometimes a bit later. After his dinner they drink scotch on the rocks, she flops on the couch, Dad slumps on his recliner with the foot rest extended, the television blares The Price is Right, they chat easily. They both try to figure out the showcase together, they rarely succeed.

"I thought the luggage would've been cheaper than the oven." Flo muses.

"Yeah, me too." Dad knows all too well the true cost of the luggage. During the ad breaks Flo regales Dad with our comings and goings for the day. She's very loyal to us and doesn't go on about how we ate through all of the cream biscuits leaving the yucky malt ones. After the show she downs the rest of her tipple and returns to her mostly empty two bedroom house around the corner.

"Time to feed Ragno." She waves as she leaves to feed her ginger cat.

"Has Flo gone home Dad?" I ask when he comes into my room to kiss me goodnight.

"Yes, she's gone to feed her feral cat."

"He's not feral Dad. Mum says he's spirited. Did you work out the showcase tonight Dad?"

"That "spirited cat" hissed at me the other day and no the luggage tripped us up again. Go to sleep Allie Peg."

Dad kisses my head and returns to the void in the lounge room.

As Finn and I grow older Flo only cleans our house for a few hours every week, sometimes more often during the school holidays. We still treat her like a member of the family though. We always make a fuss of her on her birthday. She reciprocates on our birthdays with a small present and a thoughtful card. It kind of makes me sad. She puts a lot more thought into her cards than Mum's quickly scrawled impersonal message of "Happy Birthday, Love Mum and Dad." Dad, Finn, and I take Flo out to dinner to the nicer of the two cafes by the beach, the one we always go for special occasions. The owners Bruno and Nicki think they know our family quite well. I don't know if they remember Mum at all, they rarely see her.

"Whose birthday is it this time?" Bruno asks as he plonks bread sticks and a fancy bottle of Italian water on the table. There's a naked lady painted on the label. Finn struggles to turn his head away from her as he nibbles his bread stick. I look at her briefly as well and wonder when I will have breasts like the lady on the label. Sometimes after the meal, they bring out free drinks for Dad and Flo and ice-cream with chocolate topping and crushed nuts for Finn and me. Nobody knows if Bruno and Nicki understand Flo is our housekeeper and not our grand-mother, how would they know? Flo's serene energy fits so perfectly within our household, I like it this way.

I imagine Flo is my actual mother. Flo's a natural at mothering. She's just like the mothers you see on television commercials.

"She's been tamed and conditioned by the patriarchy." Mum declares to the television as a calm and perfectly made up woman in a pristine white blouse presents her overly happy family with an Italian feast. I like being cared for like the kids on the spaghetti ads. It may sound harsh to say but it seems to me that Mum is a poor substitute for Flo's "conditioning".

On rainy days Flo's the one who sits on the carpet with me and helps me with a puzzle, or plays board games with me. Flo's the one who prepares our lunches with the occasional surprising treat from the confectionery aisle, she hides them in our lunch boxes with regularity.

"Mum, you should have seen how Flo made The Kings of Spain's daughters' magic crystal ball from the chocolate frog wrapper and then she told me the rhyme about the silver nutmeg and the golden pear. I wish you could have been there to see it."

"It takes a village Sweetie." Mum says when I tell her about my activities with Flo. But it isn't a village it's just Flo creating these memories for me. Flo is the one.

We sometimes sit on the cream rug in the lounge room while Flo sits on the sofa working on a cross-stitch sampler while she watches us play, her daily soap opera is silently playing out on the television.

"Why can't we hear what they're saying." I ask her. I'm curious about what's being said.

"I don't think it's suitable for you two. Some of the words are a bit "spicy"." Flo struggles to find a child friendly way to explain the sexy dialogue.

"Don't you need to hear what they're saying to know what's going on though?"

"Well, I can tell what they're up to by their expressions and anyway the story doesn't change that much over time. I've been watching this show for so many years now that I can predict what they're saying with a great deal of accuracy."

"You can listen with the sound up if you want to. I won't listen to the spicy bits, I promise."

"You don't need to listen to their ridiculous problems concentrate on your tower."

I watch the silent men and women stare into the middle distance while I build my tower. I'm bored with my bricks and the television. I turn my attention to Flo. At first the colourful threads catch my attention and even though this isn't the first time she's sewing at our house it seems to be the first time I've taken an interest.

"That's pretty. What's the wooden ring for?"

"It's to hold the fabric in place and keeps it evenly stretched." Flo continues to sew.

"Oh!" I watch Flo methodically stitch small lines into the calico. "Can I have a go? Please, please, pretty please, with sugar on top?"

Flo bends down and reaches into her sewing bag. I'm giddy with excitement, I'm not entirely sure why. She retrieves a small square of cloth, a spare needle, and a selection of threads. My eyes light up in anticipation, I'm actually going to sew something. Then the doorbell rings. Flo has to leave to answer the door.

"Salesmen, ugh, at least I can tell them to rack off. Good thing I don't have any authority around here. It saves me a lot of time and trouble." As Flo resumes her seat and before she's had a chance to instruct me, I've already threaded the needle and made three straight stitches in the fabric. "Wow, how'd you know how to do that?" Perplexed, Flo studies me.

"I dunno. I've never done it before." I shrug my shoulders and continue sewing while she shakes her head, she gently laughs to herself.

As the soap opera's closing credits run down the screen Flo gets back to her cleaning while I continue sewing.

"Well I best get on the house isn't going to clean itself now, is it?" She always says that.

After she cleans Mum and Dad's bedroom, Flo sits at the dressing table and stares into the mirror while she inspects the expensive, mainly untouched bottles of perfume bought hurriedly from airport duty free shops. Mum rarely uses these fragrances. She doesn't want to take them away with her in case the bottles smash in transit. It happened once before and her clothes smelt like a department store cosmetic section for months. Flo recognises the same expensive brands from the ads in the glossy magazines left lying around for her to tidy up.

Flo pulls the antique silver comb gently through her greying hair as she imagines a different life for herself. She gives herself a little spray of Miss Dior to cheer herself up and places it behind the rest of the full bottles to disguise its measured demise. She slowly winds the gold cylinder revealing crimson lipstick and smears the waxy stick over her ageing lips. The lipstick bleeds into the lines around her mouth so she wipes the excess lipstick with the tip of her finger and examines her art work in the mirror. "Not bad." If only she was ten years younger, no maybe twenty years younger, this could be her life.

Through the mirror she gazes at the giant four poster bed behind her. Flo examines the gaudy red, pink, orange, and lime green bedspread embroidered with gold and silver threads, filmy white netting falls from mahogany posts. The bedding's not to her taste. She imagines her younger self lying naked on the bed on a hot night. Rod by her side making her feel more alive than she's felt for years. She slides her hand slowly down the front of her throat letting it rest on her crinkly chest as she examines herself more closely in the mirror. She never used sunscreen in her youth and now she's paying the price. Flo feels hot and fuzzy in her sensible knickers while the prickly feeling travels throughout her torso. Her hand lands on her curvy stomach, menopause has not been kind to her and now she's not feeling kindly towards her ageing body. Her reflection exposes her blushing cheeks.

"Don't be so dopey you old......" Her voice trails off. "As if Rod would look at me." Isabelle has long tanned legs, long flowing shampoo commercial hair, mischief in her green eyes and a contest winning smile. Then there are Rod's glamorous co-workers to compete with, if he desired. "No, he's not looking your way fatty."

A tear falls onto her hot cheek and suddenly she feels fatter, older, and more frumpy than she has in a while. Flo glances at the perfect couple smiling at her from their honeymoon photo which sits next to the nest of perfumes. A good looking couple in white cotton, large toothy smiles, tanned skin, a turquoise ocean and white waves tumbling freely over hot sand. She feels another tear drop. Flo grabs a tissue from the silver embossed tissue box, catches the tear just in time and gives her nose a good blow. It smears the newly applied lippy all over the bottom half of her face. She takes a deep breath, fixes herself up and walks home without saying goodbye to anyone.

I'm not the only one that misses Mum's affections. My brother Finn suffers as well. He's often sick with sore throats and colds of varying degrees. Dad's so busy with his clients he often overlooks his illnesses and when he does notice him it's with some disdain.

"Oh, for God's sake Flo, leave the boy alone, he's a hypochondriac." He considers Finn's ailments a weakness, mostly an annoyance.

But luckily for Finn, Flo loves to mother him.

"I've just made him a pot of chicken soup with fresh ginger and garlic to help him feel better. They say chicken soup cures everything. Well, probably not everything I should imagine." Flo laughs as she carefully carries the tray into Finn's room.

Dad shakes his head as he studies the financial section of the newspaper. The Price is Right is just about to start and he wishes Isabelle was at home with him co-parenting their children instead of gallivanting around the world. Their relationship has suited both of them at times, the arrangement is somewhat accepted. It isn't an ideal situation by any means there's a lot of silent suffering in our hearts.

Not so deep down I'm unhappy as well knowing my parents are pseudo separated. I guess I hide it well, no one asks me how I feel. We don't inhabit a normal family home. I don't know what a normal family home even means. What does normal mean anyway? It really is a stupid expression. An absent mother and a workaholic father leaves me with the feeling that love is elusive, ephemeral even. I have to reach for love from people like Flo when it's available. Come to think about it she could so easily leave as well. It's best not to get too attached to anyone. It's too confusing for me to think about for the most part. I pretty much avoid relationships with too many new people.

Chapter 3 Leo

Leo stands by the stable door observing a barn owl swooping down to the muddy ground to collect her prize, a small brown field mouse. He holds his breath until the owl returns to its oak perch. It's early evening and he's meant to be inside with the rest of his family. Leo always longs to be outside no matter what the weather's like. He watches the owl swallow the tiny creature in one gulp and then as it travels inch by inch down the bird's gullet. His family knows that the house can't contain him, his universe is in the free spaces provided by nature. Leo's younger brother Hugo, a pudgy boy, sits happily inside at the dining room table finishing his own meal and probably some of Leo's food as well. It would have been left behind as Leo isn't a big eater.

Leo is six years old, in less than a year he'll leave his home, his mother, his father, his younger brother, and his nurse, to live in the chateau owned by the Duke. He'll become a knight in training, a destiny he aspires to, just like his older brother Miché who is eight years old. Hugo has another three years to enjoy life as a child and whether he consciously realises it or not, he never wants to relinquish the title of baby of the family.

Their father, Arthur du Bois the First, a nobleman, holds the office of provost, the executive who deals with the administration of the Lord's holdings. This role entitles his boys to serve as knights for the Duke. Their mother Catarine du Bois, a petite yet strong willed woman has survived two difficult births and a third slightly easier birth. She like most of the village women has also suffered several miscarriages. Throughout her confinements and subsequent labours she is strong in fortitude and courage. When she finds herself pregnant again, God willing, Catarine prays every day for a little girl to be born, as the du Bois name is well and truly secured by her three older offspring. Her dream is to share a little girl's companionship in her large testosterone filled manor house. Somehow she suspects the fourth baby kicking fiercely inside her belly is also a boy.

In the manner of the owl Leo understands the cycles of the earth and the heavens even from his considerable youth. To everyone's amazement he remembers that when certain flowers are abundant, particular spe-cies of butterflies and bumblebees simultaneously flutter around those plants. He knows that once every four weeks the moon is round, fat and bright, making exploring the garden at night time so much easier. From the doorway of the manor he searches for the North Star before making his way barefoot onto the cool grass and once again he is at one with nature.

Leo makes his escape into the wilderness from the boundaries of the shared family bedroom at the top of the stairs, there he plays unmissed for hours. Exposed to the elements, Leo knows that when the wind is warmer and the air feels full that it will rain soon. A quick glance at a line of ants scurrying uniformly to their home in the ground confirms that fat drops of rain will pound his strawberry blond head which he doesn't mind at all. In fact, he loves the sensation of rain on his skin and the ozone scent which releases from the earth as it opens and receives it's quenching. The squelch of his bare feet in the damp grass and ooze of mud between his toes is exquisite.

Sancta his nurse realises the finery required for a noble child isn't appropriate attire for Leo who prefers to play in the garden and muck around the stables. He has ruined much of his silk clothing so she decided to dress him in the drab brown woollen trousers and grey tunic common amongst the village children. Actually, Leo prefers to wear these clothes as he finds his house clothes too restrictive. She knows that she'll have to change him into his silk finery for occasions within the house, for dinners, and visits from other noble families. She thinks these changes of clothes are worth the effort, she's not a fan of mending his clothes. After breakfast when Leo's playing outside in his village clothes, Catarine heads outside for some much needed fresh air as the poorly ventilated house is full of smoke from the kitchen and dining hall fireplaces.

It's a still day with no breeze to sweep the smoke through the narrow glassless windows. As she reaches the doorway she sees a small village boy chasing butterflies in her garden, he's too small to be Auberi their page boy.

"Hey you!" She tries to gain the child's attention. Initially the boy doesn't respond, he's so absorbed by his butterfly catching mission. As she's about to shout out again, Catarine recognises the shape of the face that presses up against hers in evening embraces and she realises she's calling out to her own son.

"Leo, come here!" She orders. "Leo!" With her insistence, he snaps back into the world and reports to his mother. "What are you wearing? From where did you acquire these clothes? I can't have my sons wearing peasant clothes. Someone from Court might see you."

"From Sancta, Mama." He is a boy of very few words.

"What is she thinking?"

With a frustrated sigh she leads Leo inside on a quest to find the nurse. It isn't hard to find her though. Sancta stands in the kitchen by the fire wielding a heavy cast iron pot while Yolant the maid chops vegetables at the table, they are preparing lunch for the family. With her small frame Catarine pulls Sancta aside after she has placed the pot on the fire and wiped her hands on her apron.

"Can you explain to me why on earth my son is wearing peasant clothes? These children are bound for Guilliam's Court. They cannot be seen in these horrible rags."

Silently Sancta points to a pile of fine clothes resting on a small wooden stool in the far corner of the kitchen.

"It's because of these, Ma'am." Piece by piece Sancta displays the clothing showing Catarine exactly where her son has damaged the cloth with his outdoor pursuits. Post scalding Sancta remains calm as she clutches a pair of trousers with gaping holes on the rear and grass stains on the knees. Then she holds up a shirt and searches for a tear in one of the sleeves. "Here it is, look at this rip." She places the last ruined shirt on the pile as she appeals to her mistress's bottom line. "Ma'am I have to keep buying more silk from Ottho's workshop to make clothes because the lad's clothes keep ripping."

Catarine is smart and canny, she knows that silk is expensive. The more money that's wasted on her sons, the less money she has to spend on her own dresses.

"All right, let him wear the peasant clothes in the garden, however he must be dressed in his finery inside the house or when visiting others. He can continue wearing his peasant clothes when he plays outside, but the minute we have visitors he must change."

"Yes, Ma'am." Sancta already knew these would be the conditions. She is vindicated. She curtsies then places the clothing back on the stool and resumes her duties.

Catarine is fierce when it comes to her staff and anyone who gets in the way of her family's progress to the Royal Court, they will be dealt with severely. As a loving mother she cares about appearances and her position amongst the Ladies at Court. It will not do for one of her sons to be known as the noble peasant. Her sons will be held in the highest regard possible so that she too remains in high regard.

Chapter 4 Leon

"Get your hair out of your eyes, for Mary's sake."

Leon's mop of red curly hair often falls into his deep blue eyes as his mother constantly reminds him. He loves playing outside by himself or with his older brother Declan, at their mother's insistence they reluctantly include their younger sister Claire, sometimes, well only when they really have to. He lives with his family in a cosy yet isolated white washed house at Flaggy Shore, County Clare, in Ireland. From their home the three children only have to address a small road and walk across a narrow grass verge to play upon a stony beach. The game they enjoy most is skimming pebbles across the water, it's usually too cold to swim in the grey ocean.

Abutting the house is a thicket of bushes where the boys invent games of brave knights who protect a strongly held fort constructed with dead branches from the ground to engage in sword fights, bloody battles. Battles which last until someone's sword cracks and breaks from strain or they're called in for dinner. Later in the evenings if they are still outside, Leon observes the barn owl fly to roost on one of the taller trees. He watches and waits for the beautiful bird to catch a field mouse or two. Leon loves this enigmatic creature especially when she's in full flight, her handsome wing feathers, large vigilant eyes, fixed on her prize and her balanced tail manoeuvring her in for the kill.

To augment their income Leon's parents let out the cottage attached to the side of their house as a holiday rental. Dubliners arrive in the summer to relax and swim in the ocean though they usually only dip their toes into the icy water. The tourists want to get away from it all, to appreciate the peace and quiet. But there's nothing much else to do at Flaggy Shore so the cottage chiefly serves as a couples retreat. Occasionally a family with small boys will stay in the cottage which is a real bonus for Leon and Declan as there aren't any neighbourhood boys to play with. On these occasions with two knights per army a real battle ensues and they don't have to be quiet for lovey dovey honeymoon couples. Separate base camps are decided and Leon and Declan hold the home turf advantage of course, they know every nook and cranny of the woods. When the same families return the following summer the boys continue their play from the previous visit without having to explain the lay of the land or the rules of engagement.

Cathy's glad her boys can entertain themselves outside for much of the day, their house is far too small for the rumble and tumble of three kids. Add a cranky husband under her feet on the weekends, its too much. Besides, they know that if they stay inside Cathy will give them a job to do, so it's better for everyone to stay in their respective zones.

Chapter 5 Ailie

I'm not scared of the spiders which lurk in the dark corners of the chateau or the ones that perch on the wooden beams in the stables where I play. In fact, it's just the opposite. I take Araignee by the arm into the outside world and I look for silvery webs to inspect. I see the various shapes and intricate patterns different species of arachnids produce and it occupies my time for hours. I study them while they are busily working at their craft and I realise they aren't wondering if they're good enough or worrying if they are being judged by others, they simply create, without doing so they won't survive.

I'm a bit of a loner which isn't helped by the fact that I'm an only child. I consider myself a friendly soul and despite stereotypes, I willingly share my small number of toys, bar Araignee. No one else can even think to want to play with her. When my parent's friends visit the chateau with their small children my small guests generally trust me to be genial and their parents find it easy to engage me in small talk upon their arrival. However, my special gifts and talents are not yet fully realised. I know from my interactions with other children that I'm quite different. I don't know how I'm different, I just sense it.

"Did you know, that female spiders lay thousands of eggs and then they die afterwards." I explain my findings to my friends. The other little girls don't seem to appreciate spiders, or their webs. "Do you know that spiders produce the finest of silks and they use their silk for different purposes, such as making their webs and wrapping up their prey."

"Oh, that's interesting." Edithe is just trying to be nice, I can tell. "Can I look at your dolly, I see that she's wearing a beautiful dress."

"Um, no, not right now, I may have another doll that you can look at." I don't want Edithe or any of the other girls for that matter touching Araignee. At this point I try to retreat from the frivolous chit chat of my peers and contemplate the beauty of the natural world. "I think I can hear Mama calling me." I want to make an exit. The children are confused, they can't hear Mama calling me. But despite or because I feel awkward, I excuse myself anyway and take a moment outside.

I appreciate beauty in all its forms and I try to be creative in many ways. I conjure up stories of mystical beings that I've witnessed in my vivid dreams, who then became actors in my adventurous tales. I enjoy impressing my stories upon anyone who's nearby. That means Bietriz and Florrie, who gasp wide eyed as my accounts and characters become more elaborate and magical.

"So, there's this place where the air is clear and there's a tall mountain. An eagle soars above the trees, different types of trees from the ones around here though. I haven't seen this kind of tree before. There's a wagon like object, I think that's what it is and it's been left at the base of the mountain. It's like a horse and cart, but not. Oh, I don't know how to describe it." I stop to collect my thoughts because I can't think of the right words. "....But it isn't a horse and cart. It has four wide wheels that are not made from wood and it doesn't require a horse. The people who have ridden in this contraption wear bags with straps on their backs and they climb the mountain for no particular reason, and then, there's a storm...."

I become anxious by my own story and when I look up I notice Bietriz wink at Florrie. Embarrassed, I hurriedly retreat to the garden while the women return to their chores. They are still chuckling over my wild imagination as I continue to ponder my weird dream. I breathe deeply so that my heart will stop beating so hard. When I calm down a little I start to softly cry, I can't tell you why I'm crying. My dream just made me sad.

There's a storm brewing outside and the air feels heavy. I can't venture outside so I mooch about the kitchen and try not to play under Bietriz, or Florrie's feet as they hustle to complete their tasks for dinner. I sing a made up song as I float aimlessly, "and I will la la la." As I flit around the periphery of the room I happen upon a small open box of ribbons and they immediately catch my interest. I sit on the stone floor and carefully pick out the ribbons one at a time. I inspect the fineness of the cloth and observed their delicate weave. I notice the brightness and richness of the colours blue, pink, violet and white, I marvel at how the colours shimmer in the light when I twist them an action which occupies me for some time.

The ribbons are a centimetre wide and around forty centimetres long and after I've inspected them thoroughly, I begin to place them into a neat pile. Six white ribbons positioned in rows on the floor. I begin to weave the pink one under and over the floor ribbons. When the weaving reaches the final supporting ribbon, I gather the violet one and begin weaving it in the opposite direction. After all the ribbons are woven into a small mat, I arrange it on the floor and admire my handy work.

"Bietriz! Florrie! Come and see what I've made." As I admire my work I wait excitedly but also patiently for the women to finish their tasks.

"My that's a beautiful inkle Ailie." Florrie gushes a bit too much for my benefit, although I appreciate her endorsement. Bietriz quickly glances at the woven creation and offers a terse response, I know she means well.

"Bonne." She has work to get on with. I recognise this small phrase as high praise and I smile at my first weaving project with pride. "Flo, I don't know why you're so happy you're going to have to buy more ribbon next time you go shopping in the village." Bietriz snaps at Florrie.

While the women return to their chores I run to the hall to compare my weaving with the Daddy Long Legs' web. There's no comparison.

"Mine is more beautiful." I say confidently to the disinterested spider. I can't be so sure when I compare my work to the intricate web in the blue berry bush. I remain victoriously inside the chateau, it is raining after all. I lay in my familiar spot on the carpet by the fire, place the piece of fabric carefully on the floor and gently stroke the cool silky material as I drift off to sleep. Just before I wake, I have another vivid dream.

I wander upon a weaver's studio where there are people working at their looms and in the beams of the ceiling is a spider web that appears to contain diamonds. It sparkles and glints in the sunshine and makes beautiful patterns on the ceiling. Most of the people who work in the studio are happily working, though there is a cantankerous ruddy faced girl, I can tell that she's been yelling and stomping her feet. One of her feet is turned inward, There's a dark scowl on her face because the supervisor has critiqued her work, he isn't happy with her sloppy weaving. He told her to undo all of the weaving she'd accomplished that morning. Then just her face appears and she's glaring down at me with flaming red eyes.

"Who do you think you are?" She hisses at me. Sweating profusely I wake with a start.

Chapter 6 Allie

Before I leave for school each morning I straighten up my bed, scrunch my pyjamas into a ball and shove them under the pillow. I position Arachne triumphantly on the top of the pile. I haven't always been so neat. Flo used to make my bed, now I have to do it if I want any pocket money. My faithful spider sits sentry until I return to collect in the afternoon. In the garden after school, I test the strength of a real spider's web with my toy as its expanse is wide enough to accommodate Arachne. The structure holds for a little while before tearing at the sides causing her to fall to the ground cocooned in sticky threads. I feel guilty as I peel my toy out of the web. I've had a hand in destroying a fellow creature's home.

I had the same feeling when I almost fell into a fast running creek. I had to take a wide berth around a thousand millipedes enjoying the damp earth.

"Just walk through them love. What are you doing? You're going to drown at that rate."

"I can't step all over them Daddy, they're animals just like you and me."

"Of course you can, they're just stinky millipedes. Now come away from the edge of that creek. You sound like one of those flaming Buddhist monks you see on the tele, sweeping the bugs off their path. What has your mother been teaching you?"

"Nothing. I just don't want to hurt the animals." Through my peripheral vision I notice the spider climbing onto the leaf that once held its netting and I feel better knowing it's survived its home-wreck. It's definitely the same spider, at least that's what I tell myself.

When I play outside Finn doesn't play with me. The moment he gets home from school he integrates with his bedroom, flops onto his bed and continues reading his latest book which is probably a different book to the one he'd been reading in the morning. That's why Dad calls me Tom sometimes. I prefer to be outside exploring rather than playing with the dolls I've been given in vain. In fact, Dad's secretly worried for my future or rather his future without me. He knows I carry my mother's DNA for adventurer.

"Don't ever go and travel like your mother will you, then I'll be left alone with the bookish child." I feel sorry for Finn, Dad just doesn't get him and Mum is always away. Just as well, he seems pretty self sufficient.

One of my favourite things to do on a sunny day, technically I know I shouldn't, is to take Dad's expensive camera from his office to photograph creatures I find on my quests in the garden. It's funny, he doesn't call it a camera.

"Has anyone seen my SLR? It was here yesterday." I hear him calling out to the spaces between the walls and I remember that I must have put it back in the wrong place.

"Here it is Dad, you must have forgotten that you put it here yesterday." I say pointing to the top of the small filing cabinet.

"I'm starting to loose my mind in this house. There seems to be a ghost moving everything around." Dad scratches his head and walks out of the room, the search for his camera is forgotten.

"Dad, do you really think there are ghosts in our house?" But he's already gone and I've forgotten that I am the ghost.

More often than not there's no film in the camera and I happily click away at an insect, a reptile or bird knowing there's no tangible evidence to spring me for my crime. The first time I heard the now familiar click and whirr of the film moving on the reel sent panic rushing through my body, I almost dropped the camera. I realised Dad would see my work and deduce that I am indeed the ghost that had procured his prize SLR, primarily wasting his expensive film. I quickly put it back where I found it.

I don't have long to discover my father's reaction to my misdemeanours after a family gathering at Grandma and Grandpa's house. Dad brought the SLR to take photos of everyone enjoying the day even though Mum is in Ubud for a silence retreat. Dad's twitchy, my cousins won't smile for the camera, Aunty Diane and Uncle Pat are having a really loud argument, it actually frightens me a bit. I'm not used to adults yelling at each other because my parents are rarely in the same house and barely speak to each other. I don't know why Mum had to go to a silence retreat.

Uncle Pat forgot to put the presents into the car after Aunty Diane had reminded him more than six times apparently and now Aunty Diane is embarrassed that she doesn't have their gifts to give to Grandpa. They've been fighting for some time before the argument escalates.

"You drink way too much! Its not a good look at this time of the day you know?" Pat yells.

"Well, you're lazy in bed, I'm frustrated and bored. What do you expect me to do?" Diane retaliates.

"Okay kids, lets go inside and look at the birthday cake." Grandpa quickly ushers us inside for the second time this afternoon and I wonder why we can't just sing the song, blow out the candles, cut the cake, and eat it, but apparently we have to wait for something, I don't know what.

Aunty Diane has a nap after lunch because she'd drunk too much wine and my cousin Millie says she always has a nap in the afternoons to escape from everyone. I wonder if perhaps Mum could do the same thing and then she wouldn't have to travel so much. Uncle Pat's temper has settled down so Dad snaps a quick couple of shots, remembering he has twelve frames remaining. Prematurely, the camera starts winding the film canister back to the start position and with a final flourish the container is ready to be removed from the back of the camera.

"This shouldn't be happening. There should be at least ten frames left." He mumbles while he scratches his head and places the exposed film into the front pocket of the camera bag, he re-loads the camera with a new roll of film. "Bloody faulty film roll, no doubt." I remember that I had been the one to use up the film and panic surges through my gut, luckily at the same time Grandma calls us to sing Happy Birthday. I'm loaded with the medicinal properties of chocolate cake and I quickly forget about my wrongdoing.

That is until Dad returns from the photo shop. He shuffles quickly through the glossy prints. There's Mum in one of the first few photos, she was at home for once. She's blowing out the candles on a shop bought cake. The photo was snapped in our kitchen at an inconsequential birthday, then there's some photos of me at my music night at school. I play the recorder and Dad's glad it's a photo and not a video so he doesn't have to endure the cacophony all over again.

"I think if we rounded up the neighbourhood cats including Ragno and played them like bagpipes that would have sounded better than those kids." He complains to Mum in the car on the way home.

"I think Ragno sings better than kids playing the recorders too." Mum agrees.

There's a photo of Aunty Diane with her hair in her eyes when she'd just woken from her nap.

"She's gonna love this one." Dad says to himself flipping through more photos. There it is, the evidence right in front of him. He isn't going mad after all, well at least not for that reason. The photo shows Arachne encased in spider's web followed by a photo of a real spider and some pigeons performing a mating dance in our backyard. Dad quickly recognises the garden edging that he installed the previous spring. "I didn't take these." He starts flipping through the shots again and recognition re-hinges him when he reaches the photos of the family smiling happily at my grandparent's house. "Allie, Allie, come inside for a moment darling."

When I skip through the lounge room Dad calls me over to inspect the photos and with a quick intake of breath I slowly walk to my father's side. Both comfortably seated Dad displays the pictures to me one by one pointing out interesting features along the way. We laugh at Mum's funny face as she blew out the candles.

"Is that spit on the cake? Look at Aunty Diane doesn't she look funny in this one?"

Then he reaches Arachne's photograph. "This is a lovely photo of Arachne. But I don't remember taking it and I know that no one else would dare touch the SLR so this is a mystery." I squirm in my seat.

"Oh, and look at this one. A ladybird, how pretty." My arm starts to itch and my legs want to run away. He starts flicking through my photos and makes complimentary comments about each one. I can't stand it anymore I have to say something.

"It was me. I'm the ghost. I took your SLR Daddy, I didn't mean to. I just wanted to take some photos." I stare at the checked pattern on my school dress and follow the lines with my forefinger, pushing the fabric onto my leg. "I'm so sorry Daddy, I won't do it again."

"Oh, Allie Peg I wish you'd asked me to lend you the SLR. I would have said no by the way, it was expensive and you need to be older to use it properly. We might see about buying you a starter camera for your birthday. How does that sound?"

I respond to my father's mercy by burying my head into his chest and squeezing as hard as I can. I'm happy to not be in as much trouble as I'd imagined I would be. I also have the realisation that life is slightly easier knowing that I'm the apple of my father's eye. I might not have a very loving mother, but I know that my father loves me.

The camera I receive for my birthday has four extra rolls of film. Dad warns me not to run through them too quickly, processing the film is expensive. I consider his advice and carefully think about the shots I'll take. Then Dad gives me some extra hints to help me take the best pictures.

"Frame your subject and remember I told you about the rule of thirds. Consider the available light and its direction." I'm feeling antsy. I just want to take photos, Dad's lecture floats above my head.

When he collects my first set of prints from the photo shop, Dad hands them over with ceremony. I quickly open the blue and white envelope to liberate my photos.

"What're these?" I quizzically regard the slot in front of the envelope.

"They're the negatives. Let's look at your photos Allie Peg, any good ones in here?"

I examine each photo carefully.

"What's that orange smudge at the top of this one?"

"That's your finger love." Dad smiles down at me and tousles my hair. Some of my photos show some promise, but there are two more photos with a finger print in the top right hand corner and couple that aren't in focus. There's a photo of the ground taken before I was ready, I'd pushed the button anyway.

"Here, this one's better." Dad sticks the photo of the white daisy bush to the fridge with the plumber's magnet. I smile at my first photo exhibition.

Chapter 7 Leo

As the second son of three boys, Leo is used to rough housing with his older brother. Most of all he loves to practice his swordsmanship with his replica toy. He's equally happy playing on his own in the garden with the hounds, Milo and Gross, the slower older and more greedy of the two dogs. His little brother Hugo doesn't venture outside preferring to occupy the space around his nurse's skirts. His mother has given birth to another boy Darri, who as she suspected is healthy and strong.

At this tender age Leo is afraid of little. He knows his family as trustworthy and he loves the animals in and surrounding the manor. There is one animal he is terrified of. Just before Miché leaves for the Duke's chateau to begin his training the two boys have one last adventure in the forest. Before they depart they covertly venture into the kitchen while Yolant and Sancta are busy cleaning in the main hall. They procure a napkin from the sideboard to cover some bread and cheese and they creep out into the woodland with their food parcel.

The boys have a great morning exploring the forest searching for mushrooms, they know not to touch them, their father has been explicit about their poisonous qualities.

"They can make you really sick in fact you could die from eating the wrong ones so don't go eating any. Besides, we can't have Miché falling sick before he goes to Falaise."

"Take that you devilish fungi." Miché slices the mushrooms with his toy sword, especially the red capped ones while Leo searches the trees boughs for birds.

"I'll be Sir Magnificent and you Leo shall be Sir Younger Brother. Together we will capture Vikings and put them to their death with our swords."

"I think I'd like a better name than that." Leo sulks while they ride imaginary steeds. With their heads held high one hand clutching imaginary manes, the other hand wielding their flailing swords, they ride amongst the tall trees. As they ride further into the forest they hear a snuffling sound and something scratching around in the leaves at the base of a distant oak tree.

"Listen Leo. Shh!"

Miché and Leo stop still in their tracks holding their breath so as not to make a sound while they listen intently. The snuffling and scratching sounds grow louder, the boys can see the dark shadowy outline of a wild boar in the distance. Once they recognise the beast they know its potential as a runner and a deadly hunter, they quickly turn on their heels and flee from the forest. The boar sniffs the air and considers the chase, when it finally commits it starts to slowly trot towards the boys which gives them a head start. Rapidly, the boar gathers haste and closes in on the boys' trail. The boys quicken their step and the race to the edge of the forest commences. They feverishly pray the boar will stop chasing them. They call upon God for the hounds to appear to their rescue. They haven't fully considered the consequences of their prayer.

Even though it's a cold day sweat pours from their red faces and mixes with the dirt they've collected from play earlier in the day. Only one thing is going through their minds and that is to reach the edge of the forest and to stay alive. It's imperative that they arrive at the manor grounds before the boar. Miché runs faster than his younger brother, he encourages Leo to keep up.

"Come on Leo you're falling behind. Quick, come on!" Suddenly, Miché trips over a large stick. "Shit!" He doesn't quite fall to the earth. He rapidly recovers his upright running position, he's lost ground though. The brothers sprint side by side. Miché's ego stings from the fall, he knows that he has to get them both out of the forest safely. The boys hear the laboured breath of the boar as he gallops behind them, they run even faster.

Finally they see the edge of the forest and the hounds come bounding over to join in the fun. Unexpectedly, the boar suddenly changes his focus away from the boys towards the dogs particularly concentrating on Gross who can't run as fast as Milo. The boar quickly catches up with the slower dog piercing his side with his sharp tusks and removes a large chunk of meat. The boys continue running towards the house knowing that the boar has injured their companion. Milo runs with them, he doesn't interfere with the boar's bidding. Gross cries out in pain as the boar squeals in victory. Gross becomes limp, he's dying and the boar satisfied with his kill, slowly drags his evening meal back into the forest.

The boys continue sprinting for their lives. They arrive at the house shaking but relieved they're alive. Immediately, Miché is worried about his imminent report to their father. How does he tell him that one of his hunting hounds has been killed by the boar? Leo hasn't thought about his father instead he is instantly grieving his beloved dog. It's the first time Leo has witnessed the death of a family member, even though he was one of the pets animals are his family and he loved Gross with all his heart. It's remarkable that he hadn't experienced more death in his family. Of noble stock he's been somewhat protected from the realities of life which affects so many of the villagers. Leo suddenly feels shock and grief engulf his body, bitterness rises in his throat, he retches across the dry leaves which are scattered on the ground, he wipes his mouth with his sleeve.

A tear rolls down his face, his beloved pet lies dead on the forest floor, his belly ripped open, intestinal organs and blood in turmoil on the ground, it's horrifying to think about. With his free hand, Leo quickly wipes a tear away while he clutches his toy sword, he doesn't want his father to think that his son, a future knight, isn't resilient, another tear defies him and pours down his ruddy cheek. The tear is rapidly flicked away as he snorts up liquid snot travelling rapidly down his nasal passages.

"What is it boy? What happened to my dog? Their father addresses Miché as he approaches the pair. "Why is Leo retching like that? What on earth?"

"It's the boar Father, he got Gross." Milo bounds up to the trio as Miché explains the other dog's fate.

"Right, come inside and for goodness sake don't let your mother see you like that."

Leo can't help feelings of grief engulf him. He now realises bravery is expected of him at all times. He witnessed his stoic older brother face the facts of life with no trace of emotion. Miché honestly admitted the truth to their father. As he walks into the manor house Leo vows that he'll be as brave as his brother, as courageous as a chivalrous knight.

Chapter 8 Leon

Leon enjoys a mainly carefree childhood in Ireland, the rugged natural environment suits him. In fact, the outdoors relieves him from the blaring television news reporting the troubles from up north which streams through the house from the front sitting room. He's heard his parents discussing the bombings and subsequent killings in a country that neighbours his. The reports render him anxious especially in the quite of night. He's terrified that the troubles will spill into his country then possibly progress into his county as well. Living by the ocean is his saving grace from all the angst, it calms him. He sits for hours on the green tufts of grass playing with rocks and perfecting his pebble skipping skills. He's only managed two maybe three skips before the stone plunges into the briny depths.

One unusually sunny day during the holidays there's a young teacher couple staying at the cottage on their honeymoon. With no other children to play with Leon skims rocks into the ocean for most of the morning. When Declan turns up they both sit silently on the grassy verge. They stare at the grey blue sea before Declan breaks the calming sound of the waves sloshing over pebbles.

"S'up?"

"Nut'n." The pair sit in silence for a few more minutes before Declan stands to skim some pebbles onto the water.

"Bet I can do more skips than you."

"Right." Leon stands and searches for a winning pebble. "You go first." Leon offers because he sees his brother poised to start. Declan gives his arm a few false swings to get the feel of his pebble and to practice his shot before he lets the stone go, it skips three times before it plops into the water.

"Game on!" Declan boasts. He's clearly pleased with himself because he hasn't really expected such a good result.

Leon finds a good position to throw his rock, he feels a lot of pressure, he's never achieved anymore than three skips. Like his brother he attempts a few practice shots and when he feels ready to let his pebble skim across the water, to his surprise his rock skips five times before falling into the water.

"Mary and Joe! Did you see that?" Leon chuffed with his efforts, jumps up and down on the rocky beach.

"Just beginner's luck." Declan is peevish. They consider a rematch, at Declan's insistence. The deliberation is cut short as their mother calls them from across the road, they are required inside for lunch.

Leon is pleased to hold the number one position, for the meantime anyway. In contrast, Declan drags his feet sulkily across the bitumen road before they enter the kitchen for lunch. Archie and Claire are already sitting at the table as the boys are seated. Cathy places their food in front of them while León excitedly recounts his amazing feats as the champion pebble skimmer. His parents try to listen attentively as they share concerned glances. They smile broadly as the boys retell their epic story, the children have no idea that their day is about to turn to cac.

"I'll beat you next time. After lunch, we'll go back out and I'll definitely win." Declan challenges his younger brother through a mouthful of mash potato, cabbage, sausages and gravy.

When the family finishes eating the first course, Cathy offers her family slices of banana cake which they wolf down in seconds.

"Is there any more Love?" Archie loves cake, more importantly he's trying to delay the inevitable. Silently Cathy cuts five more slices, leaves them on the cutting board and places the whole lot in the middle of the table. Four hands shoot out immediately claiming their second piece of cake.

"Right!" Cathy announces, she pours herself a glass of wine for fortification and fiddles with her necklace. "Before you all take off again your Da and I have something to say to you. Don't we Arch?"

"Yeah love, we do."

This is unusual, they weren't in the habit of holding family meetings and Cathy normally waits until dinner time to have her glass of wine. Leon wonders what's going on and is nervous about what his dad is going to say to them.

"Archie." Cathy hands the floor over to her husband as she takes a tentative sip of her wine. He stalls again and lights a post meal cigarette.

"Righto, we've a bit of news." He blows the first plume of smoke away from the table, he doesn't want his kids breathing the smoke directly.

"What is it Dad?" Claire and Declan chorus, Leon waits patiently for the news, with his sibling's constant interruptions he knows they won't hear it any faster. Archie takes another nervous drag.

"So you know your Ma's sister, Aunty Maeve lives in Australia?" The children are well aware. They receive letters and photos from Australia every couple of months. On their mother's birthday and at Christmas time there's a phone call from Australia. They speak briefly to their Aunty Maeve, Uncle Will and two cousins, Yolanda and Sasha. "Well, we're going to visit them." Archie says with a new found enthusiasm.

"Yay! We're going on holiday." Claire is looking forward to being able to play with her older female cousins and wear her red bathers which she never gets to wear in Ireland. She hopes they still fit, it's been a while since it's been warm enough to wear them.

"There's warm water there, we can swim for a change." Leon adds as though he's been reading his sister's mind. The children are excited at the prospect of a holiday on the other side of the world where they'll experience sunshine and a lifestyle they've all heard about from their relatives. Cathy shoots her husband a look encouraging him to reiterate his previous statement. Archie straightens his posture and stamps out his cigarette.

"Well, when I say visit, I mean we're going to live there. Granny and Gramps are coming with us." He offers the sweetener at the end to soften his blow, the children haven't even thought of their grand-parents. The kids are more concerned about themselves. They sit in stunned silence for a while, then hit their parents with a barrage of questions.

All three children are afraid they'll no longer be able to see their school friends. With a rapid protest bombardment, Cathy and Archie try to calm them as best they can. Knowing her children need a practical solutions Cathy suggests something that she hopes will pacify the situation.

"You know, you could become pen pals with your friends? Remember my pen pal Kirsten? I wrote to her for years when I was in primary school. I even visited Kirsten and her family in Germany once, no twice in fact."

"That sounds like shite. I hate writing." Declan mumbles under his breath. "I'm not going to sit and write Darragh a sodding love letter am I?"

Cathy sees Claire welling up, she tries not to laugh out loud at the thought of her son sitting down to write Darragh a letter. It's hard enough to get him to put pen to paper for his school work, but she's standing by her suggestion.

"This is so unfair, I hate you!" Claire runs to her room sobbing. Cathy follows her, ready to comfort her distraught daughter. As Declan slumps his head into the palms of his hands, Archie gently slaps him on the back of his head for swearing at his mother. Leon stands up and walks outside to his happy place by the side of the ocean, the memory of his triumphant skimming competition is all but forgotten.

Chapter 9 Ailie

"Look at you my dear. I think you grew in the middle of the night and your hair, it's reaching down to the middle of your back." Florrie muses as she indicates to me to sit at the table so she can brush my hair and fix my ribbons.

"I think I'm the same as I was yesterday Florrie."

"Yes of course, but I think I'm noticing you more today for some reason."

But it is a new day according to my father. It is time for me to learn how to become a lady of the Court. I'll be taught by my mother to manage the household, to sew garments, to play an instrument, in my case a small wooden flute.

"What is that infernal noise." Papa calls out over my music during my first lesson. "Could you not have chosen a more melodic activity. It sounds like she's strangling a barn cat." He complains to Florrie as she wanders through the hall. Despite my lack of musical talent, I am taught to dance and sing. Usually I would have been taught to care for smaller children by now as well, but as Mama is no longer able to take a pregnancy to full term this aspect of my education is lacking somewhat.

Her last pregnancy and subsequent miscarriage has left Mama with debilitating depression. Both she and Papa are resigned to the prospect of no sons to bear his name. As Mama's only child she wants to keep me at home for as long as she can. She doesn't want to send me to the Duke's chateau for additional instruction, she knows she will endure pressure from Papa that I learn to socialise with the other ladies of the Court. Ironically, the more depressed Mama becomes the more she distances herself from me. Already an independent child who likes my own company I feel my mother emotionally casting me adrift.

"Go outside and play." She says as I wander aimlessly around the hall. My father is distant and distracted. He doesn't seem to see me at all I'm sure. His time is spent organising Amis in the yard and the stables, he's occupied with court business, there are visits to farmers to collect his taxes, in his spare time he regularly drinks and philanders at the tavern. There's no time allotted for me.

As I play in the garden a man with a small boy rides up to the chateau on a beautiful black stallion. Being a bit shy I hide behind one of the taller chestnut trees as I watch the man descend from his horse, he assists the boy to the ground. Florrie greets the pair at the door before they are swallowed up by the house. So as not to be identified I decide to run stealthily from tree to tree on my way to the stables. The pockets of my pinafore are full of chestnuts and they jiggle on my leg when I run. In the stables I'm ensconced in my favourite stall lined with fresh straw. I empty my pockets of chestnuts onto the ground and begin to practice counting one, two, three, four...

As I count the young boy pokes his head around the corner of the stall.

"Hello." He says confidently. I guess he's slightly older than me. I see he's dressed in noble's clothes. I can't work out why he, a boy of titled birth, is standing before me in my family's stables. This is the domain of the horse hands and stable boys. I feel strange around this boy. Should I know him from somewhere? I know I've never met him before. Embarrassed, I quickly avert my gaze towards my chestnuts.

"Hello." I stammer without making eye contact. He stands awkwardly for a moment, shuffling on his feet, scrutinising the new environment. The men talk and I notice the boy's father is a distinguished looking nobleman. He speaks to Papa about hounds, boars, something about pups and asks for recommendations as to where he can find a reliable supplier of hunting dogs? I can only make out parts of the conversation. I'm distracted by the boy in my sanctuary. The adult discussion ends abruptly and the boy is whisked away by his father. The two ride away down the drive on their black stallion. I return to my chestnuts.

Chapter 10 Allie

"How does that look?" The hairdresser holds up a round hand mirror at the back of my head so I can see how much hair she's cut off. It's quite a lot. I'm trying to be brave, resisting the urge to cry. My long curly hair has been cut to just below my shoulders so I can easily care for it. While Mum is away my hair gets pretty knotty sometimes.

"Please don't be upset. Your hair looks so pretty." The hairdresser senses my distress, then Dad steps in to offer his words of wisdom.

"Oh what's the matter now. Stop your crying. It doesn't matter. It'll grow back soon. It's only hair after all." He reaches into his back pocket for his wallet and pays for my haircut at the counter. The hairdresser places her hands on my shoulders and squeezes them while she smiles at me through the large mirror to let me know that she understands that Dad's can say stupid stuff sometimes.

Much to Dad's listening pleasure I've stopped playing the recorder in preference for honing my skills with my camera, it shadows me wherever I go. Mum thinks I should be learning a musical instrument to broaden my character. When the instrument paperwork comes home from school she's away on one of her trips, Fiji perhaps, Dad files the form into the kitchen bin.

Mum has been away a lot lately and not for the first time Dad wonders about the state of his marriage. He's lonely, worried about Finn and me who don't have our mother around for the important moments in our lives, lives that are flying by so quickly. When she's at home the house becomes awkward, routines are thrown slightly off kilter. She doesn't remember timetables, or where things are kept. We've changed our activities since she was home previously and we've reached new levels of maturity. We've grown taller, increased our knowledge of the world, have new friends, play new games, have new in jokes between us that Mum hasn't been privy to.

"Don't sneeze out a peanut, will you?" Finn laughs as he warns Flo one morning, Mum is home. Flo snorts and has to get her hanky out of her apron pocket to wipe her nose.

"Huh, why was that so funny?" Mum wants to know. We've explained it to her before of course, but her mind is on other things, other places, other people.

"Oh, Mum!"

We have to remind her of our routines, again and again, we aren't mature enough so show her patience. "Mum, I have Netball practice on Tuesday nights now not on Wednesday nights like before. Oh yeah, I need new sneakers and you have to sign my school camp form before tomorrow morning. You have to put the deposit in the envelope, I think it's in my bag."

"I also need $10." Finn adds to the list without elaborating why he needs the money. He's the detached ghost in our family. When he asks for something he usually gets it with no further questions. People have other things to do.

"We keep the vacuum cleaner in the laundry cupboard not in the linen press anymore, if that's what you're looking for?"

"Can you take me to the library please? I desperately need some more books."

"Oh my Goddess, anything else you two?"

"Well, there is one thing." I want to ask her for a hug but she's out of the room, she's grabbed her keys and handbag before the words are out of my mouth. Mum loves us in an indifferent way. I hope she loves us on some level. Her inability to deal with the humdrum of our daily lives has her itching to jump on a plane again.

"I think we should travel as family sometimes." She used to suggest to Dad.

"You know I can't take time off like you to gallivant around the world. What if one of my clients wants to contact me and I'm on the other side of the earth and it's 3am in the morning. Besides, we can't keep taking the kids out of school all the time."

"But travel is better for their learning. Rather than reading about a country from an outdated library book they can experience geography, cultures and languages first hand." Sometimes she can persuade Dad to take a holiday, she soon realises she doesn't have the same freedoms she normally has when we're along for the ride.

Going on a night out with a husband and two kids in tow doesn't quite have the same appeal as catching up with a group of new friends to dance the night away in a Brazilian night club. The times she enjoys as a single traveller can't be replicated in a family environment. Especially the hours she spends perusing her love which is examining the minutiae of art in galleries. This become a quick scan accompanied by restless kids and a disinterested husband.

"When are we having lunch Mum?" I ask hungry as anything.

"We just ate a massive breakfast. Come and look at this painting. The dress fabric on this little girl is amazing. Do you know who painted it Allie?"

"Mum, I need to go to the toilet. It says there, Manet, can you see that?" I point to the plaque next to the painting and wonder why mum hasn't discovered this resource before.

"Well I know that. I was wondering if you knew who painted it without looking at the information plaque. Anyway, you just went to the toilet. Here, this Dali is amazing, you must see this."

"That was at the restaurant this morning. Why is that ladies face melting. This stuff is weird."

"No darling it's not weird, its art. Finn, stop touching the painting. Oh my goddess I didn't realise this was going to be so hard. It's supposed to be a relaxing time enjoying the art. Rod take the kids to the toilet and get them something to eat. I'm going to meditate in front of the Pollock."

"Anything to get away from this "art"." Dad signs air quotes at Mum then hauls us down stairs to the cafe. Taking us on her kind of holiday is a battle she isn't going to win, her requests to travel as a family soon become much less frequent.

Off she goes on her own again, I don't know where she is exactly. I'm in our front yard taking photos with my camera when a lady with a red haired boy approaches our gateway. On a mission, the lady unlatches the gate and paces up the concrete path, the boy trailing behind her. The strange woman has her eyes fixed on our front door, she doesn't see me standing under the lemon scented gum tree. In the heat of the day the tree releases its heady lemon scent, I inhale its perfume. The boy notices me and gives a shy wave as he follows his mother to the door. Stupidly, I drop my camera on the grass, I quickly bend over to pick it up.

When I've righted myself I remember social protocol dictates I'm required to return a wave, he's moved on. Cathy knocks on our wooden door and waits patiently for a response. Shirtless, Dad answers the door in his shorts. It's a stinking hot day, Cathy's face is red, not just because she'd found a half-naked man at the door, the incessant heat is oppressive. She naturally flushes easily, she isn't used to these extremely hot temperatures. Droplets of sweat dribble into her eyes from her forehead, she pats the area above her eyebrows with her finger tips and searches her handbag for a hanky, she can't find one amongst the clutter of receipts, pens, lipstick, keys, and her purse.

"Bit warm today, hey." Dad greets the unknown pair. The temperature is reported to reach forty two degrees by three o'clock.

"Yes, it is." Cathy has given up her search for a hanky and fiddles with her necklace instead to help her think, the metal is irritating her skin.

"What can I do for you?" He hopes she isn't one of those wandering religious types, trying to share the Good News. Why do they always bring their kids with them he thinks? Is she here to attempt to sell him a new vacuum cleaner? They already have two of the blasted things. Isabelle couldn't find the one we already have and without asking she just went down to Crazy Bob's Electrics and bought a new one. It's weird she doesn't even do the vacuuming.

Is the lady on the porch an insurance sales person, selling art, or here to request a donation to a random charity he's never heard of? He's already shown a couple of people the door earlier in the day, he can't wait to hear what this one's selling. He's about to tell her where to go and shut the door in her face when Cathy finds her voice through the thick air. The heat has rendered her head foggy, she feels slow and listless.

"Yes, grand. Are you the person selling the single bed advertised in the local rag?"

"That's a new one." Dad's impressed by the new subject matter, he doesn't think they are selling anything. He never knows what Mum's up to. "Allie, come here a minute. I'm sorry, I don't think that's us, I'll just check with my daughter to see if her mother has put an ad in. I never know what she's up to these days. Do you need a vacuum cleaner by chance." He asks the stranger as I skip to the porch.

I arrive on the dusty red concrete verandah and stand in front of my father while he wraps his arms around me. It's far too hot for this kind of bodily contact. I adore him so I allow my father's arms to remain. The boy is next to his mother and hasn't uttered a word since they arrived, but now he looks as though he's about to speak.

"Hey Ma, I noticed on the gate, its number seven, weren't we after number seventeen." Leon finally realises their error.

"Oh my God!" The heat must've been playing tricks with her eyes. She's in the process of removing her necklace, it's really irritating her now. "I do beg your pardon. What am I like?" She flusters. Cathy looks around in an attempt to gather herself and her child as she places the jewellery into her handbag. "I'll have to wait until winter to put this on again I suppose." Leon tugs on Cathy's sleeve. "What is it now?" She replies a little too testily.

"Will you look at that spider Ma." Leon points to a rather large black spider resting on the beading board between the wall and the eves.

"That's just Henry, he's a huntsman he won't bite you, but I do hope he catches a few more of these bloody flies." Rod waves his hand around his face to swat away the blowflies. Leon recently read that the flies are only trying to collect salts and sugars from people's skin for nourishment. Fascinated, he examines the way they land on Rod's face. "Would you like a glass of water? You look like you could do with one."

Dad doesn't want the strange lady passing out on the front porch. Despite her ruddy complexion, her lips look a bit pale, she seems agitated. The boy is staring at his face and he doesn't know why. Perhaps he's already in the early stages of heat stroke.

"A glass of cool water would be grand." Cathy agrees.

"You have to be careful you don't get heat stroke. It can make you crook."

"Yes indeed, its another thing to think about when you live here isn't it? I didn't think it would be this hot though."

Dad motions to me to run down the passage and get the nice lady and her son a glass of water. I return quickly with the cool refreshments, Cathy and Leon down the water in one gulp. They haven't yet realised that they need to drink more water in Australia, certainly a lot more than they did in Ireland. They return their empty glasses and Cathy thanks us for the water. The pair make their way down the path and out onto the footpath.

When they're out of sight we go inside and place the used glasses into the kitchen sink. Dad grabs some clean glasses out of the cupboard and pours cold water from the jug in the fridge then retrieves a can of beer to follow his water.

"That lady had a funny accent. I liked it. Where's she from?" I ask rapid fire as I sit at the kitchen table my drink in one hand and my camera in the other. Dad takes a sip of water from his glass and leans against the sink.

"She said, she and her husband have just moved from Ireland. Get any good photos today Love?"

Chapter 11 Leo

Leo's been sent to the Duke's chateau for training and is reunited with his older brother, Miché. Darri is now tottering around the manor in the position of baby of the family. Hugo dejected, isn't the baby of the family anymore, he's relegated to some vague middle child position. With his older brothers absent, for the most part puzzles him, is he actually the oldest child now? And are his parents planning to send him away as well? There are so many questions left unanswered.

On his first day at the chateau his master Roland helps Leo orientate himself.

"You'll have to eat more for starters. You won't be able to do everything that you're expected to do on that skinny little frame." Roland shows him where the pages and squires eat their meals.

"Yes Sir." Leo responds weakly. It's difficult for him to comply at first. He watches the other boys scoffing themselves. In time with the extra exertion that chateau life brings he actually appreciates the extra food. If he doesn't eat quickly and take his share of the food it will all be gone from the table, there will be nothing left to eat. He doesn't have a nursemaid anymore to ensure there are leftovers just for him.

Leo learnt to ride as a young boy, he has a natural affinity with animals of all types. However, Roland is most impressed with the way he handles himself around the horses. He's gentle and sensitive enough not to make any sudden movements or loud noises as some of the other pages do. Roland doesn't suffer fools and Leo's glad to be on his good side, for the moment. He's heard from the other boys that he can be cantankerous, he sometimes slaps them if they don't perform as they should. Besides working with the horses, Leo will be schooled in weaponry, using smaller swords and lances, and reluctantly he has to study inside the chateau from time to time for French and Latin lessons. There are also more socially driven studies in the arts such as dancing and learning the rules of chivalry, the decree for honourable knights, these particular teachings he takes to heart.

Used to living in a household full of men, he misses his mother momentarily, he's soon used to sleeping on the stone floor with the other farty boys and young men who will become his new tribe. Leo's glad to be reunited with his brother, occasionally they return home for religious holidays set by the church to see their family, it doesn't happen very often though.

"Oh, my sons I know you have to return to the Chateau, I hate to see you go." Catarine cries into her handkerchief while her growing sons embrace her.

"We shall return before you know it Mother." Miché takes his turn to hug his mother and shakes his father's hand. Despite the external confinement at the Duke's chateau, a few days ride away, Catarine can see that her sons will grow into fine young men, her plans for their success at Court are well and truly going to plan.

Chapter 12 Leon

On their arrival in Australia, Cathy and Archie bought a beautiful B&B in the foothills of Kaurna Country. They have always operated B&Bs, which means their holidays are few and far between. The family generally ventures to the same seaside camp ground every year, out of season of course, when all the tourists have packed up and deserted the region for the winter. Most of the good restaurants are closed and any child friendly attractions are boarded shut until the following summer. Cathy and Archie like it that way though, they prefer a more secluded peaceful holiday. The family amuses themselves by playing cards, walking on the cold grey windy beaches and eating fish and chips from the one fish shop that remains open. But they don't eat out much. Cathy cooks familiar dinners on the aged electric twin hobs in the cabin's small kitchen. The holiday is slow and easy, the dreary weather and grey beaches often find them homesick for Ireland.

On really wet days their parents chat endlessly with the park managers, Wendy and Duncan. They perch on stools around the office desk, Duncan sits on the nice leather office chair and they spend hours in the stuffy over heated office. Duncan, Archie and Wendy are smokers, they add to the fugginess of the office. Clouds of smoke plume from their chains of cigarettes while Cathy inhales second hand smoke from them all. Sometimes, they open the window if it isn't too cold and make feeble attempts to blow the smoke through the window to save Cathy from breathing in the fumes, after a while they don't bother with the charade and smoke contentedly.

Mugs of steaming tea rest on their laps. Later in the day tea is replaced with cheap cask wine.

"Anyone else for a glass of Chateau de Cardboard?" Duncan asks. They sip their wine from their mugs. At first cup always has some dregs of tea at the bottom which slightly changes the taste of the already suspect wine. "I don't mind the tea taste at the end, it's got that je ne sais quoi aspect to it." Duncan remarks.

"Mmm, it's definitely different." Cathy adds.

"Chateau Cardboard though hey?"

It never grows old for Duncan and Archie, Cathy is tired of having to pretend it's funny every time. Wendy notices that Duncan gets on Cathy's nerves, he gets on Wendy's nerves as well that's for sure.

The talk revolves around the ups and downs of the Tourism Industries in Ireland and Australia. However, they're mostly mad gossipers as well, the summer residents their main targets.

"You should've seen those two. You know the one that always wears that cheap red satin top, she has a gecko tat on her shoulder. She goes with the bald guy, he has muscles on the outside of his shirt." Wendy pauses for a group laugh, its not as hearty as she was expecting. "Well, they slink off into all those different cabins with God knows who?"

"Oh yeah, I've seen them." Archie remembers.

"Perhaps they're part of a larger group staying here. I met her the other day by the shower block, Kali's her name. She's actually a really nice lady. She lent me her apple scented shampoo."

Cathy doesn't like gossip and certainly doesn't like making assumptions about people just because of their appearance. Thankfully for Cathy the gossipy conversation wanes. The discussion segues to Wendy's love of cake making. The banana cake recipes are the most deliberated.

"Is it bread or is it cake?" Archie wonders. Duncan wants to talk about kick boxing, he knows from previous experience that no one else is really interested, he sticks to the food topic.

"I fancy some apple pie."

The children know the battered game of Monopoly like an old friend. Most of the good pieces like the dog and the race car are missing. It's the only offering in the games room besides the broken table tennis table, one bat and no table tennis balls. But they manage to keep out of their parent's way for most of the day exploring the beach for treasures as fearsome pirates. Playing Knights of the Round Table, they ride their imaginary horses up and down the beach searching for adventure.

Two weeks into their settlement in Australia, Cathy enrols the children into the local primary school, a school that is poles apart from the one they attended in Ireland. At the beginning of all the assemblies the principal acknowledges the local Indigenous people, caretakers of the land. One of the Kaurna kids gives a greeting in his own language. Leon has never seen, or heard, anything like it. It makes him happy to think that his new school is so friendly towards the people who have been shunted from their lands and treated so badly by colonisers. The first time he hears the ancient language echo around the assembly hall a tingling sensation runs around the top of his head, he feels his heart expand.

Leon's envious of the Indigenous kids when he hears about their camp held in the remote sand dunes of the southern coast beaches. Tom talks about it at the assembly while the student body listens intently, well most of them do.

"We went fishing with Uncle and Maddie caught a couple of small bream. I caught a perch, this big." Tom holds his hands out wide and the kids gasp their approval. "Uncle said it was about 12 kilos, it was very heavy. We put it on hot coals wrapped in wet paperbark. The girls wove baskets with Aunty and for tucker they collected muntries, quandongs, bush tomatoes, and um, there was another one, oh yeah, warrigal greens which we ate with the fish. Uncle made a bonfire, the uncles and aunties told us dreaming stories and we danced around the fire."

The kids who went on camp show the assembly their baskets and sing one of the songs they'd learnt at camp. At the end of the song Leon wants to stand up and cheer for Tom because he thinks the camp sounds like the best thing ever. But the other kids clap limply at the end of the presentation while the principal takes his place at the lectern again.

When the students return to class Miss Brown introduces the new student.

"Class this is Leon. Welcome to the class Leon. Leon's from Ireland, he'll need your help finding his way around the school. I'm sure you'll do your best to make him feel welcome. Okay, why don't you tell us something about yourself Leon."

"I don't know Miss, what do you want to know?" Some of the children giggle at Leon's accent.

"Why don't you tell us what you want to do when you leave school."

"Okay Miss. Well, I want to go to Peru and hike the Inca trail into Machu Pichu, sit on a mountain and draw what I see in front of me."

"That's amazing Leon, I think I'd like to do that to."

Billy raises his hand.

"Yes Billy."

"What's a Machu Pichu?"

Miss Brown spends the next half an hour talking about Machu Pichu and the Inca civilisation which she obviously has an interest in.

After lunch, Leon struggles to understand his teacher. It seems that Miss Brown isn't speaking English or at least the English he understands. It's hard to comprehend the Australian accent sometimes and some of the things she says are really confusing, confronting even. As she gives out the permission slips for swimming lessons, Miss Brown informs the students that they will need to wear their thongs to the pool. Leon starts to panic, he wonders what kind of school his parents has sent him to, he timidly raises his hand.

"Yes Leon."

"Why do we have to wear a thong, shouldn't we be wearing our swimmers in the pool Miss?"

Miss Brown laughs and his classmates giggle.

"Oh yeah sorry Leon, in Australia we call flip-flops, thongs."

A wave of relief washes over him, he tries to erase the mental picture of swimming in a skimpy bathing suit.

Besides swimming lessons, physical education is different as well. Lessons are always outside on the oval, fitness is only conducted in the gym in the depths of winter which Leon loves. After talking to his new friends the brothers are eager to play Australian Rules football, a game similar to Gaelic football which they'd played in Ireland. Claire is playing netball as well and their games are held on Saturday mornings. Afterwards they go to the local bakery for lunch to debrief their wins and losses.

"You should have seen the mothers from the Lions. They all stand on the side of the court and yell abuse at Claire's team. I can't believe it."

Cathy starts to nibble her pasty forgetting her aversion to gossip, she's truly shocked at their behaviour.

"I know. The parents at football aren't much better. One dad had to be ejected from the ground this morning for swearing at some of the boys on our team. They're in primary school for Pete's sake not in The AFL Grand Final. Mind you, it's nothing I haven't heard before. But the kids shouldn't be hearing that kind of language on a regular basis. Fuck, Declan! Watch what you're doing with that sauce packet will you!" The kids wolf down their food as Archie wipes his jeans with his hand.

"Can we play in park now?" The kids chorus. With his jeans smeared with sauce, Archie lights a cigarette.

"Off you go now, we'll watch you from here."

Leon and Declan take to their new sport and excel at it. Despite his younger age, his talents and camaraderie with his team mates wins Leon the role of vice captain, Declan sulks. The brothers enjoy the solidarity of playing in a team where they make good friends, their teammates become allies in the playground which helps their assimilation into the team. There are a couple of bullies who tease them about their funny accent and Leon's red hair.

"Yo Ginger!"

"Ginga"

"Red Nuts!"

The bullying causes Leon angst at the beginning, he has a few sleepless nights worrying about the taunts. He'd never been teased for having an accent before and hardly ever teased for having red hair. Both were quite normal in Ireland.

"G'day mate." Leon says to Archie one morning.

"What the hell, what's with the accent." Archie replies, dumbfounded.

"I'm trying to sound more Aussie."

"What on earth for the women here love an Irish accent. Don't be daft get ready for school."

But his football mates have witnessed the ribbing long enough. They decide at recess time that they can't let it continue, they look after their own. Billie rounds up the team after school. The team mates lay in wait for the bullies behind the bike shed. When the bullies appear around the corner they squirt red paint, stolen from the art room, onto the front of the ringleader's pants.

"Now you have red nuts. Now fuck off."

Leon doesn't have a problem with the bullies any more.

Chapter 13 Ailie

Weaving fabric from singular threads is my favourite pastime. I've learnt a great deal at home but there isn't anyone in the chateau with the expertise to extend my embroidery and weaving skills. When she has errands to run Florrie takes me to the weaver's guild in the village so that I can observe the craftsmen and women at work. It's heaven, she leaves me at the studio while she shops at the market. It's definitely my favourite time of the week.

I watch the weaver's deft hands work at their looms for a while, but the time passes way too quickly before Florrie returns to collect me. In fact, sometimes a few hours rapidly pass by. I'm never bored. I never feel alone. I love being in the presence of these creative artists, skilfully manipulating their colourful silks, the joyful camaraderie which I miss out on at home.

"Why do we have to go home now?" I frown at Florrie.

"Come along child, I've got chores to do. Your father won't be happy if his supper isn't on the table when he gets home, now will 'e?"

It becomes a regular occurrence that Florrie leaves me at the weaving studio, runs her errands, visits her family then returns to collect me in time for lunch. If she's met with a boy, she'll be a bit later, I'm not supposed to know about that. I guess it to be true when her hair is messy and she smells like the stables. I'm glad she's late though, it means that I have more time to observe the weavers.

Ottho the supervisor loves my passion for weaving. He's given me a little loom to work on with some of the scrap silk threads that have been swept from the floor. He encourages me to develop my own designs and not rely on the depictions I've seen around the room. At first, I'm almost afraid to touch the loom as I've watched the craftsmen produce beautiful fabrics. I'm in awe of their talents, though I don't want to be perceived as inferior either, a conundrum for such a young child.

Ottho hovers over me as I sit on the little wooden stool he's brought out from behind his work table. I tentatively select a piece of red silk from the threads I've been supplied. I wind the thread around the shuttle which I then feed over and under the main warp threads. Ottho hands me a wooden comb which I use to push the threads towards the base of my work, I've seen the craftsmen do this many times. I understand the required actions to make fabric and I've replayed these movements in my head many, many times. My mentor gently pats me on the shoulder with encouragement and when the red weft is completed I select a green thread, wrap it around the shuttle and begin to weave the thread into my work.

Ottho leaves my side to help one of the craftsmen when his loom snaps a warp thread. When he returns I've completed a section of fabric of about fifteen centimetres wide.

"Woah, you're a fast worker. Now pull it all out and start again. This time think about which colours better complement each other and make sure you comb your work a little more neatly. And forget what I said before, perhaps to start with you should copy some of the work on the wall, just to get a feel for how it's done." He's a nice man, however I'm momentarily taken aback, I'm not used to critique from anyone. I inspect my work momentarily and think it looks quite beautiful.

"Do I really have to take it all apart Ottho?"

"Yes, now don't quibble." Smiling, he walks away.

Reluctantly, I do what I'm told and begin to pull all of my work apart. This time I look at the threads, start playing with different colours, placing complementary combinations together to see how they look. When I'm happy with my new selections, I begin to weave my fabric from scratch. As I'm working Ottho returns to inspect my weaving.

"Colours are nice, hmm, better work this time, but you still need to work on your neatness, start again."

I'm happy that Ottho thinks I've shown improvement, though I'm disappointed that my second attempt doesn't demonstrate as much talent as the master's work. I have high expectations for myself and I want to be the best weaver that I can be. Reluctantly, I pull the silk threads from the loom and notice that some of them are starting to fray with use. I inspect the threads and wonder how many more times

I'll have to start my weaving from scratch. With this thought, Florrie appears at the doorway, my heart sinks. It's time to go home and I won't be able to return to my haven at the loom for another week.

"Oh, do we have to go so soon? Why is there straw on your skirts Florrie?" Florrie flushes as she quickly ushers me out of the workshop. Ottho laughs as he packs away my loom.

It's time to petition my parents to work at the studio on a more permanent basis, as an apprentice. As the only daughter of a nobleman, I instinctively know that in order to illicit a positive response to my request, I will require keen skills of persuasion. I'm going to be ten years old soon. I know in my heart, I desperately want to work with Ottho. It will be an opportunity to develop my craft, but I'm keenly aware that my experience is three years behind the other two apprentices, who are about my age.

When I meet Sarra, one of the two apprentices, the other a boy named Bertram, Bertie for short, I have a similar feeling to how I felt when I met the noble boy in our stables. It is a feeling of knowing them well, from another time perhaps. But meeting Sarra doesn't illicit a nice feeling at all.

"You going to be working here now are you?" Sarra snarls.

"Well, I hope so. My name is Ailie by the way, so nice to meet you......?" Sarra doesn't click that I want to know her name as well. This interaction isn't going the way I've been taught, it's throwing me off kilter. Then Sarra throws me completely off balance with her next question.

"What on earth do you want to work here for? You don't look as though you would have to work a day in your life?" Sarra's gaze penetrates mine for a split second before she scurries away. Afterwards I remember I've seen those penetrating eyes before. A shiver spirals down my spine.

Chapter 14 Allie

For me, high school was a natural progression from one of the communities' primary schools, that progression isn't the same for everyone. On the first day of school an assembly is held in the quadrangle where the year eights stand nervously around the peripheries of the older students who feel at home in their usual gathering spot under the shade of the pepper trees. I've previously visited the school for orientation, but it's quite a different story now that I'm here for real. I could barely eat my breakfast this morning and now I gather nervously with my friends from primary school.

As my stomach rumbles we chat about our holidays. Lee remembers getting a CD player and Brooke went on family holiday to Bali for Christmas, however most of us have long forgotten what we received, or where we went. We giggle uneasily, shuffle our feet in our stiff new shoes, we adjust the heaviness of our shiny backpacks which heave with books, pencil cases, and lunches. I consider for a minute, or two, whether it would be okay if I just reached into my bag and started eating my cheese and Vegemite sandwich. I don't think that would be a good idea. Knowing me I'll get it all over my face and I'll start the new year, at a new school, with suspect brown smears all over my mouth. I can hear the taunts and see the finger pointing already.

"Oh my God, she's got pooh on her face!"

No definitely not a good idea.

Out of the corner of my eye I notice a new girl standing on her own. Not only does she stand alone I see that her uniform is slightly off making her stick out from the other girls. I can't put my finger on the difference, but it's there. The new girl stares at the year twelve girls who are applying shiny pink lip gloss and gossiping about their summers. They laugh confidently while they point out the new kids and discuss the ones they now know intimately.

The new girl notices that the older girl's dresses are a lot shorter than hers. The hem of her dress brushes the top of her knees while the older girl's socks are rolled down to the top of their shoes. The new girl's socks are stretched to the bottom of her knees, only her knee caps are exposed. She quickly rolls down her socks to her ankles and hitches her dress around her waist. But with nothing to hold it up, it falls down to her knees again. The year twelve girls giggle amongst themselves, the new girl thinks they are laughing at her, they haven't even noticed her.

The new girl appears kind of awkward which I like a lot, I feel awkward too. I consider introducing myself to her when the Principal stands at the lectern and announces into a screeching microphone that all students are to assemble into their form groups. When the microphone settles down the principal makes his announcements. He welcomes the year eights and the other new students, he wishes the year twelve students good luck in their final year; he introduces three new teachers and the new canteen manager. At the end of the announcements I move to my classroom with my classmates. I take a seat in the middle of the room. I've placed myself under the radar, not with the cool kids at the back and not with the try hards in the front, but in a vague middle position. When the shuffling for seats and noise has died down I notice the new girl from the quadrangle has sat next to me.

Ms Osanna welcomes the students and has everyone introduce themselves then say what primary school we've come from and what our most enjoyable activity is. Most of the class has originated from feeder primary schools in the local area, while about a third of the class went to my old primary school. Sara is the only student from a Steiner primary school. Luckily for Sara, Ms Osanna is pressed for time, she doesn't call on her to explain to the rest of the class what a Steiner School is. She already feels very different to her new class mates, trying to explain an alternative schooling system will make her stand out even more.

As the teacher speaks I observe my new classroom. My gaze falls upon Sara's uniform. The material looks soft and well-worn, as if it has been washed many times, unlike the fabric of my dress which is starchy and stiff. I look around at the other girl's dresses, I notice they are mainly brand new except for the girls who I know to have older sisters. I wonder perhaps if the new girl has an older sister. My mind is drifting again. I look out of the window to the quadrangle where we'd just been standing. I look at the drooping leaves on the pepper trees, my eyes land on a pair of galahs which are perched on one of the middle branches. They seem to be cuddling and having a lovely morning chatting to each other.

After a minute or two, the galahs have flown away. I suddenly realise that I've missed everything Ms Osanna has said. I chide myself for having been distracted so early on the first day. This isn't the way I wanted to start the new school year. I vow to stay focused from now on. Everyone starts to shuffle in their seats, they rise to move into the corridor. I have no idea where we're going, or why. My face must've revealed my confusion as Sara announces blankly, "tour of the school". Sara and I drift towards the back of the group and make our introductions while our teacher points out where the toilets are.

Chapter 15 Leo

Leo and Miché are frequently called upon to run errands for the knights and sometimes the Duke himself asks them to clean his weaponry and wash his clothing, although that isn't often. They continue to receive academic instructions in reading, writing, languages and the social graces of Court, Leo prefers to ride the horses whenever he can whereas Miché, prefers weaponry and falconry which he learns from one of the older knights.

While the boys are busy with their studies, the chateau is awash with movement as the community goes about their own duties. The nobility congregate in the hall while they entertain friends with games of cards, conduct business and strategize plans for the future with the senior knights. Cooks and maids complete their chores in the kitchen, pages can be observed running between the chateau and the stables, while the hounds have free reign over the two floors of the chateau. The lap dogs lounge over chaises, while the hunting dogs make use of the vast grounds.

Leo loves to frolic with the hounds when he has spare time, he misses his own dogs from home. They have always shown him unconditional love and companionship, however the hunting dogs at the chateau can be somewhat aloof, they only yield to the knights as the alphas of the pack. Leo wanders into the stables and sees that one of the bitches has a new litter of puppies who are suckling furiously at her teats. Leo watches the puppies for a long time before a squire interrupts his meditation.

"Hey, Leo come back inside, you have a French lesson now." The squires calls.

"Okay."

Leo manages to tear himself away from the puppies, he thinks about them all afternoon, he can't concentrate on his French lesson. Before supper is due to be served he returns to the stables to talk to the squire about a dog.

"Do you think I could train one of the pups?" He begins without preamble.

"Hello Leo, how was your French class? I heard you were a bit distracted."

"A little, I guess. But do you think that I could train one of the pups?"

"Are you interested in the pups Leo?"

Leo gives the squire an exasperated look, it's a strain not to roll his eyes, he doesn't want to appear to be disrespectful.

"Yes of course I am."

He also manages to keep his voice on an even keel, even though he's terribly anxious to have one of the pups for himself.

"Well, they'll be with their mother for a few more weeks, then we'll see. Probably that little one over there could be yours to look after." The squire points to a mottled runt which is almost hidden by its siblings.

"Perfect. That one will be perfect."

Leo spends early mornings and late afternoons in the stables, tending to the bitch and her growing pups. The squire notes Leo's dedication to his pup who has developed quite a personality. Despite being the smallest pup, he attracts attention away from the other puppies and manages to elicit laughter from the squires who work in the stables. They know that he won't make a serious hunting dog, they're glad Leo is going to take him under his wing. There's no telling what his fate would have been otherwise.

"What are you going to call him?" The squire asks Leo as he brushes down one of the horses.

"Really, I get to keep him? Jaimin is what I'm going to call him." Leo, beyond excited has been thinking of this name for days.

"Conflict to triumph and love, that seems apt don't you think considering his potential fate."

Jaimin shadows Leo everywhere except when Leo rides his horse, then he trots alongside, careful not to get under the horse's hooves. The traumatic memory of Gross and the boar means that Leo is obsessively protective of his dog, he's glad that Jaimin doesn't stray too far away. Leo is definitely Jaimin's alpha, if a page boy even looks as though he is going to taunt Jaimin, he pulls his dog close to him and walks away. The thought of confrontation is foreign to his nature, though he will have to learn sooner or later given his training.

Catarine and Arthur are at the chateau to hear Mass said by the visiting bishop, while they are here they make time to reunite with their boys.

"Look Mama, Papa, this is Jaimin my new hound."

"What a funny looking pup Leo. But he will have to wait outside the chapel while we attend Mass."

"Of course, Mama." Leo reluctantly instructs Jaimin to wait outside until the service is over.

Most of the villagers have renounced Paganism for Christianity the preferred religion which has swept throughout France. However, there are people who still hold firm to their Pagan beliefs. They live on the fringe of the forest, an area which hasn't been cleared for township development.

Chapter 16 Sarra

The black bird perches on the edge of the narrow window ledge waiting patiently for his benefactor. His pause is short as Sarra arrives to feed her raven, Corbeau, a morsel of rabbit meat which she found in the kitchen, afterwards she reclines on her wooden stool. With her back against the timber wall she watches the raven gobble his meat before he flies away to his family in the forest.

Sarra is the only female child in her family even though she has a brother of the same age she feels his intellectual superior. She's the dominant sibling to her slightly smaller, slightly younger twin brother, Bertram, who shares the same strawberry blond hair and bewitching hazel eyes. Her baby brother Andre's looks follow a similar genetic pattern. Neither Bertram, or the baby, is of any interest to her even though she is expected to look after the baby when her parents are busy. Sarra is considered a beautiful child by the villagers, however she feels flawed because of her turned in left foot. It was the result of a confined gestation and difficult birth which affects her with a slight limp. She lives with her mother Luna and father Ragno, in a small bungalow at the edge of the forest on the road to Rouen.

"They aren't like us." Papa would say. People from the village worry about the Pagan rituals that Luna and Ragno practise. They think the herbal remedies they prepare are derived using witch related spells, not prayer. They refuse to adopt Christianity as their primary belief system which angers Father Jean. They have to keep their heads down, not be too obvious around the village, it would be so easy for the Church to accuse them of witchcraft. They could be put to death because of their beliefs. Something they've been running from for quite some time. Previously drifters, this is certainly not the first village they've settled into. This place is different, they like Breteuil. It's close to a forest full of animals for food and a freshwater stream that houses aquatic animals, most importantly fresh drinking water.

Ragno knows how to relate to the mischiefs who wander past their modest house on their way to Rouen. To hide from the law, Ragno advises transients to use the feint pathways in the forest behind their house instead of travelling on the open main roads out of town. The villagers know Ragno's habits, they mostly keep their distance due to fear and ignorance. The Church has made sure of that.

When the twins are seven years old, Ragno accompanies them to the village to begin an apprenticeship with Ottho. Life has become more urbanised and many people are turning their backs on the land. Ragno and Luna understand that their children need to develop a craft so they can support themselves later on in life. Ragno himself isn't qualified in a particular trade, he hunts for food, does odd jobs for people and works on building sites. Every now and then he plays his fiddle in the tavern to earn extra money. The more orthodox activities the family participates in the better their reputation in the village.

Even though Ottho usually only takes on one apprentice at a time he's happy to employ the twins, he doesn't want to have to choose between them. To Ottho, Ragno appears to be a large and capable man, he doesn't want to offend him unnecessarily. He's heard the rumours and is a little wary of the Pagan family, he's also an artist himself, a fair man. He believes that the children should be given the opportunity to prove themselves as honest workers. Ottho supposes the young girl possesses an intelligent appearance, he hopes that her limp won't affect her ability to work because she'll be running errands and helping the weavers before she'll work on commissions of her own.

"Don't mind her gummy foot, she's a capable young girl, she'll get the job done." Ragno assures Ottho while they both consider his daughter.

She possesses a bright spark in her eyes, not a look of kindness but one of alertness and deep understanding. The boy doesn't appear as intelligent as his sister, a bit simple perhaps, he displays a good demeanour and looks as though he'll be a hard worker. They both seem to be healthy, no spots or open sores.

"Send the children to me tomorrow morning at dawn. I'll get them working on a solid craft." Ottho offers them a job on the spot because his fabric business is thriving, the more trained workers he has, the better. His staff aren't getting any younger.

Sarra is keen to go to work, she's bored at home, she'll be glad to be as far away from the crying baby as she can. Not that she'd say anything to her parents, but she's jealous of Bertram who has been invited by their father to abscond domestic responsibilities for hunting expeditions. It's amazing to Sarra that Ragno actually suggested that she too should learn a craft. Now that the two children will be working at the same studio they'll be on a more equal footing.

Sarra presumes that she is the more talented twin. All her life she's had the feeling that she's destined for greatness. She will move onto a better life, better than her parents could ever imagine. Little does she know her parents are quite happy with their lives and couldn't have asked for more. Sarra wants so much more than a shack on the edge of a forest. Sarra wants to transform herself into another realm of existence.

Chapter 17 Sara

Purple is her favourite colour, it reminds her of the shimmer on the raven's breast feathers. It's common to see an unkindness of ravens feasting on carrion on the road side verges close to her home. Sara's world is contained mainly within the family cottage at the edge of the outer suburbs surrounded by hobby farms and eucalyptus woodlands over rolling hills.

Outside of their small community, their lifestyle is considered alternative, her mother Lilly, a Reiki master, healer, and light worker, her father Raff, grows vegetables, makes candles, and hosts men's spiritual weekends. It's hard for Sara to explain to her friends exactly what her parents do to earn money. Sometimes she makes up corporate sounding jobs for them, then her friends seem more satisfied with her responses and they leave the topic alone. They were a sugar free, vegan family, before it had become popular and there is definitely no television in the house. They don't have a lot of clothes. The ones they have Lilly either makes, buys them at the local market held in the village lane ways on weekends or she adapts clothing that she's found in op shops.

Lilly rarely shops in shopping malls or supermarkets either, the energy in these places always gives her a headache. Instead, she opts for the local health food bulk store where she buys the majority of their supplies and ingredients to make everyday groceries, like toothpaste and general cleaning products using vinegar and bi-carb soda. She uses cold pressed oils for skin and hair products, rice, grains and stone ground flours for baking to augment the legumes, fruit and vegetables they grow themselves. Instead of using plastic bags or containers, Lilly recycles jars and brown paper bags, groceries are carried home in calico, shopping bags she sews and hand dyes herself.

Sara, and her brother Bodhi, attended the Steiner primary school where they played and discovered life, with children from diverse backgrounds. When it was time to go to high school, Sara discovered a world in which she has no idea, but is desperate to learn more about. Understanding the girls at her new school is going to take some time, though she's made an instant friend in me on the first day. I'm not like the other girls I guess. I appear more natural somehow, not influenced by trends, fashion or make-up. Sara is definitely curious about these mysterious trappings. For the time being I'll help her transition from the spiritual realm into the material world.

Since we've became best friends we hang out together on holidays, weekends and sometimes during the week. Lilly isn't overly excited about the amount of sugar Sara consumes at my house, she understands that will happen more and more as her daughter socialises with people outside of their community. Lilly suggests that Sara goes for a run when she returns home from my house because she's usually pretty hyped up on sweets, she can't sit still for long. She fidgets and speaks non-stop gibberish as far as Lilly's concerned. These behaviours aren't solely the sugar's fault. Her excitement results from the discovery of activities she has missed out on as a younger child, sedentary activities such as watching television and eating salt and vinegar chips which sting her mouth a little. Sara is willing to put up with it though because she's eating chips her mother can't stop her here.

The box is always on. In winter, football fills the screen, in summer it's cricket. Dad watches both the slower and faster moving games from the comfort of his black leather recliner which he always tilts backwards. Sometimes he falls asleep in his chair. More than once I've dropped potato chips into his open mouth, but Flo catches me red handed and reprimands me.

"Don't you know he could choke to death on those things?" Not wanting to wake her boss she scolds me in hushed tones. Something she doesn't do very often, so it comes as a bit of a shock when it happens. I think I hide it well. We giggle nervously as we run to my bedroom, we flop on my bed with a bowl of full fat, heavily salted, flavoured chips, we flip through Mum's travel and fashion magazines. Sara's in heaven as her mouth tingles with intense artificial flavourings.

When we're older we hold regular sleep overs, mainly at my house for Sara's benefit.

"Why don't you ask Allie over to our house?" Lilly asks her daughter.

"She doesn't like to leave her dad alone too much." Sara says to appease her mother, she's also correct.

We often huddle around my desk equipped with multi-coloured pens and rolls of computer paper sequestered from Dad's printer to draw and plan the ideal house we envisage living in when we grow up. Sara secretly gobbles the lollies I've hidden in the drawer on her side of the desk. She thinks that I don't notice her, I do. Lilly notices her daughter changing and moving towards everything they despise about mainstream life, she feels helpless to do anything about it. They know Sara is going to be Sara, there isn't anything they can do to stop her. Her parents are enlightened enough to know that it's her journey to take alone.

We've decided that one day we'll share a flat, or better yet, a house. Each time we meet our plans become more grandiose.

"Look at this house Allie." Sara flips through a glossy decor magazine.

"Ooh, look at that large foyer, oh and the atrium. See that aquarium built into the wall."

"We should have five bathrooms and five bedrooms, two pools, one for doing laps and one for playing games in, a spa and a home theatre with a sunken lounge on the side as a chill out zone."

"Cool, what about an ice-cream stand storing every flavour known to man, dance music pumping out from a huge sound system...."

"Sounds amazing. I also think we should have disco balls in all of the bathrooms and most importantly a puppy room. Look at this page everyone's wearing black tights, white high top sneakers and black crop tops with net t-shirts over the top."

"Oh yes, defs a puppy room." I agree with Sara about the puppies, I'm not that interested in the outfits.

"Can we look at your mum's copies of Vogue now?"

I go to my parent's room to fetch the fashion magazines for Sara, I grab the travel ones for myself. I see Mum looking at me from her honeymoon photo, I feel a pang of sadness.

Chapter 18 Mitch

It's hard to pin Mitchell down, Mitch for short, he's an extremely energetic child.

"Stop running around the furniture Mitch! I think he might be hyperactive." Jacquie says to John as she files her perfect fingernails.

His attention span doesn't linger on one task for very long. He constantly moves from his puzzles, to a game, plays with them for a minute, tires of them, then moves onto the next enticement from his overflowing toy box. Unlike his future adult friends, Mitch an only child, born into an upper middle class family to Jacquie his mum, a socialite who frequently appears in the society pages of the weekend newspapers, sometimes for her charity work, mostly she's seen at the right cocktail parties. Her influential husband John, is a global property developer, philanthropist and winning player of the stock market.

Mitch has everything a kid would want, all the latest toys, he's socialised into the best play groups, enrolled at the finest kindergarten, which is attached to his privileged Anglican college in the leafy eastern suburbs. He knows how to behave in restaurants and cafes, he's used to flying Business Class and their luxury European cars are never more than two years old.

"It must be time to change the car Darling, the ashtray's full." John announces with a wink.

"Oh, I was just getting used to how this one works." Jacquie laments. Jacquie and John wear their money with taste and decorum. It's clear to all who observe them that they are abundant in all areas of their life without being flashy or crass, they're old money Darling.

Mitch's family employ a cleaner, a gardener for their extensive grounds and a child minder for the many days and evenings that Jacquie hosts charity events. John's work dictates that he travels for work and if it coincides with his holidays, Mitch sometimes accompanies him, he's being groomed for the family business. John is a man's man and is training his only son to be the same.

Mitch's home companion is a Border collie named Belanger. John named the dog because he thought it sounded dignified, it's a name that he's proud to hear his family yell out in a park or down at the beach, not that he ever goes to either places unless to visit a work site. He has a bugger of a time trying to develop some of the parks around town, those environmental groups can be trouble. He's been egged more than once by protesters, he now leaves the park developments to his partner Wayne. Parks are for polo matches where both he and Jacquie are there with their ears pinned back, champagne in hand, winning smiles, photographer ready.

As a personable child, Mitch attracts a lot of friends despite his only child status their house is always bustling with friends and cousins, he's never really alone. John and Jacquie understand the economic need to socialise Mitch to provide him with a diverse range of networking opportunities that stem back to childhood, so they enrolled Mitch in Wolf Cubs. Mitch loves all of the escapades and new skills he learns at Wolf Cubs. He especially excels at tying ropes and masters tying different knots, starting camp fires, raising tents, identifying animal tracks and understanding which plants are safe to eat.

"You should never try to identify your own mushrooms, they can be poisonous and you'll die." Wolf Cub leader Rolland warns the pack, Mitch raises his hand.

"What about truffles? Do we have to get them identified as well? When the dogs find them in the forest Dad has a man who gets them for us when we're in Alba."

"Where's that?" Bodhi asks. "Is it in Western Australia?"

"No, not Albany, Alba, it's in the most famous truffle region, in Italy." Mitch thinks that's a perfectly normal question to ask. Rolland has no idea what truffles are, he tries to steer the conversation in another direction.

"Hmm.... I'm not sure. Now lets move on to nettles. Now don't..." But before Rolland can say anything Bodhi shoots his hand up.

"My Mum says that nettles are the most nutritious plant in the forest around our house and we have them in stir fries all the time. Dandelion tea is good too apparently. Dad says it makes him piss too much, he sticks to his kombucha. He keeps his mother under the sink."

"Yes well, um, that's great, thanks Bodhi. Now that's enough about food lets get the compasses out shall we." Rolland wonders whether he needs to call in Bodhi's parents or the police.

The best aspect of Wolf Cubs is the annual camp into the scrub where the cubs sleep in swags under the Milky Way, cook meals on the camp fire, tell tall tales after they finish eating their meals while they toast marshmallows in the yellow flames. They talk about the phases of the moon, search the inky sky for the Southern Cross and the saucepan constellations, find Mars by its red shiny vibe and track satellites across the sky before zipping themselves into their two man tents. After breakfast the next day they hike into the bush carrying all of their supplies in their backpacks.

Chapter 19 Ailie

Papa doesn't show any enthusiasm towards my passion for weaving. He's aware of how much I love it, I talk about it incessantly. We've had many robust discussions about my desire to work, although I try not to interject too many times, I want to get my point across. I know my father will accede to the idea eventually but I don't want to anger him in the process.

"Papa, can I please go and work with Ottho, I'm there every week anyway?" I let this information sink in for a minute.

"I don't know Ailie, you should be at home with your mother."

Mama turns away from the both of us facing the fire. She stares into the flames and disassociates herself from the argument.

"Papa, I love weaving and I know I'm good at it, please consider it." I know better than to remind him that I would be earning money for my craft. He holds pride in his position of provider to our family. I desperately try again. "Papa, you know that I'll be leaving soon anyway, if it's with Ottho in the village or at the Dukes Chateau, wouldn't you prefer that I stay closer to home nearer to you and Mama?"

Mama is eager to regain the void of the house during the day, to reel in her shadows, she's happy for me to go to work. My vivid imagination and untamed curiosity leaves Mama mentally weary, her attempts at childbirth have left her physically drained.

"Let her go." Is my mother's only contribution to the discussion.

"Very well off you go and do your day's work, but don't forget where you've come from." Papa warns.

Ottho greets me at the workroom door and promptly hands me a straw broom. It isn't what I've been expecting at all but I'm excited about my first day. I look forward to eventually creating something beautiful at the loom. I've dressed as plainly as I can given my status in life, I don't want to draw attention to my station, nor do I want the other workers to assume that I'll be granted an easy progress through the ranks. Ottho apparently agrees with me. I begin my working journey right from the bottom rung, as had Sarra and Bertram who have now been elevated to positions above me. Sarra grins when she sees me, a noble girl with an old broom in her hand. However, Bertram barely turns his head, he walks past me with an armful of threads, he may have grunted hello, I'm not entirely sure.

I try not to show it, my ego is slightly bruised. I set about sweeping the studio thinking that I should be sitting at a loom creating beautiful carpets and fabrics. As I sweep I'm careful not to interrupt the crafts-men too much. I've never swept floors before and I try to picture the many times I've seen Bietriz and Florrie sweeping the chateau. It's a skill I've learnt via observation rather than first-hand experience. Sarra watches the exercise unfold in front of her, she waits for me her sub-ordinate to make a mistake or do something unexpected. As I make my way around the studio many of the workers acknowledge me, say hello, welcome me and wish me well, while wondering why on earth the daughter of a nobleman works amongst them. When my sweeping is complete I admire my achievement for a minute before I ask Ottho for another task, hoping now I'll be allowed to weave.

Ottho re-introduces me to Marc, one of the master weavers, a small dark haired man of about thirty years old. When he stands to greet me I see he has a slight humpback from many years of hunching over his loom. I bow my head to show my mentor reverence.

"Ailie, you remember Marc, he'll be your mentor. He'll tell you what to do and he'll give you weaving instruction in the afternoons. Initially you'll work on the loom that you used for your weekly visits until you have the skills to progress onto a bigger one."

I'm excited to know that I'll soon be able to create fabric on my own loom. Marc is pleased to be able to stand and stretch, his muscles twinge and relax as he moves. He loves his job, but after more than twenty years stooped over his loom from sunrise to sunset every day, he's glad to be slightly more upright even if it's only for a few minutes.

"How was your day husband?" Marc's wife Jehanne asks when he walks through the door at the end of the day.

"Good thank you. I have a new apprentice named Ailie, she's very keen to learn everything and is very excited about starting her own projects. She kind of reminds me of myself when I first started.

Although, it won't take long for the back aches and twinges to take the shine off it all." Marc muses. He's honoured with his new teaching role, although Jehanne isn't as positive.

"Well, I hope she doesn't give you any trouble. You know what the nobility can be like, lording it over us. She'll want your job before long."

"No, Ailie's different. She's not like her father at all. I think she'll be an asset to the studio."

"Do you now?" Jehanne stirs the pot of stew on the fire then stops talking, she knows her thoughts are heading down a dangerous path. She loves her husband but he can be a bit naive. Like everyone else she can't fathom why a girl and a noble one at that, wants to work outside of the home when she can be entertained by the other ladies at Court.

The morning moves along steadily until I notice the weavers leaving their stations for lunch. Marc motions to me to take my food into the small dining room next to the studio. Florrie's packed me a small parcel containing a thick slice of bread, some cheese and a crisp red apple. My mouth is salivating as I unwrap my lunch from the square of fabric. Sarra sidles next to me with her food. She says nothing as she takes the apple right from my lap and begins to munch loudly. Wow, what just happened? Being an only child, I've never come across this kind of behaviour before and despite having her own food, Sarra takes another bite of my apple then waits for my response. I'm rendered mute.

I am too well bred and possess excellent manners. I'm not about to confront or accuse anyone of stealing my food. I wonder if anyone else had seen what happened. Being younger and educated in etiquette I wait for Sarra to start the conversation, in particular with an explanation as to why she stole my apple. While I wait for her apology, I see through the window that Bertram isn't eating his lunch inside the confines of the building with the rest of us, I wonder if he finds his sister's behaviour odd as well.

After lunch I'm still a little hungry. I search the studio for my loom and stool for a few minutes, they aren't where I'd left them, I have my suspicions though. Once I've recovered my equipment from the far corner of the workshop, I admire the little box of threads Ottho has supplied to practice my weaving. My concentration is broken when Marc calls me to take a more formal tour of the studio. During the tour he names all of the different equipment and shows me where all of the materials, threads, spare combs and shuttles are kept, then he shows me where the finished products are stored for the customers. He really enjoys standing up and passing on his knowledge, while some of his instructions are familiar, easy to understand, there's a lot of new information to consider as well. I'm worried that I won't remember it all.

"Do you have any questions Ailie?"

"No, I don't think so." I lie. I am overwhelmed with all this new information and can't think of one specific question.

"Well then you can go and clean the materials cupboard."

When I finish my cleaning chores for the day, Marc asks me to make a strip of weaving on my loom which he'll critique when I've finished. As I select my threads, a shiny glimmer catches my eye from the window. I smile warmly to myself. A web has captured a few drops of rain in a sun shower, it glistens throughout the room. I can't see the craftsman who's made the web, I know she's there somewhere, an ally in art and sustenance. Sarra watches me intently from her loom, she notices my smile. She turns towards the direction of my gaze and spots the sparkling web, from her angle she only sees the web of a common spider, she doesn't appreciate the twinkle of lights that I've seen. From my apparent strange behaviours, my lack of reaction towards her misdemeanours and my choice to work despite my nobility, Sarra's conclusion is that I'm a bit simple. I haven't questioned her apple theft and now I'm smiling weirdly at a spider's web. An easy target for her ire, she suddenly seizes the straw broom which I had lent against the wall and she sweeps the web away with one clean movement, she serenely observes my face. I try not to let her see that I'm appalled by her behaviour, but I don't have the confidence to say anything about it. Yet she does.

"You'll need to sweep this area more thoroughly in future or I'll have to have words with Ottho about your sloppy work." Sarra spits her words leaving me gobsmacked, mainly because I could never purposely destroy a spider's web.

At the end of the day Marc honestly critiques my work. Some of the feedback is positive, some not so positive, it's only my first day. I have a lot to learn and according to Sarra, not just about weaving. Florrie arrives way too quickly and waits patiently for me to finish. She's juggling a heavy bag of vegetables in both hands while trying to find a comfortable standing position. She's collected the vegetables from her mother's garden, she's keen to return to the chateau quickly, they are awkward to carry. Unaccompanied, Sarra and Bertram begin to walk towards their home in the forest. I follow them out of the studio feeling happy yet exhausted.

"Can we pack another apple for lunch tomorrow?" I ask Florrie as I fall into step with my nurse.

"Sure. But why? Were you still hungry after all the food I packed for you?" I don't respond, Sarra smiles to herself as she ambles homewards.

I climb the stairs to the loft where I sleep with Mama and Papa. I flop down onto my deer skin which lays on the floor and I close my eyes. I'm physically and mentally weary. Mama has been resting on her fur, I don't even see or hear her ask me how my day has been. I sleep through the evening meal until dawn's early light enters the window, it gently warms my face.

I wriggle my toes a little and feel the heaviness of a fur on my body, somebody must have covered me after I was asleep. I'm still wearing all of the clothes I'd worn the day before and I'm secretly delighted that I don't have to re-dress again, it takes so long. I splash some water onto my face and descend the stairs for breakfast. Having missed supper, I suddenly realise I'm starving which is perfect timing, Florrie and Bietriz begin to stir. They're making moves to prepare the morning meal for the household.

"What are you doing up so early Miss?" Bietriz scratches the back of her head and saunters into the kitchen to light the fire.

"Don't you remember? I'm going to work Bietriz."

"Oh, yes that's right." She can't help wondering why the daughter of a nobleman wants to work.

"It was quiet around here without you though." Florrie quips as she lights the fire and collects a pot to fetch water from the stream. "I miss your funny stories about those weird dreams of yours."

However, Bietriz knows my life to be exceptionally privileged, learning foreign languages, dancing and singing, making embroideries, fannying about with Mama. Life is grand for the rich. Bietriz knows why she has to work. Her role affords her with adequate clothing, food and a roof over her head for which she is grateful. It's more than some of her relatives have in life. Her bosses are kind, if not a little absent in body and spirit. The Lord can be a bit obnoxious when he comes home from the tavern, he's tried it on with her at least twice but she's managed to talk her way out of it before he passes out on the rug next to the fireplace in the hall.

"It's a wonder he didn't crack his head open on the mantle piece on the way down." She tells Florrie all about her experiences with the Lord mainly to relieve herself of the shame.

"Might be a blessing in disguise, don't you think?" Florrie wonders.

"If his Lordship is out of action, who is going to keep a roof over our heads?"

"Oh yeah, I hadn't thought about it that way."

"You never do Florrie. You're a rainbow chaser you know that." Bietriz doesn't mean that as a compliment.

"I know." Florrie giggles, she takes it as one.

The Lady of the House gives Bietriz little to worry about in a physical sense. She keeps to herself and is low maintenance for a Lady of the Manor. However, the mood is often dark due to her depressive mood. All in all, Bietriz has a relatively easy life for a peasant woman. She works hard, but she works in a chateau, it isn't all bad.

Chapter 20 Allie

My photographic hobby has become quite expensive. Dad thinks it's time I learn the value of a dollar.

"You're going to have to get a job Allie. I can't keep shelling out for film and processing."

"Where am I going to get a job? I don't have any skills. I've never had a job before."

"Go down to the supermarket at the shopping centre they'll give you a job."

"What makes you say that? How do you know?"

"Because, that's what I did when I was your age, that's what everyone does if they want to get ahead in life."

"Oh okay, I guess I can. I'll go with Sara tomorrow afternoon, after school."

I haven't really thought about looking for a part-time job before. All of my economic needs have been taken care of by Dad but gaining a bit of independence and having my own money is an attractive prospect. Much to my surprise I'm given a job on the spot. I'm told that training and induction will commence the following week.

Sara doesn't go for the job in the end, Lilly doesn't think it's a good idea for her to be exposed to the harsh chemicals in the laundry aisle, the toxins given off by the plastic wraps and bags, the herbicides and pesticides in the gardening aisle, hormones and antibiotics in the meat and dairy sections, the horror of caged eggs, the non-organic produce, don't get her started on the toxicity rife in the confectionery aisle. Lilly suggests that she find a job at the health food store instead, but Sara is more interested in the fashion stores. They're going to have to have a family workshop to discuss Sara's work life, Sara isn't looking forward to it. She knows her perspectives will be poles apart from her parents views. In the end they'll honour her decision with love and light even though they don't agree.

"Just promise me you won't work in fast fashion Sara."

"Oh Mum, you just don't understand."

At the induction training my supervisor Janet, a middle aged full-timer, informs me of all of the dos and don'ts then tells me to report to work in black pants, they'll supply me with a black polo top. But Mum's on a trip to Paris to visit her friend Trudi so Dad takes me shopping for black pants. We search the cheaper department stores, but I'm so gangly any pants that fit my waist are too short and the pants which are long enough are too roomy around the waist. Methodically we work our way around all of the appropriate stores in the mall without any luck.

Dad is exasperated, he doesn't have the patience for this.

"You would think they'd have a size and shape to fit you, you're not a physical anomaly or anything weird. Why is this so hard?"

"Welcome to my world Dad. It's always been this hard to buy clothes. Perhaps we should've brought Flo along with us."

"Hmm, yes, perhaps you're right." Dad agrees. "Honey, let's get a coffee and come back another time?"

"A, I don't drink coffee and B, I have to get these pants for Saturday morning. I can't go to work without them."

"Okay then. Let's just get a drink, then we can regroup and see if we can find you some pants later on."

As we sit in one of the scuffed leather booths in a café adjacent to the food court Dad places his coffee on the table then adjusts the positions of the salt and pepper shakers until they're sitting to his satisfaction. He obviously has something on his mind besides my work pants.

"I have something to tell you Allie Peg."

Knew it.

"What is it Dad?"

He can't find the words so he pauses to think. He takes his time tentatively sipping his scalding hot coffee then manages to speak.

"Oh my lord, that's hot. I think I've burnt my tongue."

"What is it?" I'm becoming agitated by Dad's agitation, his stalling tactics.

"It's your mother Allie. She's not coming home to live with us after this trip." He releases an audible exhalation as the final word escapes his mouth then he stares at me with pity, he waits for my response. The first thing to cross my mind is that this isn't the best location for this kind of talk. Doesn't he know that one of my friends from school could have walked into the cafe at any minute.

His confession gives him instant relief then he observes how quickly shock has engulfed me even though I haven't fully registered it. I instinctively knew this day would come, I'm not blind. I can see that my parents are polar opposites, I understand that my mother abhors everything Dad stands for but it doesn't stop the tears from streaming down my face.

"Is she coming home from France though? She'll come home to visit us, won't she?" I heave through giant sobs.

There are so many questions but the emotion of my mother's rejection can't be fully explained. Dad hands me his hanky as I search for understanding.

"What about Finn, does he know?"

"Not yet Sweetie, I'll tell him tonight."

I worry for my brother, he isn't strong like I am. He will bury himself deeper into his books to protect himself from the pain of Mum's abandonment. He's definitely a mummy's boy. He knows that his father isn't going to offer him any solace.

Dad's anxiety starts to bubble up again, I blow my nose loud enough for people to start looking our way.

"I think it's time to leave." Dad employs the family motto. If in doubt keep moving.

"Yep." I manage to say through the snotty tears. "Why did you have to make me cry here at the Food Court where the possibility of seeing my friends from school is incredibly high."

"Come on, lets go." Dad doesn't know what to do to help me emotionally. He's good at fixing things with money, he utilises that tactic.

As we leave the coffee shop Dad spies an upmarket boutique whose sole customer base are tall skinny women according to the window decals featuring tall skinny women. I wipe the remaining tears from my cheeks just as we enter the shop.

"Jackpot, if they don't have what we want in here, you'll just have to get another job." "Not funny Dad." I sniff.

The salesgirl Joanna reads Dad like a cheap novel and assumes correctly, that he's loaded and newly single, therefore she's very attentive. As a group we select three pairs of pants for me to try on. While I'm in the fitting room Joanna pounces on the opportunity to talk to Dad while he's alone.

"You're a terrific father, taking the time to shop with your daughter like that." Joanna pauses, she doesn't know how to ask where my mother is without sounding indelicate, so she just comes out with it anyway.

"Where's her mother tonight?"

"In France, we're newly separated."

"Really?" Joanna gushes while she runs her long slender fingers through her hair.

"Yes it's new actually, only a couple of weeks."

"Oh, you poor thing. If you ever need someone to talk to I would love to listen."

Before he can respond, I emerge from the fitting room. I've heard everything. I try to let their conversation wash away from my overcrowded brain. I'm pissed off that Joanna, a stranger, has found out about my parents separation minutes after I've just heard the news, before the rest of my family knows. My anger finds a home very quickly.

"I've tried them all on and I think these are the best." I maintain a level voice through the fitting room door, although I'm shaking inside. I model the most expensive pair of pants.

"You look amazing." Joanna tries to flatter me but my attention is turned towards my Dad.

"You look quite grown up. Look at you."

"So can I have these ones then?" I ask wearily.

Dad doesn't even look at the $170 price tag. He hands Joanna his gold credit card and slips a business card underneath it. He thinks he's being discrete. I see what he's done on the same night that he has dropped the separation bomb on me.

"Thank you Rodger." Joanna purrs then hands me the parcel. "I look forward to seeing you again."

"I don't think so." I say to the indifferent mannequin as we leave the shop.

"What Honey?" Dad seems distracted.

"Nothing, I just want to go home."

I'm still feeling a little tender, but my first day at the supermarket begins on a busy Saturday morning, I'm just glad to be out of the house. The first task given to me is to clean and tidy the shelves. I'm instructed by Janet to make sure that all of the tins, jars and bottles face the correct way. Flo usually does all the cleaning, I try to remember how she goes about it. It doesn't seem that hard but the shelves are long and high so Janet finds me a plastic stool to stand on to reach the top shelves. They are pretty grubby. There's all sorts of stuff that customers have thrown up there thinking that no one has seen them. It's pretty gross. I can see Matt from school who's working in the next aisle. He's tearing open boxes with his knife like Pete Townsend shreds chords.

"Labels must face the customer." Janet brings me to focus as she inspects my work. I want to tell her that I haven't got to those ones yet. I hold my tongue. Old stock has to be brought forward from the back of the shelves to the front. I have to mop the floor when there's a spill. I think it's funny the first time I hear, "Allie, spill aisle seven!" over the tannoy. It makes me think of, "Allie, come on down!" from the Price is Right. But the thrill of hearing my name blasted throughout the store wears thin pretty quickly, it means I have a disgusting cleaning job ahead of me.

By noon my stomach starts to audibly grumble. I'm feeling a bit lightheaded. If I had been at school we would've had recess by now. I'm not used to going for so many hours without food. I'm starving and wonder when I'll be able to leave the shop floor for lunch. To help me understand my deprivation more fully, I count the number of hours I've worked. Eight thirty to twelve so three and a half hours in total. Goddess, it seems so much longer. At one thirty Janet appears.

"Have you been on your break Allie?"

"No, I wasn't sure when I was supposed to go." I'm sure that I am going to wither away if I don't get to eat soon.

"Right, sorry about that. You'd better go now then. You've got half an hour."

I make a hasty bee line to the food court. The sight of the cafe triggers the pain of Dad's talk but I continue on towards the food. On the way to the salad and sandwich bar I bump into Sara who's shopping with Brittany, one of our school friends, we exchange awkward greetings. I'm irrationally embarrassed in my black work uniform, I don't know why. I've forgotten to remove my name badge which has me pinned as a supermarket worker straight away, I feel rattled. Sara and Brittany clutch plastic bags filled with cheap fast fashion and they've had a gaudy make-up makeover at the cosmetic counter of the department store.

"I'm just on my way to get some lunch, do you want to join me?" I try to sound light as I stare at Brittany's orange and green eye shadow. Wow, those purple lips. I want to laugh out loud, I don't. I haven't told anyone at school about Mum and Dad. I'm still raw and trying to process it myself. It's a difficult situation. I want to tell my friends, I do, to share the news but the shopping centre isn't the place even if Dad had thought it was a good idea.

"Oh, we've already eaten, we had sushi. It's new in Adelaide." Brittany declares. Sara can't name the strange feelings she has, was it the raw fish, or was it Brittany? She doesn't know what to say, she remains silent but she knows there's something off between us.

"I don't have long for lunch, I'll have to go. See ya at school next week." I flee from my friends.

Chapter 21 Leo

The senior knights present Leo and Miché with more responsibilities to test their newly acquired knowledge and skills. They both know the rules of chivalry which are to defend the Church of Rome, to live by its teachings, to assist women, in particular widows, to protect orphans, to serve and protect the king, to always be honest, to be generous with their time and wealth, to live honourably for glory.

Odo wants to assess the young squires further and has them kit themselves out with chain mail and spears, then instructs them to wait for him in the yard, next to the stables. The lads fetch their armour and conical helmets from the grand hall, before they proceed to the yard to meet Odo for their next instructions. There they wait patiently in the biting cold for more than an hour, there's no sign of the Duke's step brother. They understand they aren't to leave their post, but to wait as instructed. Leo begins to shiver, he calls Jaimin over to keep him warm, the dog isn't willing to be held for too long, he wriggles loose after a few minutes.

"What's going on? How long do we have to stand here before something happens, or my balls freeze off?" Miché has itchy feet and wants to continue with the mission. Feeling conflicted, he knows there's a hotly contested card game playing in the hall, he's missing out on the action. But despite the grey sky and light misty rain, the brothers know they have to stay put in the yard. While they wait, Leo watches Jaimin sniff purposefully around the stables for rats and mice. After another hour, Odo makes his appearance by the stable doors and the young men's blue ears prick up in anticipation of their orders. Instead of approaching the boys, he speaks to a squire just out of earshot. The squire disappears into the stables and returns with two saddled horses.

"Here take these." The squire hands Miché a leather purse with some coins and a note from Odo with instructions to travel to Breteuil.

"At last, thank you." Miché opens the letter, while Leo tries to see what it says. "The note says that we are to visit Ottho in Breteuil, to collect a tapestry for the Duke. We're going home Brother, well, well, well."

After waiting for so long, the brothers are slightly disappointed that their epic quest is no more than an errand, but they understand that they're required to wait and carryout instructions without complaint.

"We best be off then." Leo says to his brother without any thought to their commitment they mount their horses.

The young men begin their two day journey immediately. After a few minutes riding they quickly return to the castle. Miché has had a sudden realisation.

"Oh my God Leo we need some rope to tie the tapestry to one of the saddles." They return to the stables and find the equipment they need for the return journey.

"Won't we need some food and water as well? It's a long way to Breteuil." Again, they stop and return to the castle, via the kitchen this time. False starts by the wayside, the brothers ride out of the castle gates across the draw bridge and down the road through the forest.

"I hope Odo didn't see us coming and going." Miché is annoyed and embarrassed by their initial lack of foresight.

The squire has been instructed to watch Leo and Miché's movements, he reports to Odo.

"Sir, the brothers took off without any supplies. They had to return several times before they were finally on their way." Odo is concerned when he hears about the brothers mis-steps, but as a man of God, he tries to think about their positive attributes instead of dismissing them as fools. He has a sense that one day these brothers will play key roles in the Duke's army.

"It's a positive sign that they're raring to go. They did return to the chateau when they'd considered their requirements, it shows they're thinking at least. Let's see how they fare from now on, shall we?"

The morning drizzle clears, the ride to Breteuil is luckily uneventful. The squires carry the Duke's colours on their horses which keeps them safe from robbers. Jaimin runs ahead of the horses and every now and then he turns around to ensure Leo is still following his lead. After camping out on the first night they arrive at their parent's manor as the sun set on the second day. However, with no word of warning Catarine is surprised to see her sons and almost doesn't recognise them in their armour. She embraces each son, then calls for the maid.

"Yolant, bring the boys some supper and fetch them a jug of ale pomme!"

Hugo eats his evening meal at the table almost ignoring his older brothers, his dinner is far more important, he'll talk to them later. He's a chubby lad and Arthur doesn't think that he'll make a suitable knight candidate, he is kept at the manor to learn the business of becoming a lord instead. Even though they're almost strangers to him, Darri runs around excitedly to see his older brothers. Leo sweeps his younger brother in his arms and swings him around the room, Catarine laughs nervously.

"How's the littlest knight going? It won't be long before you join us at Falaise." Leo swings him around again.

"Careful, he'll lose his dinner at that rate." Miché warns. Leo gently drops his younger brother onto his feet and sits down to eat. Giddy, Darri falls giggling backwards onto the flagstones.

In the grand room the boys re-embrace their mother and begin to chat about castle life. After they've talked for some time their father arrives home. As he passes through the room, Arthur steadies himself on the table, he's been drinking at the tavern, it's market day and the taxes he's collected are brilliant. Like his wife, he can't believe his two oldest sons are standing before him.

"My sons!" He shakes their hands heartily and takes a chair by the fire. Catarine excuses herself while her husband engages their sons in conversation. "What's news from the Chateau boys?"

The next morning they ride into town to collect the tapestry for the Duke and when they arrive, Ottho is busy in the back of the workshop. Bertram escorts the squires to his boss. Ottho is startled to see the young men in their chain mail, it seems too formal and a bit over the top to be dressed that way, however a necessary precaution when travelling on the dangerous highways. Bertram tries to contain a small laugh behind his hand as he walks away, it's funny to see his employer jump in fright.

While Ottho gathers himself, Leo and Miché scan the workroom to see who's working in the studio. Miché notices Sarra straight away and locks his gaze upon her, Ottho brings the two boys back to attention with a little cough.

"Right, you're here to collect the tapestry for the Duke, yes? Come this way." He leads the boys to a back room where the commission for the Duke hangs on the wall. It isn't terribly large, however the colours are vibrant and the details reflect a different style from the tapestries they'd previously seen at the chateau.

"This tapestry was made by my head weaver Marc and his new apprentice Ailie." As Ottho speaks, Leo peruses the room and sees Sarra, the only other young person who could be an apprentice. Ottho notices him look in Sarra's direction. "No, that's not her. She's not the apprentice who worked on this tapestry." Ottho leads the brothers to Marc to learn more about the weaving. "Ailie is the best apprentice I've seen for many years, a good little worker. Unfortunately she's absent at the moment due to her mother's illness."

After their consultation with Marc, the brothers are instructed to go to the tavern while the tapestry is packed for its journey to the castle. They leave their horses tied to a post at the workshop. Jaimin walks the short distance to the tavern with the brothers, then waits patiently outside with the other village dogs. As they delve in to the dark tavern, they see a woman sitting in the corner, a black cat purring on her lap, a small baby boy playing on the floor by her feet. She keeps her sights set on the squires as they sit at a nearby table.

The jolly innkeeper's wife Marie knows the young men and brings them a jug of ale, a pot of stew with some freshly made bread.

"How's life at the Chateau boys?"

"All good, thanks Marie." The boys chorus before they tuck into their food. Marie continues to chat as they eat.

"What brings you back to Breteuil?" They talk briefly before she moves on to some of the other customers. As they finish their meal they sense it's time to collect the tapestry from Ottho's workshop, Leo and Miché rise to leave.

While they walk through the busy lunchtime crowd, the woman in the corner also rises and gives Miché an apple wrapped in a white hanky.

"Please, give this parcel to my daughter at the workshop."

"But I don't know who your daughter is? How did you know we were going to the workshop?"

"You know who she is." The woman scoops up the baby and the cat follows her. As she leaves the tavern, Leo and Miché look at each other and laugh nervously.

"What the hell?" But the weird thing is, he does know who he's supposed to gift the apple.

The pair stride back to the workshop with trotting Jaimin at their heels. Before they collect the tapestry, Miché has a task to perform. Instinctively, he knows she is the intended recipient of the apple. Miché marches up to Sarra and confidently presents her with the fruit laden handkerchief, he bows before her with affected humility. She instantly recognises the familiar fabric, smiles in recognition of her mother's embroidery and she takes a large bite out of the apple. Immediately she returns both the hanky and the apple to Miché then continues working on her tapestry in silence. Miché is dismissed.

Miché gratefully accepts the package, hiding it in his pocket for the journey home. He doesn't want word flowing back to his boss that he's accepted an apple from a young girl at the workshop. They're here to do a job after all. The boys collect the tapestry, pay for it and pack it as best they can along the right flank of Leo's horse. However, the package makes riding difficult, Leo has to raise his leg over the top of the tapestry. On the short ride to his parent's house he regrets offering to carry the important parcel on his horse.

That night he encourages Miché, who needs no encouragement, to play a game of cards for the right not to carry the tapestry on his horse.

It's really very uncomfortable on the short ride back from the workshop to their manor house, he imagines a difficult journey back to Falaise.

"Hey Miché, how about a game of Mouche and the winner rides tomorrow without the encumbrance of the tapestry."

"Yes, absolutely I'm in, deal the cards." An excellent card player, Miché easily wins the first game.

"Double or nothing?" Leo really doesn't want to ride with the tapestry.

"You're on." Miché wins the next two games and Leo is forced to carry the awkward tapestry back to the castle the next morning. While riding Miché munches on his apple and thinks about the mysterious girl in the workshop.

Within seconds of taking his second bite a raven flies down from a branch, in a chestnut tree and swoops up his apple. Jaimin barks warily at the bird.

"What the hell?" He calls out for the second time in twenty four hours. The raven has the apple wedged in its beak and glares at Miché. Leo laughs at his brother as he rides with his right leg higher in his saddle. Miché laughs at his brother as he wipes the remaining apple juice from his hand onto his trousers.

They return safely to Falaise and deliver the precious cargo to its new owner, satisfied in the knowledge that they've survived the journey with the tapestry still in tact.

"I feel that you're equipped with the skills and most importantly, as you've reached the age of twenty one Miché, it's time to receive your knighthoods." Odo states to the brothers a few weeks after their return from Breteuil.

"I haven't based your eligibility solely on your successful mission to Ottho's workshop, but your continued improvement of your skills and the impeccable way you've conducted yourselves in all areas of your life." The brothers are indeed chivalrous and inspiring role models for the squires below them. "The ceremony will be in one week, but we have many preparations to consider before then." Odo warns them.

"Thank you for recognising our progress, Your Grace."

"We are most honoured, Your Grace." Leo also bows before the Duke's step-brother.

White vestments to represent purity and red robes to signify nobility and black hose and shoes to represent the death of their former lives as squires are collected by valets for Leo and Miché to wear at the Order of the Knighthood service. On the day before the ritual the brothers bathe thoroughly to purify their bodies before they meditate in an overnight vigil in the chapel to cleanse their spirits. While they kneel in silent prayer, Odo places two shields and two swords upon the altar without disturbing the brother's meditation.

In the morning of the brand new day, the brothers are to be inducted as men into the fold of the Inner Circle. Most of the noble inhabitants of the chateau congregate in the chapel to witness the service.

"Miché and Leo remember it's very important to always conduct oneself as a chivalrous knight. Dear Lord, bless these shields and swords, and may they never have to be used in war." Odo hands the swords to a sponsor who transfers them to the Duke. "Please come forth, Miché and Leo." Odo calls for the brothers to be presented to Guilliam, from the pews, Catarine whispers to her husband.

"Look at our handsome sons." Arthur beams at his wife, pats her knee and feels immense pride as his sons are presented to the Duke.

Leo and Miché nervously make their way to the front of the chapel and kneel in front of the Duke before Odo instructs them.

"You now declare your vows." The brothers repeat their vow after the bishop.

"*We vow on our faith in God that we will be obedient to the Duke, we will not injure him, we will respect him absolutely, with our word, without dishonesty.*"

With their vows spoken and felt, Miché is the first to be dubbed. Guilliam receives the sword from the sponsor and taps the flat edge on both of Miché's shoulders before declaring aloud.

"I dub thee, Sir Knight. Arise, Sir Miché." Miché stands, his sponsor attaches spurs to his leg where his sword will be attached. The Duke turns his attention to Leo. Once again he takes the blessed sword from the sponsor and places the flat edge on Leo's shoulders, he makes a declaration to the congregation.

"I dub thee, Sir Knight. Arise Sir Leo." The sponsor repeats his actions with the spurs and the newly dubbed knights are presented to the congregation with fanfare.

Chapter 22 Leon

Given their religious faith and showing promise academically and on the football field, Cathy and Archie think it's best to send their boys to the Catholic school in the city, St. Marks. Cathy has heard some disturbing rumours, she shudders at the thought of her boys being exposed to the apparent prolific sex and drugs, available at the local high school.

"You know Archie, I really don't want our kids going to that school. Especially now that Angie told me about that year eleven girl with a baby and that younger boy who overdosed on, God's knows what. That school's probably not the best for the kids, what do you reckon?" Cathy sips her wine as she prepares dinner and presents her case to Archie.

"Your probably right Love, whatever you reckon."

"Well, you could sound a little more interested, its only their entire future we're discussing here." Cathy starts to fidget with her necklace while she decides which vegetable to cut up next and Archie is fossicking through the draws to find something very important.

"I am interested Love, but I need to find a pen so that I can let the school know that we're interested as well." Archie waves the paperwork in Cathy's face while he continues his search for a pen.

At first both boys resist the change, they're looking forward to going to the local high school with their friends.

"Oh, do we have to? Why do you always punish us like this? There'll be no girls and no fun at that school." Declan as always is the first to protest.

"Exactly. You can focus on your schoolwork for a change instead of girls." Cathy reminds her eldest son.

"Yes, but why can't we go to our local high school with our friends? Besides, just because one girl has a baby, its not her fault and it doesn't mean its the schools fault either." Leon backs his brother.

"What about the drugs though?" Cathy counters.

"Well, kids at private schools can afford better drugs so they don't get as sick and its not reported as much. Their families keep it quite. Anyway, its not something that I'm interested in."

"I don't think that's how it works Leon." Cathy is agitated, her son has illuminated her prejudices.

"Let's just go to the Open Night and see how you like it before you strike it out of contention. And Declan, there will be plenty of girls to ignore you when you leave school." Archie offers with a chuckle, Leon punches Declan's arm.

"Ha, you'll be lucky if you ever get a girlfriend with your gross farts."

"Well at least I can talk to girls, not like you......" Declan is about say something mean before Archie interjects. He knows how sensitive Leon is and he knows that Declan can injure him with his words.

"Right shut up and set the table for dinner. Not another word."

When they inspect the college facilities at the information night, Leon has a change of heart.

"Declan, did you hear about the international exchange programme? Think of the travel." Leon can't stop talking about the things he's seen and heard. "What about the art classes, I would love to do that. We can learn French, or Spanish, which one do you reckon Dec?"

"I dunno. Definitely not art."

"Well, we could play football against some of the other colleges which is a better comp than the high school rounds." Leon can now see the potential of a private school and in his spare time over the following days he tries to convince Declan that change might be a good thing. Finally Leon's marketing works, but at the end of the day it doesn't really matter, their parents are sending them to the college regardless of their wishes.

Term two is the first of the two football terms at St. Marks and even though he isn't the captain, Leon is selected to play on the team every Saturday. As the competition is better in this league, Declan struggles for selection early on in the season, but he shows promise throughout the year, by the end of term he plays every week, as other player's injuries cement Declan's place on the team. St. Marks College is well matched against most of the other schools in the area, except for one, the Anglican college in the leafy eastern suburb, St. Bertram's, or St. Bert's for short.

Even though the St. Bert's footballers are only in middle school they stand tall muscular and athletic. They possess rare skills for their age group with the ability to read where the ball is headed before the ball knows itself. They are legendary and undefeated at the grand final for many years. Simply playing in the final with them has become the honour. Most students hate playing against St. Bert's. There is the assumption that before the game has even begun they will have no chance of winning, strangely Leon sees this challenge as an opportunity to improve his game.

"Look at it this way Dec, we can see how a winning side performs differently from us. Much of St. Bert's advantage stems from their height and power, things that Coach Jones can't possibly change overnight, but there are some other things we can improve on. For example, we can work on our ball skills or at the very least we could keep our eye on the ball instead of faffing about. We could consider our position in relation to members of the other team and be more discerning of our next steps."

"Is that right Leon? What bloody magazines have you been reading? What a wanker." Declan mumbles as he walks away. He often wonders if he really is the older brother.

Leon's team plays St. Bert's in week four which means they can secure a few confident wins before meeting with the undefeated champions.

"Leon, you're to stand number seventeen." Coach Jones reads the play list before the game. Number seventeen is much taller than Leon, a rugged looking boy standing assertively on the earth. As Leon walks towards him the lad surveys the landscape and the other players, he adjusts his socks then performs some side stretches. Slightly intimidated, Leon arrives next to his opponent and offers him a firm handshake.

"Hello, I'm Mitch." Still wrapped in his tight grip Leon responds with the most confident voice he can muster, his voice breaks.

"Leon." They turn their focus towards the coin toss in the middle of the field.

St. Bert's win the game convincingly of course and at the final siren Mitch seeks out Leon to shake his hand again.

"Good effort. You're not a bad player." Mitch offers in condolence.

"No, you were the better players." Leon concedes gracefully. When the singing of the St. Bert's team song refrains the players disperse and Leon doesn't see Mitch again, until they play against each other in the third term.

Paired again, Leon approaches Mitch and shakes his hand.

"Are you ready to be beaten?" Mitch laughs.

"Wanker." Leon mumbles in to a fake cough.

The next time they meet they play on the St. Bert's oval and the facilities are nothing short of magnificent. Leon thinks the amenities are comparable to a professional AFL team.

"When have you ever seen AFL facilities, dumb arse?" Declan tries to cut his brother down.

"On telly, idiot."

"Ooh, burn."

The St. Mark's change rooms have hot showers, pristine toilets, a locker room with a kitchen, warm up and recovery areas, and state of the art gym equipment. When the boys enter the change rooms they inspect the facilities as if they are in a high end hotel for the first time.

"You know, I could move in here, but I wonder what the home team's change room is like if this is just the visitor's room." Leon says to the boys around him.

"They probably have gold toilets." Billie quips.

At the end of the game, Mitch shakes Leon's hand.

"Good try. See you next time."

"Thanks Mitch, No you played well. See ya."

Chapter 22 Ailie

I cherish my work at the loom and I appreciate having Marc as my mentor. He's kind and considers my ideas which gives me confidence despite my young age and inexperience. I feel so satisfied and inspired by my work, however Marc has toiled at the loom for many years, he thinks his work is tired and repetitive.

"I find your input of new ideas refreshing Ailie." They've incorporated some of my concepts into the tapestry we've undertaken for the Duke of Normandy which is very exciting. I can't wait to tell my parents that I'm working on something so special for the Duke.

Mama and Papa don't know what to do with this information though, how can they be proud of their working daughter. What will the Lords and Ladies at Court say? Papa can just imagine the men at the card tables.

"Old Belanger had to send his daughter out to work. Times must be tough for the old bugger." So my parents say nothing and I ask for nothing. I don't want to jeopardise my position at the workshop. I keep my head down and keep working at my craft. I have to learn to appreciate my own talents and be happy for myself. What more can I do?

The tapestry we are working on isn't overly grand though the colours are vivid and the details are highly original. It's to be a gift for the Duke's bride, Matilda of Flanders on the occasion of their marriage and it gratifies me to know that some of my ideas are assimilated into such an important piece of work. Ottho says that it will hang for all to see at the wedding festivities.

Work has become a vital refuge from the darkness at home, Mama has sunk deeper into depression, Papa is a sloppy drinker and philanderer. It's more apparent to everyone, my working life is the least of his worries. Papa has become the subject of town gossip which has finally reached the weaver's workshop. The artists speak of his misdemeanours in hushed tones, away from me of course. I know I'm pitied, I've have been shown compassion for my situation. Most of my colleagues seem to have forgotten that I was born of privilege, well above their station, perhaps because I never behave in a snooty way. I try to remain humble.

They see me as an equal of sorts, as a child whose parents have overlooked her, at least that's the impression I have.

Luckily I have Bietriz and Florrie to care for my physical requirements, however they don't have to care for my emotional needs as well. It's ironic, Mama mourns all of her lost babies, but doesn't seem interested in caring for the one she's successfully borne. Mama sees me as a thriving child not requiring the services of a mother. She believes that all of my needs are met by my inner fortitude, my food, and clothing provided by the servants and companionship received from work colleagues. Most of that is true, but I want her to love me as well. Nothing can replace a mother's love.

Wanting to be alone, Mama eats her meals on the top floor where the family sleeps which creates extra work for Bietriz and Florrie who have to climb the stairs at least three times a day to deliver her food and retrieve dirty plates back to the kitchen. Most of the time Mama hardly touches her food, the servants have to re-carry nearly full plates on a return journey to the kitchen. These excursions to the second floor are in addition to their trips to empty chamber pots, tidy and sweep, collect clothing for mending and laundering, and any other errands Mama demands. The servants are exhausted by her illness, I never hear them complain. In fact they do everything in their power to help Mama.

As she appears so pale and wan, Bietriz suggests something new to help Mama.

"Perhaps, the Pagan woman Luna should visit you to concoct an herbal remedy for your....um..sadness?" Bietriz broaches the subject tactfully. Via the town grapevine Bietriz learns that Luna prepares tonics for villagers who experience various maladies. Bietriz thinks anything at this point is worth trying, once. "If it means I can stop climbing those blessed stairs all day it shall be worth it." She grumbles to Florrie.

At first, Mama resists Bietriz suggestions.

"I don't know, what would it look like, the Lady of the Chateau, a good Christian woman, entertaining a heathen woman here in my home." Mama rationalises with her maid. Bietriz has planted a small seed. When she mentions Luna again a few days later, Mama actually toys with the idea. "Send for Amis, I want to send a note to that Pagan woman you speak of, to visit me."

"Yes Ma'am." Poker faced Bietriz retreats once more to the staircase to fetch the writing implements for Mama.

When Luna arrives at the chateau she is shown into the great hall to a sit by the fire. Mama washes and changes the dress she's been wearing for many days and takes her time to gather herself before descending the stairs. It's been a long time since she's entertained her friends, let alone a complete stranger, she feels she needs to be more like her former self in front of her new visitor which is ironic because that is the reason for Luna's call in the first place. With this sober realisation, Mama descends the stairs and makes her way down to the hall. As she hasn't moved far in the past few weeks, she's a little unsteady on her feet, she keeps her right hand in contact with the wall at all times to save herself from falling.

As Mama enters the hall Luna rises from her chair and walks over to greet her.

"Good morning, Lady Belanger."

"Good morning, Luna, isn't it?"

"Yes, Ma'am. You seem to be quite cold. Are you alright?" Sensing the cold in her host's hands and ignoring protocol Luna clasps Mama's cold fingers in both of her hands that she'd just warmed by the fireplace. Luna rubs them gently before lowering them to her side. Luna can feel the warmth spread out to her host's fingers while Mama's hands sting a little, as her visitor's warmth replaces the bitter cold. As Luna lets Mama's hands go both women try to process what she thinks about the woman standing before her.

"Yes, I'm fine thank you. Please take a seat over here." Feeling a little confused by this close personal contact from a stranger, Mama motions to Luna to return to her seat while she tries to compose herself as the head of a stately home. Mama finds relief in her tired body when she finally sits in front of the fire, but with the increased light Mama squints at first finding it hard to see clearly. However, it doesn't take long for her sight to return to normal. She observes Luna who's been silently absorbing her new surroundings and her host.

Luna sits perfectly still as she watches Mama fiddle, adjust and finally smooth her clothing, she gently itches her face, neck and ears, runs her fingers through her hair, tries to feel the warmth in her hands from the handshake that has long since dissipated and finally her eyes rest on Luna's serene face. Luna is about the same age as Mama, however their lives are vastly different. Luna has three children and a husband to care for without the benefit of servants. She lives in a small wooden bungalow house, makes herbal remedies and observes seasonal events set by Mother Nature, rather than those of the Church of Rome. Uncomfortable with the silence, Mama is the first to speak.

"I trust you've had a pleasant journey this morning?" Mama enquires of her guest's two and a half kilometres walk.

"Yes, though it was a little frosty to start with, I soon warmed up. But if I may?" Luna begins, she wants to get to the heart of the matter. "You're a little sad, yes?" Mama peers at the silk threads of her dress and returns her gaze to Luna.

"Well yes, but only a little." She tries to smile, her attempt is weak, she isn't fooling Luna.

"Tell me if I'm speaking out of turn Ma'am, but I fear you carry a great deal of pain in your heart." Luna's approach is kind and caring, as she speaks she moves from her chair to sit on the padded sofa next to Mama. Mama inches over to allow her guest more room on her seat. Mama has a wide personal space, but it's comforting to share the sofa with such a kind woman. Mama tries to remain calm and composed, but she can feel evidence of her sadness betraying her, a fat tear starts to roll down her cheek. Mama swipes at it with her hand, the flood gates open, she can no longer control the flow.

When Mama's sobs subside she takes a deep breath before she begins to enlighten Luna of her failed pregnancies, her husband's increased drinking and infidelities.

"It's been rumoured amongst the villagers that some of the waifs in town bear a stunning resemblance to the Master of the Chateau. The shame of it at Court is terrible you know. I can't stand those haughty woman gossiping about my family like that." Mama states blandly. Luna can't relate to her woes, but she listens anyway. "Sometimes I am not able to leave the second floor of the chateau for days on end, my body aches too much."

"Your worry and grief have manifested pain inside of your body because you bottle everything up inside. I'm glad that you called for me, hopefully we can move some of that grief and worry from your soul." Luna feels more confident commenting as a friend. She listens patiently to Mama for nearly an hour and when she finally stops confiding in her, Luna asks Mama another question.

"Can we call for Bietriz? I need her to bring some boiling water and a bowl."

When the maid arrives with the required items, Luna reaches into her bag and produces a handful of herbs.

"What are these plants?" Mama wants to know.

"This one is chamomile, this is St. John's wort, rosemary and thyme." Luna holds each plant for Mama to see and smell. Luna then picks a little bit of each herb, crushes them between her palms, swirls them in the boiling water clockwise three times and then reverses the procedure. As she agitates the infusion with a wooden spoon she mumbles some words of prayer. At least Mama thinks it's a prayer, she can't be sure. Luna places the herbs into the boiling water to steep and passes her free hand over the bowl three times, she murmurs another incantation.

"Fire, water, earth and air. Fire, water, earth and air, the sun and moon, Infinite Oneness, Minerva, Mother Earth bless and heal the soul of Isabea. Thank you, Great Mother."

Mama thinks that Luna should have said Lady Belanger instead of the more familiar Isabea, but she doesn't think it right to correct a Pagan incantation, she doesn't know how they work after all. Luna places the bowl onto a table to allow the tea to infuse for a few minutes and when it's cool enough to drink she hands the bowl to Mama.

Mama inhales the aroma of the tea. It has a pleasant floral scent and the aroma soon helps to clear the tightness around the crown of her head which relaxes her. She takes a few tentative sips and feels the warm liquid sooth her soul. Calmer, Mama forever regal reclines slightly on the sofa. She realises she's held onto a lot of tension and now she senses it oozing from her soul as she continues to sip the tea. Colour slowly returns to her cheeks and for once in a long while her smile is genuine and endures for the afternoon. The gloom hasn't completely vanished, but she feels so much better. While Mama stares into the fire, Luna hands Bietriz more of the herbs and issues detailed instructions as to how she should make the tea for her mistress.

"I'm not sure about the incantation bit. I think that I'll remember the fire and water part though." Bietriz knows that she's already forgotten Luna's chant.

"As long as you have the right intention you can't go wrong, Bietriz." Luna reassures her.

When Bietriz leaves the room Luna returns to Mama's side and holds her hands again until she is reassured the warmth is returning to her body. Luna releases one of Mama's hands and with the back of her own hand caresses Mama's newly pink cheeks, the flush has spread down her face and onto her neck and chest. Mama doesn't know how to respond or know what to think, her mind races. What's happening? This woman makes her feel alive and warm, she's stirred her in a way her husband once made her feel, but it isn't her husband touching her. With instinctual reflexes, Luna quickly stands by the fire just as Bietriz returns to the room with more tea.

"You have a lovely glow about you Mistress. The tea must be doing you good."

"Yes, I feel much better thank you Bietriz." Mama flushes again.

When I return home from work I'm shocked to see Mama sitting by the fire on the ground floor of the chateau. It looks so strange seeing her on the sofa staring into the flames, I haven't seen her in this room for months. I embrace her and share my day with her, but I have to remind her of the people I work with, she's rarely taken any notice of my work stories. It's as if she's hearing about these people for the first time and in a sense that's true.

Papa arrives home on time for once and we all eat our dinner together in the grand hall sharing stories from our day. Papa and I both
wonder what's happened to snap Mama out of her funk, but we dare
not ask her why for fear that we'll break the spell. Our little family
hasn't sat at the table, for dinner like this, for many weeks and Mama
eats her supper, a small amount, she consumes food none the less and
as we climb the stairs for bed, we laugh at the hounds who chase their
tails by the fire, we sleep in the hope that life has returned to normal.

In the morning, Mama is still asleep when I rise and Papa's in the
yard talking to Amis about the horses. I think about Mama being well
and how lovely eating dinner as a family had been, it puts me in a
happy mood and I can't wait to see Mama bright again when I return
from work. After breakfast, I skip into town with Florrie who will visit
the market in the town square, we part ways while I continue skipping
down the lane to the workshop. However, Florrie is still concerned
about Mama and when she returns to the chateau later in the day she
enquires about Mama's well being.

"Is her ladyship up this morning?" She asks Bietriz.

"No, I haven't seen her yet. Perhaps you should take up her breakfast,
see how she is?" Florrie agrees and places her shopping on the table,
grabs a tray from the sideboard and arranges some bread, a bowl of
soup from the pot near the fire, and a jug of ale.

"Shall I make some of her Pagan brew?" Florrie asks, but Bietriz has
already stepped outside to collect more fire wood, she doesn't hear the
request. Florrie decides she will go ahead with her plan and places the
jug of ale to one side. She pours some hot water from the pot, which
always sits on the fire, into a wooden bowl, and crushes up some of
the herbs. Florrie places the crushed herbs, without confidence, into
the bowl of hot water. She doesn't know about the incantation, so she
carries the tray of food and drinks upstairs to her mistress.

When Florrie enters the room, a strong noxious smell almost knocks
her over and she can see vomit on the ground next to where her
mistress sleeps. Florrie quickly puts the tray down and rushes to see her
mistress. Mama's asleep, but her face is pale and clammy. Discovering

her mistress in this state, Florrie doesn't know what to do and for a minute she thinks that she might be dead, she can't see her chest rise and fall. In the next moment, Mama takes a deep shuddering breath, Florrie exhales vocally as well. She needs help, Florrie sprints downstairs to fetch Bietriz. They gather material to clean up Mama and the floor where she's been sick.

When she returns to the kitchen, Bietriz notices that the remaining herbs look different to the ones that Luna had left them. The purple star shaped flowers are a giveaway for starters.

"Florrie, come here at once." Bietriz calls for the maid.

"These are not the herbs that Luna left here. This looks like hemlock and this one here, with the purple flowers, is belladonna. They're extremely poisonous. Did you give them to Lady Isabea?"

"I don't know, perhaps." Florrie stammers. "I don't know how they got here though, I didn't collect any herbs. I thought these were Luna's herbs." Florrie is distraught and doesn't know what to do or know where to turn. Bietriz grabs her by the shoulders to settle her.

"Get a grip girl, somebody has swapped Luna's plants for these ones. It isn't your fault. Now get the tea on, young Ailie will be home soon." As Bietriz throws out the rest of the plants, she has an inkling as to how the medicinal herbs were replaced with poisonous ones, but she doesn't know for sure. She does know that Florrie had nothing to do with Mama's relapse, she doesn't have an evil bone in her body.

"Miss, your mother is very ill and she's been sleeping for most of the day." Florrie informs me, I hook my cape on the back of the door when I return from work.

I'm shocked to hear that Mama has taken such a dramatic turn for the worse. I thought that life was going to return to normal and she will be, well I don't know what she will be, I think she has always been sad and depressed, but I was so looking forward to everything being better.

"How can this be, especially after seeing her improvement last night?"

Florrie brings my dinner to the table. "I don't know what could have caused it Miss. She was looking so good, wasn't she?" After my meal,

I sit with Mama and wipe her brow with a damp cloth. Even though Mama travels in and out of consciousness, I assure her that I'll stay by her side until she is well. Papa joins us later in the night and lays on his deer skin.

"Papa, there's a purple flower stuck to your shoe." I say to him, but he's already drifted off to asleep.

"Don't touch that flower Ailie." Mama whispers.

"But its so pretty."

"Promise me Ailie." Mama says as she drifts off to sleep.

"Yes Mama."

Chapter 23 Allie

Even though Mum and Dad are now officially separated, everyday life remains fairly normal for us all. However, Finn seems to be studying harder, Dad works even more, well that's what he's telling us. God only knows where, what or who, he's doing and sadly we hardly see Flo anymore. Mum rented a flat in the city which she rarely uses, but the funny thing is, we see her just as much as when she and Dad were together, which is to say not much. I still work at the supermarket and I like most of the people I work with, which is just as well, it's pretty quiet at home. During the school holidays, I work every day until five o'clock which are long days, but I like not being at home in the void. I'm grateful that I don't have to work on Sundays though. That's the one day when I can go to the beach, or to a park, and take photographs with my camera.

Given my role models, most relationships are difficult to navigate in high school. My friendships are fine, but there's the added peer pressure to date someone. A scant number of boyfriends come and go, if you can call them that. As a bit of an introvert, I'm too nervous to approach anyone, besides I'm content just hanging out with my friends, Belinda's the opposite. She never seems to understand, or looking back, perhaps she doesn't care, that the year ten cohort just aren't that interested in her.

Sara overhears some of the other girls talking about their boyfriends who go to private schools and play on the football team.

"Allie, let's do something different and watch the footy at St. Bert's this weekend."

"I don't know. I'm not that interested to be honest. And I have to work." Throughout the day, Sara drops not so subtle hints and is so annoying, that I finally agree to catch the bus to the leafy suburbs with her after my shift at work.

We're impressed with the school grounds and fantasise about attending a posh college like this one. After walking for what seemed like a kilometre, we eventually find our way to the well-groomed oval. We perch in the grandstand with the more affluent looking supporters of the home team. Well, we actually sit slightly to one side of them, we feel a little out of place amongst the casually well-dressed crowd. Most of them wear the de rigueur, faux rugby tops, collar up of course and we giggle when we hear one posh mother talking to her husband.

"Oh Jeremy, do pass the Thermos, I'm so dehydrated. Where did you put the crudités and the salmon terrine?"

"What accent is that?" Sara asks me.

"Eastern suburbs, money, Darling."

After the first quarter, we begin to understand the game a little more than the zero understanding we had at the first siren and we're delighted to have sat amongst the supporters of the winning team. It's a very uplifting atmosphere, as the parents scream out encouragement to their sons. It reminds me of when Dad shouted out his encouragements to me when I played primary school netball, it made me a little misty eyed.

"Stick to your man, Alexander!"

"Keep your eye on the ball Jonathon!"

"Run for the ball Simon!"

"Bloody hell Aaron, RUN!!!"

"No Ump, holding the ball!" Even though St. Bert's are well in front, they're not prepared to squander a single point.

At the start of the next quarter, the teams change sides and Sara notices two boys playing on the oval directly in front of us. Boys she hadn't spotted before.

"Look over there at number seventeen, cute hey?" I peer at the boy from the other team, number four, who's alongside number seventeen.

"Hmm." I sigh.

When the siren signals the end of the half, the teams disperse into their respective change rooms, Sara gets up, dusts her bum and starts to leave.

"Where're you going? Toilet? Canteen? Can you get me some hot chips?"

"It's finished, isn't it? At least I hope it is, because it's so boring."

"Well the first half has finished, there's still another half to go." I don't know much, but this much I do know. Sara and I laugh at her lack of knowledge of the game, we decide to leave anyway, it's so cold, the metal seats are hard on our bums and we're pretty bored. We decide to catch the bus back into town. It's just as well we left early, I have a homework assignment that's due on Monday, and I haven't even started it.

In terms of my academic interests, I'm not exactly an A grade student, by any stretch of the imagination. I mainly fly under the radar, sitting on solid Cs and Bs, there's little expectation from home in terms of my abilities, which means that I enjoy a certain level of freedom from the usual parental pressures some of my peers experience. I make sure my homework is mostly completed on time, however my teacher's attention is generally focused on students who struggle, act out, or are disobedient. Sometimes, the teacher offers extension work for the students who excel, but I'm definitely not one of those students. In a forty-five minute lesson, containing thirty students, she doesn't have time to address the performance of the moderate students, which suits me, I like to remain anonymous.

My key interests at high school are home economics and camera club. I particularly enjoy sewing and I seem to have a knack for it. This is the only class that I will get the occasional A, which feels really good and makes me wonder why getting an A isn't as easy in my other classes. The teacher, Ms Marks is impressed with my neat needlework and has me help the other students who are struggling with some of the more difficult stitches. For my end of term project, I made a cushion and embroidered small flowers in blue, pink and violet, around the corners.

"This is such beautiful work Allie. Are you sure you haven't done anything like this before.

"Not really Miss. Just some mucking around with needles and threads when I was younger."

"I would swear that you've been trained in embroidery for years. Well done Allie." Ms Marks moves on to the next student.

Even though camera club occurs after school, it's an opportunity for me to better understand the new SLR camera Dad gave me for my birthday and to use the school dark room where I process my photos.

My photographic skills have steadily progressed, from the Instamatic shots of blurry spiders, to in focus shots of birds and spiders. Sadie from the Year Book Committee asked me if I can take some photos at school events throughout the year, at first I'm a little unsure of my abilities. What standard are they expecting, coffee table book quality? However, I'm proud when my photograph of students raising money at the cake stall is published in the school newsletter and I'm asked to be a regular contributor. Not exactly Rolling Stone, but it's a start.

The photos I've taken with Sara over the past three years take up most of the real estate on the pin board, above my desk. While I do my homework, on Medieval France, I glance up at the photo of us at the football match, I had one of the mothers take our picture. For the first time, I notice behind Sara's head, the two boys she pointed out. They have their backs to the camera, I can just make out a fuzzy number four on one of the jumpers.

Chapter 24 Leo

On the checklist of his life's journey, Guilliam needs a bride to fulfil the role of Duchess of Normandy. He searches far and wide for a suitable candidate, eventually finding his love in Bruges, Flanders. Matilda is nineteen years old, of high birth, while Guilliam is twenty three and has been the Duke of Normandy since he was eight years old. According to his family, it's time for him to be married.

"Matilda will you take my hand in marriage."

"Guilliam, I'm afraid I cannot marry you, because you were.... born a bastard. You are not a suitable match for my status."

"How dare you, I have the same breeding as you."

Guilliam scorned, angrily rides back to Normandy. However, the long distance gives him time to ponder his true love's thoughts and with little warning, he turns his horse around. Guilliam is enraged, he's been so easily dismissed, he returns to Matilda's father's house in Flanders, storms into her room, and in a show of dominance, he violently drags her by her hair, from her bed, down onto the floor.

"Who do you think you are, speaking to me that way? I am The Duke of Normandy and one day, I will be King of England." He violently throws her down and leaves her sobbing on the floor.

In the dawn after his attack, Matilda has time to think about her feelings for the Duke. She reacts extraordinarily to Guilliam's vicious advances, his ferocious power and his determined manner seem to have won her love, she soon yields to his commanding ways. Moreover, once they became a courting couple, it's apparent that Matilda's family aren't the only ones who oppose the pairing. The Church in Rome, vehemently opposes the union, however their shared contempt for authority brings the couple even closer. At the Council of Reims, Pope Leo IX bans the marriage between the third cousins, once removed, as they will likely break consanguinity laws. But their love proves too strong, they are desperate to be married. Both strong willed and determined, they defy the Church, plan to marry and build an empire.

When the time for their nuptials arrives, there's great excitement at the chateau, there will be a festival lasting several days with delicious banquets, acts of strength, dancing, and a jousting competition. Leo practises jousting when he has the time, he's learnt to balance his lance while riding his horse so he can face his opponents without looking like a fool. To begin with, the pole feels unstable and unwieldy in his hand, but with some instruction from the older knights, it isn't long before he has the hang of it.

On the eve of the wedding, important families from all over Normandy travel for many days to witness the nuptials. Food, wine, ale and apple cider, have been gathered and prepared by the servants for many weeks, colourful pavilions are erected in the garden, a Berfrois is built on the field outside of the Chateau. This exclusive grandstand hosts the noble audience. The Duke's red and gold flags flutter from the castle towers and from the towers at the end of the draw bridge. Floors are swept, horses groomed, armour polished, and the new tapestry from Ottho's workshop hangs in the grand hall for all to admire. Everyone has a job to do to ensure that the wedding is magnificent enough to befit Duke Guilliam, and his bride to be.

When they arrive at the gates, Arthur and Catarine du Bois are shown to their quarters by their sons. When Roger Belanger arrives, it is noted by the Court that he has travelled alone. Everyone is wondering why Lady Isabea has not attended the festivities.

"Will your wife be joining us for the celebrations?" Leo asks Roger.

Papa mumbles something inaudible into his chin. To be polite, Leo retires the conversation as he ushers Papa to his quarters, in the same wing as his parents. While Leo is absent, Miché takes command of the welcoming duties. First in line are the artisans who have produced the wedding commemoration tapestry.

Ottho, Marc and I, are shown to the tents at the back of the chateau, where non-noble, yet valued guests, are asked to reside for the festivities. Miché notices me at the back of our little group and when he speaks to Ottho, he doesn't think I can hear them.

"Her beauty is hard to miss, is it not? There are many knights at Falaise who would like to court her."

"Yes, quite." Ottho squirms, he sees me as a surrogate granddaughter, not an object of lust, he makes a mental note to look out for me during the festivities. Although Miché isn't interested in me, he wonders if he should enquire about Sarra. He thinks she's pretty and feisty, his perfect combination of attractive qualities. It's a festive occasion, so he quickly engages his natural confidence.

"Was the other maiden not able to make the journey?" Miché tries to sound nonchalant.

"Oh no, only the artists who worked on the tapestry were invited, you just get us I'm afraid." Ottho grimaces. His staff have been remembered, but he realises, of course, Miché has a liking for his young worker.

Page boys and squires welcome guests, who are neither noble, nor artistically qualified, for a more regal greeting. The commoners are shown to the group of tents on a small field at the back of the chateau, where the horses are tethered en mass. The hoi polloi are high-spirited for three days of the festivities, however the area soon becomes quite pungent. There is much drinking and dancing, and for the most part, the commoners thoroughly enjoy themselves, despite the squalid conditions of their designated area. When everyone has had too much food, ale, wine and merriment, the castle and the grounds eventually fall quiet, despite a few sonorous snorers interrupting the silence throughout the various sleeping quarters.

However, not everyone sleeps soundly. Leo is restless and still wide awake. He decides that he wants to exchange jousting tactics with Miché, though he doesn't wish to disturb the slumbering guests, he suggests they take a stroll onto the field. It's a beautiful night to be outside, an almost full moon shines a silvery beam across the damp grass. Entering their first tournament brings forth some nerves and the young men talk for some time about the rules of engagement, they compare notes regarding the other knights who are to be their opponents.

"Watch out for the Black Knight of Caen, he's the one to beat."

"Yeah, okay will do. Anyone else I have to look out for?" As they continue their discussion, they hear a high pitched sound from the grove of trees, at the edge of the field. "It must be a goldfinch that hasn't roosted for the night." Leo explains the strange whistling noise. Miché laughs, he's always astounded by Leo's rapport for nature.

The wedding is celebrated in the chapel the following morning, conducted by the Bishop, however only the knights and nobility are in attendance. The Duke and Duchess are resplendent in their fine wedding clothes. Matilda wears a delicate gold crown, while the Duke's crown is more robust and festooned with rubies. Once they're married, they understand that they have broken Church laws, but the Duke and Duchess know they are above the law, they are now the Royal Family of Normandy. And with his sights set on England, Guilliam has the upper hand with an army on his side. He is not to be messed with, it's a brave Pope who tries to arrest them.

The wedding breakfast is served in the grand hall, followed by festivities in the grounds. Troubadours and minstrels play their music for the guests, the chateau's fool divulges indelicate jokes, causing some of the noble maidens to flush with colour, acrobats and jugglers display their skills, while they wander the grounds to entertain the guests. The Lord and Lady du Bois, and Papa, sit at the Duke's long breakfast table which takes up much of the grand hall, while the artisans and other less noble guests, eat their meal at smaller tables in an adjoining hall.

The joust a plaisance, advertised via a wandering herald, is scheduled to commence after lunch. Leo changes into his jousting armour and attends to his horse in the stables. When the bugle alerts the gathering crowd of the imminent event, Leo and the other jousters ride to the holding area. As it's an exhibition tournament, and he's known most of the other riders since he was a small boy, Leo's in a jovial mood, despite his nerves.

"Hey Tristian, who are you betting against today. Fancy some money on Sir Alain of Rouen?" He jokes with his mentor. The older knights ignore him, they're stern and upright. They are not joking around as there is serious prize money to be won, more importantly, prestige is at stake. Leo soon cottons on to the business at hand and settles down, he waits for his turn to perform.

The Invocation of Horsemen begins and the excited crowd sit in accordance to their station. The Duke and other nobles watch the competition from the Berfrois, while some of the nobles watch the events from the towers and battlements, the commoners show their appreciation by waving their supporter flags in the surrounding fields. They bellow the names of their favourite knights and toot their horns.

In order of their seniority, the knights form a single line for the parade and with the nervous energy of their first tournament, Miché and Leo fall into line close to the head of the group.

"Hey! You two nonces, move down to your proper place!" The older knights quickly put them in their place, they need to understand the pecking order.

"Sorry, sorry. We're going." The brothers don't quibble, they've made an honest mistake, they soon find their rightful place in the parade. Leo grins nervously.

After the opening procession, the first pair of knights make their way to the course and hold their positions, lances aloft. When the bugle signals the commencement of the tournament, the riders drop their lances to their sides and charge their horses towards each other. The feared Black Knight of Caen sits taller, stronger, and more centred than his opponent, he easily topples Alain of Rouen. The crowd show their appreciation for the winning knight with a loud roar.

The Black Knight trots victoriously to his starting position, while Alain jumps from his horse, when he lands, his feet connect awkwardly with the ground. He limps while he leads his horse to the holding area. With mixed emotions, he reluctantly surrenders his armour to the winner in defeat, yet with some relief to be free of its heaviness.

"Just as well you didn't put money on him hey, Tristian." Leo whispers with a grin.

"Shut up Leo." He scolds the younger knight as he takes his place in line. Tristian fights his nerves as he takes his place against The Black Knight.

The flag drops, the bugle calls, both riders begin to joust. The Black Knight, again victorious, causes the crowd to go wild, he's clearly the spectator's favourite. With three more rounds, the knight from Caen remains undefeated. It's now Miché's opportunity to joust, the younger knight is confident, yet unsure he'll be able to pitch the more popular knight from his horse.

Miché finds his place at the northern end of the field and raises his lance to show his readiness to begin. The bugle sounds, the riders charge. The Black Knight hurtles down the field and when his horse spots a hare, frantically hopping in front of him, his mount bolts to the right. Miché is able to aim his lance squarely at the Black Knight, striking him in the chest, causing him to lose balance and he tumbles to the ground. The crowd collectively gasp, they can't believe their favourite knight has been beaten. In an instant, The Black Knight has been humbled, for the first time in many years.

"Lucky break, you were saved by a hare's width." Leo calls to Miché. The fight is now on between brothers.

Miché remains in the northern position, while Leo assumes the south. The brothers tip their helmets in a show of mutual respect, they raise their lances. The bugle sounds and the knights charge their horses, their brotherhood dissolves. Miché assumes he's stronger than his younger brother, he doesn't want to lose face in front of the Duke, his family, and especially not before the ladies who stand in admiration in the grandstand. Leo's just as focused on the prize and is determined to knock his older brother from his perch. As they ride towards each other and approach the contact point, an invisible force field operates between the pair, their lances fail to make contact. The crowd jeers and laughs, this isn't what they'd come to see. Embarrassed, the young men return their horses to their starting positions. They raise their lances, the bugle calls and they're off.

As they ride to the contact point, Miché's lance catches the end of Leo's lance and Leo's made unsteady in his saddle, he remains rooted in his seat. Leo grins at his brother.

"That was close, but you'll have to do better than that." At the starting lines, for the third time, the brothers mean business. Leo crosses himself in a silent prayer, the crowd cheer, while Miché raises his lance high into the air, inciting the audience to roar even louder. The bugle calls, the brothers charge their horses towards each other as the crowd hold their breath, a hush hangs in the air. At the contact point, Leo catches Miché's lance first, but with his extra strength, Miché is able to hook Leo's lance free with a turn of his forearm, he's thrown off balance and falls from his horse. The crowd erupts, stamp their feet and clap. Miché raises his lance in a salute of victory towards the Duke, then turns to face the ladies in the grandstand.

Leo dusts himself off and removes his armour to present to Miché, the winner. As the tournament progresses, Miché triumphs in each of his rounds to win the entire competition, in the process he acquires quite a bounty of armour. Leo gathers with the other knights and calls out to Tristian again.

"You should have had your money on my brother!"

"Who said I didn't?" Tristian shakes his purse in the air for Leo's amusement.

As Miché leaves the field, spectators surround his horse as they try to embrace the winning knight. Men look to Miché with admiration, for his show of strength and women swoon as he passes them. From the grandstand, his mother and father, brothers Hugo and Darri, regard him with pride, as they wave to Miché. Guilliam and Matilda offer their congratulations to the proud parents and with no sons to represent him, Papa feels stabs of pain and envy in his gut.

Leo arrives by his brother's side, shakes his hand and thumps his back with genuine admiration for his success. Miché, on a winning high, waves enthusiastically to the crowd, as he struts proudly towards the Duke's grandstand. Miché bows before him, Guilliam shakes his hand firmly before he pivots towards the Duchess, who offers her hand for Miché to kiss. Again, the spectators roar their approval as the nobles make their way into the chateau to begin the next round of festivities.

The wine and ale flow freely all night, as people from all walks of life, toast the newlyweds. Despite the wedding, Miché is the man of the moment, people are excited to speak with him about his winning performances. Girls and women vie to sit next to the brave knight, however this honour is reserved for the Duke's younger step sister, Adelaide, an eligible maiden, according to Catarine, although to Miché's eyes, not as beguiling as Sarra.

Chapter 25 Leon

There's excitement at St Mark's, the football team has qualified for the Grand Final against St. Bert's. Students make banners and buy streamers for the big game. Walking on to the oval, on their way to practice and feeling confident of a win, Leon tries to remember the team song.

"We're as strong as Lions, we're at the top of the ..... What comes next Billy?" Leon warbles, he doesn't really know the song that well.

"We're as strong as Lions, we're at the top of our game...da..de. Look, I usually rely on the other guys knowing the exact words, to be honest." As captain of the team, Billy's a bit embarrassed that he doesn't know all of the words, but he hums the tune very well.

"Shut up you two, there will be plenty of time to sing later. Now, before we get on the ground, I want to remind you, you need to get here early in the morning for the bus which will take us all to the ground. If you are late, you will miss the game entirely." Coach Jones warns his team. "Got that Declan?"

"What? Why did he call me out? Glen is always late. Wanker." Declan mumbles to himself. He can see Glen grinning at him from the other side of the semi-circle of boys.

"Settle down over there. Okay it's pretty simple, just be here on time. That's not too hard to understand, is it Glen?" Coach Jones has trouble with his blood pressure and he starts to lose it with his team. Declan returns Glen's previous grin.

"Right, three laps around the oval for warm up, then we'll practice drills." The boys groan. "What are you all standing around for, GO!" Coach Jones wakes the boys out of their stupor, they begin to jog around the oval while he finds his blood pressure tablets in his sports bag.

Families make plans to meet at the grounds, car-pooling and transport arrangements are considered, sisters are informed to make it a social occasion in the hope that they'll bring their friends, most importantly, after party ideas are discussed. It's finally decided, the after party should be held at Billy's place, he has the quintessential party house with a pool, a large rumpus room with a bar, a pool table, and most importantly, two beer fridges in the garage. His parents, mainly his mum, isn't entirely sure she wants the whole football team and their friends in her house for a party, begrudgingly she agrees.

"What harm could it do? We can share our castle with Billy's friends." Billy's dad says, with a wink to his mum. Billy's mum still isn't sure.

Cathy makes sure the boys go to bed early, she'll be up at the crack of dawn before the rest of the house has risen, so that she can pack each of the boys' sports bags with a sandwich, clean underwear, footy socks and a change of clothes to wear after the game. Jenny Carter is on laundry duty, she'll take the uniforms to the ground. When he finally saunters into the kitchen, Leon pokes his nose through his bag, while his mother isn't looking, he swaps the faded yellow t-shirt for his favourite steel grey one and replaces the old brown corduroys with his favourite jeans.

"What is she thinking?" He smiles to himself as he places his mother's selections into his brother's sports bag and removes any other options. Freshly cleaned, shoelaces tied together, he shoves his football boots into his bag.

Immersed in their own thoughts, the family eat their breakfast in relative silence, with varying degrees of nervousness. As he finishes the dregs of his instant coffee, Archie places his cup on the table and makes an announcement.

"Righto, front door in five everyone." He speeds to the toilet, where he sits for at least ten minutes. This is an opportunity for the boys to grab their sports bags, Claire returns to her bedroom to check her outfit and makeup once more in front of her full length mirror, Cathy clears the breakfast dishes and quickly cleans the kitchen. The inevitable swish of spray from the air-freshener and the creak of the bathroom door, herald their imminent departure.

"I call shotgun." Declan runs past his family to claim the front seat.

"Sucked in loser, Mum and Claire are coming, get your arse in the backseat." Leon grins, opens the back door wide to allow his older brother to squeeze into the car first.

Declan's about to protest at having to sit in between his younger siblings, when Archie throws him "the look", Declan immediately shuts his mouth and pours himself into the middle of the snug blue sedan. To retaliate, he crosses his arms as wide as possible, his bony elbows stick into both his sibling's ribs.

"Stop it!" Claire pushes him back and pinches his arm.

"Oww! Put your arms down!" Leon demands.

"It's not fair. I'm the oldest. I shouldn't have to put up with this shite."

"No, I'm the oldest and I shouldn't have to put up with this shite." Archie clarifies the situation for Declan as Cathy arrives, she wonders why they hadn't bought a larger car when they arrived in Australia. She arrives at the conclusion that her children were smaller and better behaved then.

"I thought you kids would have stopped fighting over your place in the car by now." Cathy says to nobody in particular, she lowers herself into the front passenger seat.

She spins around in her seat and captures a mental picture of her three gangly babies and realises this chapter of her life is due to close soon. Archie revs the engine.

"Righto, all belted up?" He reverses out of the drive-way anyway, before any of them can answer, and he drives them to the school so that the boys can continue the rest of the journey by coach. "I don't see why the school has to fork out for a coach, waste of bloody money if you ask me. We still have to drive to the oval." Archie complains.

"Some of the kids need the transport Archie. Plus, it's a nice way of gathering the boys together for a bit of team spirit on the journey to the oval. You know, those St. Bert's boys will have had breakfast together since early this morning." Cathy argues.

"I guess so." Archie concedes.

In the school car park, Claire's excited to meet up with her best friend, Shannon, they travel to the game with Shannon's parents. With a wave of despondency, Cathy peers into the rear of the car again and realises that all of her children have dispersed. Her empty nest has occurred more rapidly than she'd imagined and she sighs audibly, puts on a smile and looks over at her husband, he alone is her future.

"At least I still have you love."

"What's that now?" Archie is focused on getting them out of the small car park without nudging the other cars, he can't hear his wife.

"Nothing Love." Cathy can't name the empty feeling she has, it's too painful.

As the crowd filter into the ground, the teams don their uniforms in the change rooms and fifteen minutes before the game is due to start, Coach Jones herds his nervous team on to the oval to begin their warm up exercises. There's an eruption of applause from their cheer squad. The St. Bert's boys appear at ease on the field, they've been doing their warm-ups for a few minutes before the St. Mark's boys emerge. The St. Bert's boys, in their navy and red uniforms, tower in height above the St. Marks boys, kitted out in royal blue and yellow.

Most of the St. Bert's supporters sit expectantly in the grandstand, their cheer squad claimed the space early in the morning, when they hosted the team breakfast. As Archie suspected, the St. Mark's supporters are relegated to the bleachers surrounding the rest of the oval.

"It's typical of those toffs, sitting up there in their ivory tower." Archie points out the prize real estate to his wife.

"They're welcome to it." Cathy replies. "I feel closer to the action down here." Archie gives his wife's hand a gentle squeeze. She always focuses on the positive side of life.

"Just hope the rain holds off." He peers at the sky as Cathy opens her handbag, just a little, to reveal two wrapped plastic ponchos. "You think of everything Love."

Archie turns his attention to the field where his sons are warming up, Cathy waves to their daughter who is standing with her friends on the opposite side of the field. Claire limply waves back to her mother. The cheer squads make final adjustments to their banners at the side of the oval, the support staff begin to leave the oval while the players search for their game positions. Archie gives Cathy's knee a squeeze.

The team captains meet with the head umpire in the centre of the oval for the coin toss, to determine which team will gain their preferred direction for the first quarter. The umpire throws the coin into the air, and Mitch, from the team at the top of the leader board, calls heads. The coin finds a resting position in the grass, a couple of meters from the official group, they all step aside to inspect the coin. It's tails and Billy confidently gestures towards the southern goals, where the light northerly breeze may give them a slight advantage. The St. Mark's supporters roar, as the cheer squads lift their banners, the war chants begin. The siren at the top of the grandstand blares, it's game on. As is the tradition, Leon stands his man, Mitch.

"Hey there Leon. Ready to get crushed?" Mitch playfully pummels Leon's bicep in jest.

"Hi." Leon grabs his own arm, trying not to reveal to Mitch how much it already hurts. The umpire is about to bounce the ball, their conversation cut short. In the centre square, a lanky St. Bert's boy knocks the ball towards the northern goals.

By the final siren, St. Mark's initial advantage didn't amount to anything and the St. Bert's boys win convincingly, their supporters go crazy. When the excitement has died down a little, the association committee walk out onto the field to present the trophy, the two teams line up on either side of the podium. Mitch is called upon to accept the cup on behalf of his team and missing most of the steps, he bounds up to the podium in one giant leap. While shaking the President's hand, he accepts the team's prize. Mitch grasps the trophy's handles with both hands and raises it above his head to cheers of appreciation from the crowd. In his short acceptance speech, he thanks all of the important people, coaches and parents, then gives special thanks to the St. Mark's team.

"St Marks, guys you were worthy opponents, thanks for bringing your best game today. St Bert's, WE ARE THE CHAMPIONS!"

There's a roar from the crowd, as he descends the podium stairs in one leap to re-join his team to celebrate.

The formalities over, the St. Mark's team and their support crew relocate to the change rooms, while the St. Bert's team continue to celebrate their win with their friends and families on the oval. The mood in the losers change room is sombre to say the least, though not sad.

Everyone knows it's an achievement to make their way into the grand final, it was a big ask to topple St. Bert's. Huddled inside the change room, Billy gathers his team.

"We did our best out there today, despite the final score. Now, we can either be sad, or we can cheer up and enjoy the party tonight. Who cares about the final score anyway? We got to play in a grand final, which is more than I can say about all the other teams in the comp." He doesn't want miserable team mates at his party, he hopes his pep talk buoys his sad looking team.

"YES!" Declan replies. "Bugger the game, let's party!" With that proclamation, the boys clap their captain and a little later, Declan reaches into his bag to find an old yellow t-shirt and brown corduroy trousers.

"What the hell are Leon's old clothes doing in here?" Leon laughs to himself as he makes his way to the showers.

"And where the hell are the beers I took from Dad's beer fridge?" He yells after Leon.

In the car park, Cathy shows Archie her haul, hidden under the picnic rug in the boot of the car.

"Look what I found in Declan's bag this morning."

"How did he think he was going to get away with that?" Archie shakes his head. "Bloody hell, now I'm going to have to have a word with him. Give us one of those beers will ya love."

Chapter 26 Ailie

I'm proud of my small contribution, on Guilliam and Matilda's wedding tapestry, though Mama's illness has squashed any feelings of achievement. Marc and I have worked long hard hours to complete the work by the appointed deadline, much to Ottho's delight, he was worried that it wouldn't be finished on time. Actually, we managed to complete our important task, with a few weeks to spare, which is lucky because Mama has taken a turn for the worse. I spend the next week sitting by her side, she has no desire to eat which renders her pale and gaunt, her body has given up the quest to live. During this time, a series of measures are taken by everyone to try to alleviate some of her symptoms.

On Tuesday, the butcher, who doubles as the town's doctor, is called to bleed Mama, but this process leaves her frail body even weaker. On Wednesday, Luna is called to give Mama purging herbs, again she has nothing left to eliminate, instead Luna brings in some lavender and rosemary fronds to help clear the fetid smell from the room. On Thursday, Mama is given the opportunity to spiritually purge herself as Father Jean listens to her confession and performs her last rites. Mama is so weak she can barely speak, but father Jean listens intently to her as best as he can. As Mama tries to speak, Father Jean notices something odd in the corner of the room. At first, he thinks there is someone sitting in the corner, but that can't be, it's only the top half of the person. Confused, he looks again and realises it's his own face reflected back to him. Well at least he assumes it's his own face, he has never seen it like this before, except in still pond water.

"What's that thing in the corner of the room?"

"Mama calls it her mirror?" I offer.

"A mirror? Does she look into it often?"

"I guess so. I'm not really sure." I'm out of my depth here, I call Bietriz. When she arrives, Father Jean asks Bietriz to remove the mirror and have Amis smash it into a thousand pieces. Father Jean is also out of his depth, he feels smashing the mirror is the right thing to do because if the woman's soul is trapped in the glass, surely smashing it up will release her of its grasp.

"Her soul has been imprisoned in the glass and the devil is pulling her from the other side. We need to free her from the glass for her to have any chance of survival."

The priest looks worried as he informs us of the evils of mirrors and he wonders why we still own one when the Church had ordered their removal from homes for this very reason.

The cleric remains with our family for most of the day, chanting and summonsing help from the Divine Holy Trinity, Mother Mary and the angels, to release my mother's soul from the mirror. However, his efforts are mainly to console me, I've already begun to build a wall of protection around myself from future grief and pain.

"I've smashed the mirror, it's in hundreds of pieces!" Amis lets everyone know that he's successfully carried out his important, spiritual task.

"Okay good, perhaps now that the mirror has been destroyed, your mother's soul will slowly return." The priest directs his words to me, my father is disconnected from the proceedings. He sits silently in the corner of the room, a jug of ale perched by his side, the hounds lay maudlin at his feet.

However, Mama's soul doesn't return as Father Jean said it would. On Friday morning before sunrise, Mama leaves her failing body and joins her unborn babies in an unimaginable paradise. We don't know for sure that's where she went, but that's what I tell myself. I need to know that she is somewhere beautiful.

When I wake up on this brand new day, I can see from her colour and stillness, Mama is dead. I lay on my deer skin for a while and allow a tear to escape, but the pressure of holding on to so many emotions causes my head and throat to ache. Papa's absent from the room, I venture downstairs where I find Bietriz and Florrie preparing a fire in the kitchen fireplace.

"Mother has passed." I announce blankly as I approach the staff. The two older women immediately seize me in an embrace of love and comfort; they've anticipated this news for some time, it's still a shock to everyone. Bietriz and Florrie wipe their tears of sorrow from their cheeks, then fully notice me, the detached daughter, standing before them.

"Right, we'll go upstairs to prepare your mother, and Florrie, you call Amis to fetch Father Jean." Bietriz has snapped into a coping mechanism of action, my father's coping mechanism is to disappear and get drunk. He's nowhere to be seen, so I engage my coping mechanism and leave the chateau for my happy place. I return to the workshop in a dazed silence.

Ottho is shocked to see me walk through the door, as word of Mama's passing has rapidly spread throughout the village.

"What are you doing here Ailie?" He scoops me up into his arms and gives me a big hug. My eyes are dry, my body is unresponsive to his kindness.

"I need to work." I reply calmly, as I release myself from Ottho's embrace. I sit down at my loom and begin to inspect my threads. I sense his pity try to penetrate my heart, but I'm not going to let it in. Another tear falls silently from my eyes, I quickly swipe it away. Throughout the morning, other workers offer their condolences. Sarra shows her sympathies by staying out of my way, but when Bertram sweeps the floor around my loom, he gently places his hand on the centre of my back, for just a few seconds, before he moves on. This small action causes my tears flow, grief pours from my soul. When I have finished releasing my tears, I wipe my face with my pinafore and stare down at my work.

On the following Sunday morning, a requiem Mass is held for Mama at the village church. As light rain falls, parishioners stand behind Papa, who is barely sober and me, barely present. I'm now known by the community as Lady of the Manor, the level of responsibilities I bear have increased immensely. I stand dutifully sombre as Father Jean and the congregation offer their prayers to us and Mama's soul. After the Mass, Mama's body, which has been dressed in her finest purple silk gown, is carted to the burial ground as the villagers follow by foot.

I throw a sheaf of lavender into the hole my mother lays in, to sweeten her journey to her new home. I spot a barn owl high upon a branch of an old oak tree. It's a fitting symbol of status, intelligence and wealth, more importantly the protector of the dead has witnessed this moment with me. I feel a deep connection with the bird and as I slowly return to Papa's side, I feel a shiver run up my spine to the crown of my head, I quiver as the owl flies away. On Monday morning, I return to work.

Ottho has made plans with Marc to attend the Duke of Normandy's nuptials, to be held on the following weekend. As artisans of the wedding tapestry, we've been invited to attend this prestigious event and I can hear the two men discussing the itinerary, I boldly approach my mentors.

"Ottho, would it be too much to ask, that I accompany you on your journey? I was included on Papa's invitation, but I would much rather travel with you, as a weaver." With Mama gone, life at home is lonely and I long to be far away from the cavernous chateau.

"Oh, we didn't think you would want to travel so soon after burying your mother."

Ottho places his hand gently on my shoulder and looks to Marc for support. Marc accepts the proposal with a nod and smiles warmly at Ottho, and me. I'm overjoyed to be going to the wedding with them. I give my boss and mentor a quick hug before returning to my loom.

Papa travels to Falaise earlier than we do, as his liberation from the ties of marriage give him the freedom to drink and fornicate, guilt free, all the way towards the west. He isn't fooling anyone though, he numbs incessant thoughts of his weaknesses, fears of inadequacy, his lack of care for his child, and late his wife with ale. He had provided our economic needs handsomely, emotionally speaking, we dwelt in deep poverty.

He knows that I'll attend the wedding, but he's embarrassed, I'll be attending the ceremony as a commoner, not as Lady of the Manor de Belanger. We have arguments about this of course, we are both depleted from grief and exhaustion. Our quarrels are short lived and my role as an artist, rather than a noble woman, remains firm, only because I am younger and more persistent. After the decision has been deemed final, there are few words spoken between us of our impending travels to Falaise, we are both content to keep our journeys separate. The attributes that ultimately keep us separate, my strength, determination, independence and humility, annoy and threaten him at the same time. I've learnt from an early age that I have to live my own life, without my father's approval.

When he makes his way to the Chateau's drawbridge, a young knight helps Papa dismount his horse, but despite the aid, he nearly tumbles to the ground.

"Hello Sir, my name is Leo and I'll be showing you to your quarters today. Will your wife be joining us for the celebrations?" Not wanting to draw attention to Papa's insobriety, Leo doesn't mention the near fall.

"Highly unlikely, unless you want a ghost rattling around your towers." Papa slurs his words into his chin and the kind young knight falls silent while he escorts Papa to his quarters. When he enters the room, he stumbles on his way down to his deer skin, narrowly missing the wall with the top of his head. Lord and Lady Du Bois, and their younger children, are unpacking their clothing for the wedding when they see Papa enter the room, before they offer salutations, Papa has passed out on his pelt and begins snoring loudly.

Weary from the long ride, we're glad to see Sir Miché greet us at the gate of the drawbridge, before showing us to our sleeping quarters, a pavilion at the rear of the chateau. He inquires about Sarra and gives me the feeling that he likes her for some reason, I can't work out why. When we arrive at the pavilion, we see the other artists and invited guests lounging on their deer skins. Musicians tune their instruments and some lower gentry, who don't qualify for quarters in the castle, rest in the marquee. Technically, I'm eligible to stay in the chatcau with Papa, but I am content to be amongst the artists in the pavilion. In fact, the further the distance between us, the better it is for both of us.

Exhausted, I find room in the corner of the tent and lie down on my deer skin.

"Are you going to see your father?" Marc asks. I'm not going to make any effort to interact with Papa, especially since he'll be in no fit state to conduct a coherent conversation.

"Maybe later, I'm tired from the journey." I close my eyes to the world and turn my body to face the side panel of the tent. Marc shoots Ottho a concerned look as I settle down to sleep, they understand why I'm in no hurry to greet Papa. I fall asleep quickly and experience another one of my dreams.

A wooden vessel floats on the water, in a huge open sea, strange in itself, I've never seen a sea. The calmness that the sea brings me soon changes to anxiety, the waves begin to chop. There are hundreds of brave knights in full armour, some holding shields, most wielding lances, swords, bows and arrows. The knights have sailed to a strange land and when they land on the beach, a bloody battle ensues against the knights of the other land. I'm fearful for the French knights, not only because I am French, but also, I know my heart belongs to one of them. I can't see him in the crowd of fighting men. I begin to search the beach, running up and down its length, looking into the faces of the knights who lie dead on the pebbles and sand, my love is nowhere to be seen, I can't find him anywhere. Out of nowhere, a raven flies down and rests patiently at my feet, and I know. My heart races, I struggle for breath, with a jolt, my body transports back to the pavilion.

I awake with an audible gasp, sitting upright I wipe dribble from my mouth. The tent is dark, despite light shining from the almost full moon outside. I figure it's the middle of the night, judging by all the snoring around me. I tiptoe quietly over the sleeping guests to go outside to pee. I find a grove of trees to give myself some privacy and bend down to relieve myself. When I finish, I stand tall and stretch out my tired limbs. Squatting down has reminded me that my bottom and thighs are still sore from the journey. I'm not used to the rigours of riding, let alone for days at a time. It's a delicious feeling, to stand on my own in the moonlight, breathing in the cool night air.

I take in a deep breath and watch millions of twinkling stars in the cloudless sky, I relax a little when I spot the North Star. A small spider sits in wait for the morning influx of insects, attracted to its web, I appreciate its exquisite weaving skills.

"How are you this pleasant night?" Shaking my head in disbelief, I think the spider has responded to me, but I've actually heard two muffled voices carried on the soft breeze from the next field. When I try to see where the voices have come from, I slip on the dewy grass and let out a high pitched yelp. After I've righted myself, I can see two dark figures returning towards the castle.

Chapter 27 Allie

At the end of our final year of high school, Sara and I are invited to a lot of parties and we attend most of them. Some of Sara's friends from St. Bernadette's, are invited to the College's Grand Final after party, but we decide to attend another party instead. When we find each other in class on Monday morning, Sara can hardly contain her excitement.

"We should've definitely gone to the St. Bert's after party. Apparently, it was epic. Adele said, the captain of St. Bert's was hilarious .... blah blah blah." I can't hear Sara at this point, I've tuned her out. I'm ready to start the next chapter of my life and I'm tired of high school parties, where the focus is on getting smashed as fast as possible, hooking up with boys, then gossiping about it the next day. I know there has to be something more, I don't know what that thing is yet.

In the mean time, high school certificate in hand, I find a job as a receptionist in a naturopath clinic. By the end of my secondary schooling, I've had enough of formal learning and the thought of three to four more years at university, fills me with dread. Besides, Finn's mission in life to remain a perpetual student, fills that position in our family dynamic.

"Why don't you study photography at uni, Allie Peg, you're so talented? Dad continuously asks. "I think you should give it a go at least."

"But Dad, I don't want photography to turn into a chore, where I have to submit assignments and do exams. I want to keep it fun. It's just a hobby."

"Fair enough love. Bit of a waste of talent though." Dad grunts over his newspaper and much to my relief, perhaps my detriment, he drops the subject.

Besides the normal reception activities, my most important job of the day is to ensure the urn is full of water and switched on, if Trish doesn't get her morning Jasmine tea before the first client has checked in, there's a distinct lack of calmness in the air. The work isn't rocket science, but there is no more homework to do and best of all, I have plenty of time on the weekends to do whatever the hell I want. I love my new way of life, although for the first week it's a stretch to make the jump from a 3:15pm finish, to my new knock off time at 5:30pm.

I am even able to smile and look interested when the odd client launches into the reason why they're at the clinic in the first place.

"The olive trees around here cause me a terrible rash, but this cream is doing the trick." Stan says, every time he returns to my desk to pay his bill.

"Trish is a wonder and I can see my eczema clearing up, but there's not really much left for me to eat anymore. Is there a good bakery around here that you'd recommend?" Clients, not so subtly inform me, they aren't sticking strictly to the diets that Trish put them on.

"You know dear, I can't eat cheese any more, it causes a terrible reaction on my bowel and I can't be cut short when I go out. Last week I had some of ...." I have to cut her short before she really tells me what's going on with her bowel.

"Excuse me Mrs Wilson, for just a minute. Mrs Taylor, Trish will see you now." I can never work out why they would want to share this kind of information with me. It's the last thing in the world I'd reveal to someone else, except maybe Sara.

My boss Trish, is a lovely lady, she sometimes gives me the freedom to leave early, if there are no more clients for the day and I've finished all of my work. Needless to say, that isn't very often, but she is flexible. Trish believes, if her employees are happy, her business will be an enjoyable place and with all of that good energy circulating through the clinic, she'll attract more clients. It seems to work out for her, she has a thriving business.

I've worked at the clinic for about six months, when Trish is invited to a wedding on one of the Whitsunday islands in Queensland. It's an event that's not only life changing for the happy couple, but for me as well.

"Allie, my friends Matt and Willie are getting married in Queensland and we're going to make it an excuse for a family holiday. Do you think you'd mind looking after our house while we're away?" She asks, knowing that I have no other responsibilities. "We're all going to Queensland, there will be no one at home to feed Chappy." Trish worries about her terrier who's getting a bit old and forgetful. "I think he has dementia. I might have to switch his food to a healthier brand." She's starting to drift from the main topic of conversation.

"That sounds wonderful, I really love dogs. Can I ask my friend Sara to stay with me?"

"Sure Allie, I was going to ask if you wanted to have someone stay with you. It'd be a bit lonely otherwise." Sara and I still live at home with our respective families and we jump at the chance to fulfil our childhood dream of living by ourselves for two weeks.

When she isn't travelling, Mum occupies a two bedroom apartment in the city, she's away now of course, I don't think she's too concerned by my news. However, by the time I've broken the news of my imminent departure to Dad, he's distracted with an urgent work issue. I've probably got this wrong, Dad was in quite a flap when he was telling us, a business man from Hong Kong, signed a contract for some shares, then skipped the country and hasn't paid the balance for the portfolio at settlement. The people who were selling the shares were going to use the money for a small start up and now the deal might not go ahead, it's pandemonium.

This nightmare spins Dad into full panic mode. The method he uses to overcome his problems, ensure he's oblivious to the information I have to share with him later that night. Dad drinks every evening to take the edge off, to relieve the anxiety from his professional and personal problems. But twenty years of taking the edge off, has done just that. His short-term memory is shot, his concentration span is limited to only small bits of data, especially in the latter parts of the evening. It has never dawned on him, his little girl and the apple of his eye, is effectively moving out of the family nest for good, leaving him with the bookish child for company. The day he's been dreading for many years, has finally dawned.

I liberate my suitcase, just as Mum has modelled, leaving home for good, clanking the roller bag down the porch steps with one hand, carrying a large box in the other. I'm headed to Sara's already jam packed car.

"I'll see you soon, don't worry." I say to Dad, as I plant a kiss on his cheek and give him a quick hug.

"I'll miss you love." Dad returns my kiss and gives me a quick squeeze. I can see his mind is elsewhere. He will confide with me later that he was so sad I was leaving, he couldn't say anything. Part of me regrets not taking more time to say goodbye properly, but I'm young and more than keen to start my independent adult life. Dad returns to his dwindling family home to finish his scotch, promptly pours himself another as he flicks on the telly and for the first time in his life becomes immersed in a late night re-run of Neighbours.

As soon as we move into Trish's house, Sara and I scour the papers for an apartment of our own to rent, there's no moving back home now. We both feel ready to move out on our own, Trish's offer is the perfect diving board to launch us into the wider world. We quickly find an apartment close by. It's a little more expensive than we'd have liked, but at least it's going to be ours after Trish returns from her holiday.

"Now we just have to fill in the application form and get our parents to give us a reference." I say to Sara.

"That shouldn't be too hard. Don't you think?"

"Well, perhaps not that easy. Hmm.... Dad's not going to be happy."

Initially, Sara and I keep our transition from home a secret from most of our friends, the last thing we want is a huge, outrageous party. Well, we'd love that, but I love my job even more, I respect Trish and her home. Damn shame I think, imagining the fun we could have had. In the mean time, we fall a little bit in love with Trish's court-yard and eat our meals al fresco on the jarrah, table setting, beneath a grape vine canopy. Chappy flopped at our feet, sometimes begging for scraps. Happiness at last, I think. Free from the grumpy males that I've been living with for the past, I don't know how long? My whole life.

Eventually, we cook our own dinners which keep our costs down, our first shopping expedition had been a harsh lesson in economics. At the trendy gourmet deli on the main street, we buy smoked salmon, dips, pate, domestic sparkling wine, lots of gorgeous nibbley things, in the end not a lot of real food. We'd catered for a small gourmet party, ourselves as the only guests and at the beautifully appointed check out, we realise this is going to be a once off occurrence, for the mean time anyway.

Our introductory two hundred dollar shopping expedition, is followed by a no frills supermarket shop where we gather some real food.

"Sara, I don't think we should eat this left over dip for breakfast." I inspect the suspect crust forming on top of the formally delicious spread. Considering our food budget for the next two weeks, was blown in one day, our shopping trips will have to be more meagre next time around.

We plant ourselves in the courtyard that first night, sipping our bubbly and staring at the stars through the gaps in the grapevine above our heads. Shooting stars swish across the sky, satellites steadily orbit around, and around, the earth. The craters of the gibbous moon, beckon the eye to search and explore the mysterious light and dark shadows, while Mars shines red against the indigo night, like an angry pimple on the face of a love struck teen.

My thoughts drift away, my focus travels into the ether. I sense my soul rise up and out of my body, even though I've remained firmly on the seat cushion. I leave Sara to play with a stray thread which has escaped from the hem of her top, she considers the current sales, advertised loudly on the main street shop windows. Meanwhile, I float through the black nothingness, diving between stars, moons, satellites and space junk. While I'm floating, I see a seven foot shimmering angel and distant family members, who have returned to their origins many years before. A familiar man's face smiles coyly at me, I sense we may have already met.

"See you soon." He fades into the deep blackness of the sky, silently my Nana Betty smiles at me. With lightning speed, I spiral back to earth and return to my body with a jolt.

"Allie." Silence. "Allie." No answer. "Allie. ALLIE!" Sara yells, as the wine masks her usual decorum.

"Huh." I shiver a little, my head swims in waves of energy, I wriggle myself back into the present.

"Where the hell were you?" Sara demands.

"Up in space somewhere. I don't know." I demonstrate exactly where I've been, extending my pointer finger above the rim of my glass, towards the sky. I take a deep drag on one of the herbal cigarettes I found in the pantry. I don't normally smoke, though I've taken to it without too much coughing.

"Where do you go when you do that?" Sara stares at me. Despite her upbringing, she's become too grounded in the material world to understand where I can possibly go in my mind. Spending so much time on my own as a child, I can propel myself anywhere at a moment's notice, which makes it easy for me to visualise and meditate, also to escape from the stark realities of my life.

"What do you know about the Bayeux Tapestry?" I ask Sara.

"The what now?" Sara screws up her face and we crack up, laughing uncontrollably, until fat tears roll down our cheeks.

Our laughter subsides, we sit in calm silence for a while. The laughter and the tears have washed through us like an emotional cleanse. Suddenly I'm exhausted, but lighter somehow.

"Those smokes smell like shit you know, my Dad used to smoke them." Sara screws up her nose again, she always does when she's being a little judgy.

"Charming." I actually agree with her, and smile before I take another drag, cough a little, then glance skyward once again, the divine moment has past. Sara and I are good friends, but we get on each other's nerves sometimes, a bit too much yin and yin. Being in each other's space full time is going to take some adjustment, and compromise, I'm used to living in a mainly masculine household where I could be invisible from time to time, and I need to be. But Sara requires constant stimulation from the people around her, as validation of her existence. Now I'm being judgy.

"I think I need to go to bed, I'm really tired for some reason. We can do the dishes in the morning, yeah? Goodnight Housemate." I wave to Sara, leaving her on the patio with Chappy.

"Goodnight Housemate." Sara finds that really funny and starts giggling quietly to herself as she pats Chappy.

Chapter 28 Leo

After the wedding at Falaise, life for the knights, in some respects, has reverted to their normal routine. However, via his winning prowess and growing leadership skills, Miché is chosen by the Court as a knight of special note. Leo is also taken aside and trained to be invested into the Duke's protective Inner Circle. New blood and strength of character are crucial to the Norman Army, there are wars coming. Guilliam is to claim England for France, and for himself. He wants the strongest and fittest men by his side.

Granted a few days leave, the newly conferred knights travel home for Easter, to visit their parents, and at Miché's insistence, they visit the weaver's workshop to supposedly catch up with Ottho. However, Leo knows they're walking towards the workshop so that Miché can woo Sarra with his jousting tales. As they cross the threshold of the studio, Ottho greets the pair of adventurers akin to returning family. On the way to Ottho's office, Miché's head madly swivels from one side to the other in an attempt to see if Sarra is working at her loom, Ottho produces a jug of ale.

Sarra's at her loom and watches Miché closely from the time he enters the studio. When the knights have been in Ottho's company for some time, Bertram appears at the door.

"Sir, Miss Sarra requests an audience with the champion knight." The boy makes his announcement to the three men, who stand before a large tapestry depicting a great castle and a busy hamlet scene. Ottho sees that Sarra has crossed a line, calling for the knights while he is entertaining them in his office, he will not release them immediately, least not at the whim of his young worker. Miché grins while Bertram retreats from his master's room, it doesn't take long after Bertram's departure, Ottho senses the older of the two knights is no longer listening to his diatribe. It's not lost on Leo though, Ottho mentioned more than once, the tapestry had been commissioned by the King himself.

Ottho concedes, wrapping up his meeting with the knights, and leaves. He's disappointed that the opportunity to crow about the King's tapestry has ended so quickly, but quietly satisfied that he hadn't yielded to Sarra's will, straightaway. He makes a mental note to have a word with her later. In the meantime, who is he to fight new love? Besides, in these uncertain times, it is prudent to stay on the right side of Guilliam's men, *n'est pas*.

While Miché ventures into the main workroom to visit Sarra, Leo scans the general workspace from Ottho's doorway, Bertram sweeps the flagstone floor around the weaver's feet. Leo observes Marc, who's working on a spectacular tapestry depicting village life. It's so full of life and colour. Marc senses the knight watching him, he looks up from his loom and waves cheerily, relishing the opportunity to stand and stretch his back. The knight takes this action as an invitation to meet with the weaver and to talk about their lives since the Duke's wedding. Then according to Leo, the most elegant commoner he's ever seen, approaches the pair.

"Leo, this is my apprentice, Ailie." I bow my head slightly, to acknowledge the knight, I address Marc.

"I have a question, but I can see that you're busy, I'll go and ask Ottho." And before anyone can protest, I've dissolved into the busyness of the workshop. Leo's head is fuzzy and confused, he wonders if he already knows me from somewhere, he can't think from where.

After the knights say goodbye to their friends at the studio, Leo and Miché amble to the tavern for lunch. At the door, they are greeted as heroes by the landlord, word of Miché's jousting success has circulated the village.

"Sit down, right here." Marie wipes down the bench with her rag, as they sit at the best end of the largest table. "Here's a jug of ale on the house. Congratulations on your performance Miché, you've made Breteuil proud. A bit of a shame you both couldn't win, but there you go, that's life for you." Leo shrugs in resignation and Marie leaves their sides to fetch bowls of soup, a plate of mutton with cabbage, and two large chunks of fresh bread.

The afternoon crowd vie for the opportunity to congratulate the local man who defeated the Black Knight, one by one they approach

Miché to say hello, congratulate him, and slap him on the back. After the twentieth person applauds him, Miché's cheeks hurt from smiling so much and senses a dull ache in the centre of his back. Leo looks on bemused, as his brother tests his new found celebrity status. The horde of people thin giving the knights an opportunity to dip their bread into their bowls of tepid soup, realising they are both starving, the soup is inhaled quickly before they tackle the lukewarm stew. When they finish their meal, they glance around the room and notice Papa chatting to some merchants at another table. Out of respect, the knights re-introduce themselves.

When they arrive at Papa's table, they see a dark haired woman sitting next to him. She had been screened from view by a rather large wool merchant, Papa is in the middle of a bawdy joke, he slurs his words.

".....And that's how they do it in Flanders!" Awkward laughter spills from his audience.

"Good day Lord Belanger." The knights chorus, as Papa delivers his feeble punchline. Papa carefully scrutinises the brothers, but has no recall of their faces. Although, one of the merchants immediately recognises Miché and shakes his hand roughly.

"It's an honour to meet the knight who brought the Black Knight to his knees. Well done young man." The merchant excitedly pumps Miché's hand.

"Oh, yes, hello." Papa replies. He still doesn't remember where, or when, he'd been introduced to the knights. The woman giggles nervously and runs her fingers through her long ebony hair, then raises her skirt ever so slightly, just above her ankles, as she keenly observes the dashing knights. Papa flashes Sabine a stern look, she quickly adjusts her gown and gazes at the floor. Sensing his confusion and unease, the knights bid the Lord and his table mates farewell.

Laughing to themselves as they leave the tavern, the brothers walk through the town square on their way back to their parent's manor. At the edge of the square, grows an old gnarly oak tree, a cawing raven is perched in a high bough, the brothers nearly walk straight past it. As they are purposefully striding, they hear a voice emanating from the other side of the wide trunk.

"Think you're going to pass me by without saying hello?" Sarra asks covertly. She knows she's startled them. Miché grins at her, Leo rolls his eyes, he knows they'll be here for some time.

"Wow, you just have a habit of turning up, don't you? Is that your raven by the way. I have to take umbrage with him."

"Corbeau? I don't own him, he's free to fly and return as he pleases. Like me, he won't be tamed."

Sarra extends her right hand for the knight to help her stand and Miché takes this action as an excuse to kiss her outstretched hand, Sarra does not mind at all.

"It's easy to be untamed, when you're the daughter of the town witch." She winks. Remembering the woman in the tavern, and the apple, God fearing Miché, isn't sure if she's joking, he laughs anyway, a niggle of worry lodges in his brain.

The infatuated pair chat for some time before Leo interrupts them to remind his brother that the purpose of their visit was to spend time with their parents. Miché bites his lip with annoyance, but remains calm and chivalrous as he returns his attention to Sarra.

"Yes, my brother is correct, we must be away to see our parents. May I visit you again when we return to Breteuil?"

"But of course you will." Sarra walks back to the workshop and when she's out of sight, Miché hits his brother hard on the shoulder.

"Oww! What was that for?"

"Why did you have to say that and cut our time together?"

"What? We do have to get home Miché." Leo rubs his arm where a black and blue bruise is sure to surface.

Chapter 29 Leon

With final exams to prepare for, Leon finds term four quite stressful, he has the added pressure of wanting to qualify for a fine arts degree at one of the few universities in the city. Drawing has always been his passion, he loves to express himself in that way. Early on, when they'd leave the house, Cathy learnt to bring paper and pencils with her, to keep her creative son occupied, otherwise he'd be tempted to tease his older brother which would ultimately end in a scuffle on the floor.

That would be fine if they were at home, though usually a fight would erupt after twenty minutes of sitting nicely at Grandma's house, or worse, when they were out in public. Over time, Cathy learnt the signals her sons sent her when they couldn't sit passively any longer. A wriggle, then a jab in the ribs, it was very quick to the untrained eye, the signs could be easily missed. Cathy usually responded immediately with activities and snacks for her children, to avoid the embarrassment of them fighting in front of her hosts.

Cathy ensures that Declan and Claire are quiet as church mice while Leon studies, she puts an immediate stop to any tomfoolery, no matter how joyful it is. She also buys him packets of his favourite brand of licorice, to eat during his finals, to give him an extra boost of energy. No one in her family has ever been to university and it's exciting to think that her son will be the first one to achieve that important academic status. She's doing all she can to guarantee a positive outcome, not only for Leon, but for her own sense of pride as well.

The day after he completed his exams, Leon leaves Australia to backpack around the world, alone. He's going to have an adventure before he's expected to become a man and commence his studies the following March. It will be the first time he's travelled without the security, and comfort, of his family. He has always had the urge to travel independently, now is his chance to stretch his wings. He is free from the restraints of formal education and institutional routine for a couple of months. Cathy is worried sick, knowing her son is about to launch himself into the world without her protection. Archie is just glad that his son is adventurous enough to take the plunge.

It's hard to know what to pack into his brand new backpack, it's so stiff and shiny, he knows it won't take too many journeys around airport carousels to become more rugged looking. He'll encounter cold to freezing weather in the Northern Hemisphere, heat in the Tropics, and pleasant to hot climes in the Temperate zones, he has to make sure that he has packed clothes to accommodate a variety of climates.

"You need layers sweetheart." Cathy warns him. Her voice wavers, as she educates her son on the importance of clothing strata.

"Now, have you got Aunty Siobhan's address and phone number in Dublin, just in case you get into a pickle? You'll call her now, won't you? Because I promised her that you will."

"Yes Mum, you gave me the sheet of paper with all of her information. I don't think I'll need the emergency numbers for every country in the world, but I will visit her, I promise." It's actually reassuring for Leon, to know there's some family on the other side of the world that he can contact, if the need arises.

After a tearful departure, mainly on Cathy's part, Leon is all packed and ready to fly. His first stopover is in Singapore, where he sweats profusely in the jeans he's wearing. He wishes he'd changed into his shorts before exiting the air-conditioned airport terminal, into the humid and sweltering morning, he really had no idea that it would be this hot. He looks forward to eventually arriving in Europe, where it will be significantly colder and kinder to his fair Irish skin. Since living in Australia, he's never really acclimatised to the incessant heat, tropical heat is another animal altogether and even though he doesn't particularly like shopping, he can't wait for the relief provided by the icy, air-conditioned, multi-tiered, malls.

The sights and smells attack his senses at first, after a day of sightseeing and sampling exotic food, he soon discovers that he actually likes spicy food, even though the chillies make his lips tingle and his nose run. Cathy hasn't been adventurous in her culinary pursuits, she mainly cooks traditional Irish fare with the exception of her one foreign speciality, spaghetti Bolognese. This trip is Leon's first foray into Singaporean, Chinese, Indian and Malaysian food, which he buys from the night markets and street stalls dotted around his hotel, despite strict instructions from Cathy, not to do so.

His onward flight to Greece is scheduled for the following night, giving Leon just enough time to explore some of the bustling little country before his next flight and arrival in Athens, at four am the next morning. When he arrives in the ancient city, he only has to wait thirteen hours until the youth hostel reopens for check in at five pm., considering his cumulative jet lag, it's going to be a very long day. It doesn't phase him though, he's ready to discover Europe. He leaves his backpack at the youth hostel, zips his grey fleece jacket up to his neck, to buffer from the bracing morning winter wind. He soon finds his way by foot, to The Plaka, and search the shop fronts for a breakfast souvlaki, or two, and a very strong Greek coffee.

The bonus of a winter journey, is fewer tourists competing for a bed in the hostels. In fact, the hostels aren't as smelly, or as bedbug ridden, as they may have been in the summer, but the dormitories are freezing. Leon's glad he'd listened to his mum, who'd warned him against chilblains and packed his thongs for the walk across the frozen bathroom floor tiles in the mornings. But it would have been nice if the hostel wardens could dial up the temperature on the water heater as well. Morning showers consist of a quick dance under a cold dribble of water, certainly not enough pressure to wash his hair. He starts to miss Singapore's heat.

It doesn't take long for him to make friends in the youth hostel as other backpackers become travelling companions, making the journey a lot more enjoyable. It's nice to share his experiences with other people as his stint in Singapore had been lonely. Over the course of the three month travelling period, companions come and go depending on their itineraries. However, it's fellow Australians who travel for the longest time frames and therefore, his companions tend to be compatriots.

After exploring Athens for a few days, Leon and his new friends make their way to Port Pireas, he's keen to discover some of the stunning Greek Islands he's seen on Cathy's favourite travel show. As a potential art student, and someone with an eye for beauty, he appreciates the stark contrast between the whitewashed buildings and the sparkling azure sea. On the islands, he parties with his new friends, nervously rides ancient mopeds on the mainly dirt roads, eats fetta rich Greek salads, grilled octopus and lamb from a spit. He drinks ice coffee in the mornings, retsina and ouzo at night. They soon find the taverna with the best Greek salad, a litmus test for the other food on the menu and strike up a friendship with the waiter, Con.

"Oh, you are from Australia, Leon yes? I have the cousins in Melbourne, perhaps you know him, he lives in Moreland, I think." He pronounces it, more land. "His name is Nick. Do you know this one?"

"Sorry Con, I don't as it happens."

One warmish afternoon, when his travel buddies are enjoying an afternoon nap, Leon ventures into the clear blue water for a swim. The water is far too cold to fully immerse his body, instead, he suns himself on the black volcanic stones. For a moment, he allows melancholy to float between his heart and mind as the cold water and the pebbly beach remind him of skimming stones with his brother in Ireland, he wonders what his family are doing now. Disappointed, he realises they'd be fast asleep on the other side of the world.

The time is ticking on, for the most part Leon is having fun, reluctantly he knows he has to move on from the party islands, eventually. He has spent a good month and a half travelling around Europe on his Eurorail Pass, but when he arrives in France, he has the funniest feeling.

Paris overwhelms him to start with, the beauty of the lit trees on the broad shopping boulevards, the Eiffel Tower twinkling its light show every night, on the hour, the Metro system, which he considers one of the better transport systems he's encountered so far, the delicious food and wine, he can't get enough of the apricot jam crepes, not to mention all of the tasty cheeses, the beautiful women, he's too timid to talk to, the art featured in famous galleries and on exterior brick walls, travellers and locals who've originated from all over the world, dressed exquisitely in the fashionable districts, under-dressed in Pigalle and Montmartre. It's his favourite city on the journey so far. He always knew that he would like it here, however not for the reasons that he thought.

He installs himself on park benches while he sketches the locals, tourists, food and flower stalls in the markets, iconic buildings, and trees in the parks. When he ventures into the cafes and restaurants, he's able to practise his high school French using his manners of course. Leon seems to have a natural affinity for the French language, although he can understand a lot more than he can speak. He visits as many art galleries as he can, his favourite is the Musee d'Orsay, he tries to recall the stories that his art history teacher had imparted as he wanders past his favourite Toulouse Lautrec paintings.

When he pauses at L' Origine du Monde by Gustave Courbet, it occurs to him that he hasn't seen much of this part of a woman's anatomy, except for a couple of times at Billy's house. Billy's dad has a stash of magazines in a trunk in the rumpus room and Leon has had girlfriends in high school, but never anyone serious, no one has really been able to capture his heart so far. He certainly doesn't have a good grasp on women's anatomies from personal experience.

He could've stayed in Paris indefinitely, but he knows that his time is limited, he has to continue roaming if he's going to see South America before the new university year. He is going to fulfil his childhood dream, to hike the Inca trail into Machu Pichu, sit on a mountainside and draw. In the next couple of days, Leon plans to stay with his Aunty Siobhan in Ireland, he's really looking forward to spending some time with his aunty, uncle, and cousins, he's starting to miss his family at home and he wants to keep his journey moving forwards. He's been surrounded by a lot of people, especially in the youth hostels, he isn't alone per se, but he is missing the comfort of people who speak his familial language of home. The family banter that can't be replicated by other people, until that is, they become part of the family.

As Leon travels by train, from Paris to Le Havre, to board the afternoon ferry, bound for Rosslare, he suddenly has the urge to disembark, despite being only halfway to his destination. At Rouen station, he grabs his backpack from the rack above his head and rushes from the train, jumping the step onto the platform. While he stands on the platform, dumbfounded, the train pulls away from the station to the west, immediately the area clears of passengers.

Leon doesn't fully understand what he's just done, frozen for a while, his mind is blank. He was supposed to catch the ferry to Ireland, visit his family and continue his journey. Now that's impossible, there are no more train services today. Rattled, he has to find a telephone to call his Aunty. Leon shakes himself free of the shock of his previous actions and finds his way to the station arrivals hall where he seizes the one working telephone.

"Listen Aunty, there's been a change in plans."

"But we've made arrangements to come and collect you."

"Yes, yep, I know, um I'm sorry Aunty. I'll let you know when I'm coming across."

Leon has the urge to explore Rouen, but first he has to secure a bed for the night, he makes his way to the *auberge de jeuness* to unload his backpack. When he arrives at the imposing red brick building, he finds it's way too early to claim a bunk. He leaves his bag in a holding room near the reception desk until they're officially open, he knows the drill. He walks to the centre of town carrying his much lighter day pack and as he strolls along Route de Darnétal, he notices the large variation in the age and architecture of the buildings, ranging from medieval to modern. It's great to be walking through a different town again, making new discoveries. As he wanders down Rue Saint Hilaire, he spots more shops and his internal compass leads him in a specific direction. Even though, intellectually, he doesn't really know where he's heading, his internal compass has definitely honed in on a specific destination.

Strolling through the medieval town, Leon has a strange feeling, like *deja vu*, he's been here before and strangely he's at ease with his direction as he ventures west through the town. As the streets merge with each other, he notices that he's standing straighter, somehow taller, he's alert and at peace with the decision he's made to stop in this town, even though it seemed mad at the time, that he'd disembarked from the train. He's meant to be here, he knows it from deep within his core. As Leon passes the Church of St. Ouen, he pauses for a while and admires the stonework, he isn't compelled to linger for too long. Instinctively, he continues down Rue de la Republique to Rue Saint-Romain, as he walks, he can feel his pace quicken, his heart races a little faster. His soul has a destination in mind, but he still doesn't know where he's going. Closer to his destination, he looks up and audibly gasps. He can see the spires of the Rouen Notre Dame Cathedral in the distance, he begins to shake a little. It's beautiful, yes. But why is he reacting in that way, to something he's never seen, or even heard of before? This makes no sense to him at all.

Leon stops to collect himself before proceeding to the front of the cathedral and when he arrives in Place de la Cathédrale, he stands before the imposing structure, he tries to take stock of how he's feeling, he can't find the words. After a few minutes, he notices a tree encased by a concrete boarder, he sits down in its shade to catch his breath and to take in his surroundings. He notices the medieval style buildings and wonders if they're original, or replicas, built for the tourists, but he just can't shake the feeling that he has been here before. It's all so familiar.

Growling sounds rumble in his stomach, Leon realises that he hasn't eaten since breakfast, in Paris, a croissant and coffee. He collects his day pack and heads towards the bank of cafes situated alongside the Cathedral, he's drawn to a cheerful brasserie with a terrace on the corner. He sits at an outside table and places his day pack on the spare chair. Leon's at home on the terrace, basking in the winter sun, he eats chicken *cassoulet* from the *menu de jour* and sips his beer. During his sojourn, another young backpacker approaches him.

"Excuse me, do you mind if I take this seat here. There doesn't seem to be any free tables."

"Of course." Leon removes his pack from the free seat, happy to have some company.

"Impressive Cathedral isn't it? My name's Tom by the way."

"Hi, Leon." A waiter passes by and Tom orders the same meal that Leon's been eating.

"I arrived yesterday." Tom begins. "Did you know this church is medieval and was consecrated in 1063 by William the Conqueror? Nothing as old as that in Australia, hey?"

"Yeah, no way except maybe Indigenous rock art and stuff." Leon notices that Tom's accent is similar to his adopted compatriots which he is used to hearing a lot of this far into his travels, but Tom also looks oddly familiar. "You're an Aussie aren't you?" Leon guesses.

"Got me, I'm from Kaurna Country actually."

"No way! Me too."

"Oh, I thought you were Irish."

Leon tries to place where he's met Tom before, but he's struggling. Tom is going through the same process, but arrives at the correct answer before Leon has the chance.

"Did we go to primary school together?"

"Oh my God, we did. I remember you from the school assembly about the Indigenous Camp. I wanted to be Indigenous so badly. I wanted to go with you guys, it looked like so much fun."

"Yep, it was. I loved those camps."

"Where did you end up going to high school?"

"St. Berts."

"No way, I was at St. Marks. Did you play footy?"

During their second beer, they realise they'd played football against each other and Tom hopes to qualify for a Law Arts Degree at the same university Leon expects to attend. "Small world." They muse.

As the two boys reflect on their commonalities, another backpacker approaches them through the trees of the small park.

"Mitch mate. Over here!" Tom calls out to his friend.

"Oh my God, Mitch." Leon hollers to his former football opponent and attracts the waiter's attention at the same time. "*Un de plus, s'il vous plaît,*" He asks pointing to his beer. The boys find another chair and Mitch hunkers down with the pair. "Where are you guys staying?" Leon asks.

"At the *Chateau de Auberge.*" Mitch replies with a smile and when their beers arrive the three lads charge their glasses, and cheer.

"*Santé!*"

"You know, I've had a funny feeling here in Rouen, especially in front of the Cathedral." Mitch explains.

"Yeah, I felt the same way. Feels like I've been here before, it's all so familiar, yet not. I've never been here before and to be honest, I wasn't even meant to stop here, but something told me to get off the train." Tom and Mitch listen carefully before Mitch has to interject.

"Yes, us too! We were supposed to catch the ferry yesterday, except we had to get off the train because of the strike. The train just wasn't going any further." From that point on, the boys are inseparable, together they continue their travels through Normandy where they persist to feel at home in their surroundings.

After finally boarding the ferry at Le Havre, the young men are on their way to Ireland, but because his Euro Rail Pass doesn't allow for a cabin, like Tom and Mitch, Leon intends to sleep on a chair, or on the floor in the main part of the ferry. On the deck, watching France grow smaller in the distance, he feels a bit strange, stirred up, but Leon isn't sure if it's the after effects of last night's drinking, or if it's his anxiety due to his homecoming to Ireland that has his stomach retching.

Leon's feelings are mixed, it's the first time that he's been back to Ireland since his family left all those years ago and as the vessel passes through the calm English Channel, Leon begins to feel panic rise up, his stomach cramps but he can't say why.

"I feel really crook." He utters to Tom and Mitch weakly as they head towards the bar. "I think I'll just stay out here in the fresh air for a while." His face turns sage green, then he relieves himself over the railing into the grey sea below. He has the thought that he doesn't normally suffer from sea sickness, though here he is purging into the sea. Leon hurls another three times, the fourth time there's little to materialise. He rests his head against the coolness of the metal railing. He reposes here for a few minutes, gathering enough energy to find a place to settle in the general seating area inside the ferry. He promptly falls asleep, using his backpack as a pillow.

Feeling more human on arrival, Leon can see his aunty in the distance, on the other side of the arrivals hall. Mitch and Tom are fresh from their night of sleep in their cabin, despite their hangovers. Leon unfortunately, isn't so fresh.

"My, you've grown haven't you, your teeth could do with a brush though." Siobhan screws up nose as she hugs her nephew.

"I was sick crossing the channel Aunty."

"Well now, that'll explain it."

"Have you got room for these guys?" Leon asks sheepishly, pointing to his two burly mates standing behind him.

"Sure it'll be a bit of a squeeze now though, but pile in." She gestures to the Fiat panda on the curb. "Luckily, I didn't bring the whole tribe with me today." She says seriously.

The boys stay in Dublin for a week, sleeping on mattresses on the living room floor which is okay with Siobhan, socialising is always conducted in the kitchen. The front room is only for Christmas and special occasions. While they're here, Leon receives a phone call from home.

"It's your Ma." Siobhan shouts above the din, she passes the new cordless phone to her nephew, he automatically fears the worst. Why are they ringing him here, he thinks? Hideous scenarios play out in his mind. Is his father ill, or worse yet, dying, is there something wrong with Declan, or Claire? His mother swiftly relieves him of his despair, as he puts his hand over his left ear, he finds some peace and quiet in the good room.

"Hi Ma, How are you? What's happening?"

"You got in, Leon, you got in!" Cathy excitedly screeches down the phone without saying hello, or asking about his travels.

"What now? Ma, what're you talking about?"

"Your university entrance." She slows down and tries to moderate her speech as she reads out the letter from the university.

"You've been accepted into the Fine Arts degree and you start classes on March 3rd. Congratulations Leon, you did it, well done! Make sure you tell Siobhan." Her excitement rises again, Archie grabs the phone from his wife and speaks to his son for a while, not for too long though, the call is costing him a small fortune.

"Woo hoo!" Leon pumps the air as he switches off the phone and returns to the kitchen. When he explains the call to his friends, they wonder if they've received their acceptance letters as well and ask Siobhan if they can make a phone call to Australia.

"Sure, that shouldn't be too expensive." Siobhan quips sarcastically.

All week, Siobhan treats Tom, Mitch and Leon like long lost sons. She ensures they're fed solidly, three times a day, with snacks and pints of Guinness. The evenings in the pub are spent discussing their onward travels. Not ready to end their adventure, Mitch and Tom decide that they will go to Machu Pichu with Leon. They spend a harried morning trying to change their flights home. When the time arrives for them to leave, Siobhan drops the boys at the airport, giving each of them a bear hug. Out of the blue, she smacks Mitch on the bum.

"You cheeky devil you." Siobhan chides Mitch.

"What's that all about?" Leon wants to know. Mitch winks and touches the side of his nose, signifying a confidence shared only between Mitch and Siobhan. The boys present their host with a bottle of Baileys and a bouquet of flowers, bought the night before and had hidden in the kid's room. Leon is secretly pleased his cousins hadn't cracked the seal on the Baileys before they could present it to his aunty.

From Dublin, the trio flies to the US. and tentatively party in un-gentrified, early nineties New York, for a few days before making their way to Cusco, via Lima, and Machu Pichu. As they hike into the sacred World Heritage listed site, the normally rambunctious trio become silent and continue on the last kilometre of the four day trek in awe. When they arrive at the Inca site, the three young men celebrate with a photo and a group hug, before they continue on their separate ways to explore the site.

They've been in each other's pockets for too long now, ever the extrovert Mitch can't be alone for too long, he stumbles upon a group of mainly female backpackers. Mitch talks to them, Tom and Leon wander off on their own. Tom instantly connects to the powerful ener-gies at the site and sits in quiet meditation for a while, it will take Leon a little longer to settle in. He needs to be alone to shake off everyone's excitement before he can fully immerse himself in the energies.

Sitting on an ancient stone wall, bearing a massive smile on his face, finally realising his childhood dream, Leon unpacks his drawing gear from his day pack and begins some rough sketches of the Inca ruins. Almost immediately, he notices an eagle circling above his head which he includes in his drawing. From the cloud encircled mountains, to the verdant grass terraces where llamas graze, and the ruins themselves, provide him with many artistic options. He makes a few attempts with his sketches, but after a while, he realises he can't capture what lies before him, to his satisfaction anyway. He packs away his art journal and pencils and sits in quiet contemplation. The scene has exceeded his childhood dream, the joy he feels is heavenly.

Leon enjoys the silence and the view, though the peace is swiftly shattered when Mitch and Tom bound towards him like overgrown puppies.

"Come on Matisse. Let's get our hike on. There are three beers with our names on them down in the village." Mitch shakes Leon out of his contemplative state and the three exhilarated friends float back to the bus stop. The bus ferries them to the village of Aguas Calientes where they'll catch the afternoon train to Cusco.

"Hey Leon, where are you living when you get home?" Mitch sips his beer.

"Home, I guess." Leon says between slurps.

"I don't think so. Come and live with us. We've got a spare bedroom, we all get on well, it's settled." Mitch contends.

"Hmm. Yes it's settled." Leon replies nervously, he knows Cathy won't be happy.

Chapter 30 Ailie

I'm working diligently at my loom and from the corner of my eye, I see the entire state of affairs unfolding from the comfort of my wooden stool. Resembling celebrities, the knights from the jousting competition at Guilliam's wedding, wander in from the street, I hear the audible gasps of admiration from the other weavers. I gently laugh to myself, as Ottho greets them with pride and steers them into his workshop. Half an hour later, I notice Sarra motion to Bertram, when he arrives at her side, she whispers into his ear. Bertram walks into Ottho's workroom and within a few minutes, he returns and waves conspiratorially to Sarra.

Ten minutes pass before the knights return to the general workroom, from Ottho's office, the taller knight saunters over to Sarra, he speaks to her for a while. The quieter, more handsome knight, talks to Marc. While I watch these vignettes play out before me, I attempt to concentrate on my weaving when one of the warp threads snaps on my loom.

"Damn!" I absently go to Marc for assistance, forgetting that he's entertaining noble company, I suddenly realise he's probably too busy to help me. Embarrassed, I excuse myself and retreat into Ottho's workroom.

Giddy from his meeting with the knight's, Ottho tries to focus on my question.

"Yes of course, ask Marc to help you with that this afternoon." He slowly returns to his usual composure and motions for me to take a seat because he wants to have a chat. "How have you been since the wedding, my dear? You've been very quiet." I know he's concerned, because he says wedding, but he really means Mama's funeral, I don't correct him. Both events were close together and it doesn't seem right to correct my boss somehow.

"Oh, you know me Ottho, I just like to get on with my work. I'm okay." He nods in agreement, he doesn't completely believe me. How can he, I don't believe myself.

"By the way, I was going to ask you something, it's fortuitous that you appeared. How is your embroidery coming along? I know it was something you used to do with your mother and.....” He pauses, lowers his head in reverence for Mama's soul, as I lower my eyes and allow a little wave of sadness to engulf me. After a quiet moment, he coughs softly, begins to speak, I'm comfortable returning my gaze to his face. “With more commissions likely from the Duke, he may ask for a tapestry, or an embroidery, or two, in the future, embroidery would be a useful skill to have.”

I remember the times, when I'd sit with Mama by the fire, while she demonstrated how to sew silk threads onto squares of fabric, I would prick my fingers, especially when I was learning to manage the material, the needle and thread.

“Well, I haven't embroidered for a long time. But I'm keen to learn again.”

“Done. I'll ask Osanna to continue with your embroidery lessons and you can start working with her soon.” He pauses for a while. “Some of the older artists are losing their eyesight and I'll need new artists to take their place. I see your potential Ailie, I want you to be prepared.” I'm glad that he thinks I'm a worthy candidate for this craft and we chat about village life for a while before I return to my loom in the main workroom.

The afternoon is less eventful as the knights had departed while I was in Ottho's workroom. Marc and I manage to fix the broken thread on my loom and because it's such a beautiful day, many of the workers decide to eat their lunch under the copse near the workshop. However, Sarra's the last person to return to work, when she enters the workroom, she smiles conspiratorially at me, I don't know what we're smiling about. Learning about Sarra's mannerisms is teaching me to guard myself from Sarra's changing moods, I simply nod in acknowledgement as she walks by.

When I arrive home later that evening, I'm surprised to see Papa sitting at the dining room table. Since Mama's death, I've taken to eating dinner with Bietriz, Florrie, and Amis, Papa isn't usually at home on time to eat with me. The servants have become my family, now more than ever.

"The local celebrities were in town today." Papa gnaws on a lamb shank.

"Yes, I saw them when they came into work to see Ottho."

"Did they indeed? Bloody du Bois won't stop boasting about his sons." Papa spits. "Who do they think they are, parading around town like that?" His jealousy is palpable. If he had any sons, born to women in the village, they are illegitimate, he can't acknowledge them in open society, let alone have them eligible for induction into the realm of Knights, at Falaise. I wonder how many brothers and sisters I have in the village. I wonder, are there people that I interact with on a daily basis that could be my siblings?

With no consideration to his station, he muses that Sabine might marry him, she'll produce him an heir. His son will become a knight and he too will be as proud as Arthur du Bois. Then reality hits him between the eyes. No, she won't do, she's far too common for his chateau, his title. He needs to search further afield for a more suitable candidate, someone he'll be proud to present in royal circles.

The next day at work is routine, until Ottho sends me to meet with Osanna, the embroiderer. I greet the tiny fair haired lady, she reminds me of a pixie from the stories that Florrie used to tell me. Osanna motions for me to sit on the stool next to her, when I'm comfortably seated, Osanna begins to explain some of the fundamental aspects of her craft. With nimble fingers, she gives me a demonstration, then asks to see a sample of my work. She sets about assigning a task for me to complete. Something simple to begin with, three rows of neat stitching. I can't help myself, this is too basic. When I bring my work to Osanna, I've included tiny blue flowers and two green leaves per flower.

"This is such beautiful work Ailie. Are you sure you haven't done anything like this before.

"Not really. Mama gave me some instruction with needles and threads when I was younger. But not too much towards the end, she was so sick."

"I would swear that you've been trained in embroidery for years. Well done Ailie. I think I'll have to start you at a higher level next time."

At lunch time, I sit outside under the grove of oak trees, eating my bread and cheese, followed by a crisp red apple. Sarra sidles next to me to eat her own lunch. On hearing the crunch of my apple, Sarra considers not taking the fruit from me this time, that's an old trick. But she has a sudden change of heart and snatches it out of my hand, just as I'm about to take another bite. Overlooking my usual decorum, I'm tired of Sarra's poor manners, I cry out.

"Hey, what are you doing?" Sarra grins and continues munching loudly on my apple. I sigh, brushing the bread crumbs from my lap onto the grass, some spry sparrows quickly advance towards the food, gobble it up and fly away.

"What're you doing with Osanna then?" Sarra asks abruptly. I want to point out how rude she's been, instead I reply as tactfully as I can.

"She's teaching me embroidery, Ottho wants his artists to have embroidery skills in case we receive orders from the Duke, the King, or other nobles."

"Well, ooh la la."

"Would you like to learn as well?" I offer, despite Sarra's insolence. "I could ask Osanna for you this afternoon."

"Don't bother. Unlike you, I'm not going to be working in the workshop my whole life you know." I don't take this comment as an affront, I'm genuinely content working at the workshop, for the rest of my life if possible.

"Sir Miché is going to ask for my hand in marriage soon and I'll live with him at Falaise. I won't have to work another day in my life." I have the feeling that she can't marry outside of her station, but knowing Sarra she can make anything happen. I decide to stay silent on the matter.

Life at the castle has changed significantly since Mama's death, out of desperation, I commission Amis, who's developed building skills out of necessity, to maintain the ageing chateau, to build me a separate room on the second floor. I can't bear the thought of Papa bringing home another drunken woman from the tavern, to have sex in the same chamber where I sleep. Luckily, the act never lasts long. I hate to say it, Papa and his women act the same way as the village dogs, then they either leave, or fall asleep within seconds of their copulation concluding. Separate sleeping rooms are generally reserved for dukes and kings, but I'm determined to sleep in my own quarters. Amis does a fine job constructing the room and I line the walls with some of my practice tapestries and embroidery samples. Finally, I can enjoy some peace at last.

Papa's actually happy with this new arrangement, he can see the prestige in having separate quarters on the top floor of his chateau. The extra space also seems to lessen some of the guilt he experiences when he brings women into his deceased, wife's chamber. However, he knows he has to stop drinking, be more diligent, and collect his taxes, but his main priority is to procure a suitable wife to bear him an heir. Finally, he is determined to do better with all that he has. To my surprise, he managed to turn his life around within a few months. The debts were collected, his ale belly disappeared, and more importantly, Papa met a young lady at the Du Bois manor, where he had been reluctantly invited to play cards. They needed him to make up numbers for the table. Catarine only just tolerates the disgraced Lord in her home. However, the gentlemen consider him a fair player and he's somewhat entertaining.

Papa courts Belle, the daughter of a Norman noble family, who is appropriately aligned to the Duke's political ethos. I like Belle, though I know she'll never take the place of Mama. Belle is only slightly older than me, but her father is keen to have her married as soon as possible, he doesn't want her left on the shelf like her older sister. It's too expensive to support girls at home.

"I shouldn't have to pay that scoundrel any more funds. He's skinned me too many times at the card table." Belle's father says to his wife. With my token blessing, the couple were married by Father Jean in the local church. It was a low key affair, with only close friends of our family invited including the Lord and Lady du Bois, they had introduced the newlyweds after all. Their sons, Sir Miché and Sir Leo, were also reluctantly invited. Papa thinks they are a bit too showy for his liking, however much to his relief they can't leave Falaise as they are preparing for battle.

It is less than a year into their marriage before Belle falls pregnant, a situation which finally makes Papa proud. He's excited at the prospect of a potential son and heir. Belle is young and healthy, with anticipation her confinement continues well for the whole term. Luckily for every-one concerned, she gives birth to a boy they name Flynn. I'm thrilled to finally have a baby in the household, a breath of new life and cause for celebration, at the same time there's a piece of me which mourns that he wasn't born to Mama. I'm disappointed that I'm no longer young enough to be a play mate. Although when he smiles, my heart melts which makes up for much of the sadness.

No one can wipe the smile from Papa's face, as he buys ale for every-one at the tavern to celebrate the birth of his son. He then personally tours the village, starting at the village butcher. He has Gillet, prepare a hog for roasting and then orders his driver to take him to a vineyard where he purchases a barrel of wine to be drunk at his son's christening party. Most of the community is invited to attend the festivities at the chateau, however Lord and Lady du Bois' can't attend as they've been summoned by Sir Miché to attend victory celebrations at Falaise. Fi-nally there's contentment at the Belanger Chateau as most of the dark-ness of the previous years has been lifted by the birth of a baby boy.

Papa's over the moon to finally have an heir, but he's aware that at his age, it's possible that he may not live long enough to see his grand dream, of Flynn's induction into the Duke's Inner Circle, come to fruition. He's acutely aware that if the situation had been different, he could have become a grandfather, not a father for the second time. Although, I'm glad it wasn't me having a baby, I have no intentions of marrying and having children right now. Papa has made great strides in turning his life around, but he's done a lot damage to himself, his previous drinking and partying lifestyle, will have lingering effects.

After all he's been through, he's grateful to have a son to carry his name forward.

However, Flynn's first winter foretells a life wracked with bronchial issues, not life threatening illness, though the condition renders him weak. There's little hope of the boy becoming a knight, but Papa always holds firm to his dream. Despite his lack of strength, Flynn proves to be a very intelligent boy and develops a love of reading, he definitely has a thirst for knowledge. For hours on end, he sits by the fire and reads the few books that we own, much to the annoyance of Papa who wants to take his son hunting, teach him horsemanship, and have him practice defence skills, using swords and lances. Flynn tries to feign interest in these activities sometimes, for Papa's sake, but he much prefers to immerse himself in literature, safely within the walls of the chateau.

Chapter 31 Allie

On the last night of our house sitting adventure, Sara and I go out to celebrate the fact that the house is still intact and we've survived the experience, without calling on our parents, or emergency services for help. We spend the day tidying up our messy rooms and in the evening we prepare for a night out as music pumps throughout the house. We dance and pose, as we curl our hair, lacquer and paint ourselves. As she applies her make-up, Sara tries to quiet the voice of her mother in her head.

"If you can't eat it, don't put it on your skin."

Sara has recently broken up with her boyfriend Stuart, they weren't that serious anyway, she isn't unhappy. She's definitely happy to be free to play. David is an apprentice with a construction company, our relationship is new, definitely uncertain. We've only been dating for about three months, he works on a building project in the bush, however I'm quietly glad he's away for work at the moment. I haven't laid eyes on him since I moved out of home. Even though it has only been two weeks, I have a different life now, I'm different. With hindsight, I actually don't want David to fit into my new life, but because this is my first real relationship, I don't know how to kindly end it either. The example shown to me, is to flee to Paris and let someone else do it, but that isn't a viable option right now.

There have been warning bells that he isn't right for me, of course there have. He's loud, domineering and clever at manipulating every situation, so that he appears in a positive light to everyone else. When I want to explain myself, I become tongue tired and lose my train of thought. When he has erred in my eyes, David is able to explain away the situation, to ensure that I'm compelled to accept him back into my life, I'll apologise to him for Goddess' sake. In front of friends and family, he's an angel, but there are times when he knows how to twist the knife of my emotions. Through therapy sessions later on in life, I learn that he's a narcissistic, gas lighter and just one more person to have caused me emotional trauma, besides my mother.

As we walk through the park one sunny afternoon, he says this to me.

"Your family's really fucked up, isn't it? Your brother is a socially stunted Goth, does he ever come out of his room?" This is just for starters, then the particularly hurtful questions fly out. "Is your Dad an alcoholic? Does he bring other women back to your place?" He'll drop these random thoughts into the conversation from nowhere, I'm too gobsmacked to counter them. "How could you think your mum even loves you when she's never there?" Ouch! This arrow connects. This point has crossed my mind before, but it isn't okay for someone else to say so.

My gut has often told me he isn't right for me, I can't put my finger on what it is that bothers me exactly. But actually I do, I'm in denial up to my armpits. I hate that about myself, this wishy washiness is a weakness I abhor in others, it reflects my own inner turbulence. Yet, I don't have the gumption, or the maturity, to move on just yet. I need to learn to love myself first, but that'll take a few more years to come.

Chapter 31 Leo

Word reaches Falaise, that faction groups of noblemen who live in the south west, are critical of Guilliam's possession of the lion's share of the region's power. These splintered, noble families, have conspired with the Bishop of Rouen to the north east, who have also gained much influence over the population of the duchy. The powerful Lord decides, he'll put a stop to his opposition by invading their lands, take control of their chateaus, and replace the resistant aristocracy with his own men. The Duke orders all available knights to assemble in the great hall for a meeting and as Miché and Leo place their helmets on the wooden table, Guilliam begins his meeting.

"There'll be two invading armies." The Duke addresses the meeting. "I'll head the first army, we'll travel to Alençon and from there to Domfront, to seize the lands from the Bellême family. We will insist they yield to our Norman values. The second army will travel north to Rouen Cathedral, there we'll displace the Bishop. Miché, you'll lead the northern army with one hundred men to gain back our power. Odo will be ordained as the resident bishop when you succeed in your quest. We'll ride out tomorrow morning before dawn." The Duke finishes his conference, then leaves the hall to make preparations for the impending invasions. "Miché, come walk with me."

Guilliam wants to ensure his number one knight fully understands the mission.

For the rest of the afternoon and well into the night, the armies gather supplies, armour and weapons, so they can confidently advance to the battle fields by morning. Miché is honoured and excited to be chosen as the leader of the northern army. In his first line of duty, he assigns Leo as his right hand man. As the more senior knight, Sir Roland is furious that he hasn't been assigned a key role in the battles, but he has vowed to the Duke, to uphold chivalry, therefore he doesn't make a scene, just yet. Guilliam didn't chose Sir Roland because he's not as strong and agile as he'd once been. Leo feels for his former mentor and approaches the older knight to mitigate the situation before they turn in for the night.

"Sir Roland, I look to you for wisdom and support during this mission. Your many years of experience will not be wasted."

"Leo, your youth and enthusiasm are admiral, but your tactics and strategies are not a match to mine. You know, your strength and courage does not match that of your brother's." Scorned and humbled, Leo bows his head, he didn't approach Roland to start something with the older knight, he just wanted to show his respect. However, Roland quite pleased with his disparaging comments, turns on his heels and retires for the night.

Before first light, the Duke's army of one hundred and fifty men, ride south in a bid to take over the King's sympathiser fortresses. Miché gathers his men and issue his last instructions before daylight. It'll be a long, two day ride to Rouen, but his men are fit and strong, he's buoyant that they'll be successful. As they prepare, Leo is proud of his brother's achievements, he looks forward to utilising the skills that he's been training for with his brother by his side. However, Sir Roland's words from the previous evening niggle at him, he tries to concentrate on his mission to support his brother in the best way he can.

In full battle armour, Miché and Leo ride out of the chateau on their magnificent horses, their flanks draped in the Duke's colours of red and gold. Flag bearers grip their flags, adorned with the Norman crest of two golden lions on a red background. The insignia warns passers-by that their army rides on behalf of The Duke of Normandy, the rest of the men fall into line behind them. Miché has an excellent rapport with his men, they respect his authority, even Leo, who now has to officially take orders from his older brother.

As they travel through towns and villages, the townsfolk cheer them on and provide them with food and sustenance for their horses. When they arrive in Rouen, before dawn, the army halts on the banks of the River Seine and await their instructions from Miché. They can see the spire of the Cathedral in the near distance and when he gives the signal, his men set off across a wooden bridge to the bank on the other side of the river. It doesn't take long before they circle the Cathedral, but they can't see another army in site, the roads are clear of people. As the Duke's knights dismount their horses, they raise their swords and storm the church.

The cathedral bells ring out ominously, warning parishioners of the imminent battle, word has spread throughout Rouen of the impending invasion. The townsfolk have hunkered down in their homes and the anxious bishop seeks refuge at the top of the tower which is sheltered by twenty armed guards. Despite initially feeling protected, the bishop's men are outnumbered, under-prepared, and under-armed. Miché and his men rage their way to the top of the tower and within a short time of the attack commencing, Miché's men have toppled the bishop's army and removed the cleric from his post through sheer numbers alone.

The men are jubilant. They step over the fallen and injured guards, as they descend the stairs, carrying the deposed bishop out into the harsh light of day. The men roar and cheer for their leader, Leo slaps Miché's back in triumph, pages and squires see to the horses. The triumphant knights are keen to celebrate their victory, they cross over to the tavern opposite the Cathedral, where they assemble to drink, but also to alert the townsfolk that Guilliam has now taken control of Rouen. The inn-keeper doesn't know if he's happy with the extra business, or scared of the fierce knights drinking in his tavern, but there's no way he'll complain either way.

Much ale is drunk that night, except by the sentries who guard the bishop, as leaders, Miché and Leo limit the amount of ale they consume. It's a long ride back to Falaise, they want to keep their wits about them, especially as it's their first battle assignment for the Duke. Before the celebrations begin, Miché sends a messenger to his Lord to inform him of their success and installs his own guards to protect the cathedral, until Odo is ordained the Bishop of Rouen.

Leo sees that none of their troops have suffered any major injuries, though it's evident from all of the blood, that one of the knights has received a nasty lash to his upper left arm, from one of the bishop's guards. Leo quickly attends to the wounded soldier before the knights raise their jugs of ale to the Duke's health. Sir Roland scowls at Leo as he ensconces with his cronies, nursing his ale and his pride. He isn't happy that Leo and his brother, has had a successful mission, in fact, he knows this win will cement his role as a support act, rather than the premier knight he had once been.

The next morning, the ousted bishop is hoisted onto a spare horse, the army returns him to Falaise, where he'll be imprisoned in the chateau's dungeon, alongside other shackled prisoners. By the end of the first day's riding, word has reached Miché and Leo, that Guilliam has also been successful in his quest to gain back his territories in the south, as the lords of both overthrown castles flee in fear of their lives and the Duke installs his own men to run his new stake holds. Guilliam is gaining more and more power in Normandy, as the King's power diminishes in Paris, but he has his sights set on a bigger empire across The Channel.

When both armies return to Falaise, plans are devised for a huge celebration. Villagers and the knight's families are invited to the feast to witness the Duchess Matilda present Miché with a banner of honour and grant him land adjacent to his father's holdings in Breteuil. This bounty further increased his families' wealth, making Papa most upset. Amongst the maidens, Miché is considered to be quite the catch, with his winnings from the jousting competition, his leadership qualities, and his land hold entitlements, combined with his charm and good looks, he's certainly caught the eye of many of the young noble ladies, including Adelaide who entertained him at the previous royal party. Leo could bask in his brother's limelight, if he wanted to, however he's never tempted by the maidens at Court, his heart has someone specific in mind, though she always seems to be at an unbridgeable distance.

Miché openly enjoys his popularity, but like his younger brother, he keeps his eye out for one girl in particular. She intrigues the knight to distraction, so much so, that he sends a messenger to fetch Sarra, and her family, for the party. When they arrive, Luna and Ragno feel somewhat out of place in the royal setting, but after a few jugs of cider they loosen up and are more confident with those of noble birth. Ragno captivates the lords with tall tales of hunting, his adventures, and life on the road, while Luna is amused when she overhears the complaints of the wealthy women. Even though these noble women have more money and titles, they're still not happy. Luna is thankful for her happy family and contented home life, but she wonders how the trappings of Court life might change her daughter if she is to marry the wealthy knight.

Sarra's family have worn their best clothes to the party, though their attire is still considered beneath that of the beautiful silk gowns and fine trousered coat suits of the gentry. Sarra doesn't care that her clothes aren't a match to the noble ladies' attire, she has the attention of the celebrated bachelor, which more than compensates for her less than favourable apparel. However, she is more concerned with her turned in foot. As she's grown, she's learned to hide her deformity by turning out her whole leg, giving the appearance of a normal foot. It means that under her gown, her knee is twisted outwardly, causing her some pain, she hides it well, although not always successfully.

During a lull in proceedings, Miché presents Luna and Ragno to his parents, Lord and Lady du Bois, who greet their potential in-laws with dignified respect. Sarra is also presented to her potential, future in-laws and again, the du Bois' act with the decorum required of their station, however when Sarra retreats to be with her mother, Catarine du Bois seeks out her other son for counsel.

"What do you think of Sarra? She will not do for Miché. She isn't suitable at all, with no breeding, or ancestral land. I can't imagine she'd have a dowry. No, I'm sorry, this cannot happen. I will not allow it." And with her last statement, his mother turns abruptly to find mutual support from another haughty noble woman. But before she's completely out of ear shot, Leo defends his brother.

"I think he's fond of her though, that should count for something. He loves her." Catarine rolls her eyes and shakes her head.

"No, no, no. You're too soft Leo, she'll never do for our family." Close by, Luna turns to her husband and smiles.

"I told you so."

Chapter 32 Leon

When Cathy greets her son in the arrivals hall at the airport, she's stunned to see how much he's changed, not just physically, but also in demeanour. He appears more mature, wiser somehow. Settled in the kitchen, despite the heat, cups of hot tea circle a banana cake in the middle of the table. Leon shares his travel tales and distributes presents to his family which have been thoughtfully gathered on his journey. Declan is presented with a New York baseball cap, some French perfume for Cathy and Claire, and a little clay statuette of a llama for Archie. After he's doled out all of the gifts from his bag, he finds some rolls of undeveloped film which he places on the sideboard, as a prompt to drop them into the photo shop. Feeling around inside his pack, he discovers a snow dome containing a replica of the Rouen Cathedral, he bought as a reminder of the emotions, déjà vu and the serendipity of meeting Tom and Mitch.

He inspects the dome and gives it a shake. Plastic snow cascades onto the cathedral and he's instantly transported back to France.

"Can I have a go?" Cathy asks, shaking him out of his reverie.

"Sure." Leon hands her the souvenir and she gives the small dome a jiggle. She watches in wonder as the plastic flakes float lethargically about the church.

"Look, it's beautiful. Well, we certainly missed you while you were away." Cathy is misty eyed when she hands the snow dome back to Leon. She kisses the top of his head and begins to clear the table before he clears his throat, he quickly rips off the band aid.

"Mum, Dad, the fellas have asked me to move in with them." The cup and saucer tremble between Cathy's hands, but she's able to right the crockery just in time. She knew this day was approaching, it's all too soon.

"When do you think you'll be moving out then?" All eyes are fixed on Leon again.

Leon's news causes mixed reactions amongst his family. Declan has enjoyed the extra bedroom space that a travelling brother affords him, he looks forward to settling into his own room indefinitely, at least until he moves out as well. Archie happily considers the reduced grocery and utility bills, with one less hungry mouth to feed, clothe and wash. Claire will miss her older brother, but it really makes no difference to her, she wonders if Shannon is able to go shopping with her this afternoon. It hits Cathy the hardest though, hot tears start welling, she grabs a tea towel from the drainer and wipes her eyes.

"What's the matter love?" Archie has actually noticed her, he's suddenly concerned for his wife.

"Oh, it's nothing, I think I have something in my eye." She sniffs as she rushes to the bathroom to have a proper sob. Leon knows he's made his mother cry and he feels terrible for it, he also knows he has a life to live outside of the family home, he can't wait to begin.

Semester one is due to start in less than a week and Leon is eager to settle in with the boys before his classes commence. There isn't much furniture to move, but Archie helps his son lug it all to his new room and when they have finished unpacking, Archie clears his throat.

"Make sure you come home from time to time, please visit your mother, we'll all miss you. Here, she wants you to have this bag of meat trays to use for your paints. I'm not sure what you're going to do with them. You can just throw them away if you like."

"Thanks Dad. No, I won't throw them away. Mum is trying to recycle them in a useful way. I'll use them to put my paints on, like a palette."

"Oh yeah, good idea."

Archie awkwardly reaches for his son's hand, finally making a connection. He shakes his hand, then pulls him in for a hug. Churned up, he turns around and leaves silently. Leon sits on his unmade bed, removes the snow dome from his backpack and carefully places it on top of his dresser. This is the first decoration he adds to his new room, a room that he doesn't have to share with his brother, he is beginning to feel like an independent adult as the next segment of his life commences.

However, his contemplation time is over apparently, Mitch abruptly enters Leon's room while he's deep in thought and announces that they're headed to the pub before going to the O Week celebrations at the university. It's a party for the new academic year where there will be bands, bars and dancing.

"Give me ten minutes to have a shower and I'll be there." Leon says, he searches for the clean towel Cathy packed for him.

Chapter 33 Ailie

Life has improved for a change, our chateau in Breteuil is a much calmer place than it has been for quite some time. Papa and Belle have become comfortable in their new roles as newlyweds and new parents. However, Bietriz took a little while to warm up to the new Lady of the Manor, considering the bride's young age and the maid's love of her former mistress. It was confusing for Bietriz, up until the wedding, I was the Lady of the Manor, household questions were directed to me, but after the wedding, Bietriz was still coming to me for directions.

"What do you want me to cook for the dinner Lord Belanger has planned for the weekend, Ma'am?"

"You need to speak to Belle about the dinner arrangements now Bietriz. I'm no longer Lady of the Manor."

"Very well, yes of course. I will ask her."

However, it was my new baby brother that eventually brought the maid and her mistress together. Belle had a lot of trouble settling the little boy, especially when he has a cold, which is often, but Bietriz has the magic touch with babies, she knows exactly what to do to alleviate his snuffly breathing, using rosemary and mint infusions from the kitchen. Belle is eternally grateful to Bietriz, she and the baby can finally get some sleep. It makes such a difference to both their moods.

"Wow, Bietriz you know so much about babies. I don't really understand how you did it, but you really helped Flynn with his snuffles. Where did you learn to make these infusions?"

"Oh, it's nothing Ma'am. I've picked up some things from here and there." With a little praise from Belle, a chasm of misunderstanding was bridged, Bietriz's heart was won. However, there was no mention of Mama and the infusions Luna made for her. The tea which saw her momentarily well, then so sick again. It will forever remain a mystery to me.

Florrie also loves Flynn, he is often found in the kitchen by her side, snuggled under a blanket in the washing basket, where he kicks his legs and coos happily as she cooks and cleans. As I walk through the kitchen, I notice Araignee, lying in the basket with Flynn. Florrie has used my old toy to elicit smiles from the baby, but when I see the inert doll next to my sleeping brother, I feel a surge of anger, I want to swipe the doll back for myself. Taking a deep breath, I quickly realise that would be silly, he's just a baby and I'm of marriageable age. My irritation surprises me and I see that my upbringing has left me with some painful issues that I will need to address at some point. I wish that Florrie had asked me for the doll though, Araignee has been such a special part of my childhood. I pick up the doll, inspect her all over, she's aged a bit, I inhale the scent of the worn fabric, give her a quick kiss and place her down beside the sleeping baby before walking into the garden and down the path to work. It seems that I have a bit to learn about sibling rivalry, even at my age.

I spend the morning working with Marc, then I work on my own designs, at the end of the day, I'm consumed with Osanna's embroidery lessons.

"You've progressed brilliantly Ailie, keep it up. You're going to be one of my chief artists before you know it. You have such natural ability and already, you've achieved so much. To be asked to Guilliam's wedding, as an artist of note, is a huge honour for someone so young." Ottho gushes, as he walks through the workshop.

"Thanks Ottho." I blush.

Sarra was the next weaver to be recognised, but not for her work. She has received a request from one of the Duke's messengers to travel to Falaise, to spend some time with her love, Miché. The news creates great excitement amongst the weavers, especially Sarra, who has waited impatiently for this day since the victory party. When the talk of Sarra's love life dies down a little, Ottho remembers he has an embroidery piece which needs some alterations, it requires delivery to Duchess Matilda by emissary.

"As you've worked on this piece Ailie, I think this journey is a golden opportunity for my star apprentice to gain favour within the Duke's household. With your sense of colour and style, your quiet and attentive manner, I think that you can persuade the Duchess to create an order from our workshop. You will travel with Sarra to the castle." Little did I know that this journey would change the course of my life.

"What the..?" To begin with, Sarra isn't entirely happy with this arrangement.

"Oh my Goddess, you can't let me have five minutes of attention without having to weasel your way in." Sarra spits.

"I don't wish to take anything away from you Sarra. Consider this, I'll be your companion on the highway. You're going to a royal castle, you'll need a suitable companion. It wouldn't look right to arrive on your own. I will be a part of your entourage." I planted a seed for Sarra's contemplation.

"Yes, perhaps you're right. You'll be my lady in waiting, you can serve me." When she's thought about it, she realises how amusing it is to consider me as her travelling companion. The tables have turned, she's going to relish lording it over me. For once, Sarra will know what it's like to appoint an underling. This journey will be the first of many opportunities where she'll be the Lady of her realm, perhaps, if not my superior, an equal. Her potential marriage to Miché, is a means of escape from Breteuil, to live a life she's always aspired to, as a Lady of the Court de Falaise.

To guard us from highwaymen, Ragno travels with us to Falaise and from our stables, Papa lends us a sturdy cart and one of the older mares to transport our belongings, including the embroideries for the Duchess. It seems that everything is happening so easily, it all falls into place.

"Goodbye Breteuil, I won't be returning. Falaise will be my home from now on." She's keen to begin her new life as a lady, but something tells me that it won't be that simple. Sarra is optimistic, she takes the ease of the journey as a sign of her future success.

When we arrive at the chateau, food and drink have been arranged for we weary travellers in the grand hall, while some of the knights mill around the room. From a circle of men, Miché appears before Sarra, knowing that he matters a great deal in this situation, his first port of call is Sarra's father. He pumps Ragno's hand heartily.

"Good day Sir. Welcome to Falaise. My dear Sarra." He kisses Sarra's outstretched hand before turning his attention to me.

"Good day, Ailie isn't it?" We respectfully bow towards each other, he grasps my hand, which I'm not expecting, he lightly kisses it. Sarra's usual cool confidence is rattled at this show of affection towards her supposed underling, but then she realises that I'm only being treated in accordance with my true station in life, although Miché doesn't know that. Miché bows to us, then leaves us to rest in the chateau as he guides Ragno out into the yard to talk, man to man.

Sarra departs to her room with a page to unpack her small bag of belongings, I remain on my own at the table. After I've picked at some of the bread and butter, I pivot on the bench seat to observe the grand hall. I notice that not much has changed since our hosts wedding. I see the tapestry I worked on with Marc, from the corner of my eye, it holds pride of place on the eastern wall, I rise from my seat to inspect it more closely. I regard the piece intently for a few moments before I sense a presence behind me.

"It's such a charming tapestry. You're so talented." The young knight whispers from a close distance, making my cheeks burn as I turn around to see who's standing behind me. "My name's Leo, pleased to make your acquaintance." I hold out my hand to the young knight which he promptly kisses.

Chapter 34 Allie and Mitch

Thanks to Dad, Sara and I have scraped together enough money for the first month's rent on our new home. He's a bit upset that we didn't used his preferred real estate agent, but in a way, he's glad that I'd showed an independent spirit, he knows that I'll be able to survive on my own, for the time being at least. Our new home is close to the clinic where I work, the shops, and most importantly, the pub is within walking distance. Our new home is a modern, white rendered, two bedroom townhouse with a small fenced off courtyard in a group of four. We had to have a courtyard, a place where we'll spend our time entertaining and contemplating our futures, on sunny afternoons and balmy nights.

At dinner, in a café further down the high street, we nibble on salads and warm bread rolls, we chat furiously about our plans to furnish the apartment.

"I can enlarge some of my photos, print them in black and white, frame them and make a gallery wall in the living room." I suggest.

"We have to include that funny one of us at the football that day, remember I didn't know it was only half time when I got up to leave. And we were wearing those baggy overalls with white cropped t-shirts and navy basketball boots, we were so matchy matchy." Sara chuckles to herself.

"No wonder we were so cold." I laugh.

After our shared piece of hummingbird cake, we contentedly stroll arm in arm to the pub and like a predatory animal that he is, the moment we enter the bar, Mitch takes a mental picture of the prey who have wandered into his territory. He pays careful attention not to stare, but keeps us in his peripheral vision. He has already decided in the time that I take to cross the threshold, I'll be his conquest for the evening. Civilly, Mitch waits for us to get ourselves a drink and be seated, before he makes direct eye contact. At first, he smiles at us while he continues to talk to his friends, as adrenaline courses through his body, excited by the impending chase. The hunt has begun.

The bar fills and a loud party atmosphere engulfs the room. We have changed the topic of conversation from the new flat, to a deliberation of the people sitting around us. We must have been sitting there for a while, because suddenly I have the urge to pee, I make my way to the ladies. Not looking anywhere in particular, I crash into Mitch's fridge like chest on my way and of course, he does nothing to avoid me because he knows damn well, I was positioned directly on his collision course. He'd put himself here after all.

He holds my bare shoulders in his massive hands and gives me a confident smile before he points me in the right direction towards the toilets. I try to be casual and not giggle.

"Is that where you're headed?"

"Yep." I manage to say, I blush deeply. At his touch, a buzz of electricity surges through my belly, or is it the urge to pee. Not an overly sexual feeling, but a flirtatious recognition of something, maybe. On my way back, I'm astonished, but not really surprised, when I see Mitch sitting at our table with Sara, deep in conversation. He's a fast worker.

"This is Mitch, number seventeen!" Sara not so discretely whispers and points above his head, as I resume my chair. I suppress a smile because I know his type. I coyly replace the fallen spaghetti strap from my dress as I sit down, however Sara has been won over, she's overtly smitten by Mitch's charm and wit.

"So, you're moving into the area?" Mitch asks, before I can answer, he fires off another question. "Quel est tom nom? He gazes directly into my eyes, I blush again. Damn Irish skin.

"Allie. Her name's Allie." Sara offers far too quickly before I can answer for myself.

"Yes. We just signed on the flat today." I nervously find my voice, as I extend my hand to Mitch's large out stretched palm, even though we'd met minutes ago, be it a little less formally.

"Great. So, this will be your local as well then." He beams, planting a quick kiss on the back of my hand. Bloody didn't kiss my hand, thought Sara, who's turned a lovely shade of emerald.

"I guess so." Sara decides to remain cheerful, despite her obvious envy, this is just the beginning after all. We all shout a round and became progressively intoxicated, our conversation is peppered with flirtation, good humour and happy bullshit.

Sitting at the bar, Sara's ex watches the scene unfold before him, he doesn't like what he observes. He definitely isn't over Sara and her lack of yearning is wounding his bruised ego, he's generally in pain all over. She hasn't even noticed his presence, though Stuart is going to make sure that she sees him. He finishes the dregs of his beer and rises unsteadily to confront her, but it isn't because he's drunk that he is unsteady on his feet, it's because he is slightly frazzled by the whole situation. With newly mustered confidence, he appears to the observer, to have brazenly marched over to our table and there he stands, silently waiting for a break in the conversation to announce his existence.

He's invisible for an eternity. We, the merry threesome, are encased in a bubble of joy and we certainly don't respond to him while he stands humiliatingly rigid. Can't they see me here? He thinks to himself, fuming, Sara laughs loudly at one of Mitch's corny jokes. That's the final straw. Stuart delivers an edgy salutation.

"HELLO!" He yells during the break between songs. "Sara!" The music resumes its frenetic pace.

"What?" She cups her ear towards him, in a pretence to hear him more clearly, albeit a trifle pissed off, he's broken the snugness of our trio.

"Hi!" Stuart shouts back. He nervously shuffles his feet as the music suddenly silences again, as well as the general hubbub and conversation. At the bar, Maria calls number 97 to collect their chicken schnitzel with mushroom gravy, Stuarts "Hi" hangs loudly in the air.

Choosing the right breaks in the songs has become a tiresome game.

"Hi." Sara waves. She quickly resumes her conversation with Mitch and me, then I suddenly regain consciousness of my surroundings. I see Stuart standing by our table. Oh, this is going to be interesting, I think.

"Hello." Mitch, forever the gentleman, pulls out the remaining empty chair for Stuart. "Hi I'm Mitch, nice to meet you. Do you have a drink? Um, I don't know your name sorry?"

"Stuart." Stuart searches Sara's face for approval to sit down, but he quickly decides he isn't going to wait for permission, he knows approval won't be forthcoming. With residual shreds of self-respect, Stuart claims the remaining chair, knowing that Sara doesn't want him there, but their new friend has invited him into the fold, luckily. However, Mitch isn't really a gentleman, he angling to catch me. "Yeah, a beer would be great thanks." Stuart yells to the waiter.

Introductions over, our small group orders another round of drinks and the good humour quickly resumes. Stuart watches Sara moonily over the top of his pint, like a love sick beagle. With the help of the alcohol, his anger diffuses into a sickly lovey feeling. Over the course of the evening, Sara becomes increasingly irritated by Stuart's existence, he catches her more than once, giving him the evil eye, but in the company of Mitch and her new commitment to being graceful, she tries hard to tolerate his very being.

Sara struggles to hide her not so secret jealousy of Mitch's attraction to me, I know what she's thinking, but I don't say anything. I'm weak, a coward and selfish. I've had too many drinks to stop the attention. Yes, I like it actually and what's the harm in a little flirtation, I rationalise with myself. A switch suddenly goes off in Sara's brain, she realises she's either going to make a fool of herself by directing her attention where it won't be reciprocated, or she can cut her loses and guarantee herself a night of fumbling sex with Stuart, for which she'll hate herself for in the morning.

With little energy to fight remaining, she chooses the latter scenario. Sara's drunk and her thoughts turn to the maudlin. She starts to question her attractiveness, she knows that she definitely has a feisty personality to win Mitch over in the long run, it will just take some time. She's more than prepared to play the long game. It's obvious where his intentions lie tonight, she places her sword down and leaves with Stuart who is grinning smugly.

"Stop that Stuart, it's not cool." Sara chides him.

"What? What am I doing?" Stuart's confused, he can't see how goofy he looks.

"Oh, it's nothing really. Come on, lets go." Actually, Sara wants to go home and cry, though she doesn't consider it a viable option.

Mitch and I remain at the table, sipping our drinks, engaging in flirty banter, until closing time. Declan drops in after indoor cricket and leaves pretty quickly. I don't really look at him and certainly don't commit his face to memory. If there was a police line-up tomorrow, I wouldn't be able to identify him. Being responsible, Declan takes his role as assistant to the manager at the credit union very seriously, he leaves after one drink. He also knows that if he doesn't give Mitch space with me, he'll hear about it tomorrow.

At last drinks, Mitch escorts me to the door.

"Where shall we go now?"

"Shall we see what's going on out there?" The street is jumping with people who are dancing to the rhythmic beats supplied by the bands at the annual music festival. Adding to the music, a DJ is spinning house music at the end of the street. In the spirit of the evening, Mitch pulls me closer to him, so close, I can feel the heat of his burly body. He places his giant arms around my waist and suddenly I can feel my feet lifting from the ground. I expect a lingering kiss, I purse my lips in anticipation, but my body continues into the air until I'm over his shoulder and I'm staring down at the ground behind him. I giggle and burp at the same time, he laughs. He's caught his prize.

My drunken eyes meet with a strange reflection in the water that's running through the gutter. A little girl, perhaps six years old, with long curly hair, regards me from the stream. Her face looks so sad, tears begin to trickle down her cheeks. Then gentle sobs flow from her soulful eyes, her face is so sad, she knows something that I don't. The little girl is just about to share her secret with me when a festival reveller stomps into the puddle and splashes her image away. In the same instance, I relieve myself of the night's alcohol, salad and hummingbird cake, into the dirty gutter.

Feeling my stomach lurch, Mitch immediately places me on to terra firma and holds my face in his hands. He studies me and using his semi clean hanky, wipes the spit from my chin before he carefully places my wayward hair back into some normal semblance. He gives me the once over and declares me passable.

"You're still beautiful you know, even after a big vomit." In his state, anyone would be attractive. However, he's seen past the drunken haze and into my inner worth which I am yet to see, he gently leads me by the hand through the crowd.

In his bedroom, my summer dress slips easily from my shoulders and I stand next to his bed in my white knickers. Mitch immerses himself in the vision before him, with hungry eyes and unsteady stupor. He scans my tussled hair, down to my painted blue toenails, making sure to include everything in between. His eyes linger for an awkward length of time at my breasts which I suddenly realise by his goofy grin. I quickly cover myself with my arms. Unperturbed, he gathers me up and sloppily plonks me onto the middle of the half made bed. I'm woozy, but my mind is willing. We kiss widely and deeply, grope each other for a few minutes, then promptly fall asleep.

The next morning, I wake feeling disorientated, especially when I find myself alone in a strange king size bed. My head pounds and so does my heart. Is it from the alcohol, or anxiety? Perhaps a bit of both. Why do I get myself into these stupid situations? Satisfying an itch on my leg, I realise I'm only wearing knickers, I quickly pull the white cotton sheet above my breasts. I take a moment to look around the room and notice a full glass of water sitting on the opposite bedside table. My mouth is desert dry, I reach over and drink the water in one big gulp. At the end of the bed, I spot a large bath towel, I wish it was a large paper bag to cover my throbbing head as well.

I drag myself out of bed, wrap the stray towel around my body and collect my things. Thank Goddess some people don't tidy up after themselves. I hope that I can find my way to the bathroom without having to ask anyone. I have no idea where it is, though I'm guided by expectation and some intuition, I really need to pee. As I exit the bedroom, I clutch my dress, purse and shoes, with as much dignity as I can muster, which is not much at all by this stage. As I approach the bathroom, I look up to see a nice man's face, it isn't Mitch staring back at me and even though he's a stranger, he seems oddly familiar and comforting.

"Um, hi. Bathroom's that way." He points down the hall.

"Hello. Thanks." I nervously reply. Realising my state of undress, I somehow manage to find the bathroom door, walk through it and snap the door shut. I pee, then quickly re-dress. Without interacting with anyone, I quietly steel away from the house. With my reasoning returning slowly, I wonder why on earth I didn't get dressed in the bedroom and leave from there, but there's no reasoning at this point.

Feeling pretty seedy, I walk back to Trish's house to find it empty and peaceful, to which I'm forever grateful. Sara is still ensconced with Stuart, so I retreat meekly into the comfort of the bedroom, the nice man's face still etched on my mind. I try to erase the night with Mitch, my mind keeps going back to the other man. Guilt flashes across my mind for a split second, with regards to David. Have I cheated on him? Who am I kidding, I don't really care. Wasn't I trying to break up with him anyway? Have I cheated Sara? Definitely. She's liked Mitch since we were at high school, but only based on a once off, far off sighting on a football field. But if I hadn't gone home with Mitch I never would have seen him, the stranger.

Justifications aside, what I know for sure, is that I am a bad friend and this will need to be processed when I'm older, I'll just add it to the list. However at this time, what the nice man in Mitch's house thinks of me, matters. It's a bizarre feeling, I only laid eyes on him for a few seconds, he seems so familiar, already I'm aware of his spirit enveloping mine. Perhaps that's how Sara feels about Mitch. I feel terrible again.

Chapter 35 Leo

After the party from Breteuil arrives, Leo and some of the other knights are in deep discussion regarding the battles they've engaged in, while Miché connects with Sarra. When I'm alone, Leo looks over and notices me as the girl from Ottho's workshop. He watches me pick at my bread from the far side of the great hall for some time before I get up to look at the wedding tapestry. He wants to meet me properly, he quietly approaches my side of the hall, but he's nervous, he hasn't had many interactions with women, besides his mother and his nurse. Trying to pluck up the courage, he lingers for a moment before speaking and in nearly a whisper, Leo compliments the tapestry and my skills. He then introduces himself and nervously lifts my hand to kiss it.

As he's about to ask me another question, Odo, now the Bishop of Rouen, storms into the hall and demands to speak to Miché.

"Where is your brother? I need to speak to him urgently. Go and find him with haste."

"I'll fetch him for you, Your Grace. Please excuse me Ailie?" And just like that, Leo leaves my side immediately to search for his brother.

He eventually finds Miché, talking to Sarra, in the grove of oak trees next to the field. Upon seeing the couple, Leo's first impression is of their indiscretion, considering they haven't employed a chaperone, a consideration they have been taught throughout their training. Although he needn't have been concerned, just out of eye sight, Ragno is only a short distance away.

"Hey Miché! Odo wants to see you in the Grand Hall."

"What on Earth for?"

"I'm not entirely sure." Miché looks pensively at his maiden

"Okay, I best go and speak to Odo. Please excuse me." Miché bids Sarra farewell.

Ragno appears from the grove of trees carrying a small stick in his hand. While he's been waiting for his daughter, he's whittled a raven's head into the soft wood and has meditated on the niggling feeling he has had since they arrived at the chateau. His instincts are telling him that trouble is brewing, he knows his instincts are never wrong.

"I don't think the upper echelons are happy with my daughter being here with Miché. Well, our family in particular, we're not suitable stock for the likes of your brother and especially not your family."

"Why ever not?" Leo asks, as they approach each other.

"Well, for one thing, we're not Catholic, let alone Christian, Odo won't be happy with that state of affairs, him being the bishop and all."

"Hmm, yes." Leo has to agree.

Leo hasn't even considered that the class, or religion, of potential suitors will be an issue for his family. However, he then remembers what his mother said to him at the battle of Rouen celebrations, how she believed that Sarra isn't a suitable marriage candidate for her son, it all makes horrible sense now. He's worried, and sad, for his brother all at once, his heart is heavy, he can see there will be no way that Guilliam and Odo will grant permission for the relationship to continue, let alone a wedding.

When Leo arrives back inside the chateau, Odo and Miché are deep in conversation.

"I'm afraid it's not possible, Miché you cannot marry her. It's fortunate for them that I don't imprison the whole family as heretics." Miché drops his head into his hands in disbelief.

"I understand your Grace, however I'm saddened by the news. Is there nothing we can do? Can she convert? Tell me, what can I do?"

"Nothing my son. The Church is insisting that we don't allow any mixed marriages to occur, especially not with those Pagans, they will not convert to Christianity and anyway, their hearts are impure, I can't take them in, even if I wanted to. They need to leave immediately, or I shall have them declared to the Church Council for their non-Christian values. If tried, and found guilty, her mother will be burnt alive at the stake for witchcraft. So, as your counsel, I instruct you to stay well away from Sarra and her entire family. I know it's hard Miché, but you must leave her be."

He knows Sarra is his one true love, the girl he wants to marry, but now he knows that he has invited his beloved into a very dangerous situation. What was supposed to be a beautiful encounter, is now ugly and dark.

"Is there any way we can negotiate this situation?" Miché pleads with his cleric. Leo watches his brother from the sidelines, willing a positive response from the bishop. But the bishop's compassion is wearing thin, he's becoming angry and will not yield.

"I'm sorry my son, they're a family of heathens, we cannot invite them into the Church. As a servant of the Pope in Rome, I cannot allow this union, ever. Do not invite anyone like them into this chateau again as it brings shame to The Duke and our community." As a faithful knight, who's pledged his faith to the Church, he knows the bishop speaks the truth, but it doesn't stop the agonising pain stabbing him in the chest.

While Miché has been pleading with the bishop, Ragno collects his despondent daughter from her chamber. She's been sobbing for some time and was in a crumpled heap on the floor since hearing of her fate. Her dream of escaping Breteuil is in ashes. Her father is repacking the cart for their looming departure, while they wait for me to return from my meeting with Matilda. When she has gathered enough energy, Sarra flops onto the cart in floods of tears, it's humiliating to be sent away in this manner. To be so close to her happiness, a potential future with a celebrated knight and to have him ripped away in an instant, is too much for her to bear. Ragno knows they have to lie low and return quietly to their old life, otherwise his wife and daughter will be in mortal danger.

When Odo leaves the two knights in the grand hall, Leo tries to console his older brother, but there's nothing he can say, or do, to make Miché's pain diminish, especially so soon after the lance has been thrust into his heart, he knows it will take some time. Instead, Leo sits with his brother in silence and within a few minutes, Miché senses a shiver run through his body. He rises and resumes his daily routine as if nothing has happened. Leo doesn't think that Miché's recovery will be quite so fast.

"Hey where are you going?" Leo wants to make sure that his brother is okay.

"I have work to do, leave me be." He has to shake off this awful feeling, bury it and continue as Guilliam's lead knight of the Inner Circle, he has an important job to do. But Leo is worried for his brother, he knows he's strong and will find love again, someday, but he also knows that Miché is suffering terribly. In the meantime, Leo searches the chateau for me, but apparently I seemed to have vanished as well.

Chapter 36 Leon

In a share house, on an inner-suburban street, Mitch showers while he sings Roxanne at the top of his voice, he likes the classics. Leon is staying at home to finish an assignment, he doesn't want to disturb the flow of his writing, so he continues with his art essay on 19th Century Impressionists, it's due on Monday.

Mitch observes his usual Thursday night pilgrimage to the local pub, The Hammer and Trowel. A builder's pub back in the fifties and sixties, and now during the late eighties, the Yuppie revolution has come to town, the pub was sold and renovated to look more or less the same, but somehow more expensive and upmarket. He has a large assortment of friends that stem from nowhere and everywhere, and he'll arrive at the pub just at the right moment to shout a round and share a funny story. Mitch is a flirt pure and simple, always keeping his eyes open for pretty women amongst the patrons. Most of the regulars know Mitch intimately and to be fair, he treats them like princesses, in turn they think he's charming, harmless fun. This particular Thursday night, the bar is bustling and the local music festival is at its height, the crowds are out for a good time.

Since the end of high school, Mitch has become more aware of his attractiveness to the opposite sex, unlike Leon, Mitch knows it and capitalises on his looks. He has different women emerge from his bedroom door at least four mornings a week. The other days of the week, he stays at their houses. It isn't a surprise that Leon saw me escaping from Mitch's bedroom, but for some reason it is. Leon recalls the next morning, when I, a tallish girl, with bed hair, a towel wrapped tightly around my chest, and a face that wasn't quite ready to start the day, creeps sheepishly from Mitch's door. After a brief "hello", I'd fled to the bathroom with my clothes held closely to my chest. I closed the door and melted away.

"A strange girl, leaving the house in the morning isn't unusual, but a girl like her?" Leon is at home for dinner, chatting with Declan in the lounge room after the meal. "She isn't one of Mitch's usual conquests, she appeared genuinely mortified as she emerged from his bedroom. She seemed truly embarrassed and awkward."

"Bloody hell, you're gone aren't you. I've never heard you go on like that about anyone. How long did you talk to her? What's her name?"

"The thing is, I didn't really talk to her and I don't know who she is. It'd be a miracle if Mitch even knows who she is."

"Oi, you two, you need to come and do the washing up for your mother!" Archie yells out to his sons from the kitchen.

The next morning, Mitch is at the breakfast table, scouring the morning paper with a large mug of steaming coffee cradled in his hands. A plate of half eaten toast marks the midway point of the paper.

"So, who is she?" Leon asks as he comes in for breakfast.

"Um, good-morning to you too." Mitch scratches the two day stubble on his chin. "I think I must've scared her off."

"Yeah you did." Leon pours himself a mug of coffee from the nearly depleted, stove top, coffee pot and snatches half of the paper from under Mitch's toast. But it doesn't come away cleanly, he has to adjust the plate so that he can grab the rest of the pages. Sitting opposite Mitch, after he's rearranged the pages of the newspaper, Leon tries to study an article on the current demarcation disputes at the inter-city bus terminal, but his mind keeps wandering back to the bathroom door.

"No really, who is that girl?" Leon asks again, a little too impatiently.

"Oh, um, Katy, or Pia was it, no, maybe Karlie, Allie. That's it, Allie, I think." Mitch yawns. "It's weird you know? She comes back with me from the pub, nothing happens and we just fall asleep. Oh, we fumbled around for a while and then it's lights out. It could've been that we'd had one too many disco slammers, maybe. She couldn't wait to get out of here though, could she? Bit unusual." He shrugs thoughtfully and scratches his crotch as he drains the last mouthfuls of coffee from his mug.

Girls who disappear so easily don't exist in Mitch's experience, he usually has to scheme and suggest subtle ways for them to leave. Over the years, he's become proficient at convincing them to depart, ensuring they feel special at the same time. But when they leave early and of their own accord, it has him wondering if he's losing his mojo.

Leon puts his empty mug onto the table, collects his sketch pad and pencil from the dresser and walks through the French doors into the Boston ivy covered courtyard. As he sits down, he notices a clear puddle that he needs to step over to reach the chair. As he looks down, he notices a distorted reflection mirroring him for a brief second. Is it his reflection? Shaking his thoughts free, he begins to sketch the girl in white towelling from memory. Leon's hand moves the 6B pencil in quick sharp movements and within a moment, he's captured my likeness perfectly. He then adds shade and tone and when he's finished the drawing, he looks away from the image and back to the puddle. This time, he overlooks his reflection and sees right to the bottom of the water through to the structure of the paving bricks below. He's deep in thought again.

Leon scribbles out a poem on a separate piece of paper and puts the poem and the drawing together. He gathers up the tools of his trade and steps over the pool of water. Back inside the house, he tucks the drawing and poem under some undies in the top drawer of his bedside table.

Chapter 37 Ailie

Once again, I find myself alone in the grand hall at Falaise, Leo is in the yard with Ragno, and Miché is in deep discussions with the Bishop in the far corner. The bishop seems to be riled up and the air around them is very tense. Luckily a page appears, requesting my presence with the Duchess, I'm relieved that I can leave the strained environment. With the thought of meeting Matilda, a different type of anxiety rises in my stomach, though I'm pleased to be called upon, I'm adrift in the vastness of the Duke's home and all its drama. I leave the hall to fetch the embroidery Ottho dispatched with me and handling the fabric and threads centres me, I feel a lot calmer. While I collect all of the required supplies for my meeting, a page boy meets me at the doorway to my room.

I follow the young boy down a series of passageways to the Duchess' chamber, he confidently knocks on the door to herald our arrival. A young maiden opens the large oak door from inside the room. The Duchess heavily pregnant, reclines on a large padded chair upholstered in a fine vermilion fabric. From this proximity, I notice Matilda's fine features, in particular her slender nose and her long flowing ebony hair. The Duchess rises to receive my hand and I notice that she's slightly shorter than me, but perhaps only one, or two years older.

"Thank you for meeting me at our chateau Ailie, I adore the piece you completed for our wedding tapestry. It means a great deal to us both."

"Thank you Ma'am." I bow my head in reverence. "But it was the master weaver Marc, who completed the majority of the work."

"You're too humble Ailie. Ottho told me you would be. He also said, you are a great artist and a diligent worker. I look forward to seeing more of your work."

"Thank you Ma'am. I have the piece from the workshop that you wanted to see." We chat easily for some time before a page requests, via Ragno, my leave from the chateau.

Running back through the corridors and down the stairs, I quickly make my way to the horse and cart without seeing anyone. The hall has mostly emptied, apart from a few older knights who chat and play cards around the enormous fire place. I haven't heard about Sarra's plight and I'm surprised to see her crying in the cart when I arrive outside, but now I wonder if it has anything to do with the argument I'd overheard between Odo and Miché.

"What's the matter Sarra? What's happened? Where are you going?" I direct my questions mainly to Ragno, as I observe his final preparations for departure and Sarra's failure to respond.

"We must go home immediately. Our lives are in mortal danger if we remain here."

"Why? How can that be?" I'm so confused. Everything was so happy and cordial an hour ago.

"Sarra is of the wrong birth to marry a noble such as Sir Miché. We're Pagans and Odo perceives us as heretics. We....." He starts to stumble over his words. "We could be put to death and I've put my family at great risk by coming here." Ragno pauses and casts his eyes to the ground near his feet. I'm dumbfounded.

"Odo is somewhat compassionate, but he's not willing to turn a blind eye. We have to return home and not engage with the Duke's community at the Chateau, including Sir Miché." I know Sarra is not of the right standing to marry Miché, but I thought all of that would be overlooked for the love they shared. I believe Miché's standing at the Chateau would have granted him some favour, especially given the Duke and Duchess's forbidden, and somewhat rebellious, marriage. However, personally, he can't disobey the vow he had made to the Catholic Church, despite his lord's misdemeanours.

In an attempt to comfort her, I climb up onto the cart and put my arm around Sarra's shoulders. Everything that she's done to me in the past dissolves, I truly want to pacify my co-worker. However, my efforts to help ease her pain are shrugged off immediately.

"You're just the same as those people." Sarra snaps. "You think you're so much better than us because of your titles, your money and your religion." I softly shake my head, but I don't try to defend myself verbally. Ragno allows his daughter to take her anger out on me, while she catches her breath and discharges her tirade at a more ferocious level. "Where are your families' Christian values? Your father whored around town when your mother was ill. God only knows how many bastards he's sired. He was always drunk while your mother was sick of living, they both neglected you. How are they Christian values? And yet, you are free to marry whomever you want."

Venom pours out of Sara like bile, while I sit ramrod still and take her abuse like bitter medicine. I'm not hearing anything new, though it's still shocking to hear these words from the mouth of my companion, she obviously hasn't finished.

"You work in a workshop alongside me, and you are better than me? Go back to your so called royalty, leave us alone. GO!"

Shocked and humiliated, I don't know what to do. How can I return to Breteuil with Sarra and Ragno? It would be an awkward journey, to say the least, and I wonder whether I should leave the cart and identify another mode of transport? It appears, Ragno can hear my thoughts.

"What do you want to do girl?"

I grab my bag and climb down from the cart. When my feet touch the earth, Ragno gives the reins a snap, a signal for the old chestnut mare to walk on. I'm stupefied by this turn of events. My day has gone from a successful meeting with the Duchess, to turned out of my own cart, with no transport to take me home. I watch Ragno, Sarra, and the horse and cart grow smaller in the distance. As I ponder my options, a page requests my return to the chateau. In silent disbelief, I return through the tower gates.

Chapter 38 Allie

Well into the late afternoon, Sara finally returns, neither of us have the energy to discuss what happened the night before. In fact, we say very little. Sara isn't ready to admit that she's been with Stuart, or was he with her? She doesn't really know anymore, she's disappointed that she didn't manage to win Mitch's affections. I don't gloat that I'd spent the night with him, because I'm not proud of my behaviour, actually I don't covet Mitch at all, though I think that he'll make a fun friend. It's the other nice man in his house that holds far more appeal.

The mood hangs heavily in relative silence, while we complete the necessary finishing touches to ready Trish's house for her return from the Whitsundays.

"Oh my Goddess, look at this house. I don't think it's ever been this clean." Trish observes her immaculate interior. "Would you two like a regular cleaning job?" The compliment washes over our heads as we stand in a heavy, awkward silence and not just because the offer isn't appealing to us.

"Are you two okay?"

"Yep, we're fine." I lie. Sara's silent treatment is embarrassing.

"Well, goodbye then. I'll see you on Monday morning." I walk down the steps with my stuff, Sara has already packed her things into the car.

"Yes, see you. See you on Monday." Trish waves to us from the porch, Chappy flops down by her feet. What should have been an exciting new beginning, has manifested into an awkwardly, silent journey to our new home.

The air around Sara is icy to begin with, but when we immerse ourselves into our new townhouse, the chilliness gradually thaws. Over the next week, Sara and I work to make our new apartment a home, as we arrange the few pieces of furniture we've collected from our parent's homes, that fit sparsely into the large spaces of our roomy new apartment. We soon realise that we'll need to start collecting some more furniture. From our respective homes, we've brought our own bedroom furniture, though the rest of the apartment contains too much negative space for our liking.

"There's a bit too much chi frolicking around this flat." Sara announces, after she's read a magazine article on Feng Shui at the dentists.

Dad gives us the old beer fridge from the garage. It's noisy as hell and cranks up to life at three in the morning, but it works and holds the required amount of food, and bubbles. We sit on two old deck chairs in the lounge room, in place of a sofa and dinning suite, and all of our dining and social needs, are met by those two chairs. When we entertain friends, we give up our chairs for our guests, we sit on the floor, or sometimes on the old brown corduroy bean bag that Finn no longer wants. The bean bag contains too few foam balls to be comfortable, the sitter has to constantly rearrange and bunch up the beads, to provide some padding underneath their bum. Needless to say, nobody wants to sit on it very often. Over a few months, we gradually gather more furniture, kitchen gadgets from op-shops, garage sales, and leftovers from our family homes.

Our apartment becomes a funky space, full of quirky things we've collected, though its mainly a lot of cheap stuff, but I've channelled my high school home economics skills by sewing some cushions and soft furnishings on Mum's old sewing machine. The old Singer was pretty dusty, but I spend an afternoon cleaning it and I eventually work out how to use it, it's different to the one I'd learnt on. Our friends seem to appreciate my supposedly, new found talent and they put in their requests for some colourful cushions as well.

"You could set up a stall at the Equinox Market with these." Sara marvels at a colourful throw cushion I'd sewn in a matter of minutes.

"Oh, they're not good enough for that." I'm not confident in my abilities, but she makes me wonder if they are good enough to sell to the public.

The business with Mitch aside, we manage to stay fairly friendly with each other considering we've never lived with anyone else, besides our own families of course. As long as we avoid each other first thing in the morning and we've drunk our first coffee, our day works out fairly well. Especially as Sara slowly rekindles her friendship with Stuart, has singing classes, does a jungle dance class, and has an active social life, she isn't around the house that much anyway.

I see David when he works in town, although deep down we both know this arrangement is mainly for his convenience, not mine. David has his eye on a country girl, where his construction job is located. I know that, I've seen him hiding in the bathroom to text her. He says that he likes me, his words and actions prove otherwise. However, according to him, I've changed, apparently.

"I need an uncomplicated, low maintenance relationship, with a simple country girl, you're a lot more complicated." He complains when I ask him to put his dishes in the kitchen sink, subtext, he wants a slave to do his dirty work.

"That's insulting to everyone. And no, you just want another person to clean up after you." I say, but he manages to turn it back around.

"You're just too sensitive. You need to toughen up a bit." And boom there it is, a dagger. My patience for him is wearing thin, it's about time. Perhaps I'm slowly waking up to his crap and I'm not even sad about it, just angry at myself.

About four months after we'd moved out of home, Trish is offered a partnership in a big corporate clinic on the other side of the city, where they already employ several receptionists.

"Allie, I'm so sorry, but they don't need any more receptionists. If anything comes up, I will definitely let you know." Trish is apologetic, but the opportunity for her is too good. Trish gives me a glowing reference, however there aren't many jobs at the moment, I've found myself unemployed and quickly running out of my ample, but finite, severance payout. I refuse to ask my parents for any more money and I only reluctantly, borrow money from Sara when I find myself flat broke, which isn't often.

Once again, I see this situation as an opportunity to start my life afresh. Emotionally and financially, I can't support David's city trips anymore. I don't know where it had been hiding, but I find the courage to tell him that he'll have to find somewhere else to stay when he's in town. He receives this information a little too well though. It would have been nice, if he protested just a little, but we both know the split had been imminent. He'd been anticipating this moment for some time, my place was pretty convenient when he was in town. I don't let my newly found bravery go to waste and do the next predictable item on the list in this situation. I have my hair cut to my shoulders and layered around my face. I don't cry at the hairdressers this time, even though it isn't a messy, or sad break up, it's definitely time for a change, and a new look.

Chapter 39 Leo

From a window in the grand hall, Leo notices me standing un-accompanied by the tower gate, he gazes at me for some time, then he sees a page boy running to my side. Where are Ragno and Sarra? He notices their horse and cart are no longer in front of the chateau, but mysteriously, I have remained. Leo can't divine why they'd leave me stranded, so far away from my home, with no manner of return. The page boy and I return through the gates of the chateau and a maid brings me refreshments in a small room next to the grand hall.

After everything that has happened with his brother, and Sarra, Leo avails me some time to collect myself, to eat in peace. He doesn't think it is appropriate, to venture into the small room unaccompanied, so he waits patiently for me in the grand hall. While he rests by the fire, Leo chats with the other knights and wonders where his brother has gone, suddenly Miché appears in the hall.

"She's gone and for good this time." Miché is heartsick.

"Yes, I know."

"But they didn't all leave."

"Huh, who's still here?" Miché is suddenly buoyed that Sarra might still be in the chateau, somewhere.

"Well, Ragno and Sarra left, but Ailie is still here, it seems they've left her behind."

"Why? Oh, that's probably my fault."

"How could it be your fault Miché, you didn't force her off the cart?"

"Well really, it's because she's one of us."

"What are you talking about, one of us, she's a commoner, a weaver?"

"No, she's nobility and works as a weaver, there's a big difference."

Leo is stunned. He had no idea that I was of noble birth.

"Who is her family then?"

"Belanger." Miché informs his younger brother as Leo slumps down onto a bench seat. This is a lot of information to take in.

"This beautiful, talented girl is Roger Belanger's daughter?" He wonders out loud. "How is that possible?"

Chapter 40 Leon

Leon scoops up his backpack from his bed, retrieves his hacked up mountain bike from the small shed in the backyard and goes to work at the local community art college. Leon has been an art teacher since he finished university and had taken another back-packing trip around Europe. He really enjoys teaching, as there is a relaxed atmosphere to his mainly practical lessons. He teaches his students how to use different types of mediums, including charcoal, oils, acrylics and watercolours, how to draw, and occasionally he throws in pottery and sculpture classes, to change things up. Field trips are arranged so that his students can escape the confines of the Besser block walls of the classrooms, to immerse themselves in the natural environment, Leon's favourite environment.

A disused railway yard is a favourite haunt for his students, where they can capture a mixture of the built and natural environments. There is so much to absorb, and draw, everything from the dirty pebbles under the tracks, to smashed coloured glass from the signal lights and the hard steel tracks that travel forever into the distance. Fat grey pigeons fan their tail feathers, coo, and flirt, with each other before perching noisily on the rotting station roof. Thick layers of guano hold the tiled roof of the station house intact, concealing its original colour. The smell of oil mixes with diesel and wafts from the ground when kicked and exposed. If he listens carefully enough, Leon can hear the whistle blow and imagines steam pouring from the smoke stack of the 4:05pm leaving from the blue stone station, many life times ago. On these days, he wistfully remembers the Rouen train station.

"Did I tell you about the time I hopped off the train in Rouen?"

"Yes, I believe you have Leon. Once or twice." His students try to focus on drawing the lines of the ticket office.

The beach is a natural environment where the colours and movement of the water changes constantly, it's Leon's favourite place to take his students. The smell of the salty air, the crest of a wave, washing turquoise and white foamy film onto the land, gulls, terns, pelicans, and dotterels scratch and screech, busy crabs scuttle across the shoreline, returning to the surf, the heat of the sun on his broad shoulders and face make him happy. It reminds him of his childhood in Ireland, he keeps that piece of information to himself though.

His chocolate lab Hugo, who's a bit of a guts, loves the beach as much as Leon. He frolics along the shore, chasing gulls before switching back, suddenly he attacks a piece of sedentary driftwood. He barks loudly and frantically splashes water over everyone, most of the students adore him. Except for Carol, she has an animal dander allergy and sneezes wildly if Hugo ventures too close. Generally, Hugo receives a lot of friendly pats, scratches, tummy rubs, and left overs from morning tea. During cold wintry days, Leon confines his class to the studio to paint still-life, or a model will be booked, his preference is to be out in nature.

Chapter 41 Ailie

Upon hearing of my predicament, the Duchess calls a page to fetch me. When I arrive, Matilda embraces me as best she can, given her pregnant belly. Proximity to the Duke's wife has been granted, she knows deep in her heart that I will become a trusted confident and friend. Matilda also recognises my outstanding education by the manner in which I conduct myself and speak, qualities she values highly in a person.

"You may stay here as long as you like Ailie, please do not fear, you shall be looked after as my guest. I'll send word to your father that you'll be residing with me as my guest for a few days."

"Thank you Ma'am." I bow to the Duchess in gratitude and respect.

"Oow!"

"What is it Ma'am?"

"The baby is strong. It kicks me all day long."

I ask for permission to touch Matilda's bump where the baby is kicking, the duchess happily guides my hand onto her bulging abdomen. Nervously, I feel the stirrings of a robust baby within.

"Oh my Lord, that must feel peculiar?" I laugh.

"It did to begin with and now I feel it's kicking to be free of me." Matilda laughs nervously as well. This will be her first baby and she's unsure of the birthing process, she's scared, but she never voices her fear.

Matilda instructs her maids to help me settle into a suitable room, adjacent to her chamber, and for the first time in ages, I sleep long and deep. It's wonderful to be away from home for a while, but I do miss my work. I don't know what I'm going to do next, but for the moment I don't care.

When I wake, I'm asked by one of the maids, Millie, to visit the Duchess in her chamber. When I arrive in Matilda's room, the Duchess is sitting up in bed with the bedding folded to her waist, when she sees me, she taps the side of her divan for me sit beside her. As I sit, a wet nurse returns to the room with a baby. For a minute, I wonder whose baby it is, then I remember Matilda's pregnancy.

"Oh, my goodness!" I exclaim in a hushed voice. I place my hands in the prayer position, covering my mouth and nose. I really had slept well, I hadn't heard a thing throughout Matilda's labour.

"It's a boy, we're calling him Robert after Guilliam's step-brother." Matilda informs me.

"He's beautiful." I quietly observe the little cherub while he snuffles and wriggles in his mother's arms. "Did it hurt?" I've been studying the size of the robust newborn and contemplate his improbable entry into the world, I wince with the thought. Although, I don't know why I'd grimace, I know nothing of the birthing process myself.

"Yes, it caused a great deal of discomfort, but the pain has subsided, and look, I have this delightful little boy in my arms. Would you like to hold him?"

"Hmm, okay, yes please." I haven't had much experience with babies, except for my new step-brother. I'm anxious about holding such a new baby, especially a royal baby, it wouldn't be good to drop him. The duchess expertly interprets my uneasy body language and reassures me.

"You'll be fine. Here you go."

Before I'm completely ready, she passes the newborn to me and I hold him securely in my arms, I gaze into his deep blue eyes. He has a little tuft of black hair, the same colour as his mother's and I caress it before bending over his fragile crown to inhale the scent of his skin.

"You look so at ease with him Ailie. Do you think you'll want a child of your own one day?" I've never thought about having children, I'm so involved with my weaving commissions and creating pieces of art, childbearing has never really crossed my mind. However, holding baby Robert has stirred something within me.

"I don't know. I'll have to find a husband first, I'm in no hurry." I laugh uneasily.

When Guilliam enters his wife's chamber, I return the baby to the wet nurse, bow deeply and return to my own chamber. As I enter my chamber, I realise that my only babies will be the tapestries and embroideries that I produce. I'm at ease with that thought, even though I don't know where my surety stems from.

Odo officiates at his nephew's Christening, held in the chateau's chapel, the baby's first rites are witnessed by his parents, invited nobles, including the du Bois family, and the new Belanger family. I'm pleased to be sitting with Papa, Belle, and Flynn, reunited as a family unit, even though I know Papa has brought great shame to our family in the past, it's nice to be surrounded by familiar faces. During the Mass, the knights of the chateau sit at the rear of the small chapel while the servants prepare a banquet inside the steaming kitchen.

I've been a guest of the Duchess for two weeks and in that time she now considers me a firm friend who she relies on for conversation and companionship. Guilliam is often away from the Chateau, for business, or battle. She says it comforts her to host an educated noble woman such as myself. However, even though I enjoy the Duchesses' companionship, I begin to feel restless at Falaise. I miss my work and my friends at the workshop and as the congregation prays, I decide that I'll return to Breteuil with my family after the Christening. I have one big concern though and that is how I'll be received by Sarra. We've been separated for more than a fortnight and I hope that Sarra would have cooled down by now, but perhaps not. Sarra isn't really the forgiving type.

As I've been in close quarters with the Duchess, for the duration of my visit, I haven't spoken to Leo since the day I arrived at Falaise. Now here he is, so close, but due to the circumstances, he's been so far away. Miché and Leo sit next to their parents as the parishioners bow their heads in prayer. When the service ends, Papa whispers that they'll be leaving for Breteuil at first light the next morning.

"I think I'll come with you."

"Are you sure?"

"Yes, I need to return to my work."

"It's always your work isn't it? I know you'd find a suitable husband if you stayed here a little longer."

I roll my eyes as I exit the pew and the Christening party moves into the grand hall, the servants lay out large trays of food and gallons of wine in clay jugs. Odo prays over the food and recites a special incantation for the newly Christened Robert. The party begins, minstrels, trouveres, jesters and jugglers, roam the hall, performing their artistic skills while the guests eat, drink, sing and dance, throughout the night. I'm not without attention from the knights and surprisingly a line of interested bachelors' line up to dance with me.

I soon become flustered, I'm not used to this much attention from the opposite sex. I blush and bow my head as I engage in the chaste dances, while Papa watches me with interest.

"I'm interested in which knight will claim her for his own." He says to Belle, a little too loudly. Belle is dancing with baby Flynn.

"She doesn't seem very interested in marriage at the moment, but give her time, she might change her mind. There are some very eligible bachelors here tonight. You never know what can happen at these events."

"Indeed." Papa is put out knowing his wife has noticed all of the young men in the room. Suddenly he feels quite old.

"Perhaps, that one will do her? The one she's dancing with."

"Perhaps, but only time will tell."

I have other ideas and when I glance in their direction, I see that Miché is nursing his broken heart as he sits beside his parents, much to the dismay of most of the maidens present. Leo waits patiently by his family's side for his opportunity to dance with me, as I will him to me, he never approaches, so I continue dancing with the other knights, while my attention floats above the Du Bois' table.

The final music of the evening is about to play and I use the small intermission to bow out of the dance with a dashing knight named Tristian. He tries to encourage me to continue dancing with him, but I am tired.

"It's just one more dance, surely you can keep going for just one more?" He wipes his sweaty brow with a handkerchief, I glow from the exercise and heat of the stuffy room.

"I'm sorry kind Sir, but I have to take my leave." I excuse myself and on the way out, I meet Millie. I invite her for a stroll into the crisp night air.

In the cool of the night, I shiver as the heat quickly dissipates from my body and as I peer into the moat below, I see my reflection ripple softly in the water. My watery head dances and spins, I breathe in deeply and collect my thoughts. Apart from the Duke and Duchess' wedding, when I was younger, and as it seems, not so eligible, this is the first party where I've gained so much attention from the bachelor knights. Without Mama to guide me, it's a frightening aspect of growing up that I hadn't considered before.

"You've certainly made an impression tonight." Millie confides.

"Do you think so?"

"Well yes, of course you did. They didn't leave you alone."

"I think you've caught the eye some of them as well, Millie." Millie blushes. "It's fun isn't it."

"Kind of. I feel pressure from my father to be married. Then there is all that attention which I'm not used to. I miss my mother. We never had chats about what to do in these situations."

"Your doing fine Ailie. Just relax and have some fun. Don't take it too seriously."

"I guess so."

Suddenly feeling chilly, I don't want to attract any more attention from the partying crowd, but I do want to retire for the evening. I realise I have my dignity and purity to protect, so in an act of stealth, I find my way to my chamber, via the chateau's back stairs, while Millie returns to the party, via the tower gate. She's going to take her own advice.

Chapter 41 Allie

I rise early'ish and stroll to the corner deli, purchase the morning paper and a takeaway coffee. I return home to the patio table to scan the employment section. There aren't many jobs available, but wielding a red pen, I circle the jobs I think I'll be qualified for and return inside to make phone calls and type cover letters to accompany my resume. I follow the same routine every morning, rising nice and early, buying the paper, making calls, sending out letters, and waiting patiently for a reply. By the second week, I start to lose momentum, I scan the paper with a coffee, in a real cup, at an al fresco table at a café, even though it's costing me a small fortune, who can resist real coffee and perhaps a cheeky chocolate muffin? Anyway, Sara's at work and the apartment is too secluded during the day.

Much to her mother's anti-corporate stance and disgust of patriarchal economic systems, Sara lands a role as a personal assistant for a high end PR company. She's always immaculately dressed, ready for any event that's thrust upon her at short notice. Always at her side, a comprehensive handbag holding a spare scarf, earrings, make-up, and extra tricks, which modifies her day wear, into a knockout outfit for cocktail hour. She learnt that from Mum's magazines all those years ago. Her bag though compact on the outside, seems to contain a world of elusive accessories and even if some time is required, the right accoutrements are generally found in there, somewhere.

Sara stumbled upon her job, from an offer through a friend of my Dad's. Of course he would have suggested the opening to me, but I was still working for Trish at the time and I had liked my job. Little do we know how our lives will change in the blink of an eye. Sara began her career brewing tasteless coffee resembling weak dishwater. To be fair, it isn't a beverage she's particularly familiar with. The strongest hot drink her family brews is dandelion tea, on the very odd occasion, some kind of coffee substitute from the health food store, which I think is made from some part of the dandelion as well.

"Feel free to take as many of the dandelions from the lawn as you want." Dad offers to Sara, when he discovers they drink dandelion tea.

"Don't tell Mum, she'll be around here with her foraging bucket and special scissors before you can say, free weeds."

Sara's employed as the general dog's body to a well coiffed, forty something woman, who drives a white BMW convertible, wears Channel suits, purchased in Paris, and every time I see her, she has one of those new mobile phones attached to her ear. The social aspect of the job more than makes up for the tedious errands Sara has to endure. Attending launches, where there's bags of freebies to delve into, dinners to arrange for so called important people, movie premieres, band promotions, product and book launches. To her friends it appears glamorous, but these affairs are the icing on the cake after weeks, sometimes months, of hard work.

I'm sometimes slipped an invitation, to the larger parties, where I can blend into the crowd, although I'm not too proud to admit that sometimes, I'm quite lonely amongst the throng of revellers. I generally feel uncomfortable at these events. The Glitterati dressed to the nines in uncomfortable clothes. They engage in conversations which seem shallow and trivial, often related to their occupations and incomes. The discourse never touches on who they really are, but then again perhaps it really does. How you earn and spend money speaks volumes in these circles.

For fun, bored business men like to engage me in conversation, sometimes they try to tempt me with promises of exotic holidays and gifts. Occasionally, their wives hover close by, slightly out of earshot, deep in conversation with others. I find this banter flattering, they find it exciting and risky, but I soon realise they are empty attempts to explore my knickers.

"I wonder what they'd say, if I said yes to flying off to Rome. I bet they'd try to back out of it pretty quickly?" I confide in Sara, after one event.

"No, they'd tell their wives they have a sudden work trip." Sara winks.

"Oh, perhaps I should have said yes then. But to be honest, there was no one there, that I would want to spend 23 hours with, in the confines of a long haul flight."

"I hear you." Sara agrees.

Tonight is a black tie launch for a new French perfume, held in a disused warehouse on the industrial side of the city. The warehouse is decorated with tonnes of steel and faux building site equipment to resemble a construction site.

"Industrial Chic they call it. It cost them an absolute fortune to make it look so old and rusty, when it already was in a shabby state." Sara tells me about the trend, before it's a chic species within the interior design collective. The launch is to promote a scent, aptly named Waft. The testosterone inspired warehouse pays homage to the essence of a diminishing concept, the macho man.

The waiters wear cut off denim shorts, navy blue singlets, steel capped boots, and their imperceptible sexuality as a badge. The male dancers also wear their bulging biceps very well, which are much appreciated, and discussed by most of the invitees. The hired bodies provide a stark contrast to the black tie guests and while some of the models make some of the guests feel inferior in their black penguin suits, no matter how expensive and how stylish they are, the workman look is a more powerful and sexy one, I think as I scan the room.

"Those tradies could actually create something with their hands." I say to Sara the next day.

"You know, they're not actually tradies, don't you?" Sara laughs at me.

"Of course. But being able to create something with your bare hands is sexy, don't you think?"

Embracing my feminine side, I'm normally more comfortable in jeans and a t-shirt, I wear a blue satin gown which I've borrowed from Sara's vast wardrobe. I'm wearing delicate stiletto sling backs, which aren't so delicate on my feet, they actually hurt a lot. No, the gel pads don't really provide any relief either, as the sales girl said they would. Ugh! Up-selling. I arrive at the warehouse with Stuart, Sara has been here for an hour, ensuring everything is in place for the evening to proceed smoothly.

As a first point of call, Stuart weaves his way through the crowd to the open bar and waits patiently to order a drink. I observe the decorations and sample the tester fragrances which are located on small pedestal tables around the room. However, there is really no need for testers, the air is thick with scent. A waiter passes me with a tray full of canapés just as I hear whale song emanating from my stomach. I haven't been able to eat dinner, realising that I'm starving, I shovel one of the little quiches into my mouth and quickly pinch one more of the salmon tarts from another silver tray, for later.

Another shorts clad dancer with huge muscles approaches me. He asks if I'd like to smell him as a human sampler for the new fragrance. I think that's a bit odd, but I crane my nose close to his neck and deeply inhale his aroma. According to the notes, the fragrance contains notes of cardamom, cedar, red leather, beach mist and a hint of benzene. I think it smells more like black leather, but I'm no expert. I close my eyes and dreamily draw in another long inhalation, when I languorously open my eyes, the human tester has moved on. Slightly embarrassed, I shuffle on my painful toes, pinched by my ridiculous, yet beautiful shoes.

Luckily, another waiter approaches me with a tray laden with tall glasses of champagne and pink frangipanis. I accept a glass and sip the bubbly while I scan the room, startling me, the waiter places a frangipani behind my right ear.

"Um, thanks?" I mumble my appreciation for the flower, but he doesn't hear me and is scouring the room for another punter. Stuart still waits to be served at the bar as the crowd continues to thicken. He figures the wait for a beer is worth it, it isn't offered by the roving waiters and he can't stomach champagne, no matter how expensive it is.

As I survey the room, a thinly built man approaches me.

"I see your flower's behind your right ear." He winks at me and instantly annoys me from the get go, I can't pinpoint exactly what it is about him that makes my skin crawl. However, all of my instincts tell me to be on high alert.

"Yes, it is, but I'm not sure what it means."

"Hi, I'm Paul and it looks as though you're very available tonight.

Doesn't matter about the rest of the time though. Am I right?" He winks again and snorts, he offers me a clammy loose fish handshake.

"Um, I'm not sure. Allie, Allie's my name." I reply blandly, I wipe my hand on the back of my dress and wish I was elsewhere. Suddenly, the frangipani in my hair falls to the ground and to avoid talking to Mr Skincrawl, I quickly bend down to fetch the flower as if it were a priceless heirloom hair clasp that has fallen from my head. I replace it behind my left ear.

Paul leers for way too much time and is far too obviously concentrating on the bodice area of my dress. As I right myself, I want to inform him that my eyes are positioned somewhat higher up, but it's Sara's show and I don't know where this man stands in the corporation's pecking order. Paul finally looks directly into my eyes, holding his gaze a little longer than appropriate, breathing heavily, little rivulets of sweet trickle down his brow.

I can tell he's sizing me up, he hasn't been particularly discrete about it. Mr Skincrawl is standing way too close for me, I have a large personal space at the best of times. I step backwards to afford myself some room and awkwardly bump into a glamorous woman standing behind me, she gives me a haughty stare and continues talking with her group. My flower falls from my hair again, I bend down to pick it up. If nothing else, I'm getting a workout this evening. Simultaneously, Paul reaches out with both arms to help me regain my composure. In disgust, I shake my shoulders free of his grasp, causing me to spill champagne over the both of us, to which he seems oblivious. Grappling with the frangipani and my glass of champagne, I don't know why I'm persisting with the damn flower, well, yes I do, it's a diversion tactic. But it isn't working, Paul continues talking to me as if nothing has happened.

"So, I'm with the accounting section of the company. I handle all of the in-comings and out-goings, if you know what I mean?" I brush the spilt champagne from my dress, I have no idea what he's trying to say to me. Quite frankly I don't want to know. Paul inches closer, in fear of knocking down an entire group of people, I remain rock solid in my painful shoes, holding my ground and my breath. He puts his clammy hand up to my face and places a section of my hair behind my ear where the flower had been, brushing my cheek at the same time. I can feel his alcohol laden breath on my face and his body warmth is way too close for my well-being. My whole body quivers with repulsion, he thinks I've quivered with pleasure. I struggle to keep my champagne and canapes down. Reflux erupts into my mouth and I quickly swallow it down, tasting the bitterness as it returns down my throat.

Oh my Goddess, he's still talking, impatiently, I look around to see if Stuart has progressed any further in the line at the bar. I will him to hurry up.

"Maybe we could hook up together, tonight?" Paul's hand trails from my cheek, down my neck and lingers momentarily just slightly to the right of where my left nipple is, had he any idea? I fume, I can't believe this creep thinks he can actually behave like this. Suddenly, I don't give a damn where he works, I thrust, what remains of my champagne, into his face and slap him hard with my free hand. Paul wears a drunken grin, he prefers his women a little feisty. I spin around again and accidentally bump harder into the haughty woman, pushing her into the group of haughty people. Without apology, I collect myself and make a quick exit. Stuart finally arrives with a beer in each hand, he doesn't want to line up at the bar again for a while.

"Thank God, you're here now. You should have seen the guy I had to talk to while you were gone."

As it happens, I don't have to worry about being around haughty rich people for a while. On the job front, movement is far too slow for me, I'm anxious about money, or to be honest, the lack of it. I've registered for the dole, but that only just covers my expenses, it doesn't leave much for anything else. However, despite my lack of money, I decide to take an art history class at an adult college to keep my mind alive and to interact with a different group of people. It's a stretch on my finances, but with the unemployment concession, it's just possible. I have to get out of the house and meet interesting people. Oh yeah, I hear it too. I'm starting to hear my mother's words inside my own head, something she's warned me about since I was little.

I've always wondered about the stories behind the paintings I love and I'm willing to make some sacrifices to learn more about art. Pot noodles are not that bad. Mum often told us stories about the famous art galleries from around the world when she returned from her trips. Her favourite is the Dali Museum in Figueres, Spain. It isn't just her favourite because of the wonderful pieces of art, which are genius by the way, but for the artist himself, who resided and drew his inspiration from life in the community. Living amongst the local people, Dali was inspired by the local countryside, the ocean, and his wife and muse, Gala.

The college is located on the other side of the city, so I need to endure a variety of bus trips to get there, but I figure the journey is well worth all of my spare time. I'm not doing much else with my day. Besides, I like to people watch while I travel to my class and the different kinds of commuters are fascinating. The friendly types, regulars who proffer a hello when they recognise me, or offer me a seat, the downright rude, who point out misdemeanours and tisck under their breath, particularly if they think that someone has erroneously claimed a seat they aren't entitled to, and then there are the indifferent. They seem to be the most lost and sad of all the commuters, lacking the energy to bother with anyone around them. I wonder about their stories as we travel together.

When I first see the lecturer, Freyja, I think she's a bit of a cliché. A woman in her late forties, wearing long flowing clothes, purchased from exotic locations. She wears bright head scarves, sometimes an outrageously large fabric flower, and a signature single row of amber beads around her neck which cascade around her ample bosom. Freyja, a new bohemian, reminds me of the women in Mum's stories and it's comforting, in a disturbed way, but Freyja reminds me of a slightly younger version of Mum. I'm captivated with her lectures which are more like tales about people she actually knows, rather than a stuffy oration from a slide show.

Her stories are peppered with personal anecdotes from her back-packing days and time lived in West Berlin during the seventies. Mid way through the story, she'll wander off as she contemplates the large classroom windows and we know that she's secretly reminiscing over a bygone love affair. One of the students will cough to bring her attention back into the room, she's never embarrassed by her dreamy state, instead she seamlessly continues her dialogue of the paintings displayed on the screen.

Because of her fascinating stories, classes always run over time and sometimes spill over into the college bar where we continue chatting over a glass, or two, of the cheap house red. At the end of the day, other lecturers join us which leads to divergent discourses on art, psychology, philosophy, travel, quantum mechanics, and any subject under the sun really. Some topics, I understand and there's much that I don't fathom, but that's fun too, there's always something more to learn.

"Freyja, tell me again about the essence of Surrealism."

"Wow Dan, have you got all day?" She laughs.

"For you Freyja, I've got all week." Freyja doesn't really have the time for Dan, so she turns her attention to me.

"Have you been to Figueres Allie?

"No, not yet, but its on my list."

"I love the way young people say "not yet" your world is so full of potential and first times." With the mention of first times, I can tell that her mind is searching through her memories again.

From my sessions in the bar and extra classes I take in yoga, I become familiar with some of the other lecturers. So familiar in fact, that when an opening in the office is announced, they encourage my application, which I jump at the chance. The role calls for many of the skills I already have, I'm confident of landing the job. At ease at the interview, I feel as if I'm in a discussion with friends, rather than being cross-examined by a panel of strangers. At the end of the interview, the panel immediately offer me the job which starts on the following Monday morning.

"They were always going to give you the job Allie, but we had to give you a formal interview process." Freyja tells me later.

"Yay! I have a job. Can you believe it? Oh, but now I have to catch the bus every day and I won't be able to have a chocolate muffin either, which is probably for the best."

"I can take you as far as the city, but you'll have to catch the bus from there. As far as muffins are concerned there's probably a bakery, or a cafe close by somewhere. Here's to your new job." Sara raises her glass of champagne to celebrate. However, what was once a bit of a novelty, is now turning into a more ordinary experience. Determined not to become one of the listless bus travellers, I decide that once I've saved up enough money, a car will be my first big purchase. Having a car will give me independence from Sara and Stuart, who have chauffeured me everywhere. They don't mind of course, but I don't want to stretch the friendship further than I already have. I passed my driver's licence at seventeen, when everyone else at school did, but Mum's car was always available at home, I never needed to buy my own car, until now.

On a sunny Saturday morning, Sara, Stuart and I, pile into Stuart's EH Holden to scour the car yards. At the third yard, we inspect at a small yellow Laser when Stuart spies a familiar face.

"Sara isn't that's the guy from the pub? You know, from the night of the festival?"

"Who's that love?" Sara asks, without looking up. She peering into one of the car's rear windows. She and Stuart have become closer of late. I see the guy's reflection in the car's front window where Sara has been looking.

"Oh my God! It's him. What's his name? Mitch, from the pub on the last night of the festival." I'm suddenly nervous and wonder how Sara is going to behave.

Sara straightens herself up in lightening time and wishes that she could brush her hair and reapply her lip gloss. I on the other hand, want the earth to swallow me up. Mitch is inspecting a late model Jeep and sees us in the reflection of the review mirror, at the same time we see him. He swings around from the car dealer, mid-sentence, beams an enormous grin and waves to us from the window. Sara swoons a little and has to catch her breath, Stuart notices everything. We all return his wave with various levels of excitement and with a hand shake, Mitch excuses himself from the salesman and saunters over to the yellow Laser.

"Fancy coming for a test drive in that?" He points to the red Jeep, gazing directly at me.

"You bet." Stuart returns a little too quickly. Sara jabs him in the ribs with her elbow.

"Stuart and I have made plans, but Allie'll go with you. Won't you Allie?" And before I have the chance to decline the offer, Stuart and Sara have reached Stuart's car.

"See you later Allie, Mitch. You can hitch a ride home with Mitch, can't you Allie?" Sara breezes away, giggling at her rhyme. This sudden state of affairs surprises and terrifies me, I thought Sara liked Mitch. Why would she encourage me to go out with him by myself? Also what is he going to say to me? I'm hoping that it won't be too awkward.

"I guess so." I'm drowned out by the car's engine. Stuart grumbles under his breath, something inaudible, about wanting to go on the drive as well.

"I guess that means I'm coming for a test drive with you and not looking for a car for myself today."

"We can do both, can't we?" Mitch offers. "How about we go for a test drive and you can help me decide on this beast, then I'll help you with your car. Sound like a deal?" He beams, I can't resist that face.

"Sounds like a dodgy deal to me."

I start to relax and laugh as I climb into the cab. We drive through the city and head along the coast when I have suspicions about the test drive story.

"Don't we have to return this car soon? We've been gone a long time from the dealership."

"Well to tell you the truth, I bought this car yesterday, I was at the car lot to collect it."

"Liar, Liar. Your nose will grow longer ...." And just in time, I catch myself, I can feel my face redden. Mitch grins, knowing exactly how I was going to finish the sentence. "Sorry. I meant um.., well it doesn't matter now." I'm flustered.

"How about, we stop here for a coffee?" It's a cute café perched at the top of the cliff, overlooking the teal blue ocean. He knows how to impress a girl.

Facing the ocean, we chat easily about what we've been doing since our last awkward encounter. Although, I madly hope that Mitch won't bring up that night, I'm still very uncomfortable about several aspects of that evening.

"You know my house mate Leon? He thinks you're pretty hot."

"No, I didn't know that." This news turns my face scarlet again. I've thought little of anyone else since I'd seen him in Mitch's hallway and I did wonder whether he'd noticed me. Apparently he did. "Wow, your new car looks like it's waiting to be in a car commercial, perched on the cliff like that." I quickly change the subject to Mitch's new car, the subject of Leon and that night isn't mentioned again.

We finish our second coffee and I glance at my watch to discover, by the time we drive back to the city, we won't have any time to look at cars, I've resigned myself to enjoy a beautiful day with a new friend. Somehow, I knew that there would be no more car hunting, part of me is actually a bit pissed off, it means that I'll still have to catch the bus to work for a while longer. Which isn't a problem somewhere like Paris, where public transport runs every five minutes, but this is a much smaller city, with a much smaller population. If I miss a bus, there probably won't be another one for an hour or so. Even though I'm slightly annoyed with him at that moment, I think I'll still hold Mitch to his promise, to help me buy a car.

Over the next few weekends, the ritual is coffee with Mitch on Saturday mornings, followed by car searches. He collects me, then we drive to the local car dealer precinct. We head to a nearby café for a quick coffee, required sustenance, before dealing with assertive car dealers and we chat about the week's happenings whilst scanning the paper for affordable cars in the area. Mitch rarely mentions Leon and I feel too awkward bringing up his name. Comfortable with the company, yet agitated by the numbers of coffees downed, we make an assault on the car yards. The salesmen generally treat us as a couple, directing their questions towards Mitch, which makes me furious.

"What colour are you after then, love?" Salesmen always think to ask me the high level technical questions. Better include the Misses.

"It doesn't really matter as long as it's mechanically sound." I respond testily, but they still direct most of their sales talk through Mitch.

"So Sir, are you after the sports model. This one over here has a cooling system designed by NASA."

"Look mate, don't look at me, you need to talk to Allie." I really don't know anything about cars, but it would have been nice for them to address me. It is my money after all. But I do really want a silver car.

Finally, on the fourth Saturday morning, my wish is actualised when we discover a silver hatchback, at the right price, in a car yard run by a saleswoman. This transaction ticks all the boxes. Smitten by Mitch, the dealer initially focuses on him and I thought we were so close, but when she realises the car is for me, she quickly readdresses her sales pitch. The dealer and I negotiate a price on the car which favours the car yard of course, but I'm excited to be the proud owner of a nearly new car. A visit to the credit union to secure a personal loan is my next hurdle, but I've saved a good deposit. I'm confident of approval, for once in my life.

However, there's a hitch, my excuse to catch up with Mitch has ended for the time being. He's fun to be around and I'm going to miss our Saturday morning catch ups. Of the two of us though, Sara is the most disappointed that I have a new car.

"I thought that you'd be happy that I can drive myself around now."

"I am Allie, it just that.... Well you know."

"No, I don't Sara. What is it?"

I do know, but I want her to say it. She never made Saturday morning appointments until after Mitch and I would leave, it was her one chance of the week for a flirtatious moment and now those opportunities are gone.

"It doesn't matter." She leaves to busy herself in the bathroom.

Trish occasionally delivers workshops on natural medicine at the college and we catch up for lunch in the bar. One afternoon, I introduce Trish to Freyja as she passes through the cafeteria.

"Freyja this is Trish, Trish, Freyja."

"Lovely to meet you. A friend of Allie's is a friend of mine. Ooh, look at your amazing sweater. That colour, what would you call it? What a beautiful weave, it reminds me of the fabrics one sees in the markets of Marrakesh." Freyja sees the clock on the wall. "Oh, bugger, what time is it? I have to rush to class, must be off."

"She's a wild one. I couldn't get a word in." Trish whispers as Freyja departs.

"Oh, she's really busy." I'm perturbed that Trish has formed an opinion so quickly. "Yes. I think she's great. But what makes you say wild?" I know I sound defensive.

"It's nothing I can pinpoint, it's just a feeling I have about her, an energy she exudes." Trish has heard about Freyja's famous parties from co-workers.

"I think she has great energy." I defend my friend.

"Yes, of course, I do too. I think she's in touch with her wild side is all I'm trying to say. It's a positive trait, not a negative one Allie. She looks like she knows how to have fun and that's a great attribute to have, especially in this day and age when everyone is so serious and corporate."

"Yes, she does know how to have fun. In fact she's invited Sara and me to her house for a party she's having on Saturday night." I can sense how petulant I sound, but I can't do anything about it. It's as though I'm not in charge of my own words.

"How is Sara? Trish, the more mature one, changes the subject.

We arrive at the party fashionably late, about 11:00p.m. We had planned to appear then so we wouldn't be the first to arrive and secondly because we got terribly lost. Sara and Stuart enjoyed a few drinks at our local, then we drove up the winding roads through the foothills to Freyja's house. After several wrong turns, we finally arrive at the long gravel driveway and I nervously park the car between two tall gum trees. I know their reputation for falling limbs. The hundred year old cottage is surrounded by a beautiful native gardens and a flagstone path directs us to the open front door. Revellers bejewel the property and most of the rooms, while wood fires blaze in forty-four gallon drums in the back yard to keep people warm on the cool, spring night.

We walk through the front door and scan the house for Freyja. We spot her floating through the house in a long black, figure hugging, velvet dress, adorned with her signature strand of beads. Barefoot, with a bottle of red in one hand and an empty wine glass in the other, she catches sight of us from the corner of her eye.

"Allie darling, bonsoir, entree. Come in, introduce me to your lovely friends." Freyja oozes, thrusting a wine glass into our hands.

"Hello Freyja." I kiss my friend's cheek as the generous woman fills our glasses to a meniscus.

"This is Sara, and Stuart." Freyja plants a kiss on both sides of their cheeks, while I sip my wine to a more manageable level. As Freyja welcomes him, Stuart is enveloped by her perfume and is very aware of this older, exotic, more experienced woman's aura cloaking his senses. With a murmur in his jeans, he quickly turns his attention to the laundry where he can see the beer housed in an ice filled trough.

"Go on, help yourself Stuart." Freyja purrs. Stuart tries to think about calculus.

Freyja shimmies away while Sara and I wander about the small cottage taking in the party atmosphere and appreciating the house decor. All the walls are adorned with large pieces of abstract art, colours mixed in heady mind spinning ways. The old furniture has been lived in and loved on, the hand painted eclectic furniture and throw rugs cover well-worn timber floors. The overall vibe is rooted in the early 70's bohemian heyday.

Later, in the kitchen, a blond haired wiry man of indiscriminate age, to which life has not been kind, begins to roll joints at the kitchen table. The warm, sweet, highly identifiable aroma, soon fills the small kitchen. Sara, Stuart and I decide to partake, without saying a word, we return to the kitchen. One of the many large joints is passed to us while the exhaust fan whirrs noisily on top speed. I take the joint in my left hand, my wine in my right hand and inhale deeply, closing my eyes in the process. The sweet smoke fills my core before I pass it on to Sara, who after a quick toke, passes it to Stuart. In a haze, we wander sleepily to the lounge room floor and promptly fall asleep under the feet of the other party goers, so much for a wild party.

When Sara and I rouse the next morning, we can't find Stuart anywhere, not that we are anxious, but we are curious as to his whereabouts. We wander to the kitchen to find some coffee and out of the window, we witness party goers in various states of dress and sleeping arrangements. After finding the kettle, and some coffee, I sit at the table with my head in my hands while Sara searches the house for Stuart.

Tentatively, Sara pads around the house, so as not to disturb the sound sleep of the party cohort. She confirms that no one is in the laundry, as she drains the final dregs from a bottle of sparkling Shiraz, into the melting ice of the laundry trough. Moving from room to room, reveals a similar story until she arrives at Freyja's open bedroom door. She has to cover her mouth to ensure the sound of her shock remains within. Stuart is on the bed in nothing but his tattooed arse. His head is snuggled into Freyja's bosom, still adorned with beads, of course. His tattoo of the Southern Knights Football team emblem, a roaring lion, winks at her. All Sara can do, once she's regained her composure, is to stare, not quite sure if she's repulsed, or slightly aroused. Roused to her senses, she thinks she might get caught, she quickly pads back to the kitchen.

"Quick, we have to go."

"What, what do you mean? Russell the Kitchen Dude is making breakfast later, remember, he said last night." I've only just started my much needed coffee.

"Shut up, here's your bag and keys, lets go."

"But...Okay." I'm confused, but I can tell by Sara's tone that there is no way we are staying for Russell's breakfast. I abandon my coffee, hurry over the bodies still in their slumber and drive back into town, sans Stuart.

"By the way, tell me why we left without Stuart." I ask, after feeling ten minutes of Sara's silent rage.

"Ask me later, I'm too angry to talk right now." Sara crosses her arms over her chest and stares at the passing landscapes through the side window.

Chapter 42 Leo

Leo is relieved to see his mother and father at the Christening, he hopes they'll take away some of the pressure he's been experiencing, trying to cheer up his older brother. Even though he loves him, he's growing tired of supporting Miché through his sadness, he assumes that extra moral support from his parents, will be handy. However, Catarine isn't as much help as Leo hoped for, she actually finds pleasure in her eldest son's sorrow. Well, not his sorrow per se, but the reason for his grief relieves her, as their family is no longer associated with the lowly born Pagan girl and her family. Their association has brought her shame from the other ladies at Court and Catarine is now in the process of distancing herself from the whole sordid situation.

"I told you so. She was never a suitable match for this family." She boasts to Leo when they reunite for the first time since the incident.

"Did you have something to do with Odo banning their relationship, Mother?"

"I don't know what you're talking about Leo." She feigns ignorance, a quality his mother doesn't possess. "They would have been breaking Church laws, it had nothing to do with me."

As they sit in prayer in the chapel, Leo's awareness shifts from his mother to the family who sits directly behind him. He's thought about me ever since we met in the hall, more than two weeks ago and he is fully conscious that I have been sleeping in chambers next to the Duchess. It would've been so easy for him, if his moral code permitted, to slip into my room to be with me. But as a chivalrous knight, with high principles, he's tried to busy himself with his normal routine, all the while hoping to catch a glimpse of me in the grounds. To his dismay, I spend most of my time with the Duchess, there was never an opportunity for us to talk. Even though he faces the opposite direction, he senses my eyes upon his back.

In the great hall after the ceremony, Leo is with his family for the feast while musicians play their music around them. Although the music fails to buoy Miché's spirits, so the minstrels relocate their merriment to more receptive guests. As the crowd becomes satiated from their banqueting, musicians relocate to a central part of the hall and the guests begin to dance. From his vantage point, Leo sees that I've attracted many enthusiastic dance partners, he yearns to ask me to dance, however his shyness keeps him at a heartbreaking distance.

Frustratingly, Leo watches me dance with many of his knight friends and other noble bachelors. It renders him unsettled, he just can't muster the courage to ask me to dance in front of all these people, especially his mother. He knows what she's capable of and he doesn't want to jeopardise his chances with me. Leo is prepared to to be strategic, to be slow and play the long game. He now knows I'm of noble birth, so his mother can't object to my breeding, but she can object to Papa. If she's feeling particularly nasty, she might object to the fact that I work for a living as well. For the time being, Leo will allow Miché to properly grieve before he introduces a new person into the family dynamic. The night's festivities continue while the brothers teeter on the edge of their torment.

Towards the end of the evening, Leo's previous vow to remain single for a while, leaves him as excitement heaves in his chest. He watches me move away from the dance floor through the crowd of guests. This is his chance at an encounter, he rises from his seat, but just as he has his moment to speak, from nowhere, Miché steps in beside him with a jug of wine, I continue walking outside.

"Damn. Where did you get that wine, I thought you were sitting right here." Leo quizzes his older brother.

"Come and have a drink with me brother. It's time to move on, celebrate the Christening of baby Robert. We shall wet the baby's head." Leo tries to protest and attempts to walk away, but he can see the pleading look in his brother's eyes is genuine, he dutifully follows Miché back to their table and allows him to pour them both a sizeable toast. "To the newly christened, baby Robert" Miché yells, the chink of his toast almost breaks Leo's cup.

"To Robert." Leo says weakly, watching the doorway.

The next morning, Leo frantically searches the grounds for me, but after enquiries with everyone he passes, he realises that all of the Belangers have left the compound and returned to Breteuil.

Chapter 43 Leon

Leon is only a few minutes late to the faculty meeting, but because he's rushing to get there on time, he splashes his coffee onto the table as he sits down.

"Good, you're here at last." Bob the College Principal is chairing the meeting, Leon finds a napkin in his pocket, then wipes the spilt coffee around his cup. Leon notices Ursula moving her papers to one side so they won't get wet.

"Yes, sorry Bob, I had an issue with a student and a two litre bottle of burnt umber. Total disaster, the art room looks like someone had a bad bout of gastro."

"Yes, right well, your day is about to take a turn for the better, I hope."

"Excellent, I could do with some good news Bob."

"You and Graham will be taking the art and tourism students on the trip to Europe this year. It was supposed to be mainly in Italy, but with all the train strikes they've been having, we thought lets stay away from that chaos and focus on France and Spain instead."

"Wow, that sounds great. When are we leaving." Ursula gives Leon an envious stare before sharing a conspiratorial look with Janine. They had been eyeing that trip for years and now this young new lecturer lands it before them. They are not happy, Janine makes a note and passes it to Ursula. Meeting with Bob later? Ursula nods in approval.

Bob's first announcement stands, Leo and Graham stay as leaders, Ursula and Janine get to eat sour grapes. Leon on the other hand is beyond excited about the trip. His feet always itch, but not because of athlete's foot. He longs to revisit all of the art spaces he loves, The Louvre, Musee d'Orsay, L' Orangerie, in Paris, Parc Guell, the modern art museums, The Picasso, and Dali Museums in Catalunya, and this time it's all paid for by the college. The tour will be jammed packed, as far as the schedule is concerned, even though he's an introvert who needs to seek shelter in his own corner at the end of a long day, he thinks it'll be more than worth it. There will be some free afternoons where he can draw and do his own thing. Transport, activities, and accommodation details, are all taken care of, all Leon has to do is wait for the departure date.

Leon searches the dusty top of his wardrobe for his old blue backpack. It's amazing how much dust collects up there. Resorting to climbing up on a chair, for a better view, he finds his old travelling companion waiting for its next adventure. The royal blue backpack has faded a lot since he bought it all those years ago, though it's still in good nick. It's seen a lot of the world, carried on his back through train stations, airports, bus stops, and ferry terminals. He peels open the thick black zip, revealing an empty cavity. Leon runs his hands through the inside pockets and finds several pieces of paper. He also discovers ticket stubs from museums, receipts from restaurants, drawings done on napkins, and papers from his art book. He sits down on the floor next his bed to reveal their secrets. Unfolding the quarters of yellowing art paper, Leon remembers he'd hidden the drawings in his pack the last time he'd used it, on his last day at Machu Pichu, before hiking back to Cusco.

He was sitting at the top of the Andes, below a glorious sunset of pinks, oranges, and deep purples. He sketched what lay before him, the mountains, the ruins, the departing day tourists, and a single eagle soaring on the thermals, just as it had when he was there with Tom and Mitch. Leon had perfectly captured the majesty of the magnificent bird. Drawing in the mountains was the perfect activity at the end of a perfect day. He carefully refolds the paper and places it with his other drawings under his undies, in the middle drawer of his bed side table.

He returns to the pockets and finds a moonstone crystal which he bought at the Ollantaytambo markets, just before he caught the train to Machu Pichu. There's a piece of paper that he hadn't noticed before which gives a brief explanation of the stone's properties. He reads it carefully. This stone is helpful for new beginnings, to give the owner strength, it promotes inner growth. It will bring good luck in new relationships, with love and business. It will help to reduce emotional stress and bring about calmness in stressful situations. Leon holds the cool stone in his left hand before he carefully places it back into the backpack pocket and zips it up. He could do with some good luck in a new relationship.

The night before he is due to leave, Leon, Mitch and Declan, take to the local pub for some farewell ales.

"Looking forward to Europe then?" Mitch is grinning madly which makes Leon nervous.

"Yes, I am, but damn shame you're going to miss it." Leon raises his glass in a self-congratulatory toast while Mitch winks at Declan.

"Not gunna miss it for the world Mate." Declan counters, as Mitch produces two airline tickets from his breast pocket, he waves them victoriously in the air. Leon's mouth hangs open wide. "Mate, we're coming with you. The same flight, everything. We've even managed to score the same hotel in Paris." Leon's gape morphs into a confused smile, when he fully realises the propensity of it all, his face breaks into a wide beam. "Yes!" They chorus, charging their beers to the gods.

"But seriously, how did you find out all of the travel details?" Mitch winks at Leon and sips his beer. Leon knows better than to try and dig any deeper, he lets the matter rest.

On the flight the next day, Leon's head is still thumping a little, he realises this isn't a footy trip with his mates, but a work tour. He's sharing the charge, co-leading students on a cultural visit to Europe and he has to be professional, which is going to be difficult with Declan and Mitch on board the same flight. Mitch and Declan agree, it's funny to see Leon switch roles, from their brother and friend, into a professional teacher and tour leader.

"Okay, any more questions before we settle in for the rest of the flight?" Leon directs his question to the tour group.

"Excuse me Leon. Are we likely to have any other cultural exchanges while we're there?" Mitch shouts over several rows of seats. Most of the surrounding passengers release a loud groan, others laugh. One girl doesn't grasp the context of Mitch's comment, she pretends to understand and laughs anyway. Leon shoots Mitch a look that says, shut up right now. But Mitch just laughs along with the rest of the group. Luckily for Leon, or maybe not, he's relieved that Mitch and Declan are only travelling to Paris, they won't be able to annoy him for the whole tour.

For most of the flight, Mitch has the airline's cabin crew eating out of his hands. They can't bring him enough drinks and he's consumed more than his fair share of warm nuts. The crew regularly passes by to make sure he's comfortable and just before the passengers ready themselves for sleep, a crew member sidles up to Mitch.

"Excuse me Sir, but I've noticed that you're very tall. These economy seats weren't made with men like you in mind. There's a spare seat in Business Class, we thought you might be more comfortable there, if you're interested?"

"That would be lovely." He replies with a flirtatious smile as he collects his day pack from the overhead locker. "Adios Declan." He winks at his friend.

"Are you kidding me?"

Declan is jealous that he hadn't been asked to move to Business Class and Mitch seemed to have forgotten to ask for an upgrade on his behalf as well. When the cabin crew pass his seat, Declan takes a chance.

"Excuse me, but my friend has just moved to Business, I was wondering if there's another free seat that I could use. We are both travelling together."

"Oh, I'm sorry Sir, but that was our last available seat. Perhaps you could pay the extra, or use your frequent flyer points to purchase an upgrade on your return trip home."

"Thanks." He replies weakly.

Declan stares into the bottom of the empty nut packet and fiddles with the recline button on his seat, it isn't going to lay back any further. He pushes his pillow onto the plastic curve next to the window and tries to get some sleep, but he can't find a comfortable position the whole night. By the end of his luxurious horizontal flight, Mitch has obtained the names and hotel addresses of most of the female crew, and one male crew member. He had a great night.

Chapter 44 Ailie

I sit pensively in the wagon with Papa, Belle, and baby Flynn, while our driver takes us to our chateau in Breteuil. I'm keen to return to work and relay to Ottho, Matilda's plans for orders of more tapestries and embroideries. Papa needs to collect his taxes, and Belle, and baby Flynn, will resume their quiet existence in the chateau. Even though Belle has begun to entertain the ladies of the district, she's a lot younger than Mama's old friends, she lacks confidence in terms of her experience. The other ladies' children are grown up and living their own lives, Belle is just beginning this phase of her life and even though they offer her some sound advice on child rearing and how to manage a noble household, the other women are easily bored by domestic topics of conversation. They prefer to gossip about the Royal Court.

I sit at my stool, smell the familiar scent of the workroom and smile. I'm home again. I pick up my threads and inspect my loom to remind myself of the piece I'd been working on before I left for Falaise, as I begin to work, I sense Sarra beside me. I've been dreading this moment, my stomach clenches with dread.

"What are you doing here? Why did you come back here?" She hisses at me. "You're not wanted here anymore. You don't belong, a noble working in a workroom. Haven't you played this game long enough?" It seems that Sarra is still angry about Odo banning her relationship with Miché and she accuses me of causing her misfortunes. I decide, enough is enough, I'm going to stand up for myself.

"What have I ever done to you?"

The other weavers hear the start of an altercation, their ears begin to prickle, they look up from their work. Ottho notices that the workroom has quietened considerably. There isn't the normal shuffling of threads and combs, the general hubbub that coincides with a busy day at the studio. He wanders out from his office to see what's occurring. Momentarily, Sarra is stunned that I have stood up to her, but it doesn't deter her in the slightest.

"Go home, you don't belong here!" Sarra starts to shout again.

"You're playing a game aren't you? You're a lowly worker during the day, when you go home at night you become a princess. Well it's okay for some, isn't it? You make me sick. You come in here and advance before us, working on the Duke's commissions. Did your drunken father pay Ottho for you to progress so quickly? Who are you laying with?" "Woah now, stop that at once!" Ottho finally demands. "Go to my office Sarra, Ailie my child, are you okay?" I nod silently, Ottho fumes and herds Sarra into his office.

I look down forlornly at my work while my heart beat pounds out of my dress. I feel bad for Sarra, but I also understand that her broken relationship with Miché isn't my fault. I can feel her scorn, it etches deep within me. Acutely embarrassed, the rest of the weavers resume their work, except for Osanna, who has a profound motherly instinct, joins me at my loom and grasps my hand in her own.

"That girl's evil, pay her no mind now. You're a talented weaver and embroiderer. She's just jealous of everything about you, especially your talent, and your connections with the Duke and Duchess. Don't let her bring you down to her level." "Thank you Osanna. I understand she's angry, but it's not my fault her relationship with Miché is forbidden." Osanna caresses my shoulder and hands me a handkerchief, but her show of kindness causes me to well up, then I'm embarrassed by my show of emotion.

"I guess a lot of us were confused when you started here. We couldn't work out why a noble, such as yourself, would want to work, but we see your dedication to the craft and your outstanding ability. I think you're bound for high places my dear, don't let her bitterness upset you."

Ottho's door opens, a red faced Sarra returns to her loom. Ottho appears at the door and calls me inside.

"Sit down my dear. How are you?"

"I'm okay Ottho, thank you for asking." However, my puffy red eyes tell another story.

"You're forever the little stoic one, aren't you? I don't know what to say, Sarra acted beyond reproach, but the argument is between the two of you. I know it isn't your fault, she has a dark side that one, but you managed to remain calm throughout her tirade. I'll have to think about how to proceed from here."

"I'll stay out of her way for now on, but if there are any further opportunities to travel I'd be grateful. I know, I've only just returned, but I think that I have the ability to talk to a wide range of people, from all walks of life." My train of thought is interrupted by my emotional exhaustion, besides weaving, I really don't know what I want to do. Weaving is all I have ever dreamed of doing.

"Let me see what I can do Ailie. I may have something you'd be interested in at one of the monasteries in Paris."

Chapter 45 Allie

I've worked at the college for eighteen months and now I've finally paid off my car loan. It is such a relief to be debt free, not only from the financial side of things, but the assistant to the junior manager at the credit union gives me the creeps. He reminds me of someone familiar, yet I'm not sure who. Declan's his name. Every time I have to make a repayment, he emerges from his glass walled office and sidles up to the teller.

"I hope everything's all in order?"

"Well yes, it's only a standard loan repayment." The teller replies impatiently.

"Very good, just checking to make sure we give this lovely lady our best service."

The teller who is about my age, grimaces, rage prickles at the back of her neck, she feels scrutinised by the junior administrator. But then one day, she realises that the only times he appears from his office, is for meetings, coffee breaks, lunchtimes and when attractive women conduct business at her window.

"Car going well is it?" He directs this question to me.

"Yes it is, thanks. Bye." I gather up my pay-in book, purse and keys, and flee, but little do I know, Declan isn't at the front desk to check me out, he's just saying hi to someone that he has met socially, I'd forgotten his face completely. It maddened me that I can't place him though. He's remembered me from the pub, from the night of the music festival, I have no recollection of him at all. If only I knew who he is, things may have been different.

"Goodbye!" Declan hollers from the enquiries counter as I'm half way through the door. I'm almost home before I remember where I'd met him, but I don't know who he is, not really.

For the past year, Sara and I have planned to spend our annual four week holiday in Paris. We've busily saved for months, limiting our shopping trips to the bare minimum, we rarely venture to the pub anymore. I start to catch the bus a bit more when it goes my way, it's on time, and the moon aligns with forward moving Mercury.

Since I was a little girl, I have always wanted to go to Paris. Mum often speaks fondly of the magnificent city, of the artists along the Seine, the steps of Montmartre, the cafes, the Latin Quarter, Versailles. All the stereotypes intrigue me, but it's the people in her stories that interest me the most. The Romany people, the African street vendors, the eccentrics with monkeys riding on their shoulders, the Metro musicians, the embracing lovers, the cancan dancers from the Moulin Rouge, the seedy men in Pigalle, the glamorous monsuires et madams who promenade the grand boulevards, are all characters from the fairy tales of my childhood and I can't wait to see them come to life for myself.

Sara and I have a place to stay with Mum's good friend Trudi, who lives in a fourth floor walk-up apartment, on Rue de Passay in the 16th Arrondissement, across the Seine from the Eiffel Tower. Everything is settled, we'll sleep on a pull-out sofa in Trudi's cosy apartment and we'll travel around France for three weeks, but for now, we just need to save a lot more money.

When the big day arrives, Dad takes us to the airport in his new green Jag. There's a lump in the back of his throat as he fights back conflicting emotions, his baby girl is travelling overseas for the first time, he's glad that I have the opportunity to discover France, its food and culture. Though, he's worried that I will be safe, no especially worried, that I'll be bitten by the travel bug, acquire Mum's taste for travel, never to return, lost to the world. As he kisses me goodbye, he hands me a new traveller's debit card in my name.

"Dad, I've got a credit card." I protest.

"I know, but you can use this one in case you get into any trouble. There's enough Francs on it for you to have a good time, for a little while. Better keep it separate from your other one though hey, they're always mucking up with money over there. Your Mother used to always call me, at all hours, to have her cards sorted out. It's a good idea to have a spare one, just take it. It'll make me feel a lot better." The lump in his throat becomes tighter and bigger, he can barely speak.

"Thanks Dad, it's really sweet of you. we'll be okay though, won't we Sara?" Sara beams and nods.

"We'll be tres bon, Rodger." She shoots back, in her best Aussie French.

"Sure you will. See ya love." His nose fills with snot as he gives Sara a quick hug, then turns to me for a final bear hug and kiss. He quickly leaves without waving, heads towards the car park, noisily blowing his nose.

"Au revoir, Papa!" We happily sing out to him.

After a transit in Singapore, the plane touches down at Charles de Gaulle Airport in the early hours of a new spring day. A crisp chill in the air cools our faces as we stand slightly shell shocked, brand new black trundle suit cases at our feet, waiting for the RER train to arrive and deliver us into Paris. Even though we've just travelled to the other side of the world, and we are horribly jet lagged, this is the business end of the day. We have to work out the money, check, the train and metro tickets, check, the language, check, we've both remembered a little high school French, and the metro maps, check. I dig deeper into my handbag, phone?

"Merde, I don't have my phone. Stay here with the bags Sara." I run back inside the terminal and find a booth selling mobile phones, I buy a new one on the spot. Just as well I have Dad's debit card because it isn't cheap, but at least Sara and I can communicate with each other and go our separate ways, if we want to. My phone is still on the kitchen counter at Dad's house where I'd been charging it the night before I left. It's a miracle that I remembered my tickets, passport and money.

Back in the queue for train tickets, I'm out of breath from exertion, the thought that I need to get fitter when I return to Australia crosses my mind for a millisecond.

"Huh, I'm so glad that we had that stop-over in Singapore, to stretch our legs out a bit. Can you imagine if we had to fly the whole way without stopping? A day cooped up in a plane is too much."

"Yeah, but it's even better that we're out of that stuffy tube. After all those hours, its pretty wiffy."

"I know, I don't think I could stand being cooped up in that plane, breathing other people's farts for much longer. They should push Australia a bit closer to Europe. Actually, you know what? Well, Australia is moving north a few centimetres every year, perhaps if it went west a bit as well, in a few million years, it will be close enough to Europe and a much shorter flight for everyone." I'm a bit delirious as well as unfit.

"Oh my Goddess, you're delusional and jet lagged. Come on, you ask for those tickets, your French is better than mine." Sara laughs.

"Deux billet s'il vous plait. Combien?"

We disembark at Chatelet Les Halles Metro station without too much strain. In fact, we sit in a tired, slightly numb, excited silence as we watch the outer suburbs morph into the city of Paris. However, at Chatelet Les Halles the fun begins.

"Right, we take the Pont De Neuilly, one, until Charles de Gaulle-Etoile, there we change trains to the number six." I turn the map in all directions while I nervously chew my thumb nail. I always revert to my childhood comfort when I'm deep in thought, or anxious, which is quite often and the reason why there isn't much nail left to chew.

"How about, we should've stayed on the RER until Denfert Rochereau and catch the number six from there?" Sara smugly suggests.

"Well, we're not on the RER now, are we?" Jet-lagged and hangry, I fight hard to contain my mood. More silence. After standing in the same spot with the map in hand, the morning pedestrian rush hour speeds past us in both directions. An odd beggar thrusts an empty palm towards us and pleads his poverty in fast French. Trying to ignore him, Mum has warned me before that these types are often professionals, we calmly decide to return to the RER and continue our journey to Passay from there.

We amble along Rue de Passay and even though our bags have wheels they are becoming increasingly heavy as they fail to roll smoothly over the uneven street. We search the faded numbers on the buildings, dodging dog poo and clunking over cracks in the pavement, until we eventually discover a heavy royal blue door. It's the only door without a number displayed, but it's the next door sequentially, we figure it must be the right one. A row of named buzzers catches our attention and there it is, Trudi Du Bois, apartment number nine.

I release my suitcase handle, causing it to fall onto the wet pavement.

"I hope that's just water." I say as I press my finger onto the buzzer.

"You know it probably isn't water." Sara offers.

"Well, I'm going to tell myself that it is water." A long silence echoes in our heads, we both eye each other in disbelief as the silence lengthens.

"This is the right place, isn't it?" Sara breaks the silence.

"Of course it's the right place. There's Trudi's name. I'll buzz again." I buzz again and we both hold our breath as we will Trudi to answer, another long silence fills the air.

"She must have left for work already." I sigh in resignation.

"What are we going to do with these bags then, hey? I'm not pulling them around Paris all day."

Sara's jet lag and slight PMS has made her cranky to say the least. Exhausted, we sit on the stoop and wait for a minute to think, but no sooner does the denim from our jeans touch the concrete step, the door behind us begins to swing open. Someone is leaving, we quickly collect ourselves to catch the door.

"Yes! Merci." Sara's heart lightens, we smile at each other as the man holds the door open for us. We begin to climb the four flights of stairs to Trudi's apartment.

The stairs seem to spiral up to the heavens, but luckily Sara and I, puffing and red faced from dragging our heavy suitcases, arrive at the apartment in no time. We see a note stuck to the door with sticky tape.

"Welcome to Paris girls! I'm off to work, sorry I can't get a key to you. I'll be home for lunch at 12:30. Caio Trudi."

Sara's hormones surge through her body and her jaw clenches tighter.

"I'm starving and I need a loo." She whimpers.

"You've just had breakfast on the plane." I've pushed a button, but I can't help it.

"Yes, but that doesn't mean that I'm not hungry and need to pee now, does it? I don't count that excuse for an omelette, don't get me started on the state of that coffee." Sara's blood pressure increases as her blood sugar drops, I decide not to start a fight within our first hour in the City of Light.

"Right, well let's just leave our bags here and go down and get some breakfast."

We nervously leave our bags in front of the apartment door and venture into the street in search of food. Not a difficult task, considering where we are. Shops of all kinds begin to open as we make our way to a café for our first taste of real French food. We sit inside where it's warmer and cheaper, we order our food in ancient high school French, two hot chocolates with some freshly baked brioche. In twenty years' time this cake will be used for hamburger buns, weird.

"Hey, Sara." I whisper.

"What?" I grasp Sara's hand in mine and squeeze tightly.

"We're in PARIS!" I yell with wide eyes.

None of the other patrons in the crowded café give me a second look, they're far too French for that. Thankfully Sara's mood changes once it's sunk in where we are. We're both excited to finally be in the city we've scrimped and saved for.

"Right where's the loo?" Sara suddenly remembers she's busting.

After breakfast we stroll down Rue de Passay, admiring the boulangeries, the luxury shoe shops, the elegant dress boutiques, the colourful cosmetic stores, and the dreamy chocolatiers have especially caught our attention. Even though we've just finished eating, we discover our mouths watering as we admire the decadent selection of petite chocolates. By way of ancient pont, we cross the Seine, arm in arm, before us stands the iconic Eiffel Tower. Sitting on a park bench, at the foot of the Tower, we each remove a single chocolate from the little blue box, adorned with a red satin ribbon, we place a delicious morsel into our mouths. We instantly feel better as the incredibly smooth chocolate melts in our mouths. Nothing soothes the soul like French chocolate at the foot of the Eiffel Tower. I'm so happy to be here and I think Sara's happier now as well.

Chapter 46 Leo

The Duke believes his knights have lost focus, spending too much time contemplating the fairer sex. The men need a serious diversion and Guilliam has just the operation. The King of France, Henry I, Guilliam's uncle-in-law, supported the Duke when he acquired his duchy, but since the Duke's show of strength to secure more land, the King alleges that his relative holds far too much power in France. This power is significant in Normandy, with designs on England, he can see that Guilliam may have his sights set on Paris as well. Henry has already failed to keep his strongholds in Normandy, he certainly knows his place, but Guilliam will send a contingency to Paris as a reminder of who actually controls France.

Leo, Miché, and now their little brother Darri, join the army of one hundred men on their journey to Paris.

"Are you ready for an adventure Darri?" Leo asks his younger sibling.

"Sure am." Darri, a squire, has been training with the Duke's men, he's now old enough to go on assignment with his older brothers. The journey will take a little over a week by horseback, when they reach the outskirts of Paris, they'll set up camp. Word has reached the Palace that Guilliam's men are in close proximity, but as yet, there is no threat of an attack. Henry isn't certain of his nephew's intentions, so he has his men prepare themselves, but also to hold fire until he can think of a suitable strategy of defence.

However, Guilliam hasn't sent his men to attack the King, merely to intimidate his royal relative. Yet, not everyone sees this as a serious assignment, some of the knights and squires feel the journey is a reason to celebrate, a holiday away from Falaise, where they can drink, womanise, and gamble, far away from the Duke's scrutiny. Paris is full of little side streets and alleys where they can disappear into the darkness of their desires. But Miché, Leo and Darri aren't among those knights as they venerate their vows to the Church, and the Duke, they will uphold civility and chivalry. Nevertheless, vice is difficult to avoid in the grotty capital city and as the evening grows darker, the knights ride into the centre where they eventually discover a tavern where they can fill their rumbling bellies.

The small inn is crowded, but there is a spare table, almost hidden in the corner, where they sit down. The hostess brings the young men vegetable soup, bread, and wine, they eat heartily, despite the soup being a little more watery than they are used to. The bread is tasty though so they order more. As they finish their meal, Leo sees three familiar Norsemen at the bar, though strangely these men are not to be feared, surprisingly, they are friends of the Duke.

"Keep your enemies close by." Guilliam often warns. Darri is still a little wary, he isn't sure about these men. But it's Leo who greets them, he invites the trio to sit them. Mitch knows that the Duke has conducted business with the Norsemen and is comfortable with them sitting at their table. However, the community thinks the Duke's Knights are there to protect them against the plunderers, they attract worried sideways glances, the locals dare not say anything for fear of retribution from both sides.

Another bench is placed at the end of the snug table and the brothers arrange themselves to accommodate the three Vikings. After re-introductions are made, Miché asks Eric, the senior of the three, what business they're conducting in Paris.

"We've come to sell furs at the market. We think we can make some money while we're here."

"Our grandfathers came to France, robbed and tyrannised the people. We're here to collect their money, in a more creative way." Lars chuckles.

"Here, we've also brought our own drink, Black Death. Do you want to try some?" Arne offers the drink to the brothers. Ready for new adventures, Darri is the first to respond, despite the fact that his constitution is the most immature.

"Sure, hit us with it."

From the first tentative slug, the innocuous clear liquid hits Darri with a punch. The alcohol burns as it flows down his throat, then he chokes and coughs.

"Hey, you don't drink this stuff like ale." Eric's warning is issued too late, but the rest of them still laugh at Darri's expense. The six new friends exchange jokes and tell stories well into the night. At the beginning, the du Bois brothers remember to sip their drinks, for a little while a least. However, it isn't long before they throw caution to the wind and swig the potent drink down with gusto. In direct correlation to their alcohol consumption, their stories become bawdier, their laughter louder, their friendship bond grows tighter. After only two drinks, Darri pretends to drink the Viking's spirits, he isn't going to swallow any more fire water, it's too dangerous for his liking. Instead, he sticks to his ale and nobody even notices.

Women wonder in from the darkness, into the dimly lit smoky tavern, it doesn't take long for the Norsemen to become excited by the female company. Each of the Northern men, immediately claim his own girl and disappears into the dark corners of the tavern. However, without the influence of the Vikings, the du Bois brothers sober up a little and decide to leave the tavern to return to camp. Amazingly, their horses are still tied to their posts, but only a madman would steel one of Guilliam's steeds and face a Norman's wrath. Laughing at a joke he'd remembered from earlier in the night, and feeling a bit unbalanced, the normally strong and agile knight, Miché struggles to mount his horse. Darri and Leo think they are going to have to give him a leg up, but he eventually manages to haul himself onto his patient steed.

As the brothers ride back to camp in the dark of the night, the back streets confuse them so much they become lost. However, Paris is a city of monasteries, places of safe haven, they know they can take protection in the grounds of one of the nearby holy shelters. They'll sleep off their alcohol while they wait for daylight before returning to camp. The young men eventually find a stable in the monastery grounds, loosely tie their horses and promptly fall asleep on some bales of dry hay. In the morning, their horses begin to munch on the knight's soft bedding, as they wake and collect themselves, five of the King's knights ride menacingly towards them. It's clear to Leo, that the monks must have alerted the Palace of the presence of Guilliam's knights and as their little brother still sleeps, Leo kicks Darri on his shin.

"Wake up Darri, for God's sake, wake up!"

"What is your business here?" The knight at the front of the pack is clearly the spokesman, his mere presence governs respect.

"Good day Sir. We lost our way in the night and now we're on our way." Miché replies humbly. He knows they are outnumbered, he doesn't want to start anything.

"The King bids Guilliam and his men good health, but you should be on your way."

"The Duke of Normandy bids the King and his men good health also and wishes him well." Miché responds respectfully. However, despite their civility, the King's men don't attack the brothers, they don't want to start a fracas they know they won't win, in the long run, so they grant permission for the Norman Knights to return to their camp in peace. With Darri now awake, the du Bois brothers mount their horses and swiftly make their way back to camp, relieved that their lives have been spared.

When the brothers are back at the camp, most of the other knights are also in the process of returning from the city centre, in various states of sobriety.

"We were stopped by Henry's men." Darri reports to some of the men milling around a large bonfire.

"Yes, they were here as well. I think we scared them off though." One of the older knights laughs as he warms his hands by the fire.

"We were outnumbered and they were still scared of us." Laughs Miché.

"They must've heard about your triumph over the Black Knight. That would scare anyone."

"No, they wouldn't know who I am." Miché humbly gazes deeply into the fire.

Leo pats his older brother on the back, reminding him that he's the leader of this motley group of men.

"Come on, we need to get this troop organised." Miché's head pounds from the wine and Black Death, he glances over at Darri and several other men who are green and listless.

"I think we'll wait until the afternoon before we make any plans." Leo shrugs and concedes, it's probably for the best that they wait.

Chapter 47 Leon

Leon's group arrives at Charles de Gaulle Airport, after a brief stopover in Kuala Lumpur. They have a coach awaiting their arrival, to transfer them to their hotel. As there are only fourteen people on the tour, they spread out one person to a row and luxuriate in the spacious coach that has enough room to take Mitch and Declan with them.

"You know, this coach has more leg room than my seat on the plane." Declan observes.

"No, I'm pretty sure I had more room than this."

"Okay, whatever Mister, I get everything in life." Mitch lets Declan's tantrum slide. When they arrive in the centre, Leon reminds the group that they will stay overnight in Paris before catching the train to Barcelona as the weary travellers check into their hotel in the seventh arrondissement.

The boys drop their bags in their rooms and then head out to explore the city. Apart from immigrating to Australia, Declan has never been overseas before and even though Leon and Mitch are both well seasoned travellers, they are still like children in a lolly shop. Declan can't believe all of the sleek, elegantly dressed women parading just for him, or so he thinks. He walks around the city with his tongue hanging out, almost dribbling.

"Did you see her over there in the red dress."

"Keep it in your pants, for God's sake Dec, be cool." Mitch warns.

The friends have some time with Leon before he has to meet up with Graham. He'll start his official duties with the tour group later in the morning which will give everyone a chance to shower, have some breakfast, or go for a walk and stretch their legs. Across the Seine, a cosy café beckons the boys inside to satisfy their main lust, hunger. They pour into a booth, order a hearty tourist breakfast and wait for their food to arrive. Just as the waiter approaches them with their food, Leon catches a glimpse of someone familiar through the café windows. He isn't quite sure who I am, but he knows that he's seen me from somewhere before, he fights with himself for a minute, contemplating whether to chase after me, or not. Even to Leon, it seems a little crazy to run after a complete stranger in a foreign country. What will he say to me if he does catch me? What the hell, he's in Paris and he's going to listen to his heart. He wins his inner battle and while the waiter hands out steaming plates of food, Leon gently pushes him aside so he can pass him by in the cramped space.

"*Excuse moi, désolé*".

He strides through the busy café to the door and once he's stepped onto the bustling street he breaks into a slow jog, weaving between morning pedestrians. After about fifty meters he stops dead in his tracks, realising that I've vanished, lost in the crowd. Despondently, Leon turns around and walks back to the café feeling foolish. When he returns, his mates have eaten most of their food and gulped down their now tepid café o'laits. Declan is about to grab some of Leon's toast as he resumes his seat, but Leon smacks Declan's hand away from his food just in time.

"Oi! That's mine."

"Did you catch her? Who is it by the way?" Declan mumbles, as crumbs fall from his mouth. It isn't the first bit of toast he'd swiped, Leon scrutinises his plate and sees that he only has one of four triangles left.

"It's that girl, who was in your room that night Mitch." Leon starts to eat his cold breakfast, instantly regretting having his first meal in Paris ruined.

"Ha, that narrows it down mate. Could you be a bit more specific?"

"You know the strawberry blonde, from the night of the music festival. She left in the morning without a word, you know, she didn't try to stay all morning. She didn't want to marry you straight away and have your babies. That one."

"All right, you don't have to rub it in. But yeah, Allie, I know her pretty well. I helped her buy car a while back. Well, she might be here in Paris somewhere, there's a coincidence."

"What the hell! You didn't tell me you saw her again." Leon shakes his head in disbelief as to why this information is only now forth coming. "I wonder where she's staying?" He doesn't know why I've captured his thoughts so intensely, he can't stop thinking about me, to the point of preoccupation for the rest of the day. Mitch deliberately ignores the first question and tackles the second one instead.

"I don't know if you've noticed, but Paris is a big place. She could be staying anywhere. Anyway, why don't you ring her on your mobile?" Mitch continues as if that's the most natural thing in the world to ask.

"Well for starters, I don't have her number, do I?" Leon replies a little testily, but hopeful that Mitch does have the number.

Mitch pulls his mobile phone out of his back pack as Leon holds his breath hopefully, his phone is still switched off from the flight and he's forgotten to turn it back on. After a few seconds, the phone starts to beep animatedly, all of his new text messages download all at once. Ignoring the texts, he scrolls through his contact list to find my number.

"Here it is." Mitch exclaims triumphantly.

"Quick hand it to me, I don't have much time before I have to go and find Graham." Leon is clearly anxious. He presses my number nervously, he doesn't know what he is going to say if I answer the phone, after all, I don't really know who he is.

The phone dials quickly, but I don't answer, instead he hears a recorded message saying that my phone is switched off and would he like to leave a message after the BEEP.

"Hi, you don't know me but I'm a friend of Mitch. This sounds mad, but I'm in Paris and I think I saw you this morning, on the street in front of a cafe. Are you here as well? No perhaps you're not, but anyway I'm heading down to Barcelona soon and......." He doesn't know what else to say, but the beep to end the message sounds so he presses the end call button. "Shit, that's not what I wanted to say."

"That was pretty terrible." Mitch offers.

"Smooth. Ring her back and leave another message." Declan encourages his brother.

"No, I don't have time." Despondently, Leon passes the phone back to Mitch and heads back to the hotel to collect the tour group for the day's excursions. All day he searches the crowds for just a glimpse.

Chapter 48 Ailie

Millie and I arrive at Isle de Cite, after crossing the Grand Pont which has just been reconstructed. A flood had washed the bridge away two years previously and masons are still applying their final touches to the reconstruction as our driver makes his way towards the abbey. When Matilda discovers that I have business in Paris, she insisted Millie travel with me for companionship. I'm in the capital city to work with the clergy on a series of tapestries for the monastery, but while I'm here, I will reside with the nuns in the abbey. However, my initial meeting with the bishops have to be delayed because the clergy are entrenched in meetings regarding the building of a new cathedral, to be named Notre Dame. In our spare time, Millie and I seize the opportunity to discover Paris.

As we stroll through the narrow streets, we somehow grow used to the city's pungent odours. Sometimes, we turn down a street corner and the stench of urine and waste which pours down from the houses, is overwhelming. Fish mongers positioned on nearly every corner contribute to more ripe smells emanating from the streets. While we are walking a beggar approaches us for coins, as is the custom, I happily reach into my purse and give a shiny coin to the unfortunate man. The man thanks me kindly and we continue to walk through the congested streets. Farm animals of all descriptions populate the thoroughfares, as much as the public does, it's hard for us to look at the sights and avoid stepping in sheep dung at the same time.

We also struggle to be heard, as we talk to one another on our way through the clogged city. Heralds bellow the latest news along the streets, merchants advertise their wares to potential shoppers, and animals bray, bark and moo. The cacophony is deafening.

"My goodness it's really loud here. It really makes me appreciate Breteuil."

"What?" Millie cups her ear to hear me better.

"It's too loud here." I screech. I point in the direction in which we've just walked.

"Let's go back to the abbey. It's too crazy out here." We weave our way back to the priory avoiding manure and effluent as we walk.

When we arrive at the cloisters, we smile, sighing with relief, we've found peace again. Exhausted from walking, the noise and excitement, we're glad to be in the safety and relative comfort of our small cell. As I lie down on my deer skin, I search the rafters and notice a house spider spinning its web. I knew there would be one here somewhere. Mesmerised, I watch the arachnid going about its stunning work, but it isn't long before I fall asleep, lulled into slumber by the familiar repetitious movement of threads discharging from their spinnerets.

After breakfast the next morning, a page accompanies Millie and I to the monastery which is only a short distance from the abbey. When we arrive, we overhear the clergymen, huddled in a corner, discussing some knights who were caught sleeping in the monastic stables overnight. The shocking aspect of this turn of events is that they aren't the King's Knights, but Guilliam's. Bishops, priests, and monks, speculate as to whether there will be an attack on the city by the Duke's men, they are understandably worried, Guilliam has a vicious reputation. I wait patiently for a break in the conversation before introducing myself, thinking that my Norman origins could be potentially inflammatory, given the climate, I make sure that I only refer to Ottho's workshop in my dealings, carefully omitting my associations with the Duke.

Chapter 49Allie

At lunch time, we return to the apartment on Passay to find our bags missing. Panic shoots through our jet-lagged minds before we remember that Trudi may have brought them in when she arrived home for lunch, we seriously hope and pray that's the case. I nervously wrap on the door as I look deeply into the eyes of my travelling companion, willing Trudi and our bags to be safely ensconced within the apartment. Finally, a latch clicks, the door opens and a slight brunette with a thick Parisian accent flows from the doorway.

"*Allie, ma petite.*"

Trudi grabs me by the shoulders and kisses both cheeks, then gives me a refined hug. It's nice to be embraced warmly, even though I have only met her once when she visited us in Australia. Mum has spoken about her so often that she feels like family.

"This is Sara."

"*Bonjour, Sara.*" Trudi repeats the kissing and hugging performance, then gives us a tour of the apartment, but the tour doesn't take long because the apartment is tiny. Trudi's home consists of a tiny kitchen, a tiny bedroom, and a narrow passageway linking the two.

"Just one question, where's the toilet?" Sara asks. Trudi directs her to what appears to be a cupboard, Sara opens the door and backs herself into the tiny stall. We are relieved to see our cases lined side by side along the narrow passage way and I give mine a reassuring pat as we venture into the kitchen. The cosy kitchen, with views of the city, houses the shower cubicle and a pull out sofa which Sara and I are to share. When the sofa is released to make the bed, the kitchen all but disappears.

Trudi makes coffee, while I prepare sandwiches with fresh baguettes that are still warm from the oven, ripe red heirloom tomatoes, delicious cheese, and fragrant basil leaves we've bought from a local street market a few streets away, which we noticed while walking back to the apartment. Sara relaxes on the sofa while Trudi chats airily, reliving tales about our families. Trudi then excuses herself after lunch and returns to work, leaving the spare key on the table.

"*Desole*, I'll be out this evening. I hope you don't mind exploring on your own, on your first night here, but I made these plans many months ago and can't get out of them."

We flop. Our tired bodies recoil into themselves with fatigue, and jet lag. I'm barely able to connect the cup to my lips, salvaging the last drips of coffee, I contemplate our first night in Paris. I study Freyja's favourite museums list which she had offered to me before I left Australia while Sara peruses her lists. Sara's lists were compiled by her boss, and a co-worker, who had been to Paris, but they had both enjoyed a larger budget than us. The options consists of favourite places to eat and more importantly where to drink, dance, and have fun.

Ms Coiffed's list seems to consist of up-market venues that entice rich tourists who want to play in an extravagant, yet conservative way. Sara compares this list to the "What's on" guides she's collected from the airport tourist stands which seem to confirm her thoughts exactly. Looking at Sara's friend's list, the offerings appear to be more down to earth and hopefully will provide opportunities to interact with interesting people. Sara circles a couple of bars on the map that are within stumbling distance of the apartment.

I have my own list as well. I want to see a French film in France, I secretly want to have my portrait drawn by an artist along the Seine, cheesy and as touristy as it gets, I want to stand at the top of the Arch de Triumph and watch the mad traffic weave its way around the frantic round a bout. The site of the Champs Elysee, at night, with its twinkling fairy lights circling pavement trees, is another sight Mum waxed lyrical, I'm dying to witness these spectacles for myself. The list that I'd composed on the flight from Australia, cascades down the page and at the bottom of the page is the final suggestion. A moonlit walk along the Seine with someone special, deep in my heart I don't think I'd be able to tick that one off the list, on this trip anyway, I scribble it out.

"Keep the expectations simple." I say to myself quietly.

"What?" Sara looks up from her brochures.

"Oh, it's nothing." I say sheepishly and hide the list in my handbag.

"What do you want to do now Allie?" Sara stifles a cavernous yawn.

"Well, we could have a nap so that we're good to go out tonight. Or, we could go and check out some of those shops a little more thoroughly, you know the ones we saw this morning. I think I even saw a sale sign on one, or two, of the windows."

"Well, that's final then, definitely shops first, we can have a small nanna nap when we get back." Sara declares.

Chapter 50 Leo

As he wakes from a peaceful sleep, Miché decides that his knights will return to the city centre to ensure that King Henry understands Guilliam's men aren't intimidated by the Parisian knights. The plan is to ride en mass, onto the Isle de Cite, to warn the King's men that the Normans are in charge. Their horses are draped in Guilliam's red cloth while flag bearers proudly grasp red pennants adorned with golden lions, the procession into the city commences without haste. Word has spread quickly that the parade is about to occur and the public tentatively line the streets to watch the spectacle. However, the ample crowd doesn't cheer Guilliam's men, in fear of retribution, nor do they jeer them. Rather, they watch in awe as larger than life figures ride arrogantly through their city.

At the front of the contingent, Miché and Leo ride their horses in a measured trot. In the light of day, they have a better idea of the street layout and their confidence grows as landmarks become familiar. As they ride over the Grand Pont, and onto the Isle de Cite, they notice clergymen lining the monastery's exterior. Bishops, priests and monks, stand two deep, rosary beads clutched in their hands, some with their heads bowed in prayer. However, when they pass the abbey, there are no nuns viewing the parade, yet they see two young women standing on the side of the road waving madly. In a scene of solemness, the women are conspicuous. They seem to be the only people along the route who aren't intimidated by Guilliam's men.

"Hey, that's Ailie, and Millie." Leo shouts over to Miché.

"What?"

"It's Ailie, from Ottho's workshop in Breteuil, Belanger's daughter, and Millie, one of the Duchesses' maids."

"Oh, yes." However, Miché is absorbed in his work, his thoughts are focused on the imminent passing of the King's Palace. He's concerned with what might transpire.

Leo's distracted, I am all he can think of. The Norman contingency approaches the palace where they can see a line of the King's horsemen protecting the gates. Knights protect the towers.

"What do you think she's doing here in Paris?"

"What? I don't know Leo. We're here to show strength to the King, not to worry about a maiden you barely know."

Leo tries to concentrate on the mission at hand, he struggles to focus. Although he wants to, he can't stop and return to me, he has to ride on. He twists his head to see if I'm still watching him, Miché scolds his brother.

"Look directly ahead. We don't present a strong force when you're peering around as if it's a holy day." Leo snaps back to attention and tries to push his persistent thoughts to the back of his mind, it's a challenging task.

As the procession flows past the palace, someone from the crowd throws a rotten apple at one of the knights who rides at the back of the line. Luckily, it misses the knight, but unfortunately the soft fruit whacks his horse on its rump. The shock hit causes the steed to rear, luckily, its rider manages to brace himself and manoeuvre his frightened horse back into line. The crowd gasps with appreciation for the knight's riding skills, then he turns to see where the apple thrower is stationed. Leo sees a small boy run for his life, he sees the knights searching in the boy's direction, but Leo doesn't say anything to Miché, he doesn't want to cause any further distractions to their progress.

The commotion settles as Guilliam's men pass by, the King's men raise their swords in a show of strength, even though there will not be an attack. It's a procession of intimidation only. The knights ride on, retracing their steps over the Grand Pont and when they ride past the monastery, Leo strains his head to see if I'm still waiting on the street.

"There she is!" But he has to ride on, he can't break rank. He smiles secretly to himself, he's glad to have another glimpse, he'll just have to wait a bit longer to see me again.

Chapter 51 Leon

In his busy schedule, Leon leads the tour group in a methodical appreciation of the works at The Louvre, after which he joins them for dinner to celebrate their first night in Paris, giving them yet another opportunity to discuss the art. Declan and Mitch try to wiggle him out of his evening duties, but ever the professional, Leon isn't about to shirk his responsibilities. Besides, he enjoys the company of his students and genuinely cares about their opinions. Leon, his brother, and friend, travel their separate ways for the evening.

As they walk through the city, Declan and Mitch search for somewhere cheap and cheerful to grab a bite to eat, they want to conserve their money for other things. They find a pizzeria selling reasonably priced pizza by the slice, located some distance from the main tourist strips.

"Wow, that was one of the best pizzas I've eaten in a long time." Declan wipes the sauce from his mouth with the back of his hand.

"It was pretty good. But you should try the pizza in Italy. You 'aint tasted nothing yet."

Mitch slaps his napkin down on the table and finishes the dregs of his beer.

"Right, where to now?"

"Dunno." Declan attempts to keep up with Mitch's pace, quickly finishing his beer as well. Ambling down the street, they see a sign for a bar with a red neon arrow directing them down some stairs.

"This place looks as good as any."

"Cool music." Declan gushes. Mitch notices that everyone in the bar is roughly the same age, around 21 – 22ish, over the music he hears mainly American accents. While he's waiting for his drinks, Mitch asks the bar tender why there are so many Americans.

"Apparently, this is a bar for American's students who are studying here in Paris." Mitch relays this information to Declan when he returns to the table with their drinks.

"It's great. I like American girls." Declan says wistfully.

"How many do you know?"

"Well none, but now would be as good a time as any to get to know one. Don't you think?"

The guys drink Dutch beer for a little while before they meet three Scandinavian students. One of them has been to Australia as an exchange student and when he hears the Australian accents, he introduces himself. The students carry a clear bottle with a label depicting a skull and cross bone, they call Brennivín, or Black Death. They seem quite happy to share it with Mitch and Declan, just to swap stories of Australia.

Chapter 52 Ailie

Throughout the monastery, word has spread like wildfire, that Guilliam's knights have returned to intimidate the people of Paris, in particular, the King and his Knights. With a ripple effect, my meeting is adjourned again as the clergy clamour onto the streets to pray for a peaceful procession. To scope the parade, Millie and I stand slightly apart from the religious men. Millie knows these knights well, she's seen them regularly at Falaise. I'm also familiar with some of them, through my friendship with the Duchess, though I don't know them as well as Millie. In the spirit of a parade, both of us are keen to show our support for the knights from our home region, we wait patiently for the procession to begin.

"Oh, there's Miché and Leo, they're leading the procession." I wave at the contingency as they ride past and I'm thrilled when I recognise Leo at the head of the group. Trying to remain calm, I play down my delight in front of Millie.

"So many men we know, look there's Sir Tristian." Millie smiles and waves to the knights she's most acquainted with. I can see Leo searching for someone in the crowd and I suddenly realise it's me he's searching for. I see him stare directly at me, for a moment or two at least, before he rides on. Our eyes locked for only an instant.

The clergy glance side wards at us and wonder what our association is with the Duke's men. As the contingency ride into the distance, Millie begins to ponder aloud why Guilliam's men are in Paris.

"What do you think their business is here?" There's a lull in the usual cacophony, a monk has overheard her query, he replies directly to her.

"They're here to bully us, well the King's men specifically. To let us know that Guilliam is really the leader of France. They think our King is just a figure head for the city."

"Oh, really." We'd never really considered Guilliam's reach outside of Normandy, but now we realise we are ensconced within a very powerful realm.

The parade winds its way past the monastery while Millie and I finish talking to the monk. When the knights have moved on, relative peace returns to the streets and the clergy stand in a circle and murmur prayers of thanks for the peaceful procession before returning to their quarters. Millie and I quietly follow them inside so that I can finally attend my meeting regarding the proposed tapestries for the new cathedral. I'm relieved and thankful that nobody asked me about our affiliation with the knights, for many reasons.

When the meeting concludes, Millie and I are ready to eat, we venture a short way from the monastery to find a tavern. We could have eaten at the Abby, but I had tasted the food at breakfast. Even though I appreciate the offer to eat with the nuns, their singing is a lot better than their cooking. There's a buzz at the inn, as the crowd who'd witnessed the parade of Guilliam's men, animatedly recap the day's events as they eat and drink. We quickly seize an available bench when some men leave their table. After seating ourselves, we look up to see three young men sitting on the opposite seat, they aren't knights, nor are they noble men, however they do bare a familiar appearance.

"Hello, we are Eric, Arne, and Lars, we're Norsemen here to sell furs, please do not be afraid of us." Eric says by way of introduction. Millie and I blush, while we inspect the fine grain table top, the waitress brings us soup, bread and wine. I look at Millie and she nods her approval for us to remain sitting with the Norsemen, even though she's my companion and a commoner, in my heart she's a peer and I treat her thusly.

"I know these men from the Chateau, it's alright." Millie places her hand on my arm, as she speaks. I smile nervously, I'm not so sure about them. I've been taught my whole life that men such as these are violent and dangerous, but on first appearances, they seem polite and honourable.

As we begin to eat our meal, I can see from a spill on the table, that the Vikings are drinking a clear liquid. I know it isn't water because it's too dangerous to drink from the city fonts, but it could have been. These men would have strong constitutions, I think to myself, I pluck up the courage to talk to them.

"What is that you're drinking?"

"We call this Black Death. Would you like to try some?" Arne offers me his cup. Curious, I take the vessel from the red headed man, sniff the cup and instantly know that it isn't water. Millie observes me with awe.

"I would never have risen to such a challenge." She says later. I cautiously place the cup to my lips, take a little sip and immediately splutter the liquid onto the table. The Vikings roar with laughter while I cough uncontrollably.

"Oh my Lord, that's fire water. I won't try anymore, thank you." I say when I've recovered a little.

"I say, well done for trying it fair maiden. Most maidens wouldn't even try." Lars says, regarding Millie with a wink.

"Now, you tell me." I say, my coughing subsides.

"Are you ladies from Paris, or are you visiting from somewhere else?" Eric asks, as we focus on our own food and drink.

"No, we're from Normandy."

"Yes, so are we."

"I thought you looked familiar."

"We were in here the other day with some of Guilliam's Knights."

"Oh." I'm keen to hear which knights that might have been and thankfully, Millie broaches the question.

"Do you know who they were? I work for the Duchess and I may know them." Arne, Eric, and Lars, study each other's faces while they attempt to remember the names of the knights they'd met only a few nights earlier.

"Well, one was Sir Miché, the champion of the jousting competition at the Duke's wedding, I know him for sure." Lars says. Suddenly, Arne speaks up after much contemplation.

"Leo, wasn't the other one Leo?"

"Yes, that'd be right." Millie confirms, I feel a flutter in my chest hearing his name said aloud.

"I forget the name of the other one though, he was much younger." Arne says as the other two men shake their heads, they can't remember Darri's name either.

"But being a littl'un like you, he couldn't hold his drink." The

Norsemen roar with laughter. When we finish eating, we excuse our-selves and leave the tavern.

"Say hello to Leo, Miché, and the other one, when you see them." Eric shouts.

"Yes, we will. Good luck with your sales, I hope everything goes as planned."

When Millie and I leave the tavern, Lars leans into his friends.

"I could go a piece of those two you know."

"Yes, but do you really want to end up with a lance through your gut? Guilliam's men will string you up if you touch a hair on their heads." Eric warns.

"Hmm." Lars weighs up the payoff of a brief encounter versus the retribution from the Duke's Court.

"Damn shame though." Nodding in agreement, they drain their cups and move their attention to the less noble women in the bar.

"What a small world it is." I say to Millie. We link arms on our way back to the abbey.

"What is?"

"Well, those Norsemen know Leo and Miché. We're far from home and the first people we meet know acquaintances of ours. Don't you think that's peculiar Millie?" "Well, I guess so. I only see people that I already know at the chateau, I never thought of it that way."

We walk arm in arm to our bedroom cell and chat about our day while we recline on our deer skins. When our chat fades, I wonder when I'll have the opportunity to see Leo again. In the darkened room, I strain to see the threads of the spider's web which is attached to the oak rafters above my head, the same web that was constructed the previous evening.

"Yes, you're right, I am here to work." I whisper to the spider.

"What?"

"Nothing, go to sleep."

"Goodnight Ailie."

"Goodnight Millie, sweat dreams."

Chapter 53 Allie

Shopped out, but fresh from a small afternoon siesta, we hit the night with Sara's lists concealed in her handbag. We venture into a few bars and listen to some funky music at each of them. The first bar houses a small jazz quartet, playing on a stage in the corner of the room, we feel sophisticated while we sip pastis and watch the crowd. However, my sophistication escapes as I point out a small man in the corner.

"Hey, check them out."

"They're a bit of a cliché, don't you think?"

"I reckon." Sara reviews the black skivvy beret wearing, Frenchman. He taps his hand on the table in time with the music, his beautiful girlfriend feigns indifference, smoking sexily on a Gitane.

"Oh my Goddess, the ultimate cliché" Sara laughs with a touch of envy.

We linger at the jazz bar for only one drink, we want a more vibrant venue and a younger crowd. We wander out onto the street and within a few minutes we hear a thumping beat emanating from a basement bar. We gingerly descend an old wooden stair case. At the bottom of the steps, we find the room hot and jumping. With drinks in hand, we glance at each other and smile.

"This is more like it." Sara yells as she bounces to the music.

"Mmm, nice." I check out the drummers in their baggy trousers, bare feet, and muscular chests peppered with droplets of sweat. We dance by ourselves to the hypnotic beats and then with various other dancers who drift on and off the floor.

Time seems to race ahead while we dance. We are starting to receive attention from the dancers, I'm wary. I fantasise about what it would be like to be with one guy in particular. A tall man with a cheeky grin, dreadlocks tied up in a high pony- tail, and wide, almond shaped eyes that are as deep as time.

During a break in the music, I fan myself and lightly pant to regain my breath while taking a few sips of a new drink. The dreadlocked man leans into me and starts to full-fill my dreams. That's what I call quick manifestation. Be sure of what you really want in the future, I tell myself.

"Would you like to come back to my apartment? It's just around the corner." He doesn't waste time, or mince words, as he croons into my ear in perfect English. I nearly faint with the anticipation of a hot and heavy night ahead. Instead of being sophisticated, I giggle nervously. I saw this man try the exact same move on another woman when we first arrived at the bar. This type of encounter is something that Sara and I have always joked about, but in reality, it scares me.

"I'm sorry, um, *desole. No Merci. Mon ami* over there."

I'm too tired to attempt a complete French sentence. Turns out, I'm not very sophisticated after all and I politely decline his offer. I make excuses to find Sara, who's dancing with another equally attractive man. When I find Sara, I see that my dreadlocked man has processed my rejection and effortlessly moved on, which I admire a lot.

Chapter 54 Mitch and Declan

Declan and Mitch are woozy from the Black Death, but they want to see more of Paris than the student bar has offered, they farewell the Scandinavians, climb the stairs, albeit a little shakily, to street level. The cool Parisian air smacks them in the face, offering respite from the stuffy bar. They return to the pizzeria for a few more slices, it's a long night, this time, they hungrily scoff two large pieces of pizza each.

"Righto, where to now Deco son?" Mitch is still chewing a bit of pizza.

"Let's take pot luck and find another neighbourhood gem. Let the summer wind guide us, like Sacha Distel, to find paradise up each and every by way." Declan half sings.

"Bloody hell, you are pissed aren't you?" Mitch shoots back. "And that's Frank Sinatra, you idiot." It doesn't take long before they hear an intoxicating drumming beat and they head in its direction.

Chapter 55 Allie

Wearily, we climb up to street level and are thankful for the cool Parisian night air.

"What do you want to do now, Sara my love?"

"I du'know, Allie my lovie."

"I need somewhere quiet and less noisy. I think I have a stitch from all that dancing and meeting exciting people." I grab my side as I walk and for some unknown reason, Sara pats me on the head. Our faces are red and shiny from dancing, all we want to do is to cool down before we find another venue.

"I've got this Friendy." Sara consults Jill's list while I retrieve my map of Paris from my handbag. I pinpoint approximately where we are.

"We're only a few blocks from an American student bar." Sara peers at the map.

"An American bar? I didn't come to Paris to hang out with Americans." I'm shocked that Sara has even suggested this type of bar.

"Jill said, the drinks are cheaper there and you can take a break from speaking French for a while. Come on, it could be fun. Jill said, she was pleasantly surprised. Anyway, there are people of other nationalities there as well."

"Okay, we'll go but just for a little while. I'm kind of tired." I look at my watch and see that it's 2:00am. I attempt to work out how long it's been since I've had a full night's sleep, though my tired and frazzled brain don't want to work it out.

We walk the few blocks to the student bar and have to descend some steep steps to enter, once we find the address that is. It's well hidden, especially since we are both so jet-lagged, and a little tipsy. As we cross the threshold of the bar, we can hear American pop music, I sigh. Sara who's in a more up-beat mood, scans the room and immediately sees four students gathered around the bar. Sara and I recognise that these students are not American, they have Scandinavian accents.

The students have seen us walk in and glance towards us. As we approach the bar, they ask us if we want a drink.

"Sure, are you the waiters. Shouldn't you be on the other side of the bar, or is this some kind of quirky French thing." Sara replies rapidly. I shrug my shoulders, because I'm tired, just so tired, yet I go along for the ride.

"No, we're not waiters, but we have something different that you can't buy over the bar. We thought you might like to try it with us." The boys have a clear bottle which bears a skull and cross bone label and I wonder what the hell we are in for.

"This is called Brennivín, or Black Death, it's actually Icelandic and it means burnt wine. When we are home, we drink this and eat fermented shark meat."

"Great."

"Yum, not." Sara and I have different levels of enthusiasm for this risky venture.

"Take a water glass from the counter." One of the students suggests while they walk over to a free table on the other side of the room. We conform to the request and take a glass from the counter. The student with the bottle pours a couple of centimetres of the clear liquid into everyone's glass. The boys down the liquid quickly, like shots, before we've figured out what's going on, we watch in awe, we are very tired. All of a sudden, Sara copies the students, experiencing first hand that the drink isn't poison, well not just yet anyway.

After this exhibition, the boys introduce themselves.

"I'm Arne." The most confident boy states.

"And this is Lars." Arne points to the guy sitting next to Sara.

"Eric and Bjorn." Arne gestures.

"Ooh, just like the guy from Abba." Sara squeals failing the sophistication test while I elbow her in embarrassment.

"Sorry about my friend, it's such a stereotype. You must get that all the time." I apologise, unknowingly missing my own irony.

"Well yes, I do as matter of fact, but only when I meet Australians. It seems that Abba, outside of Sweden, is most famous in Australia." Bjorn recalls.

"I'm Allie and my crass friend here is Sara."

Approaching the drink a little more cautiously than Sara, I sniff the contents and I can smell the alcohol, though I can't place the aroma. It smells a bit like dried parsley. I sip hesitantly and instantly my whole throat inflames, then goes numb. I'm not going to finish the shot, I pass it back to Lars who's eager to finish it. I excuse myself from the table and buy a soft drink from the bar, I need a bit of caffeine and a lot of sugar. Sara is not wasting time while I'm gone, by the time I've returned, she has swapped phone numbers with the Scandinavian students.

"Great, yes, we should catch up again while we're here in Paris." Sara gushes to the boys and we chat a while longer, but Sara can not keep drinking the Brennivín Death she calls it, in fact, I'm a bit woozy myself.

I scrounge for my map and realise that we've wandered far from Trudi's apartment, it's late at night or is it early in the morning? Anyway, it's too far and too late to retrace our steps. We say our goodbyes to the students and hail a taxi back to the apartment.

We just make it out of the taxi when Sara throws up into the gutter.

"Welcome to Paris, Sara. That's a beautiful way to end our first evening. Come on, I'll help you up the stairs." Further up the street, a large street cleaning truck is spraying water into the gutters and misses the opportunity to clean away the contents of Sara's boozy evening.

"Well, I've got a secret and now I'm not going to tell you." Sara slurs her words while brushing spit off her chin.

"Tell me in the morning then, but you'll probably forget anyway." I turn my face away from my friend's mouth to escape the stench of vomit and alcohol fumes.

"Okay, I'll tell you when I me-member."

We slowly begin the long climb up the stairs and enter the apartment after fumbling with the key in the lock for some minutes. I crash on the made up sofa bed and Sara curls up on the cool tiles in front of the shower cubicle.

"I fink Mitch is 'ere." Sara, barely audible, mumbles under her stinky breath, just before she passes out. I'm already comatose. Both of us sleep fully clothed.

Chapter 56 Leo

It's time for the knights to leave Paris and return to Falaise, they've managed to intimidate the King's men and most of the clergy. As they ride out through the outer city limits, a scuffle breaks out at the back of the infantry and word of the fight swiftly reaches Miché and Leo.

"Go and see what it's all about Leo. We can't be seen fighting amongst ourselves." Leo rides to the back of the group and witnesses two older men fighting each other on their horses. One of them is about to pull his lance out of its sheath when Leo arrives on the scene.

"What are you doing? Re-sheath your lance at once. You're one of Guilliam's men." "He owes me."

"Ride on, remember your vows of chivalry."

"I'll have you when we arrive at Falaise. I'll get my money." The disgruntled knight hisses at his adversary and rides on ahead of him while Leo gallops to the front of the group, he thinks that the matter has been settled for the time being.

"What was that all about?" Miché asks his brother.

"Tristian's losing at cards again I dare say."

"Roland needs to understand there's a time and place to assert himself. In front of the Parisians, is not that place. They should know fighting between ourselves makes us appear weak." Miché is fuming. This journey has been another successful mission, but he doesn't want news travelling back to Guilliam that he can't control his men.

"I'll speak with them when we return to Falaise." Leo attempts to placate his brother.

"We can't have our men turning on each other like that. They won't be reliable in battle. If they can't sort themselves out, they'll be expelled from the chateau."

Leo tries to keep an eye on Tristian and Roland for the remainder of the return journey. However, on the final night of the journey, frustration escalates as Leo witnesses Roland point his lance to Tristian's throat.

"Roland! Return your lance to your belt." Leo commands. The surrounding men become quiet and watch Leo try to pacify Roland.

"Roland stop!" But it's as if the knight has been locked in a trance and he's blocking out all surrounding noise. However, Roland is not going to take orders from Leo and he continues with vengeance. "Roland, I command thee, step away from Sir Tristian."

There is still no response from the agitated knight as the tip of his lance pierces the skin underneath Tristian's chin, blood begins to trickle down his neck onto his chain mail. Leo knows that the drawn blood is a show of defiance towards him, rather than retribution towards Tristian.

Before too much blood is shed, Leo swiftly removes his sword from its sheath and knocks the lance out of Roland's hand. Tristian is left bleeding while Leo pushes Roland to the ground and places the tip of his sword upon his heart. He will not stand for Roland's rebellion, instead he elects to uphold chivalry and honour, his duty to his brother as leader of the mission, and to Guilliam, ruler of his lands.

"You are under arrest, for the attack on one of the Duke's Knights and insubordination of your commanding officer." Leo affirms to Roland. Miché appears beside his brother with chains and they tie up the offending man and place him back onto his horse. Roland spits on the ground in front of Leo's feet.

"Well done Brother, you've certainly sent a message to the men that you are not to be messed with." Adrenalin surges through Leo and he rapidly experiences its affects as nausea strikes, he turns away from Tristian, the sight of his blood doesn't help matters. "Still not as brave as you think you are, hey brother?" Miché laughs when he sees his brother turning green, not for the first time.

At Falaise, a de-briefing meeting is called for Miché and Leo to report on their journey. Miché testifies to a successful expedition and informs Guilliam of his brother's brave encounter with Roland.

"Hmm, Roland shall be dealt with. It's not the first time he's stepped out of line. Well done both of you. I've had reports from Paris that you suitably unsettled the King's men, I don't think they'll be disturbing us for some time to come. By the way how is Tristian?"

"Well, he has lost some blood, but he'll recover, he's a resilient gentleman." Miché replies.

"Yes indeed. By the way, we'll have a visitor joining us soon." Guilliam leaves the room before the brothers can enquire about the new visitor.

"I wonder who that could be?" Leo wonders out loud.

"No idea little brother. Now I'm off to find that card game. Want to join me?"

"Um. No, I think I'll pass this one and keep my money for a change."

"You are learning little brother, you are learning."

Chapter 56 Leon, Mitch and Declan

Declan and Mitch don't linger at the African drum bar for very long, Declan is somewhat intimidated by the stunning men, and for that matter, the sleek girls are way out of his league. Mitch laughs at his unease and lack of dancing prowess. They head out again and this time, find themselves at a Jazz club. This scene is more Declan's tempo, even if he doesn't quite understand the music. Although, he identifies with the beatnik man in the corner, a beautiful woman by his side.

They stay for a couple of drinks, then stumble up the stairs, into the dawn light. By a small miracle, they find their way back to the hotel, just as Leon's tour group is ready to board the coach, to drive them to the train station. Leon checks off his students from his clip board, then ensures their luggage is properly stowed in the bottom of the bus. The students board silently, wiping sleep from their eyes. It had been a big first day in Europe, for everyone.

"Well, look at what the cat dragged in." Leon checks his watch as Declan and Mitch huff and puff up the slight incline towards the hotel. With a small wave, they head straight into the hotel and crash onto their beds where they sleep for most of the day. The coach pulls away from the curb and travels towards the train station.

Phase 2: Chapter 57 Ailie

Millie and I reside in the abbey for another week. After I return to Breteuil, Millie travels on with the driver to Falaise. I'm sad to see her go, we've fast become devoted friends. I didn't have a close friend growing up, probably because I was a bit odd. Millie tolerates my love of spiders, she looks past my quirky side and accepts me for who I am. I feel blessed to have found her.

"I shall miss you terribly." I confide to Millie.

"Yes, I'm sorry, I have to return to the Duchess, but do write to me soon and let me know what happens with your commissions from the Monastery, I want to hear all about it."

"Yes, of course I will." Millie's driver pulls away from the side of the road and begins their long journey to Falaise.

"Say hello to Leo." I whisper to the moving vehicle.

When I return to the workshop, Ottho calls me in for a meeting and while I cross the workroom floor, I notice Sarra isn't at her loom.

"So Ailie, how did you go with the bishops in Paris?"

"It was hard to organise a time for our meetings at first, but they went very well, thank you Ottho. We've negotiated an order for the new cathedral and I'll give the list of requirements and initial sketches to Marc, to help him manage the project."

"Brilliant, well done young lady, I definitely want you to assist on his team. I knew from the moment you stepped into the workshop, as a child, you'd be an asset to this workshop one day and here we are, already."

My nobility and education has provided me with liaison and negotiation skills that the other weavers don't possess. I also have experience and confidence discussing a wide range of topics, with people from all walks of life, which helps when I speak to royalty, clergy, merchants and peasants alike.

"By the way Ottho, where is Sarra?"

"She has left the workshop, taken up with a farmer and they're to be married. It's a shame to waste all of those years perfecting her skills, but what can I say, her temper impacted those around her. It's for the best. You weren't the only one she bullied, you know. If she hadn't left, I would have asked her to leave."

"Really? Wow! I didn't know any of that. It was a quick decision to leave with another, even for Sarra."

"I guess she's jumping straight back onto the horse."

"Well good for her, I hope she's a bit happier now that she's found someone."

"I don't know if that young lady will ever be happy, do you?"

"No, I suppose not."

"You know, it's funny, but Bertie has emerged from his shell now that Sarra isn't working here anymore."

"Really?" I'm not surprised at all.

"Right, back to business. Has Florrie laundered your clothes since your return?" Ottho enquires.

"I'm not sure, why do you ask, do I stink?" I want to sniff my clothes right away, I think better of it.

"Well, we've had a request from Falaise for your return to the Chateau, as soon as possible."

"Oh my goodness, my feet have barely returned to Breteuil soil and now the Duchess wants me back."

"Well no, it's not the Duchess, it's the Duke. He wants some embroidery panels made of his family, and Knights of the Inner Circle. They both loved the wedding tapestry so much that they want more panels to hang in the chateau."

"Oh my goodness, it sounds like a big job."

"You can do it, I know you can." Ottho assures me.

"When do they require me?"

"You'll leave as soon as the driver arrives for you, in a day or two."

I wonder when I'll return to my own loom in the workshop, Ottho reads my thoughts.

"There'll be plenty of time for you to continue work on your loom when you return."

"Ha..Am I that obvious?" I smile weakly because I don't think that I'll be returning anytime soon. Walking back through the workroom, I notice Bertram at his sister's old loom, he wears a beautiful smile and appears to genuinely enjoy his work. I'm glad that Bertie is content making beautiful tapestries without his bossy sister around. Silently, I gently pat him on the back as I pass by.

When I arrive at Falaise, a squire accompanies me with my luggage, to my regular chamber and as I settle in, Millie bounds into my room.

"Hello friend." Millie hugs and welcomes me back to the chateau.

"Hello friend." I grin as I embrace her.

"How was your journey?"

"It was most pleasant, thank you."

"I think the Duke will see you tomorrow, but the Duchess wants to see you tonight." "Oh yes, I can't wait to see her. Baby Robert must've grown since I've been gone." "Yes, he's growing well and smiling. His wet nurse is kept very busy."

"I'm looking forward to cuddling the baby."

"There's another person who's keen to see you as well."

"Oh, and who might that be?" I laugh nervously because I have an inkling.

"Leo of course. He asked after you the day I returned from Paris." I don't know what to say. The colour of my face has exposed my feelings as I inspect my dress to avoid direct eye contact with Millie.

"I think he has feelings for you Ailie. You know, I can arrange a meeting for you after you've seen the Duke tomorrow, if you like?"

"No! What? Whoa." It's happening all too quickly for me to process. "Give me some time to settle in and then we'll see about a meeting with Leo." Millie laughs at me. She's amused to see me squirm, I don't want to be rushed though.

Millie divulges gossip from the Chateau and I'm glad of the diversion.

"You know, Sir Roland attacked Sir Tristian on their return from their mission in Paris and now he's locked up in the dungeon with the old Bishop of Rouen and common criminals. And, you'll never guess who came to Tristian's rescue?"

"Who was it?"

"Leo." At the sound of his name, I blush again. "You really like him don't you?"

"I don't know what it is. We've only really met once, or twice, but our paths seem to cross inexplicably. There's something about him that I can't put my finger on."

"You're thinking way too much about it. How do you feel about him?" My flushed face expresses it all.

The meeting with the Duke is held in the grand hall by the fire and I wear one of my best dresses for the occasion. As I wait for him to arrive, I pick at my fingernails nervously. One by one, I begin tearing at each of my nails, starting with my thumb with the intention of progressing to my pinkie on my left hand. When I've ripped the extended nail from my middle finger, the Duke appears by my side.

"Good morning, Ailie."

"Good morning, Your Grace." I quickly stand and curtsy, hiding my ragged fingernails behind my back.

"This won't take long. I've a meeting with the Bishop."

"I want you to make a tryptic of panels depicting myself, my wife and son, my step-brother Odo, and the Knights of the Inner Circle. I'll give you access to sketch everyone and we can make a time later when I'll sit for you."

"Yes, of course Your Grace." I stammer. "It shouldn't take me long to complete a quick sketch."

"Good, right, did I say to sketch Sir Miché and Sir Leo, my lead knights as well." "Yes, Your Grace. I'll make the necessary arrangements. I hope I'll do your family justice, Sir." I begin to feel a little more confident while the Duke strokes his moustache in contemplation.

"If your other work is anything to go by, you'll do a fine job." For a man with such a vicious reputation, he can be such a nice man. We say our goodbyes and he leaves for his meeting with Odo. Then it suddenly hits me, oh my goodness, I'm going to have to sketch Leo. That's going to be awkward, but I'm also excited by the prospect.

Chapter 58 Allie

We sleep in for most of the morning and gently snore on the sofa bed as Trudi eats her breakfast, standing at the dormer window. After her breakfast, she leaves for work without interrupting our sleep. Sara and I stir around lunch time which is just as well, because Trudi's kitchen is cramped enough without the bed fully extended. With the bedding tucked away, we recline on the sofa, sipping our bowls of coffee, we are quiet and pensive. Suddenly, a shiver runs down the back of my head and shoulders, I'm roused into action.

"Right, I'll shower first and we can get on with the day." Taking a shower in the kitchen is awkward to say the least, but we manage without too much embarrassment.

For privacy sake, Sara withdraws into Trudi's bedroom to peruse her photo albums and as she flips through the photographs, Sara sees the usual fare of family photos, pets, travel and nights out. As she progresses further into the album, she recognises a familiar face which is Mum's. Sara's excited to see someone that she recognises, yet so far away from home, out of familial context. The first photograph shows Mum in a café eating escargot, appearing happy and at ease. I wonder if Allie has seen these photos? Sara thinks to herself and as she scans the pages, the photographs become increasingly intimate as if there's more to the relationship than just old friends catching up.

"I bet Allie hasn't seen these photos." Sara says to herself, inspecting a photo of Trudi kissing Mum in a passionate embrace. Sara hears the water has stopped running in the shower and quickly snaps the album shut, she jams it back into the bookshelf.

"Your turn Sara!" I call from the kitchen.

"Yep... sure, coming."

Trudi arrives home for lunch, just as I'm finally ready. Trudi and I leave Sara to shower while we head to a local cafe to eat, the kitchen is too crowded. While we eat our lunch, we make plans to visit Versailles.

"Its not just the palace you know. There are restaurants, the Court-yard of Fragrance, there are a couple of street markets and there are friends to visit, and of course we will go to the chateau as well. The queues shouldn't be too long at this time of year, but who knows?"

"It all sounds great. I can't wait to see more of the country side. Also, do you think Sara was behaving normally before we left for lunch?"

"I don't really know Allie. She was in the shower. I haven't studied her in the shower before. Anyway what's normal for me, may not be normal for her. It's all relative *n'est pas*?"

"Must be an intuitive thing. We have a funny connection."

"You certainly do. You both seem very different, but I guess that makes a connection closer. Like opposite poles of a magnet, no?"

But before an existential conversation develops, Sara walks into the cafe.

"Allie, there's this beautiful restaurant where they do the best onion soup." Trudi continues as Sara joins us after her longish shower, she needed time to fully awaken. She half listens to our plans, but gives us funny looks as she eats her Croque Monsieur.

"You know Allie, I don't think that I'll go to the country with you this weekend. I think I'll stay in Paris and see what happens."

"Are you sure Sara? Paris is a big place and you could feel quite alone here."

"Yes, I'm sure. You two go to Versailles for the weekend and catch up properly. I'll stay here and do a bit of sightseeing. I won't be lonely." Sara tests the waters to see how her suggestion is received.

"Well, I don't know Sara, it sounds great to have the freedom to explore on your own, but once you're doing it, it can be a different story."

"You know, I'll love it and hopefully, I won't be alone for too long." Sara reassures me with a cheeky smile.

"Yes, I know you'll love it, but be careful. You don't want to catch anything."

"Perhaps she does want to catch a tall dark stranger." Trudi jumps in.

"Hmm, that'd be nice." Sara laughs, hoping it to be true. "By the way Trudi, where do you work?"

"Oh, I work for the City of Paris, in the Department of Diversity."

"What's that?" Sara has sobered.

"Well, we make sure that everyone has equity in their dealings with the City, for example, people from different cultural backgrounds, I don't like the word race, it's a colonial construct after all. We make sure people with special needs are looked after and we advocate for the rights of people with gender and sexual discrimination issues against the City.

"Oh, that must be very interesting." Sara says, then gives me a sideways glance as she's seen an outrageously dressed person enter the cafe. It's the emerald green hat with a wild plume secured with a sunflower flailing from the purple hat band that has her tipping over the edge.

Sara and I giggle nervously, which quickly turns into a belly hurting laugh. Later on, we can't remember why we're laughing, I don't think it's even that funny.

"Is something funny about my job." Trudi asks, a little perturbed.

"No, not at all." I say. "I think we're just exhausted and we're finding everything funny. I'm so sorry. We don't mean to offend you. Your work sounds amazing and I wish we had more departments like that back at home."

"It's okay, I remember when I flew to Australia I was jet lagged for a solid week."

Sara wipes her eyes with the napkin from her lap as she considers our evening.

"So, where are we off to tonight then?"

"Perhaps you two are off to go fishing." Trudi suggests, we begin to laugh cry again. Trudi sighs as she sips her coffee.

Later that night Sara, Trudi and I head out to one of Trudi's regular haunts where we meet some of her friends. Her friends are nice, but they don't speak much English, conversations are strained and stilted between English and our very basic French. After a while, Trudi's friends suspend their polite English and reengage their fast Parisian tongues. Which is fair enough, I can't match their conversations in French, I shouldn't expect them to speak fluent English all night. Trudi has become ensconced with her friend's conversation, Sara and I make our excuses to look further afield.

As we walk around the quarter, Sara literally stumbles across the American student bar as there is a loose pavement stone just in front of the stair case. If she hadn't caught hold of the railing, she would have dived head first into the bar, which would have been quite an entrance, even for her.

"How did we avoid that loose stone last night?" Sara shakes her head and adjusts her dress at the same time.

"I don't know. I don't remember it either."

After righting herself, Sara and I descend the stairs in a more demure fashion and head for a small table in the middle of the room. I can't believe we are back here again and I'm peeved, there are so many more places where we could have a more authentic French experience. But I put up with it for a while, at least, knowing that I'll be exploring the countryside on the weekend and getting to know a little bit more of France.

"Why did you want to come here again?" I keep my voice light and cheerful.

"I like it here, don't you? Look at all the hot guys here. You have to admit that the odds of picking up a hot rich American boy is pretty good here."

"Well yes, that's true, but we didn't come to Paris to meet American boys, well I certainly didn't anyway." The lightness is seeping out of my voice.

"Perhaps, a cute girl then? What do you want to drink? I'm going to the bar."

"What do you mean by that?" While Sara's heads to the bar, I observe the room and fiddle with the ashtray. Sara turns around and gestures, raising her clenched hand. I take her act as, what do you want to drink?

"*Un vin rouge!*" I yell above the crowd as Sara is halfway towards the bar.

Sara returns to the table with two glasses of white wine and I laugh to myself, she obviously hadn't heard my request.

"You'll never guess what happened to me at the bar. See that guy over there?" I look in a random direction towards the bar and focus on a tall boy with spiky blonde hair and large green shoes. "No, it isn't the joker with the red pants and braces." To his right, is another tall young man wearing jeans and a pale blue shirt with the sleeves rolled to just below his elbows, brown hair with a side parting, a strong jaw line and when he turns around to wave at us, I can see the attraction straight away. He has amazing brown eyes with long, cow like eyelashes.

"Wow, okay, well done. What's the story?" Before I can grill Sara for the whole story, the tall American moseyes towards us.

"Just act cool and follow my lead." Sara pleads.

"Sure." But I'm not sure. We smile awkwardly at each other until the stranger appears at the table. "What do you mean? I would prefer a cute girl."

"Allie, this is Lincoln." Sara introduces the now, not completely total stranger. "Lincoln, this is Allie." Lincoln receives my hand in his large outstretched palm, giving it a fairly firm handshake, which I approve of straight away. Once he sits down, at Sara's insistence, Lincoln and Sara become enraptured in each other and they occasionally remember to include me in the conversation, but it becomes rapidly apparent this is a two people party and I'm not one of those two people. Perhaps how she felt, years ago, when we first met Mitch. I make my excuses, against Sara's feeble pleas for me to stay, but Sara is pleased that I depart so easily.

I leave the bar relieved, though a little dejected, it only took ten minutes for my companionship to be demoted for the evening, I slowly return to the bar where Trudi has been entrenched for the evening. I listen to Trudi's friends who are still engrossed in conversation, but I'm not sure what all the angst and gesturing is about. To amuse myself, I begin to play a game, to guess what they are saying and when I understand sections of the conversation, I feel a wave of satisfaction and award myself points, sad but true. I don't try to involve myself in the discussions as I'm happy to sit, listen and sip my wine. By the end of the night, I've amassed twenty house points and realise they're trying to figure out the best place to buy apples. Apparently, Normandy has the best apples for ale pomme, but the best eating varieties come from Pays de Loire. The weekly street market at Rue Montorgueil is good because of the adjacent cafes, chocolatiers and patisseries. I'm learning a lot about French apples and my anger towards Sara has waned somewhat with the soothing talk of French food.

When I return to the apartment, I receive a text from Sara, she is staying at The Ritz with Lincoln and not to worry about her. Worry about her? What a nerve. I've be sleeping on the uncomfortable sofa bed, in a tiny kitchen, although I now have extra room thanks to her evacuation, and Sara, will be sprawled out on a king size bed, no doubt thanks to Lincoln's daddy's Amex card. Well, I am a little bit worried about her, but bloody hell! I can feel my blood pressure rise again. As I put my phone back on the floor, I think about Sara spending the night at The Ritz and come to the conclusion, she'll be insufferable. I won't hear the end of it. Luxury this, room service that, four poster bed and gymnastics, a gold medal, and something about the Olympics, sore thighs.

At checkout time, in the cold light of day, Sara leaves the hotel alone because she can't see a future with Lincoln. Truth of the matter is, when he opens his mouth, there isn't much of interest springing forth. Not that she's been offered a second night, she thinks it's for the best that it's just this one night, she'll be able to move on. As she floats from the Ritz foyer, her graceful glide ends abruptly as she collides into Mitch's broad chest with a thump.

"Whoa there, oh crikey, Sara! What are you doing here?" Mitch demands, when he finally recognises her.

"I could say the same thing about you. Hi." Sara quickly adjusts the dress she'd worn the night before and tries not to stumble on her high heels.

"Hello, Declan." Before Declan can respond, Mitch interjects.

"We didn't know you were over here. What a head spin."

It feels natural for them to talk to each other, even if the surroundings are a little odd for them as a group.

"When you say we, who do you mean exactly?" Mitch smiles looking up toward the rooms.

"Oh no, nothing like that." Sara lies. "Allie's here in Paris with me and we're staying in the 16th."

"Ooo la la."

"Yeah." Declan agrees sagely, but not fully understanding why.

"What are you doing here boys?"

"We've crashed my housemates work trip." Mitch explains. "He's currently in Spain so we'll catch up with him later. Anyway, we just thought we'd come and have a look at the foyer to say we've been to The Ritz, although, I think I stayed here with my Dad when I was a kid. Have you had breakfast? We're just on our way to find somewhere to eat. Do you fancy coming with us?" Mitch suggests. Sara suddenly realises she is actually starving, despite the large midnight feast from room service the previous night, but she figures that she's hungry again.

"I'm starving."

They walk at a brisk pace towards a nearby cafe and the trio chat easily along the way. They talk about the last couple of days that they've spent in Paris.

"You know, it's funny, but we were in a bar and some Scandinavian students said they'd met you." Sara recalls.

"Yeah, we did, how funny." Mitch confirms.

"Such a small world." Declan muses.

"So how is Allie?" Mitch enquires as they walk into a cafe.

"She's fine, she's spending a lot of time with the lady that we're staying with. I think Trudy's a lesbian who's having an affair with Allie's Mum, but Allie doesn't know, so don't say anything to her. I don't know how she is today because I was out since last night and she left me at the American bar." Sara blurts out.

Sara suddenly realises that she doesn't know if I've returned to the flat, or where I am, she assumes that I have made my way back to Trudi's. A niggle of guilt crosses Sara's mind, but when she remembers the night of the music festival, she doesn't feel any guilt at all. But she had left her friend alone for a guy, the guilt does start to seep in.

"Wow, this is amazing." Mitch finally sighs.

"Yeah, I know." Sara replies, not really knowing what he means, but she knows the two days in Paris have been pretty amazing, in theory, she agrees.

"Yeah, now Allie can hook up with Leon." Declan says unexpectedly.

"What the?" Sara's flabbergasted. There are so many questions. For starters, who is Leon? Has Allie even met him? If he's anything like Declan, she isn't entirely sure that I'll be interested.

Mitch reins in the conversation and attempts to fill in some of the gaps in Sara's understanding as to whom Leon is. Mitch tells her about his infatuation, even though he's only seen me for a split second in their passageway at home, then for a split second the other morning at breakfast in Paris. So in total, he's seen me for a maximum of two split seconds, on two sides of the world. Does a split second work in the same way as a split atom? It hasn't caused a nuclear reaction, but a reaction none the less.

"Wow, that's amazing and a bit bizarre." Sara sighs, she thinks Mitch's story sounds romantic, she's a little envious, despite the fact that she's just had a somewhat romantic night herself. To Sara, more is more.

"Why hasn't he called her then?" Sara asks Mitch.

"Well funny you say that, he tried the other morning, but he got her voicemail."

"Oh, that would be because her old phone is at home in Australia. She bought a new one here at the airport. Cost an arm and a leg, but at least we can stay in contact with each other."

"Oh, that explains a lot. Do you want to eat that extra toast?" Mitch is still hungry, the cafe breakfasts in France are not as ample as he's used to.

"No help yourself."

As they finish their breakfast, she recalls the evening in her head again and fully realises that she doesn't know what has happened to me.

"Sorry guys, it was great catching up with you both, but I have to go." Sara could have just called me, but instead she wipes her mouth with her napkin and jumps out of her seat. She also remembers that she hasn't showered and begins to feel grotty and uncomfortable as well, it's time to leave. "Bye."

She waves from outside of the window and the boys return her farewell. Mitch and Declan sit silently with their thoughts for a while, and as if by magic, their feelings synchronise. "Shit! We forgot to get Allie's new phone number for Leon. Damn. It would have been nice to hook up with the girls while we're here." Mitch muses.

"Hmm." Declan thinks pensively, he knows that Leon is going to be annoyed with him for not securing my phone number. Instead, he says, "Do you think Sara paid, for her share of the bill, when she left the cafe?"

"Declan, you can be a dick." Mitch laughs.

When Sara arrives at Trudi's flat, there's a note on the door, saying we're out shopping and will return later. Sara sighs, retraces her steps down the four flights of stairs to collect the spare key from the concierge, who lives in the ground floor flat. An exercise we could have completed on our first day apparently, however we didn't know about concierges in apartment buildings. Sara speaks to the concierge in part sign language, part Frenglish.

"*Le key por apartment neuf.*" She says too loudly while she counts nine of her fingers, just in case the concierge is still in kindergarten.

"*Oui, bien sur, la cle por appartement neuf. Son appartement Trudi, oui?*" The concierge shows that he fully understands her, by giving her the key.

That evening over dinner, Sara regales me with the details of her evening at The Ritz and how she had literally bumped into Mitch and Declan.

"Do you know that you have a secret admirer and he's in Europe, as we speak." Sara finally reveals the headline at the end of her news report.

"Well, who could that be, apart from Mitch and Declan? I don't think it's one of them, because they've had access to my number for a long time now, besides we are just good friends. No, I can't think who it could be at all." Sara then explains, albeit disjointedly, who my secret admirer is.

"Well, you know Declan?"

"Yes of course, I know who Declan is. I just said his name didn't I?" I respond with some confusion and hope it isn't him.

"It's not him, but it is his brother, Leon."

"But I've never met his brother." I say. I scratch my head then chew the nail off my left thumb.

Sara thinks of another way to describe him when she hasn't met him either, then she remembers something important.

"Leon's Mitch's roommate." Sara relays this vital piece of information and I instantly know who he is. As the revelation hits me, clarity is removed from Sara's eyes.

"I'm glad you know who I'm talking about, because I don't." Sara laughs.

"I don't think I ever told you this, but it was on the final night of the music festival when we met Mitch. The following morning he was there in the passageway, staring at me." I start to wander in my thoughts and forgot to verbalise them for Sara.

"How exciting, but who ever thought that Declan's brother would be a mystery man?" Sara questions the air as she turns around to find another bottle of red wine on the shelf, she refills our glasses. She doesn't have to leave her seat, the kitchen is that small.

"Did you give the boys our numbers so they can catch up with us? It'd be great to see Mitch and Declan." I think aloud, although I really want to meet Leon now.

"Bugger, I was in such a hurry to leave, I forgot to give them our numbers." Sara confesses.

"Yeah, we could have rung them, but I don't remember Mitch's number. What with speed dialling and all, I don't know anybody's number anymore." I'm annoyed at myself.

"Oh well, we might bump into them again, it's not like Paris is a big, bustling city with millions of people, or anything." Sara laughs.

"Yeah, that's likely." I think about Leon and wonder if what Mitch had said is true, or is it just one of his cruel wind ups.

The following day, Trudi and I catch the train to Versailles, leaving

288 – AMANDA PANAZZOLO

Sara to fend for herself in Paris. However, Sara is suddenly disappointed and in a conundrum that she isn't coming with us, at the same time she'll be bored without the bright lights of Paris.

"You can still come with us, if you want to." I offer again.

"No, you two run along and have a good time I'll be fine." Sara doesn't sound a hundred percent convincing. Trudi doesn't mind one way or the other, if Sara comes with us or not, but she is keen to show me around, just as she'd done with Mum many years ago.

Sara's determined to be brave and have a good time in Paris. She commences her independent journey on familiar soil, ordering a *cafe au lait et une croissant* from the café we regularly frequent along Rue de Passay. Feeling more confident after her breakfast, she ventures onto the Metro and rides a train to Montmartre where she intends to climb the famous steps, alongside the funicular, and soak in the Parisian skyline from a different perspective. At the top of the steps, a little out of breath, she wanders over to the imposing Sacre Coure. Tourists speckle the steps, African vendors try to sell her copies of designer handbags, but Sara can never understand why anybody would want a designer copy of anything. At the heart of it, you know it's a fake and not the real thing.

"What's the point?" She finds herself saying out loud. How could she go back to Australia, hold her head high and walk past Ms Coiffed with an imitation designer handbag, she'd pick out a fake bag from fifty metres away.

The artist's square precinct is filled with tourists and souvenir shops which seem to be a little too contrived, even for Sara, who normally loves to shop. She scans her map and decides to make her way to Pere Lachaise, to see Jim Morrison's grave. As she turns around and begins her decent down the staircase, she recognises two familiar silhouettes in the near distance. Sara breaks into a trot, to catch up with them, when she's within a dignified yelling distance, she shouts out.

"Mitch, Declan, whoa, wait! Hello!" When she reaches the boys, Mitch scoops her up in a bear hug and swings her around in a wide circle, nearly missing some other tourists.

"Hello." Declan is less demonstrative. After Mitch replaces Sara onto terra firma she straightens herself up and strains to suppress a giggle.

Sara's out of breath, due to a number of factors, running in her small heals, being lifted into the air and swung around by a handsome man, being the main one.

"Fancy meeting you two again, in this big city, especially considering the millions of people walking around?" She beams, thinking about her recent discussion with me. I won't believe her, she thought.

"Where are you two strapping lads off to today?"

"We've just had lunch and now we're heading to Pere Lachaise." Mitch offers before Declan can collect his thoughts.

"Oh my God. No way! I was going there as well, do you mind if I join you? I'm a massive Doors fan and my dad has all of their albums." Sara continues to tell them about the Jim Morrison grave site.

"Yeah, it can be a little weird. I've been before, but Declan wants to see it for himself. It's a bit sad really, for many reasons, but there are usually some pretty interesting people sitting in vigil. We'll just have to wait and see who's there today."

Mitch wants to prepare Declan for what he might encounter at the grave site. From the metro station, the trio walk along the streets singing their favourite Doors songs in various keys and harmonies.

When the singing fades, they hum quietly to themselves.

"Where's Allie today?" Mitch asks.

"She's in Versailles for the weekend, with Trudi."

"Well, well. Why didn't you go as well? I'm glad that you didn't by the way."

"I thought it would be more fun here and turns out, I was right." Sara beams. She knew this moment would come and she can feel her connection with Mitch blossoming into something, finally.

He scoops Sara up for a second time and spins her around, it's lucky she hasn't just eaten because it would have ended up all over Declan with the amount of whirling going on.

"It looks like we're going to be hanging out for the weekend then." Mitch informs them. "That's if you're not doing anything else." Sara smiles coyly, while Declan appears pale, he instantly agrees, although he figures he's now the third wheel. Sara is more than excited. She's seriously had her eye on Mitch since forever, she's determined to finish what I hadn't wanted to.

"Yeah!!! Oh, did I actually say it like that?" Sarah grimaces. Mitch likes Sara's enthusiasm, but Declan grimaces and punches Mitch on the shoulder, a little too roughly.

"I kind of wish we hadn't gone to Morrison's grave though. It's sad isn't it? Especially that one guy, he was so wasted. I can't believe he fell and hit his head on another headstone. It was too real seeing all that blood. I hope he's okay." Declan recalls as they leave the cemetery.

"I think that's why that first aid guy was hovering about. It must happen a bit." Mitch says.

"Yes, it's pretty sad, but I can't wait to see the photo of you two, wearing my lipstick, at Noel Cowards tomb." Sara laughs to lighten the mood. Declan can be such a downer, she thinks. At the end of a fun day, arrangements are made to meet up for Sunday lunch.

"Why don't we make our way down to Monaco for a few days." Mitch suggests during the picnic in the Bois de Boulogne.

"That sounds amazing, I'd love to go."

Sara is more than eager for an adventure and the change to her solitary plans, though she's worried about my reaction. I'm due back from Versailles tonight, she'll approach the subject then. Mitch has already checked the train timetables for services heading south and he thinks the best, and cheapest bet, is to stay in Antibes as a base, then catch the local train to Monaco for entertainment.

Trudi and I appear relaxed after our weekend in the country and we're in a mellow mood after removing ourselves from the hustle and bustle of city life. Sara makes us a pot of French Earl Grey tea, puts out the remaining brioche, olives and cheese from the picnic, and listens intently to us relive the past two days of train rides, palaces, fountains, gardens, hall of mirrors, lunches, dinners, walks in the misty countryside, superb wine and good friends. Then she begins to worry about how to relay her weekend to me. She starts with a classic cliché.

"You'll never guess who I bumped into this weekend?"

I'm relieved that Sara's leaving in the morning, I've really enjoyed getting to know Trudi better and I'm not sure that would've happened if Sara was around. I also relish the idea of discovering my own version of Paris for that matter and working on knowing myself better as well. It's an opportunity to think about my own secrets and dreams. I realise I can't rely on others to be there for me, I have to show up for myself.

As Trudi and Sara discuss the pros and cons of travelling to the South of France, I begin to re-write my list of all the things that I want to do whilst I'm here. But my list starts to reach outside of the city limits, my thoughts turn quite a bit further afield. The night wears on, fatigue envelops me, but my mind races with possibilities. Suddenly, I become impatient with Sara because she still has to sort out her luggage for the next day. She plans to leave early in the morning, but I have to wait for her to finish her conversation with Trudi before that can begin. To get the ball rolling, I drop some not so subtle hints.

"Wow, I'm really tired guys." I yawn and stretch my arms above my head, but they don't get it. "What time does your train leave tomorrow morning Sara?"

"Umm, early'ish I guess." Sara actually responds, but then reengages Trudy. "How many pairs of shoes do you think I'll need Trudi." Frustrated, I start to brush my teeth at the sink and thankfully Trudi understands the message straight away. She promptly wishes us *adieu*, leaving Sara to discuss her wardrobe options for the casino, with no one in particular.

I find the bed roomier in the morning and I luxuriate in the wider space, fully extending my legs, something that I haven't been able to do during the night. Before I make coffee and stow away the bed, Trudi comes into the kitchen to prepare for work.

"So what are your plans for today?" Trudi lathers her hair in the kitchen shower.

"Where do I start? I begin to list four, or five, major museums I want to check out, as I pack away the sofa.

"Whoa there!" Trudi exclaims, wiping soap from her forehead. "That's more than enough museums to keep you going for a week. The Louvre will take at least one day. Don't forget, you won't just walk straight in, there are long queues."

"Oh really, okay, I'd better rethink my plans especially if I want to travel to Spain."

"What is it about Spain that's so appealing, there is so much to see here in France that you...." And she stops mid thought, remembering Sara's conversation from the other night. "Oh, I see there's someone you might see in Spain. But Spain's a big country, no? How will you know where to look?" My idea suddenly seems foolish, even to me but I have to have my own adventure. It's more about the journey and I don't really expect to spot my secret admirer on board a small provincial Spanish train.

The queue for the Louvre dissolves in about half an hour, even though I joined it quite early in the day. As I stand in line, I read about a short cut entry at the Porte des Lions, but I'm already at the front of this line, I stay where I am. I spend most of the day wandering through the halls and I'm surprised, not only by all of the art works, but how hot it is. Usually museums and galleries are havens from the heat, but despite the pleasant day outside, it's very warm inside. Luckily, I'd listened to Trudi who forewarned me, I've worn layers to peel off and even though I'm physically comfortable, it's hard for me to concentrate on the art. I am contemplating my impending journey to Spain.

Strolling around the galleries feels grown up, to begin with, but while I amble around Musee D'Orsay, pangs of loneliness strike and I suddenly have the urge to ring Freyja to discuss the paintings and speak to a familiar voice. After a few minutes of umming and arring, I decide that it's too expensive to phone Australia and I really have no idea of the time back at home either. Instead, I buy some postcards of my favourite paintings from the gift shop and sit in the café. Sipping my coffee, I write to Freyja, attempting to convey in the small space, how I felt wandering around the converted train station. However, my mind draws a blank, surrounded by magnificent examples of creative proficiency, I pen, *"Having a great time, wish you were here, Love Allie."*

I scribble over my banal note and shove the remaining cards into my handbag.

Chapter 59 Leo

Leo is at the breakfast table as Odo approaches him with a quizzical look on his face.

"Leo, oh dear, I wanted to talk to you, but I've forgotten. What was I going to say? Give me a moment." Odo scans the room, trying to remember why he'd come to see Leo, when he spots the wedding tapestry, he remembers why he is here. "That's it, got it. You'll need to make a time to meet with the young weaver woman so that she can sketch you for Guilliam's project."

"Oh." Leo manages to say. His mind is blank as well, but for a different reason, he can't think straight. "Right, will do." Leo responds as Odo walks away. Miché appears and sits down to eat with his brother. With his mouth full of bread, Miché asks Leo a question.

"Hey, has Odo said anything to you about Ailie sketching us for a project for the Duke?"

"Yes, he was just here, but I don't have any details. I guess we'll just have to wait and see."

As he finishes his breakfast, Leo decides to take his horse for a ride into the forest, he needs some time alone to think, to breathe fresh air, and to reconnect with nature. A squire has saddled Leo's horse and he rides out of the castle walls, down the main road before he reaches the dense forest where he directs his horse onto a smaller track that winds through tall trees. The sun glimmers through the branches, creating beautiful patterns on the ground, birds fly from branch to branch as they sing to each other. Butterflies, dragonflies, and bees buzz and flutter in the lower spaces around the bushes, while his horse's hooves disturb the earth, releasing its scent for Leo to inhale. There is joy in his surroundings and the love in his heart reaches all the way back to the chateau.

He rides through the forest until he arrives at a clearing where the grass is lush and verdant. Across the meadow is a meandering river with crystal clear water. He can see smooth, round pebbles at the bottom of the water. Leo dismounts his horse and disrobes. He hasn't bathed for a while and now seems as good a time as any to wash away the daily grime. He cautiously steps into the chilly water and winces at its iciness. Bravely, he continues to walk out deeper and deeper until the water is deep enough to immerse his body fully and with a sharp gasp, he plunges in, allowing the chilly water to envelope him. A thousand tiny knives prick his skin all at once, but after a few minutes Leo has adjusted to the difference in body temperature, he relaxes. He tilts his head back to let the water wash over his face and hair.

Leo reposes here for some time before he notices that he's starting to feel cold, he climbs out of the water and onto the river bank to fetch his clothes, but they've vanished. He thoroughly searches the vicinity, they are nowhere to be seen. A vagabond must have stealthily walked past Leo when he had his eyes closed in the water. Frustrated, he searches his horse for some spare fabric, there is none and he realises that he'll have to ride back to the chateau naked.

He appears at the tower gates, icy blue and covered in goose bumps. Here he rapidly dismounts his horse and returns to the stables.

"Fetch me some clothes, there's a good lad." Leo shivers as he instructs the squire. He isn't going to walk straight into the chateau in this state of undress, there will be too many questions from the other knights, especially from his older brother.

"What happened to your clothes?" The squire asks rather sheepishly, he fears the answer and thinks better of questioning his senior, no matter how mad the situation appears to be, he does want to know of course. "I was bathing in the river and a wandering scoundrel nicked my clothes."

"Right, Sir." The squire suppresses laughter as he runs into the chateau. "You'll never guess what happened to Sir Leo." The squire can't wait to pass on his news to the other squires in the hall.

Leo hides in a stall while he waits for the squire to return with his clothes, but he doesn't have to wait very long.

"I hope these fit you."

"They'll have to do." Leo hurriedly dresses himself and when he's done, Leo is confident enough to leave the security of the stalls, on his way out, his heart skips a beat as he sees me sketching the Duke's horse.

As he sidles up to me, he causes me to jump. "Hello." He says, but apparently I don't appear to be overjoyed to see him, or perhaps, I'm just shy, he thinks. He notices that my hand trembles a little, he decides to deflect from himself and complement my work which appears to ease the tense situation.

Leo senses the frisson between us, I can't hold eye contact with him, but he certainly feels the power behind my eyes when we do connect.

"Odo informs me that I need to sit for you at some stage. I'll need to fetch my armour." Leo issues instructions to the squire, for his horse to be dressed in Guilliam's colours, while he leaves to collect his costume. As he runs to the chateau to retrieve his armour, a wave of excitement rushes through his body, he feels alive and reborn. He looks forward to this next chapter of his life. He finds his armour, changes and returns to the stables as quickly as the confines of armour allow.

The squire returns Leo's horse to the area where I will draw him and I give him instructions as to how I want him positioned. While Leo runs his hands through his wet hair, he hopes that I won't notice it dripping, he places his helmet onto his head. Leo is immediately grateful for the metal barrier. A barrier which holds in his feelings, rather than have them flooding straight from his face.

Our time together seems to fly by in an instant, I realise that I can't pretend to draw all day, I abruptly and regretfully announce that I've completed my work.

"I think that's it. Thank you for sitting so still for me." I break his revive and he's naturally curious to see what I've drawn.

"May I see your illustration?" He dismounts from his horse while I inform him that the drawing will be used in the embroidery for the Duke, therefore it will be a surprise until it's presented to Guilliam, besides I am too shy to show him. Leo wants the moment to last, but he knows of no words to capture my attention, instead he searches my eyes. In that moment, he knows in his heart, body and soul, that he has found his partner in life, his breathing is laboured, his hands are clammy.

Frustrated, Leo stamps the ground when the squire interrupts our moment.

"Shall I take your horse away now, Sir?"

"Huh? What?"

"Can I take your horse for grooming, Sir?"

"Um.. Yes of course." Leo notices that I'm shocked out of the moment as well and I unexpectedly leave the stables while he'd been talking to the squire. Leo is suddenly alone with no one in which to divulge his encounter and he certainly doesn't want to share his news with his brother, in fear of ridicule, or jealousy, he retires to his chamber. He sits at his bureau to draft a note, when he's finished, he rolls it up, ties it with a red ribbon and calls for a page to deliver it.

Chapter 60 Leon

The coach pulls up alongside the mid-priced hotel, in the Gràcia barrio, in Barcelona and the tour group pour into the lobby. With an afternoon to himself, Leon is thankful to be able to stretch his legs, after they check in, he strolls the grand tree lined boulevards, he stops to admire the apartment buildings designed by Gaudi. Remembering the direction from his backpacking days, he finds himself at the entrance to Parc Guell. He admires the park and nothing seems to have changed since he was here years ago. He wanders to the lookout, appraises the sprawling city before him and rests on a mosaic tiled seat, before he removes his drawing gear from his day pack.

When he searches one of the pockets for an eraser, his hand touches something cool and smooth, he retrieves it from his pack. The moonstone glistens in the strong sunlight and makes rainbow patterns on his paper. He holds it in his hand for a few moments and remembers that the stone represents new beginnings, he wonders for a moment what that will be, everything in his life is running smoothly. He really doesn't want for anything. Well, if he is completely honest, there is something, someone to share this experience with, would be nice. He gives the stone another squeeze, places it back in his pack and continues drawing.

The compulsion to draw every day is innate, but it has been difficult to find a spare moment on tour and now that he's alone, Leon appreciates the freedom to draw. He breathes freely and deeply as he observes the other tourists, the city and the park. He loves being an art teacher, but this tour is next level in terms of considering other people's needs, twenty four hours a day, as an introvert he needs some space to regroup.

The day becomes hotter, there is little shade on the gravelled space, so Leon collects his art supplies and heads back down the hill to find a café with a menu del dia. It doesn't take long before he finds a little hole in the wall restaurant which offers three humble courses and a bottle of wine for 830 pesetas, less than ten dollars.

Satisfied with the delicious, but simple food, and pleasant tasting wine, Leon heads out into the late afternoon sun. It's time to dip his toes into the Mediterranean, via Las Ramblas, where he marvels at the throng of tourists, jugglers, musicians, vendors selling caged birds, flowering pot plants, souvenirs, and football merchandise, it's hectic to say the least and a bit stressful. He's relieved to arrive at Columbus' Column, where tourist numbers have thinned, buskers and touts dispersed. He can smell the briny sea and in no time he'll be scrunching his feet on the soft white beach sand. He thrusts his socks and sneakers into his backpack. His toes are instantly relieved as they escape their constraints and exposed to the cool sea breeze.

As he paddles in the cool water, he is joyous in the relative serenity, until he hears his name called from a distance.

"Leon! Leon!" Two middle aged ladies wave frantically, power walking towards him. His peace and freedom shattered.

"Hello Jenny, Karen." Leon sighs. Panting with exertion, the class mates beam with satisfaction at finding their teacher, who has no means of escape, at best, a polite level of interest. They reel off a list of all the touristy activities they've ticked off their list since they'd parted ways at the hotel. Luckily for Leon, the women sense that their teacher prefers time alone, they complete their diatribe, turn and continue their chatter as they walk up the beach.

As he looks out to sea, Leon wonders what mischief Declan and Mitch are getting up to in Paris, without him. He has no idea that they have travelled to Monaco, or have met and travelled with Sara, but then why would he, he doesn't know who Sara is. He glances at his watch and gives himself another ten minutes of free time in the coolness of the water, he thinks wistfully about Parisian footpaths.

He's become lost in his thoughts and before he knows it, he's been standing in the water for over half an hour. He can feel that his face is hot, he knows the familiar dry feeling that precursors sun burn. Thinking about his fair skin, he chastises himself for being so forgetful with the 50+SPF and makes his way back to the hotel to prepare for another evening with his tour group.

Chapter 61 Ailie

I spend the morning sketching the Duchess, and baby Robert, who by the way, has grown considerably since his Christening. The Duchess poses regally, as I make quick sketches and although her eyes are expressive, she keeps her head very still as we reunite with each other. However, baby Robert proves to be a more difficult subject, as he wriggles about in his basket, but I'm able to capture his likeness well enough for the embroidery. When I've completed my drawings, I excuse myself and go to the kitchen to see if there is something to eat.

My second favourite happy place, the kitchen, is situated in the grounds and after sitting for most of the morning, walking through the garden brings relief to my aching legs. The fresh air is a welcome respite from the stuffy conditions within the chateau. There's great hustle and bustle in the kitchen, as cooks warm large kettles of soup over the fire, knead dough on large wooden tables and prepare a roasting pig over the fire pit. The cooking smells are delicious and I'm salivating. I ask one of the younger cooks if I can take some of the fresh bread which has been cooling on the table.

"Of course, Ma'am." The servant has instantly recognised my nobility.

"Thank you." I bite into the dense wholegrain bread. "Oh my goodness, this is heavenly bread."

"Thank you Ma'am." The young servant smiles and curtsies, but I quickly flee, I know I'm in their way.

When I've finished my lunch, the grounds appear deserted, I wander into the stables to see if I can find some knights to draw from Guilliam's list. There are only squires running about the stables so I consider drawing the Duke's magnificent black horse, as a surprise for Guilliam. As I draw, I sense a presence by my side, somebody familiar, exciting and safe all at the same time.

"Hello." Leo realises he may have startled me.

"Hello." I notice my hand trembling. I place my drawing apparatus aside and wipe my hands on a damp cloth to remove the black charcoal dust.

"That's a great likeness of the Duke's horse, you're so talented."

"So you keep telling me." I laugh gently, remembering our last encounter in the great hall. I have no reason to feel nervous, he is calming to be around, comfortable, but also thrilling at the same time. "I believe I'm supposed to draw you, as well as your horse." Studying my dress, I can't hold eye contact with the handsome knight and I suddenly remember the times, when I was little and I couldn't work out why Florrie wouldn't look the messenger in the eye. Now I know now exactly how she felt.

"Yes, Odo did mention that I'd need to sit for you at some stage."

"Are you free now?"

"Why yes I am, I'll fetch my armour. Squire, dress my horse in Guilliam's colours. I'll be back, Ailie." I blush when I hear him say my name in his deep voice.

While Leo collects his armour, I contemplate my drawing and subsequent embroidery, but I can only think of my immediate subject. I wonder how I am going to focus in on him so intently, to capture his likeness. He enters the stables, in full uniform, carrying his helmet in the crook of his right arm, my heart skips. I inhale deeply to calm myself as the squire brings Leo's chestnut horse out of its stall and into a brighter area where I can draw him.

"Right, perhaps if you sit on your horse." Leo follows my instructions and adds his own touch as he places his helmet upon his head of wet hair which causes me to wonder how his hair had become wet in the first place.

I'm grateful for the metal barrier between us, although I can still see his deep blue eyes staring back at me, which at first is unnerving, but after a few deep breaths, I settle down and think that I've produced a decent enough representation of his image.

"I think that's it." I break the silence after half an hour of drawing.

"May I see your illustration?" He dismounts from his horse.

"I'm not too sure. I think it'll be a surprise." I hold the sketch close to my chest so that he can't see my work and we stand in contented silence as he looks down at me. I am finally confident enough to make steady eye contact with him. In that moment, I know I've found my partner in life. My breathing is laboured and my hands are clammy. My body confirms my emotions. It's weird, scary and lovely, all at the same time.

The squire interrupts our perfect silence.

"Shall I stable your horse now, Sir."

"Huh? What?"

"Can I take your horse for grooming, Sir?"

"Um. Yes of course." With the squire's presence, I become self-conscious again, I use the opportunity to dismiss myself from the situation. I need to breathe. In a daze I retire to my chamber and lie on my deer skin, still clutching my sketches as my heart pounds out of my chest.

From her chamber, Millie hears me climb the stairs and is excited to visit me. She knocks on the door and immediately enters my room.

"What ever's the matter?" Millie is concerned with my flushed appearance.

"Nothing and everything" I half laugh.

"What?" I can't speak coherently for a few minutes while I catch my breath. As I begin to relax, the illustration of Leo falls from my waist and appears before Millie.

"Give me a look at that!" Millie demands. Before I can snatch it back, Millie grabs the drawing. "Oh my goodness, even though you've only drawn his eyes through his helmet, you've really captured his likeness, I can tell its Leo. You're so talented you know."

"That's what he said." I laugh nervously again.

Millie connects the dots and realises that I must have met with Leo to draw him.

"Ooh, so you have seen him again."

"Well yes, obviously, to draw him. He found me in the stables for the second time in my life." Remembering the time when I was little and the visiting noble boy said hello in the stalls of my father's stables. "Oh my God, Millie, I saw Leo when I was a child. His father brought him to our stables, but it was only a brief meeting. I can't believe I'd forgotten that." I had to verbalise the story for myself as much as to explain it to Millie.

As we continued to chat, a page boy knocks on the door with a note for me.

"What does it say?" Millie is very excited. Taking a deep breath, I unfurl the scroll and read aloud to Millie.

"Fair Ailie, I enjoyed our time together today and I'd like to know you better. Please meet with me in the grove of trees, next to the field after supper and please feel free to bring a chaperone. I look forward to our meeting, with anticipation, L."

"Oh my goodness."

"I shall be your chaperone," Millie offers immediately.

"I shan't be able to eat any supper tonight."

"I'll have your share" Millie giggles as she hugs me.

Chapter 62 Allie

I board the train for Barcelona, with a light overnight bag borrowed from Trudi. When I arrive in the port town, I scour the names of the underground stations on the wall map, but I'm having a lot of difficulty with the Catalonian language. The name of the station I require, eludes me. I'm becoming increasingly frustrated. It's great being on my own, but it's times like this, when another set of eyes and a voice of reason, would be handy.

"It must be here somewhere." I grumble. I'm sorry that I hadn't written the name down, but it seemed so memorable when the lady at the ticket counter had said it.

I comb the board a few more times before an elderly gentleman recognises my distress, he points to the map with a gnarly nicotine stained finger.

"Which one you want, Signorina?"

"*Lithau.*" I attempt to pronounce it the same way the ticket booth attendant had.

"*Qué?*"

"*Lith-a-u*" I repeat it slowly and phonetically.

"*Ah si.*" Recognition spreads across the man's face, much to my relief. He points to a spot on the board reading *Liceu*, a name I've overlooked many times. All I can see is spelling that seems completely foreign to the word I've just pronounced. I don't understand how that could possibly be the same word I'd searched for, but after a few days in Barcelona, I can't comprehend how I'd missed it.

I emerge from the metro into the bright sunshine of Las Ramblas, where there's an abundance of bright colours, evocative music, bird-cages full of canaries, beautiful people from all corners of the globe, cafes selling tourist versions of sangria, paella and tapas, buckets and buckets of multi-coloured flowers, artists displaying their creativity, men with pythons lying on beds of nails, other tourists and general life, it's overwhelming, but amazing to see.

In minutes, I've found the small pension Trudi had recommended, with surprisingly little effort, however Maria the landlady is busy mopping the foyer floor when I arrive. The cool front step provides respite while I wait for Maria to complete her task and I admire the skateboarding frog splashed on the wall of the opposite building. Once the foyer floor is completely damp, Maria, a woman of indeterminate age, hands me the keys to an airy room overlooking the square. I climb the two flights of stairs to inspect my accommodation and collect my thoughts.

Walking over the threshold of my room, is like falling into a European movie set. The French doors are open to the square below and a soft breeze carries the filmy white curtains in across the room, then out over the small balcony. The white wrought iron bed beckons me to firstly sit at its precipice, to determine the firmness of its mattress. Not too hard, good, I then let it fully envelope me in a sweet caress of deep, white down. Next to the balcony windows is a small wooden table where Maria has placed a vase of delicate blue and white flowers, they beg to be inhaled. Gently picking up the vase, I bring the flowers to my face so that I can breathe in their scent, but I soon discover they don't really have one. While I'm in this position, I notice the small square below where locals are walking home from the market with bags of vegetables and bread, school children head home for lunch, old men perch on wooden benches and discuss who knows what. Life materialises all around me and I could stay here for hours watching the world go by, but I itch to see more.

Remembering I'd been on an overnight train, I pull my hands through my tangled hair and arrange it into less of a birds nest, brush my teeth and instantly have empathy for all of the people I've spoken to this morning, my breath is less than minty fresh. Applying lip gloss, I free my constricted feet from my running shoes and plunge them into sandals while I sniff my armpits and deem them just passable. I venture back to Las Ramblas to find something, or someone?

On the hectic thoroughfare, I spy a cafe selling churros, moreish Spanish doughnuts eaten with small ramekins of molten chocolate. As my stomach rumbles, I remember breakfast has eluded me and think this is going to be a delicious first meal of the day. I observe the tourist parade as I nibble my chocolate dipped churros and the next time I glance at my watch, I realise that an hour has passed and I haven't advanced in my goal of discovering Barcelona. Half of the pot of chocolate remains, but I can't finish it, it's way too rich. I collect my things and get on my way.

I stroll down Las Ramblas towards the sea, where my guide book informs me that I will find a tourist information booth. With maps and brochures in hand, I decide to board the double-decker tourist bus which stops at all of the major sites. I feel a bit guilty about taking the easy way out, not exploring the city by foot, but I only want a quick overview of the city. Okay, I'm lazy. When the bus pulls up at Parc Guell, the housing development designed by Gaudi, I disembark with some of the other tourists who are also drawn in by the unusually curved buildings and colourful mosaics.

I wander around the buildings and choose a mosaic place to park myself, is it a seat exactly? Unearthing my camera, sketch pad and pencils from my day pack, I wonder if I can actually draw something that will resemble what I see and after a few tentative moments of not knowing what to focus on, and a lack of confidence in my drawing ability, I realise that no-one else is going to look at my drawings, so why not just go for it?

Closing my eyes for a few moments gives me clarity and when I re-open them I immediately hone in on one section of a building that resembles a ginger-bread house from a fairy tale. I draw it in great detail, paying attention to the roof spires and mosaic tiles. Drawing without straight lines gives me the freedom to go with the flow of the design and I sit in a state of active meditation while I sketch. I snap a couple of photos of the ginger-bread house so that I can work on my drawing later and then glance around noticing that the other tourists have started to thin, the light has faded a little. I look at my watch in disbelief, the last tourist bus left an hour ago.

However, my drawing meditation helps me to remain calm. I'm not panicked, I know I can find my way back to my pension easily. As I walk away from the park, there's a nice neighbourhood where I observe the locals living separately from the tourist hype. Wandering further into the neighbourhood, I see the locals having their hair coloured and styled in a hairdressing salon, some are buying food from the grocers for their evening meal, everyday activities seen in any country, familiar activities. But these mundanities make me think of home, I miss my family such as it is, and my workmates. This is crazy. What am I doing here? At that moment, I decide I'll return to Paris where I won't be so lonely. But I can't leave Catalonia just yet, there's one more place that I have to see.

Chapter 63 Leo

Leo nervously paces his room while he waits for the hour when we will formally meet. He refuses to join the other knights at the dining table for supper and declines a tray of food to his quarters from the kitchen staff. His stomach is tied in knots and when the hour arrives, he inhales deeply and descends the stairs to make his way to the grove of trees. It's early summer but the day has been cool, we'll have time in the drawn out sunset to meet and declare our love.

As Leo walks through the hall, knights are eating the last morsels of their supper and are starting card games by the fire, discussions of battles past chorus throughout the cavernous room.

"Hey, Leo, why weren't you at supper?" Without waiting for a response, Miché hollers across the room. "Where do you think you're going?" The chatter within the hall silences, all eyes are upon Leo.

"Um, I'm just heading out for a walk."

"Great, I'll come with you." Miché offers with a smirk, he has his suspicions.

"No! No, I want to go on my own." Leo is too abrupt at first and then modulates his voice when he realises that he is being too defensive.

"Okay then, be on your way little brother. I shall stay here and win handsomely at cards."

The men at his table know Miché speaks the truth and therefore they aren't inclined to laugh at his statement. Before Leo can escape, his brother keeps talking and Leo can feel his agitation rise again. He is anxious that he will be late for our meeting, it's a highly charged situation.

"I hear a champion knight, wringing wet and blue from cold, rode into the chateau wearing only his birthday suit today. I wonder who that could be?" Miché is determined to embarrass his brother. The men know this to be true and roar with laughter, as Tristian flings a pair of tights around his neck like a scarf. Leo mortified, walks away and tries to muster a thread of dignity in his final steps from the hall, but his boot catches on the edge a jutting flagstone, he trips through the giant doorway. The men cheer and roar with laughter as they return to their card game. Leo is soon forgotten and the knights muse on their strategies to beat Miché at his own game, though Miché, confident that he will win hands down, wonders what his little brother is up to.

Leo stands sentry in the yard while he gathers himself.

"Right, breathe." He instructs himself before he continues through the tower gate to the grove of trees. When he arrives, he notices there is no one else around, he patiently waits for me to arrive. He bends down to pick up a stick and when he rights himself, he sees the outline of two figures walking towards him from the rear of the chateau. He sighs with relief, knowing that we will soon be together.

"That's smart, I should've done that. It would've saved a lot of trouble and the explanation I will have to provide Miché could have been avoided." He says to himself when he realises that Millie and I have taken a more discrete route to the grove of trees.

As he completes his self-admonishment, he can see us more clearly as we walk purposefully towards him. Giant moths wage battle in the depths of his guts, but on the outside he is solid, grounded. Millie tapers from me and stops some distance from Leo, for which he is grateful. He sends her a small wave in appreciation then turns his attention to me. My long curly hair flows around my face in the cool evening breeze, my gaze fixes upon Leo. Our eyes lock and suddenly, I'm only half a metre away from him.

Chapter 64 Leon

The train pulls away slowly from Barcelona Sants Station, it's on its way to Figueres. Leon and Graham perform a final head count in the second class coach. The tour group are all seated and excited to visit the Dali Museum and as Leon watches the city morph into countryside, he chats to Graham about how they are going to conduct the day.

"I think the best mode of operation is to have the students wander through the gallery at their own pace, with an audio guide, if they want it and if they have any questions we can convene at a designated time before we go to the restaurant for lunch. It's a shame we couldn't get the English speaking guide today. Apparently, she's been booked by another group, or there was a mix up of some sort. I think it's better for them to see the art at their own pace, they can form their own opinions without being told what to think. On the other hand, I know some of our group will be disappointed not to have a guide, but they can ask me for my impressions if the audio guide doesn't satisfy them."

"That sounds like a plan to me, Leon. You're the expert. It's a shame there won't be a formal tour but the students will enjoy this place, I think. Linda said its pretty amazing."

"By the way, how are Linda and the boys coping without you?"

"They're okay, I guess, but I haven't rung them much, its pretty expensive. The boys are a bit too little to understand what's going on, but Linda had her mother come over to stay and help her out." As he is talking, Graham is studying Leon's face. "Catch a bit of sun yesterday, did ya?"

"Yep, seems so. Luckily we're mostly inside today though."

The pair chat easily until the train pulls into the station at Figueres and after the group disembark, they walk towards the Museo Dali. On arrival at the impressive building, Leon issues the group with final instructions before they eagerly discover the madness and brilliance of the artworks. Initially, Leon hangs back with Graham while he pays the cashier, allowing the group to set off while he waits for the first gallery to clear a little before he wanders through. This isn't his first time to the museum, although there have been some significant changes to the building since his last visit.

With most of the tourists through the first room, Leon begins to wander through, inspecting the art work and chatting with his group. He finds nuances in some of the artworks that he hasn't seen before and lingers at each piece longer than he initially anticipated. Suddenly, he's anxious that he should speed up so that he won't fall too far behind the bulk of the group. He sees them animatedly pointing at the art-work, engaged in intense discussions, he relaxes. He was worried that the art may have been too confronting for some of the students, but his worries dissipate when he sees how absorbed they've become. He smiles to himself and remembers his reaction when he had first visited the amazing museum. Leon's decision to visit this particular museum has been validated in more ways than one.

He wanders from room to room and finds himself on the second floor. At Dali's crypt, he lingers in front of a giant painting of a man, surrounded by a body of water. Then he feels the pull of the court yard. As he walks through the wall of windows into the courtyard, he sees a familiar figure standing next to a black Cadillac.

Chapter 65 Ailie and Leo

With Millie in the near distance, respecting our need for privacy and intimacy within the confines of his vows to Odo, and the Church, and to protect my virtue, Leo and I greet each other chastely. We both tremble, as Leo fumbles for my hand which he eventually kisses. Instantly, a wave of grief engulfs him as he dreads the release of my hand, he clings on.

"I've waited anxiously for this day, for many years in fact. I have never loved another until you."

I can't respond, I clasp his hand and sense the electricity between our palms radiating down my fingertips. His skin touching mine is intense. Apart from a quick hand-shake, I've never held a man's hand for this length of time before and even though I am self-accomplished in my career, for the first time in my life, I feel held, secure and loved. Both adrift from our families and village, we've returned to a home that's far from our ancestral beginnings, we have travelled to a place that we will dwell in forever. Our threads span lifetimes.

Leo feels the magnetic force between us and longs to kiss me. As he wonders if it's appropriate to enact on his feelings, my lips are caressing his. Mid embrace we hear Millie cry out.

"Yeah!" We turn our heads to witness Millie performing a celebration dance which stops abruptly when she realises that she's been caught mid jig. Millie waves at us. "Ignore me, continue." We laugh at our friend and return to each other as Millie turns her back on us, we resume our embrace. After an eternity that spirals into an instant, we hear a loud series of coughs. We look over to Millie, who appears to be convulsing, but it's just her subtle way of alerting us of an imminent arrival.

"I thought you were playing cards." Leo and I quickly part as he addresses Miché.

"I thought I might find you here." Miché waves his purse in the air. "I was winning too much money and the others got the hump. They are planning to ride into town and visit the tavern. I thought you might like to accompany me, but I see now, that you're otherwise occupied."

Miché notices Millie approaching us. She figures it's the right thing to do, she feels a bit weird on her own.

"Good evening Millie." Miché nods in her direction and Millie blushes.

"Good evening Sir Miché."

"Well I must take my leave and ride with my men, but I shall see you dear brother, tomorrow." As he gestures with a flamboyant wave, he returns to the stables. Leo is relieved that his brother hasn't made a scene and thankful for his discretion.

When Miché is about ten meters away from the small group, he spins around and returns to us.

"Good Lord, where are my manners? Good evening Ailie."

"Good evening Miché."

"Oh, and Leo."

"Yes Miché."

"I think it's marvellous that you finally have the balls to go after what you want. You've been moping around the chateau for far too long now. Hurry up and marry this fair maiden before she realises what you are really like." He pauses for a moment. "Yes, I think that's all I wanted to say." He turns on his heels, leaving Leo, Millie and I, dumbfounded. We giggle nervously.

Millie is suddenly feeling awkward again and doesn't know where to turn. Should she stay with us? Should she wander back to her original post? She attempts eye contact with me, but my attention has quickly returned to Leo. Millie returns to her original position in the grove and waits patiently. Amongst the comfort of the trees, she considers Sir Miché, picks a wildflower from the grass and slowly plucks each petal from its stem.

"He loves me. He loves me not. He loves me. He loves me not." There is one more petal though.

Leo considers his brother's words as we embrace and then wrenches himself away, knowing what he needs to do if our relationship is to continue according to our values, he continues to hold my hands tightly.

"Ailie, I have loved you from the moment I laid eyes on you in your father's stables." My eyes light up knowing that he understands who I am. "And, since we've become reacquainted as adults, I know for sure that you are the one I have been waiting for. Ailie I don't want to be separated from you ever again. Will you honour me by marrying me?"

"Oh my goodness, yes!" He squeezes my hands so much they start to tingle.

Millie turns around and sees us in an embrace.

"Still at it." She utters as the sun is setting. She is cold, enough is enough. Millie coughs, though not as frantically as before and we look across to her and laugh. As the maiden approaches us, I run to my friend.

"Guess what?"

"What is it?"

"How would you like to stand witness to our marriage?"

"What you and me?" Millie laughs at her own joke. "You and Leo, I know that." She grasps me in a tight hug and kisses both my cheeks. "I'll most certainly be your witness."

Chapter 66 Allie

Trying to work out how to ask for a second class ticket, proves a little tricky for me, my Spanish isn't great and the attendant speaks so fast that I get flustered, I can't think properly. Originally frustrated that I'd managed to buy a first class seat to Figueres, I arrive at my single seat and I'm glad that I can sit alone and watch the countryside pass me by in peace. The train journey is just over an hour long and it seems to wiz by. Before long, I'm standing on the platform inspecting my map to determine the best way to the museum.

Regarding the platform, I notice the masses alight from the second class coaches. They chat noisily and joke, most of them seem to be part of a large group enjoying themselves. I suddenly realise, I need to visit the toilet and with few public conveniences in Spain, I consider the station amenities. All set to go, I stroll to the Museo Dali taking in the atmosphere of Figueres and I'm relieved to see most of the passengers are heading in my direction, lessening my navigation anxiety.

I arrive at the Museum, having walked more rapidly than I thought, as the large group has just arrived and are huddled in conversation. I go inside ahead of them and purchase my ticket. I find the first gallery as the tour group follows slowly behind me and at first I try too hard to interpret each piece of art. I inspect it from all angles and attempt to work out the symbolism, as I'd been taught, but I realise I'm thinking too much about it, it's impossible to interpret somebody else's intentions. I empty my mind of preconceived ideas and just be with the art, but something is niggling me to move on, so I refer to my map and realise I am never going to see everything if I spend so much time in front of each artwork.

A labyrinth of a building, I make my way through the second floor and I find myself in front of Dali's crypt. It's fascinating and disturbing at the same time, knowing that the artist who had created all of the fantastic surrealist creations, had been laid to rest in the building. I'm mesmerised by a giant painting of a man's torso, a monolith emerging from rocks, surrounded by water, his head bowed, his face shadowed with a fissure cracked through his skull, a trapezoid tunnel burrowing through his chest and a gnarly tree growing on top of the tunnel, just your regular piece of art.

I'm drawn to a wall of windows, revealing an oasis of ivy clad stone walls with inlays housing gilded goddess figurines. At first, I'm overwhelmed with the number of statues, illusions and especially the vintage black Cadillac, adorned with a figure of a busty woman, I don't know where to look. Eventually, my focus rests on the Cadillac. Inside the vehicle, is a mannequin with a strong resemblance to Elvis. A tourist feeds the car some money to make the car rain from the inside. When the rain subsides, I examine my map once more to see how much of the museum remains. There is still the Mae West room to explore. As I turn around, I see a familiar face. Abruptly my heart starts racing, I'm short of breath.

Chapter 67 Allie and Leon

Aware that Graham and the tour group are wandering around different parts of the museum, Leon greets me as if we're old friends.

"Hi, I'm Leon by the way. I've finally found you." He immediately wishes he hadn't said that and blushes violently, but to alleviate his embarrassment, I return the favour.

"Hi, I'm Allie and it appears you are correct." We smile awkwardly at each other. We have waited for this moment for a long time, but now that we're in this position, we don't really know what to say to each other, after a long pause, I break the ice.

"It seems that we have a mutual friend in Mitch."

"Yes, Mitch, he's a funny bugger. He told me you might be here, in Europe I mean. Long story short, I live with Mitch and I said hello to you in our house on the morning after the music festival." I blush, this isn't the way I want to be remembered and Leon doesn't like the way it makes him sound either. "Oh, and I think I may have seen you on a street in Paris on the morning I arrived. You're probably not a street walker, but I don't know if it was you, or not." He nervously rambles before he forces himself to stop talking.

"Yes, I remember you from Mitch's house." I reply, as we turn towards the Elvis mannequin and smile while we consider our next move. Serenely, we feel the magnetic force that has bound us together for millennia.

Suddenly, Graham arrives on the scene and unknowingly interrupts Leon and I.

"Leon, this stuff's really wild. How did Dali's mind work, I'll never know?"

"Yes, it's quite different isn't it? Not everyone's cup of tea, but I find it fascinating." Leon is tetchy with his companion as Graham lingers uncomfortably for some time. He desperately wants him to go away so he can talk to me.

Graham finally grows tired of Cadillac Elvis and wanders off to another gallery, while I scrounge through my handbag, to retrieve a pen to write on the museum brochure.

"Look, I understand that you're here to work, here's my number. Call me when you get back to Paris. I'm booked on tomorrow's train and I'll be there for a while before heading back to Australia." Leon accepts the brochure thankfully and pulls out one of his business cards from his wallet to hand to me. I glance at the card and place it in my purse for safe keeping. The tour group starts to mill around Cadillac Elvis, heralding an end to our time together.

"Well, I think duty calls sooner than I would have liked, but there you go. I'll call you when I arrive in Paris." We approach each other awkwardly to deliver a friendly peck on the cheek, but our aim is way off and our heads collide.

We laugh as we rub our sore heads and approach each other more thoughtfully. This time, our kiss is straight on target and as we have just formally met, I wonder if we are being too familiar? We both think about it for a millisecond and realise what the hell, of course it's okay. We both have the feeling that we've realigned with each other. We've found each other again. Both adrift from each other, our families and country, we have returned to a home far from our ancestral beginnings, we will travel to a place that we will dwell in forever. Our threads span lifetimes.

During our brief kiss, we hear applause and a congratulatory "Yeah!" coming from behind us and as we turn around, Leon's tour group is applauding an embryonic couple making our first moves. Karen turns to Jenny with a smile.

"Boy, he works fast doesn't he?"

"Yes, he certainly does. Who's that girl though? I thought Tammy liked him."

"Well she's going to be very disappointed. It looks like he's smitten."

Leon says goodbye and I plant another kiss on his cheek. I wave to Karen and Jenny, and the rest of the group, before floating all the way back to the train station. I can't finish the rest of the museum now, I can feel Leon's eyes follow me as I walk away.

"Oh my Goddess, he's gone." Jenny laughs. Graham arrives while the tour group gossips and laughs about their leader.

"What did I miss?"

"Oh, you'll never believe it."

Graham seeks out Leon.

"We'd better round this mob up for lunch, what do you say?"

"Hmm?" Leon's totally distracted.

"Lunch, we need to get to the restaurant for lunch."

"Yes certainly, now where did we say we'd meet?"

"At the entrance, at 2pm."

"Righto, yes of course, let's go."

Leon's thoughts are in the first class coach returning to Barcelona, he can tell the rest of the day is going to be a struggle. Graham can see that he's going to have to round up the troops and as he encounters some more group members, he reminds them to return to the entrance in ten minutes.

"What the bloody hell is wrong with Leon? He's a bit vague this afternoon. This is his jam. I thought that he would be more switched on here." Graham confides in Albie from the Tourism class.

"He probably just needs to eat something. I'm struggling with the Spanish eating times myself." Albie grumbles.

When his commitments for the day have ended with the tour group, Leon has to make a phone call. He doesn't want to wait until we return to Paris and I've also thought of nothing else all day. My attempts to engross myself in Barcelona's tourist sites have proven futile and I spend the rest of the afternoon on a sandy beach looking out to sea. When he arrives back at his hotel room, he types my number into his phone. He also adds the number to his contact list so that he won't lose me again and at the same time I've been performing similar actions, without ringing, our phones connect.

"Hello."

"Hello?"

"That's weird, the phone didn't even ring." I comment to myself.

"Hi."

"Hi." We aren't sure what to say.

"Can I meet you for dinner?" Leon breaks the greeting loop we've found ourselves circling in.

"That would be lovely, I'm in the Gothic Barrio and there's some lovely little restaurants here." We arrange to meet outside of the cathedral, so I quickly run back to the pension to prepare for our first date.

As we sit outside of the restaurant, in the plaza, on that balmy evening, we barely touch our tapas. I couldn't tell you what was on the plate in front of me. We gaze into each other's eyes and occasionally sip our vino tinto. Initially, it's hard to talk, we can't believe that we've finally found each other. Even though we were bound for each other, we've only just met in this incarnation. We are both awkwardly introverted which makes it difficult to find mutual ground, but we manage when we broach the Dali Museum's art, our experiences with Mitch, our previous travels, and our families. These topics keep us talking nonstop for hours, but then we just stop talking. Over the restaurant speaker, we hear a familiar Australian song, sung in Spanish. "*And I will, la la la la.*"

"Wow, I haven't heard that song in ages."

"Yes I know, fancy hearing an Australian song this far from home." When the song finishes, we realise the waiters are cleaning up and most of the clientele has cleared the restaurant.

"Boy, it must be really late if the waiters are cleaning up."

"Hmm." Is all I can think to say. Neither of us want the moment to end, but Leon knows he has to be back at his hotel by morning which is only a few hours away. I break the tense silence. It seems to be becoming my thing. "I know this is really forward, but do you mind walking me back to my pension, its not far?"

"Not at all my fair maiden, I shall walk you to your door."

"How chivalrous you are, kind Sir Knight." I cringe. Did I just say that? We arrive at Maria's Pension. "Well my door is on the second floor, can you walk me there because you never know who could be lurking on the stairs at night."

When we arrive, I unlock the door, he lifts me from the ground and carries me over the threshold, fireman style and places me gently on the bed. I quickly brush my dirty clothes and overnight bag aside, they fall noisily to the floor and he lies down beside me. We face each other, stare into each other's eyes and start kissing.

Before he has to make his way back to his hotel, he holds both of my hands in his.

"Allie, this is going to sound crazy, but I have loved you from the moment I laid eyes on you in Mitch's house." One day Cathy will inform us that we had already met, way before that, the week his family arrived in Australia and they mistook my house for another one further up the street.

"You know, it doesn't sound crazy to me. What's crazy is that I don't know how I'm going to be able to function and find my way back to Paris." I lament.

"I'm only going to be here for a couple of days and then I will definitely see you in Paris." He kisses me again before he has to make his way back to his tour group.

I do manage to find my way back to Paris that morning and by 8pm I'm on the platform, at Gare de León, searching for my metro connections. When I arrive at Rue de Passay, Sara, Mitch, Trudi and Declan have engulfed the tiny apartment.

"Wow, I wasn't expecting everyone to be here." I place my overnight bag on the floor in the hallway and when I return to the kitchen, I see there's no room to sit on the sofa.

"Let's go for a drink." Trudi suggests, feeling way too restricted in her own home. "Perhaps we can get something to eat as well?" Declan proposes.

As we descend the stairs, I grab Sara's hand and squeeze it meaningfully while Sara promptly returns the squeeze. When we arrive at the doorway to the street, Mitch civilly holds the door for everyone to leave, Sara makes sure she's the last to leave. As he's about to close the door, he plants a big kiss on Sara's pursed lips and it appears to me this isn't their first kiss either.

"Oi! What's going on here then?" I laugh.

"I could say the same about you actually, little birdie and all that." He smacks Sara's bum playfully as we walk towards the restaurant.

Phase 3 Chapter 68 War

At the dawn of a new millennium, a messenger races into the chateau, red faced and panting, he delivers a salient scroll from his small sweaty hand to Odo, the Duke's step-brother, Bishop of Rouen.

"What is it now?" The Duke is irritated by the interruptions to his day.

"King Edward is dead and Harold, the incumbent, has been crowned the new King of England." Odo shakes his head in disgust, knowing that his brother will be infuriated. Standing silently beside Odo, Guilliam's mind races, he was supposed to be the next King of England, but Harold has beat him to the post. Guilliam ceases to think incessantly, instead, he engages his intuition.

Roused into action, Guilliam incensed, thumps his fist onto the solid oak table.

"I am the rightful heir to the throne! I henceforth declare war against Harold and his army. He'll not get away with this." The messenger gathers the amended scroll from the enraged Duke and runs from the chateau to spread the news. With his men gathered, Guilliam begins to strategise in earnest and in the coming days, he will commission a navy of ships for the ensuing battle. Forests of trees will be felled before hundreds of carpenters shape the timber into planks for this ambitious construction project. The first steps towards his quest to conquer the throne.

Miché, Leo and Darri are to embark on the pinnacle adventure of their lifetimes, a journey they've been training for their entire lives. They, along with hundreds of other military men and volunteers hailing from Brittany, Normandy and Flanders, have been briefed at the Chateau de Falaise, by the Duke of Normandy himself.

As the sun dawns over the eastern horizon, the knights pack their weapons, food and other provisions, in preparation for their long ride ahead, reluctantly leaving their loved ones behind.

"Matilda my dear wife, while I'm away, I leave you in charge of our chateau, actually the whole of Normandy. Don't invite any of those Northern marauders in, will you? Guilliam laughs then kisses his wife passionately. "And thank you for my handsome ship, I know she'll bode well on my quest." As a parting gift for her husband, Matilda has commissioned a flagship named The Mora.

"Be safe my darling. I look forward to news of your victory." Matilda returns her husband's kiss and waves him goodbye from the drawbridge.

I'm asleep when Leo leaves our quarters, early in the dawn, we shared wretched adieus the night before, my heart still aches. I hear him rouse and before he leaves, he bends down and kisses my forehead. I sleepily kiss him back and tell him that I love him, but the gravity of what he is about to enter into, is too much, I quickly hug him.

"Be safe Leo. I'll be waiting for your return. I love you so much."

"I will be. I love you Ailie." He returns my embrace and exposes the white handkerchief hidden in his breast plate armour, when he is no longer in sight, I roll over with a heavy heart and close my eyes.

When they leave the grounds of the chateau, Guilliam rides alongside his step-brothers, Odo and Robert, along with his finest knights from the Inner Circle, the du Bois brothers, ride proudly in this contingent.

"What a glorious day to spend on the back of a horse traversing the French countryside." Miché is buoyant as they began their ride to the north of France.

"I'm looking forward to battering those English rascals." Darri, is more than eager to fight for the Duke's honour, without fully understanding the potential devastation that could be bestowed upon them. Darri doesn't look his best though, he awkwardly adjusts himself on his horse.

"All in good time young brother, we have a journey of many days before we encounter any English rascals." However, they're barely able to control their excitement, the oldest and younger brothers can't wait to ride to Saint Valery-sur-Somme, a five day journey north. When they arrive at the coast, they will board one of the Duke's many hundreds of wooden vessels to sail to Hastings on the English coast, via the Isle of White.

"What's up with you Leo?" Darri asks his brother. Leo is more introspective than his brothers and therefore fails to immediately respond. Leo knows that he has trained well and believes he is prepared for whatever lies ahead, but how can a person be truly equipped for war? Miché notices his brother's pensiveness and pounds him on the shoulder with his fist.

"Snap out of it Leo, there will be plenty of action to take your mind off Normandy when we reach England." Leo shrugs and returns a friendly thump to his brother's back. "Think about it. We will be knights of the English Royal House."

"What's up with you Darri? Did you have to go so hard on the ale last night?"

He had clearly indulged a little too much on the eve of their journey, his head aches, his mouth is parched and he really isn't looking forward to sitting on his horse's bony back for hours on end.

"I was celebrating the eve of our journey?" His brothers roll their eyes, they know better than to get drunk on the eve of a journey like this, however Miché decides to change the subject and leave his little brother alone for a while.

"What do you think of these new fangled stirrups Leo?"

"I think they'll take a while to get used to." Leo struggles to keep his feet in the metal rings, he thinks they'll need some adjustments at the next rest stop, but he doesn't let on to his brother that he hasn't mastered the new stirrups. Miché has noticed though, there isn't much that gets passed him.

"The Duke had this tack made by the smith, especially for this mission. I'm not too sure about this high saddle though." Miché says switching the bane of contention.

"Oh, stop your whining you two. At least you have new tack. Look at my old kit. I don't have any stirrups at all. I have to ride the old fashioned way with my legs flapping about the place." Darri chimes in.

As they ride, Miché sings a battle song, combat instructions for chivalrous knights. However, he isn't the greatest singer in France and his warbling voice inflames Darri's already pounding head.

"Shut up will you." Darri calls out to his older brother. But despite his little brother's malaise, he continues with the *chanson de geste*, with gusto. Leo's horse trots serenely, a few paces behind his brothers' steeds, its rider lost in thought as they make their way towards the first of many castles where they'll stay for the night and rest before heading north in the morning.

Miché finally stops singing and they ride in contented silence for a good while. Then out of the blue, the oldest and youngest brother begin to chat about everything and nothing. Darri's hangover had subsided as the du Bois brothers quickly become familiar with the other knights and volunteers who are travelling with them. They converse and joke boisterously with their new band of companions, leaving Leo riding moodily at the back of the pack.

At the end of the day's riding, the Norman army arrive at the welcoming castle where they'll lodge for the night. The hard-working servants prepare them a large banquet of suckling pigs, a variety of seafood and loaves of freshly baked bread, which have been cooking in enormous outdoor ovens.

"Before we eat, let us pray." Odo declares. The men hang their heads in reverence. "Dear Lord, bless this food, we give thanks to those who have made provisions for us." Odo prays piously while the knights dutifully perform the sign of the cross, from their heads, across their shoulders, their hands resting piously on their hearts. Famished, they dig into the abundant feast.

Later in the evening, space has been made for the knights closest to the Duke, to sleep by the fire in the grand hall, but Leo has other plans in mind.

"I'm going to sleep outside. Look at the sky, it's a great evening to be outdoors, don't you think?" Leo makes this announcement to his brothers from the doorway as he breathes in the evening air.

"What are you talking about? Get back in here Leo. You have to stay inside to protect The Duke." Miché is perplexed that Leo has even considered sleeping outside, even the lower born knights and volunteers, who are relegated to the barn, have shelter. Some men are even forced to sleep outside in the cooler elements, Leo is envious of his subordinates freedom. "You know better than that Leo, come on."

"Okay. If I have to, I'll sleep inside the chateau with you, and The Duke." He lingers by the large doorway and searches the inky sky for the North Star. "There you are, good night. I love you Ailie" He whispers to the star before retiring within the protective walls of the chateau.

The routine of riding, feasting and sleeping, continues for five days before they reach the mouth of the River Somme and the night before the army is to sail to England, they attend Mass in the Eglise Saint Martin where they are blessed by Odo. After the Mass, the men assemble on the beach and board their vessels.

"Look at the sea." Leo says to his brothers in awe. "See how calm and still it is."

"Yeah whatever." Darri is keen to jump aboard The Mora and start fighting.

"I'm so glad that it'll be smooth sailing." Leo reflects on the smooth sea again.

"No chance of throwing up today, hey brother?" Miché pounds his brother heartily on the back as they sail across the channel. He's well aware of his younger brother's delicate constitution and is quietly hoping that Leo won't embarrass himself by falling foul to the rolling ocean waves.

They arrive safely at the Isle of White and to Miché's relief, without incident. They are here to rest, refuel their bodies and to assess the situation on the English coast before making their eventual onward journey. As many of the men relax, an informant from the English mainland arrives in a small boat with a message for The Duke.

"What does it say?" Odo stands by his brother's side to hear the news more clearly.

"The King knows of our presence and has his army poised to fight us along the shoreline. We must prepare to cross to the mainland and build our fortification without haste."

As they listen to the Duke's instruction, the Frenchmen collect their conical helmets with protective nose plates, their mail shirts to guard their torsos, and retrieve their shields, spears and axes, in preparation for the next sea crossing towards the mainland. The lowly ranked volunteers gather whatever provisions they could afford before they had set off on the journey. However, the volunteer's protections are grossly inadequate from the potential dangers of the imminent war.

As they await further orders, the knights congregate on the beach while they consider their destination across the Channel. Various thoughts course through the minds of every soldier, and volunteer, but the main thought is, what hell are we headed towards? Many volunteers have abandoned their wives, and families, to do battle against the English, for countless men it's the first time they've ventured away from their homelands. Leo's mood as always, is pensive.

After all, he's left me behind as well and despite the fact that we've been connected over many lifetimes, our life together this time, has only just begun.

Above his head, various species of seabirds conduct the business of surviving. Terns, gulls, osprey and cormorants, dive into the water, to snare fish, sun their outstretched wings, stab worms with their beaks, and drag them from their homes deep within in the sandy beach, some soar majestically above the soldiers heads.

"Oh my God, what was that?" A volunteer feels a splat on the back of his black hair, he couldn't afford a helmet. Leo glances towards his brothers as they sharpen their weapons on whetstones which they've carried with them from home. They laugh heartily at the volunteer's misfortune.

With his lance sharpened, Leo replaces it into its sheath and regards the ground reflectively before he chooses a smooth grey pebble from the beach. Leo feels its flat hard, surface between his fingers. Quickly scanning the sky, he ensures there are no birds circling his head, for two reasons, one, he doesn't want to become a victim of stray excrement, and two, ever the animal lover, he doesn't want to harm a bird with his rock. He determines the coast clear and expertly skims his pebble over the water which skips across the surface four times before splashing into the blue depths.

"Not bad." Miché watches his brother from the sidelines. "Bet I could do better though."

"Come on then, show us how it's done." Leo challenges.

"Right, I'll show you."

As Miché stands, he dusts the residual sand from his bottom and legs. He selects a smooth pebble from the shoreline while he inspects the surface of the glistening water. He then blows gently on the stone for luck and skims it across the still water. It skips three times before plopping into the water.

"Ha! Not good enough." Leo declares. "Mine did four. You'll need to do better than that." Silently, Miché adjusts his footing from one leg to the other, bends down to select another pebble, taking his time to choose the correct one. He waits for a moment before crouching again, he skims his pebble across the water. It skips four times before drowning and with that, Miché raises his hands in triumph, turns towards his brother and lifts him up into the air as he proclaims himself, Champion Extraordinaire.

"He's only matched Leo, not exceeded him. What's all the fuss about?" A brave volunteer mumbles to his group. Luckily, Miché doesn't hear him as he continues to celebrate his victory with his brothers.

As their celebrations die down, Odo makes an announcement to the collective.

"Enough games! Our journey across the Channel is imminent. Board your vessels!" With that proclamation, the mood amongst the knights changes instantly. Word travels down through the ranks that their journey is about to advance. The brothers gather their weapons and head for The Mora. When they reach their ship, Miché clasps his brother's right hands, one by one, shakes them firmly.

"All the best my dear brothers." He heartily slaps them on the back before he climbs aboard. Leo winces as his brother's hand claps upon his back. He knows it's going to wind him a little, he isn't wrong.

The sea fills with hundreds of wooden ships, containing thousands of men, horses and weapons, and as they sail the final stretch towards the English coastline, the weather begins to turn for the worse. The breeze gathers force and the waves grow choppier. Within half an hour of leaving shore, some of the men become seasick and vomit over the sides of the ships. Miché and Darri are solid in their constitution though, they are able to keep seasickness at bay. However, Leo struggles with the choppy conditions, rendering him nauseated. Suddenly, a sharp cramp engulfs his abdomen, he's clammy and hot, he throws up over the side in a violent gush which by the way, makes him feel better, instantly. He reaches into the breastplate of his armour and retrieves the white handkerchief. The fabric is embroidered with our initials, surrounded by delicate blue, pink and violet flowers. Leo looks lovingly at the hanky for a moment, before he wipes the spittle from his lips and re-joins his brothers on the other side of the ship.

"You're looking a bit green there Leo." Darri laughs at his brother's discontent. Miché ever the protector of his family, slaps his little brother on the back of his helmet.

The English coast soon appears in the distance, while gull numbers increase above their heads. Guilliam's men are ready for battle. They are prepared to die for Normandy, and their Duke, if they have to. When the ships reach shore, the horses are released onto the sand and some of the knights ride to Hastings, to collect food for a feast, to ensure they have enough energy to build a base camp and eventually fight. When the men are restored from their journey, they spend their time building a motte, a temporary fortress used to protect their army before they will go forth to do battle with the English.

It's a slow building process and a fortnight passes before they are finally ready to go to war. On the morning of battle, Guilliam resplendent in his shining armour, mounts his gleaming black horse, his mace held aloft in his right hand, flag bearers at his side.

"Men you are about to go into battle against the English, to fight for the rightful owner of the throne. I know you've already sacrificed much to be here and there will be more sacrifices to come, but you are the elite, you will do me, and France, proud. I am by your side in battle and together we will defeat our foes, we will be victorious!"

The men are ready to fight for their leader. They know there will be many deaths, but they have trained for this moment their entire lives.

"Death or glory!" They roar as the Norman Army charges their horses towards the English.

The Englishmen fight their battle, mainly on foot, sheltering from Guilliam's men behind a barricade of wooden shields. Arrows and lances fly through the air like shards of icy rain in a thunderstorm and it isn't long before men, from both sides of the Channel, lie dying and bloodied on the ground. Guilliam's army surprises the English, fighting their opponents from all sides of the battlefield, the English have nowhere to turn, they have been ambushed.

The fighting continues around them, as Leo, Miché and Darri, become separated. Miché and Darri fight to the south, while despite being upon his horse, Leo is trapped by English foot soldiers, to the north of the battle. Suddenly he's cornered.

"Take that, you French bastard." Two English soldiers drive a lance into Leo's side between the gaps of his armour. His brothers are too far away to defend him. He falls from his horse and lies drowning in a pool of his own blood. Leo's breathing is laboured as he whispers to the air around his battered head.

"Dear Lord, bless me....." He knows that he won't make it back to France. This will be the end of the fight for Leo.

As he closes his eyes in elegant anguish, an eagle soars above Leo's head, then he sees me. I smile down on him as I brush aside the wet matted hair on his forehead and I caress his face. The battle rages on around us while I gently kiss him.

"Until we meet again my love."

From a deep sleep, I sit upright in my bed, my heart pounding and I let out a whimper. I've had another bad dream.

The fight continues on around him with more bodies lying inert in bloody pools. Death doesn't discriminate between stations on the battle field as it lays its heavy hand upon the King's brothers. Many horses and hounds can't escape the bloodbath either and they also lay dying on the field. Odo fights bravely alongside his men, but as a man of the cloth, he is unable to wield a sword.

"Look at that pathetic man with his wooden club." An English knight yells out to his fellow soldiers, Odo is determined to spur on Guilliam's knights to continue fighting for France, despite his encumbrance.

"For the Glory of God and the Glory of France, fight for Guilliam!"

As the day progresses, more English men are hacked to death. The Duke's men who are far superior fighters, begin to outnumber the English soldiers which becomes the Norman Army's biggest advantage. All of a sudden, King Harold is left unprotected.

"Attention Darri." Miché warns, then silently motions to his younger brother to get himself into a better position. "We have him covered, surround him!" From close proximity, Miché shoots his arrow into the King's face, without fear, or trepidation, Darri drives his lance into the King's back.

"Got him!" Darri raises his bloodied sword in victory.

As the King draws his last breath, the news of his demise is quickly relayed to The Duke. His men gather around him, Miché and Darri ride quickly towards their ruler just in time to hear the conquest verdict.

"The battle has ended and I, Guilliam, am victorious. I will be crowned the King of England on Christmas Day, in London, before the people of England." Miché and Darri are exultant for but a moment. They bask in the glory of victory as they deliver the deceased king on the back of Miché's horse to the Duke. With their offering, thrust to the ground, Miché and Darri bow before the Duke.

"Thank you, Sir Miché, Sir Darri." Guilliam appreciates the bravery displayed by his knights.

"For your Glory, and the Glory of France and England, long live the King!" Miché and Darri take their leave after bowing down to the new English leader.

"Where's Leo? He should be here to celebrate with us." Miché is agitated and nervous that he hasn't seen his brother for quite some time. "Darri! Where's Leo?"

Still in shock over his assassination of the King, Darri shrugs his shoulders as the glory of victory drains from his veins, replaced with anxiety and panic.

Where is their brother? They can't see him anywhere in their immediate vicinity. With fear and dread in their adrenaline filled hearts, the brothers return to their horses to begin their search for Leo on the blood soaked battle field. After quite some time, examining the crowded field, Miché notices a familiar form.

"He's over here." Miché is the first to spot the body of his brother. It doesn't take long before they're at his side, Leo's body is motionless in a red sea. They rapidly dismount and rush to their brother's body. He's bitterly cold and rigour has started to set in. The smell of death batters their senses.

In a state of shock, Miché tightly grasps Leo's unresponsive body, willing him to reanimate while he and Darri weep silently for their dead brother. Leo's departed forever, they can't process what's happening.

"Oh God, NO! Please don't take my brother! Come on Leo, awake from your affliction." It's the first time Miché has wailed since childhood. Since Leo was Miché's best friend, his brother, his confidante, they were a team who were supposed to continue into old age together, but their profession ensured that would not occur.

"Men it is time to begin our journey to London." Odo, sweating and bloodied, is miraculously still alive as he rallies the troops for the victory ride into London.

"Miché we have to leave Leo's body here. You have to let him go now, we're heading out. Come on." Darri pleads gently with Miché, who finds separation from his brother agonising, from a place deep within, somehow he uncovers the strength to let Leo go.

As he rises, Miché notices a piece of white fabric peeking out of Leo's breast plate. He gently draws it out of the armour and places it behind his own breast plate.

Leo's body is reluctantly discarded by his brothers on the battle field where wolves will discover him by smell, then they will feast on him. Ravens will peck out his eyes, insects, worms and fungi, will recycle his body where he'll return to the earth, the natural environment where he loved to play as a child. He will remain forever young.

A messenger races into the chateau, red faced and panting. He delivers two scrolls from his small sweaty hand to Matilda. One contains good news, the news of her husbands rise in status across The Channel; the other one, reports a tragic death within the Inner Circle. As I walk through the deserted chateau grounds on my daily walk, I feel a shiver travel from the top of my head, all the way down my spine.

Chapter 69 Into the Wilderness

On a day near the end of the millennium, the nightly weather forecast indicates clear blue skies and a cool springtime breeze.

"Why don't we take a hike up to Heartbreak Hill tomorrow boys?" Mitch suggests, as a segment about a hive of bees, taking up residence in someone's letter box, airs on the nightly news, on the silent television above the bar. The mountain range is situated near the state border, however it isn't quite a mountain, but a good sized hill, the trail is long enough to be challenging and worth the long drive. "Come on, it'll be great, just us three men, a female free zone, for once." Even though he knows he doesn't have to, Mitch pleads his case. Declan needs little persuasion to embark on an escapade with Mitch, but Leon seems ensconced in his own world, he requires more prodding.

"I don't know." Leon replies.

"You'll enjoy it. Fresh air and the opportunity to tell us all you know about birds." Mitch nudges Leon's shoulder while he continues to sip his beer. For some strange reason, or for no reason at all, he finally changes his mind about going on the hike, instead of having a lazy Saturday with me.

"Okay, but what time do we have to be up this time?" Leon is still hesitant. He doesn't really want to know the answer, he remembers too many journeys to the bush beginning well before sunrise. In fact, the last time Mitch had one of his great ideas, they had to be out of bed, not long after they'd turned in. Declan stayed up playing video games until it was time to leave. He figured it wasn't worth going to sleep for the short amount of time they had to wait.

On the morning of the walk, Declan and Mitch wake early, the crack of dawn to be precise and they drive to the next suburb to collect Leon. I'm asleep when Leon gets up, but I hear him rouse and move around the apartment. Before he leaves, he bends down and kisses me on the forehead. I sleepily kiss him back, tell him I love him, then I reach out to him for a quick hug.

"Be safe. I will be waiting for your return. I love you so much."

"I can't guarantee anything with Mitch running the show today, but

I'll try. You have so much on today, you won't give me a second thought. I love you so much." He returns my embrace and when he's no longer in sight, I roll over and go back to sleep.

They have to leave early to make the two hundred kilometre journey to the ranges, provide themselves with enough time to hike the track and return to the city. After an hour of driving, they stop on the fringes of the outer suburbs for coffee and a road house breakfast, hopefully to sustain them for a few hours, at least. While Leon and Declan use the bathroom after they've eaten, Mitch grabs a few extra snacks from the temptation trays in front of him and skims through the box of discount CDs. Back on the road, Mitch slips a new CD into the CD player.

"I picked up these little beauties at the road house. Look classics, all three of them. I haven't heard these songs in ages." He cranks up the volume on the Best of the 80s, they all sing along with gusto, even if they don't know all of the words, the effects of the roadhouse coffee has kicked in, life is good.

It's the perfect day for a hike. The sun is peaking out over the horizon as they roar along the highway, in a big grunty truck, Mitch "borrowed" from his construction job site. Mitch justifies the term "borrowed" to his friends with a wink.

"No one is using it for the weekend, so why should it sit in a parking lot going to waste?" Leon taps his brother on the shoulder and gives him a concerned look as he can never be sure if Mitch is kidding, or not. For most of the journey, Leon is worried they are driving in a stolen vehicle and he twitches with anxiety every time the police cruise past.

With loud music playing, best mates sitting side by side, cold beers stored on ice in the cooler to enjoy after the trek, it's everything they need for a successful day. Leon realises his state of contentedness and starts to relax a little. After four, or five, well known songs the singing fades. Mitch and Declan chat excitedly in the front of the cab, while Leon is silent in the back seat behind Declan. Leon's head is pressed against the cool window while he contemplates his life. He definitely has something on his mind, but Mitch and Declan don't seem to notice him, they're too immersed in their own conversation.

When the trio arrive at the conservation park entrance, Mitch parks the car in the gravel car park. They amble up to the old wooden rangers hut, file in through the squeaky fly screen door and sign the hiker's register, signing their names, the date and time, with the name of the track they intend to hike which is Goldfinch. All hikers are required to fill in their details, if they go missing on the mountain, the rangers will have some idea as to where they are, giving them a better chance of rescue.

Declan checks the weather information which is scrolling on a continuous loop on the monitor fixed to the wall above the souvenir hat stands.

"Why are you so focused on that thing for? It's a perfect day for a hike." Mitch views the crystal blue sky through the window as he models a pink bucket hat.

"Yeah, you're right. Just habit I s'pose." Declan follows his brother and friend who have already left via the whiny door.

Outside of the ranger's hut, the trio give each other an awkward high five in anticipation of their adventure ahead, then they easily find Goldfinch track to begin their hike, via the pine sign post. Their backpacks contain snacks, fruit, chocolate, and muesli bars, and each of them carries a one point five litre camel pack, filled with water. The walk is relaxed and easy to begin with, the three friends are somewhat fresh as they've finally woken up from their early start, they're raring to go.

"The adventure begins. For the glory of the summit!" Mitch raises his fist to the sky as the track turns from bitumen, to dirt, a clear sign that they are leaving behind the man made world, for the natural world.

"The glory of the summit!" Declan and Leon chorus.

The path bristles with life, as grey rabbits rustle under bushes, and large Monarch butterflies flit around their heads. An assortment of small and medium sized birds dart from branch to branch, while native bushes release familiar perfumes as the rising sun warms their hidden oils. A lone Wedge-tailed eagle, soars at a great altitude, on the thermal layers above their heads, oblivious to any human cares. It's searching for its next meal no doubt. Mitch brings their attention back to earth with a large belch, then a raucous fart. He can turn on the charm when women are around, but alone with his mates, he's suddenly ten years old again and back at Wolf Cubs.

"Are you okay Mitch. Your guts are rotten. I think you may need to see someone about that problem you have. Allie would know someone that could probably help you out. You should ask her when we see her later tonight." Declan advises, while Leon contemplates his surrounds.

"It's the exercise Declan, it loosens up everything." Mitch explains, waving his hand around his belly.

"Here's one for you. Did you know that male Superb Fairy wren's balls are up to 25% of their overall mass and they collect yellow petals to impress female wrens?"

"Right there. That's why I invite you along. Only you Leon, can come up with that gold, every time." Mitch proclaims.

"Look! Shh. There's some in the bushes over there. Can you hear them call to each other? Look at those beautiful blue feathers." Leon whispers. Declan bored with the bird talk, continues walking along the path.

The last couple of kilometres to the summit are a hard grind as the path becomes progressively steeper and narrower.

"It's just like Peru, hey Leon?" Mitch hollers down the hill.

"It's not quite as steep, but I'm not as fit as I was back then either." Leon puffs as he works his thigh muscles hard to propel himself up the hill. Lagging behind a bit, Declan is glad he hadn't hiked the mountains in Peru, especially if it's harder than this. This hike is proving tough enough for him.

"Breath through your nose. Don't mouth breath, it makes exercise harder."

"Thanks Doctor Mitch." Declan takes the advice and tries to keep his mouth shut while he walks. "Hey, it works."

"I told you didn't I? Now shut your mouth again and keep walking."

Thorny bushes cover much of the path, as they veer too close, the brambles scratch their ankles. Their calves ache, their thighs burn, and their hearts pound, as they tramp to the top. Leon is quiet for most of the journey, but it's becoming more difficult for the other two to talk as they struggle to breathe deeply, individually, they need to concentrate on breathing deeply through their noses while they take the remaining steps to the summit.

At the summit, the trio bellow like hoarse wolves, thrusting their fists into the air in triumph. Mainly, they suck in large amounts of air to catch their breath. Leon bends over with his palms to his knees to aid the process. Feeling a bit nauseated, he doesn't know if he's going to throw up, or not. His ruddy face glistens with droplets of sweat, trickling down his brow, despite the freshness of the mountain breeze. He scans the far horizon, committing to the breathtaking view. Mitch hoicks a large spit ball, casting it into the bushes at their side.

Exhausted, the trio collapse onto a large flat rock while they survey the panoramic view stretched out before them into the distance. The sun is now full and warm. They empty their backpacks onto the salmon coloured dirt in front of them and devour most of the water, and all of the snacks. The eagle has followed them to the summit and circles above their heads before it soars south. It flies to a large nest in a tall eucalyptus tree further down the hill, majestically surveying its territory.

After they've sat quietly for a while, Leon surprisingly breaks the silence.

"I've got something to run past you two."

"Yeah, are you joining a medieval inner circle or something?" Mitch asks with a grin.

"Yeah, you got me. That's exactly what I was going to say."

"Well, what is it then, because Darren joined a medieval group recently?" Declan adds.

"I'm thinking of asking Allie to marry me." Leon ignores his brother and just blurts it out.

"Wow! That's amazing, well done. You two are meant for each other." Mitch congratulates Leon with a hearty hand shake. "It's about bloody time. You've been going out with her for ages."

In a display of congratulation, Declan pummels Leon's back and shakes his hand, when it's free.

"Well that'll be a celebration beer in the car park now." Declan thinks about the well stocked beer cooler in the back of the truck.

"When are you going to ask her?" Mitch probes.

"Soon, but I'll probably have to run it past Rod and Flo first. Don't tell Sara though, I want it to be a surprise."

"Of course." Mitch confides.

"Don't you mean Rod and Isabelle?" Declan wants to correct his brother.

"No, Flo will have my guts for garters, as she always says, if I don't involve her. Allie will want that as well." The three friends silence, engaging with the magnificent view once more.

With exaggerated movements, Mitch rises and brushes the residual sand and dirt he's collected from the rock, from his bum.

"Okay champions, enough rest. Let's go!" Leon and Declan drag themselves up with a groan. They aren't as fit as Mitch and they've appreciated the short respite and quiet contemplation that the summit provides. At least they're descending the hill and not climbing it, a new set of muscles are employed on this stage of their workout, but it seems easier in this direction somehow. Although, Declan's knees are hurting, but he isn't going to tell the others, even though their throbbing thighs will remind all of them of the steep descent in days to come.

Mitch strides on ahead, Declan not far behind him. Taking a moment for himself, Leon breathes in the crisp fresh air of the summit as he enjoys the serenity. Suddenly, he feels the weight of a large firm hand upon his shoulder. The hand radiates warmth throughout his core, disturbed he whips around quickly to see who's there. He thought he was alone, and he is. Just as abruptly, the warm feeling percolates outwards again and a shiver spirals down the length of his spine. Leon is weightless, a bit spacey perhaps, but at total peace.

"What the hell was that?" He says to a disinterested wattle bird.

Awakening from his stupor, he oscillates, but to Leon's surprise, there is no one around. Mitch and Declan have already made a lot of progress from the peak. Rattled, Leon figures he must have imagined the calming hand upon his tired shoulders as he descends the hill. He's been working pretty hard lately and they did have a pretty late night. Perhaps it was his mind playing tricks on him. It happens from time to time. He's very intuitive and sometimes he can see things his friends can't, but nothing like this has happened to him before.

Leon suddenly realises that he has fallen behind, by a long way, his intention is to catch up with his mates as soon as he can. When they understand that he's so far behind them, Mitch and Declan stop a little further down the track by a clump of trees to wait for him. When they see Leon in sight, but still further up the mountain, they automatically continue on their way down the track.

Still confused and a little annoyed that Mitch and Declan aren't waiting for him, a large raindrop plops onto the middle of Leon's forehead.

"Hey, it's starting to rain!" He bellows down the hill.

"A bird must have pooped on your head. Look at the sky it's still mostly blue." Mitch gestures towards the azure horizon, but ominous clouds are forming quickly. Leon explores the top of his head for the offending crap, but his forehead is merely wet. Another droplet crashes onto his cheek, then one falls into his eye. The sky is rapidly changing from clear blue to menacing black and is beginning to empty its soggy contents onto the three hikers.

At first, the three walkers embrace the change in the weather as they turn their faces skyward, inhaling the refreshing scent of ozone. However, refreshment turns into freezing conditions as the wind changes to a southerly direction. The sun disappears in fright behind a thunderous black cloud and suddenly their clothes drip wet from precipitation, not perspiration. Leon notices that the butterflies have vanished, the birds have disappeared to shelter, and the rabbits are nowhere to be seen. Not carrying rain jackets, the torrential downpour pelts the trio, they are drenched by the deluge. On the ground, rivulets are forming in the clay path which in turn are cutting streams which are flowing swiftly down the mountain.

At this point on the trail, there are no trees of any description to shelter under so they continue to gingerly descend the slippery, mud soaked path. One after another, they lose their footing, falling into the sticky mud which bonds to their clothes like glue. Before long, they can't see the original colour of their clothes. Carefully as they can, they trudge most of the way down the mountain, the intensity of the rain increases dramatically, second by second.

The three hikers look like drowned rats. Droplets fall from their eyebrows, hair, noses, earlobes, chins and numb fingertips. Their walking pace has slowed considerably and the trio have become progressively colder while their extremities turn blue from the icy conditions. Leon still lags well behind Declan and Mitch, by about fifty meters. But that's all it takes.

An enormous thunder crack reverberates down the mountain from the heavens. A noise so loud, it echoes through their freezing skin, into their chests, it stops them cold in their tracks. Another thundering boom echoes around the bush after another blinding flash of light. The lightening strikes are happening fast. Before they have time to react to the lightning, tons of mud, boulders and rubble, slide rapidly down the side of the mountain, bringing with it broken tree branches from further up the hill. The mudslide quickly blocks the track behind Declan and Mitch. Leon has no time to run. He couldn't have out run the power of the storm. He has no time to breathe, no time to twitch, no time to pray, or think of me.

Adrenalin courses through them, Mitch and Declan are running, stumbling, and flying, down the mountain in shock. They are so close. Around the next bend, they all would have made it to the truck. When they arrive at the car park, drenched and dazed, Mitch and Declan realise that Leon is no longer behind them. Three mud soaked souls stand by the car, but only one of them realises the propensity of the storm.

I am laying on my yoga mat, in savasana, on the floor of The Valley Yoga Studio. My mind is still after the guided section of the meditation, but I sense a slight twinge at the base of my spine as a tear rolls from my eye onto the mat. It's been an intense Kundalini yoga session, I think that I have released something very powerful, but I don't know how this release is going to manifest in my life just yet. I love Audra's classes, she's such an amazing teacher, but I've never experienced a session quite like this one.

The lightening settles down as a rescue helicopter whirrs noisily above their heads. When the ranger spots Declan and Mitch in the car park, he appears somewhat relieved, however that feeling shifts rapidly when he joins the pair. He knows there are supposed to be three hikers, not two.

"Leon's still up there, on Goldfinch." Mitch shouts to the ranger above the noise of the helicopter.

"What? We can't go up there now, it's too dangerous. We'll have to wait until the storm has well and truly passed before we can get a rescue team up there. The pilot says its a no go zone at the moment."

Mitch and Declan are depleted, they fall despondently onto the mud soaked ground and sink their heads into their wet hands. The ranger radios the paramedics, then the rescue helicopter pilot to report that he's found two of the three walkers alive.

"It's not looking good for the third guy though Steve. Can you take a look over Goldfinch when you can, thanks. Over!" The ranger clicks off his walkie talkie and waits for a reply from the helicopter pilot.

My phone vibrates aggressively as I leave the yoga studio.

Chapter 70 Ailie

I examine a delicate spider's web which is hanging from the roof beams in my chamber. I can't bear to clean them away and I make sure that the servants don't do so either. Even though the maids complain at first, they assert it's their job to clean my room. I'm feeling raw and actually stamp my foot, insisting the webs must stay. As I examine the fine threads which are interwoven so expertly, I consider all of the weaving I've completed in my life and how inspired I was at such a young age by these beautiful creatures. From my purse, I remove his white handkerchief and examine the small neat stitches of my embroidery. One corner of the fabric bears his initials, L du B, reflected on the opposite side are my initials, AB. Intricate flowers in delicate blues, pinks and violet, and there is a single red heart adorning the lacy border.

As I trace over our initials with my finger, I remember the day I had gifted the handkerchief to him, on our wedding day. Our friends and family were gathered in the chapel at Falaise. Papa and Belle, Flynn, The Duke and Duchess, The Du Bois family, on one side, my small family huddled together on the other side of the chapel. I was so happy to see Ottho and Marc, who had made the long journey from Breteuil as well. We promised our vows to each other, witnessed by Odo and God. Leo placed a plain, but fine gold ring upon my finger and I gave him the handkerchief to remind him of our union.

Now, I stand numbly in the chapel until someone I don't recognise helps me to my seat. The surrounding faces are familiar, yet not, the air is heavy with knowing that his life was finite. Odo stands sentry behind the alter. His mouth moves as if he is speaking, yet I can't make out what he's saying. My ears are muffled and refuse to hear, a low hum echoes within them. Suddenly, my hearing returns and there's clarity. A recognisable prayer, chanted by the congregation, reminds me there is peace to be found in the familiar and rote.

Expectation of the congregation rests heavily upon me. I'm a noble born woman married into the realm of the Duke's Court. I'm expected to be a picture of steadfastness, but every atom of my soul wants to run from the stone church and be somewhere else. If I could have run all the way to Breteuil and sit at my loom in Ottho's workshop, I would have. But I have responsibilities to my family, to the Duke and Duchess. Of all the sorrows in my life, this is the hardest to face. There is too much emotion involved, too much to bear.

Chapter 71 Allie

I stare into the deep puddle below. My legs wobble in the reflection and shake in reality, my heart pounds. A clear, yet mournful complexion stares back at me. Who is that woman? Silence prevails through every crevice of my being, even though the city is bounding on regardless. Its throbbing vibrancy falls silent over my mind, standing still, my pulse races. I notice a serene puddle in the middle of the gravel driveway. A drop of rain batters the puddle and shatters the moment. One by one, hundreds of droplets conjoin with the puddle and the dust morphs into mud. The rain pelts down hard. It falls so hard that water is sent towards heaven with enormous force. It's been a wet year so far.

I shake free of my daze and run to cover under the chapel porch. Avoiding a near collision with other mourners, I arrive almost drenched and I stand numbly in the chapel until someone I don't recognise, helps me to my seat. While I take my place in the second row, water falls from my hair into my eyes, disguising the tears that fall in unison. I reach for the memorial card and see his face staring back at mine. I have to put it in my purse to stop everything being too real.

The surrounding faces in the congregation are familiar, yet not, the air is heavy knowing that his life was finite. Cathy, Archie, Declan, and Claire, stand sentry in the first row. Their lives have been shattered, they are shattered. When the pastor speaks, I can tell that he's speaking, his mouth is moving, yet I can't make out what he is saying. My ears are muffled, they refuse to hear clearly, a low hum echoes within them. Suddenly, my hearing returns and there is clarity. A recognisable prayer, chanted by the congregation, reminds me there is peace to be found in the familiar and rote.

I think that I'm expected to be a picture of steadfastness for Cathy, Archie, Declan and Claire, but every atom of my soul wants to run from the chapel and be somewhere else at that moment. If I could have run all the way to Barcelona and sit at a table with him in the square, I would have. But I have a responsibility to his family, to Cathy and Archie. Of all the sorrows in my life, this is the hardest to face. There is too much emotion involved, too much to bear.

Chapter 72 Leo

Throughout the grounds of Chateau de Falaise, a brave young battle scarred knight traverses the buildings and grounds in search of his love. No-one interacts with him as he desperately combs the area for her, room after room, through the top levels of the chateau, down to the bowels of the dungeon, outside to the kitchen, and through the stables. He lingers in the stalls, remembering our encounter, the horses have sensed his presence. They whinny in acknowledgement, causing the squire to look up from his work.

"What's the matter fellas?" An icy shiver runs down his spine, but he shakes it off and continues with his chores. The knight leaves the stables and continues his search. The horses calm down, the squire is left haunted.

Chapter 73 Leon

Around the corner, in a cafe on the high street, stands a young man. He holds a cup of coffee, steaming in his hands. His boots are muddy and wet, his faded jeans are spattered with dark mud. He's staring hard into space, his hips against the counter, steam rises into his angel face. His eyes are a clear, deep, dark, blue, yet totally immersed in another world. A lady walks by with her golden retriever, he barks softly in acknowledgement.

"What's up boy? No one's around. You're such a funny dog. Barking at shadows, what are you like?" She bends down and gives her pet a reassuring rub.

Leon can't make head or tail of the situation either.

Chapter 74 Ailie

I continue to live at Chateau de Falaise, even after the battle that wrenched my love from me. Guilliam is King of England and Matilda is making preparations to follow him, as his Queen. She has ruled Normandy while her husband is away, but now after almost a year apart, they are to be reunited. Millie, as her Maid in Waiting, will travel with her. Before they depart, we gather to say our farewells.

"We shall miss you terribly Ailie." Matilda holds my hands tightly.

"I shall miss you as well, but I would love to visit you in London someday." Millie's eyes well as she embraces me. She knows that I need a friend, now more than ever, but she is beholden to her mistress. All she can do is firmly hold me together for a few moments. There are no words to convey how she feels. The loss that Millie suffers is nothing compared to the loss she knows I have experienced, she wishes that she could release my burdens and throw them away.

When the royal party departs for London, the castle becomes momentarily quiet as I watch them leave through the tower gate from my window. My heart breaks again when I see little Robert wave to me from the coach, his Tatie Ailie. I blow my nose and think of all the times the baby has made me smile and laugh. He used to follow the knights around the hall with his small wooden sword which he'd trip over while he tried to keep up with his favourite knight, Leo. This thought makes me sad all over again, so to guard my emotions, I turn away from the window and wander down to the hall. Jaimin is old now too, he ambles despondently behind me. He misses Leo as much as I do.

From the stairs, I see Miché peering deeply into the fireplace. I claim my position on an adjoining seat and silently stare into the fire with my grief stricken brother-in-law.

"This is not how it was meant to be. We were meant to grow old together and watch our children play ......" He trails off, incapable of finishing his train of thought.

"I know." I reply, unable to find anything useful to say that will alleviate the situation, we return our attention to the flames, in silence.

Within minutes, Darri joins us to warm himself by the fire and with his back turned to the flames he smiles with sympathy, I manage to return a narrow smile.

As he warms himself, Miché and I can hear Darri's stomach gurgle and rumble.

"Have you eaten?" I ask with concern.

"Sounds like he's digesting a sick cow." Miché observes.

"Yes, I have eaten, thank you Ailie. I've just eaten a large bowl of cabbage and beans in the kitchen." Darri replies ignoring his brother. His face displays visible angst, his stomach grumbles, the pressure builds as the noise flows through his bowels and out through his tights. "Puuuuuft." Jaimin looks up from his place by the fire, his sense of smell is still as keen as ever.

"Oh my God, did you just fart in front of your grieving sister-in-law, Darri?" Miché accuses his brother of this heinous crime while suppressing a smile and holding his nose.

Darri's face turns beetroot and for the first time, in a long time, I can feel a chuckle rise in my throat. I can't suppress my laughter any longer, it tumbles out of me just as Darri's fart exited his buttocks. Darri's condition is still audible and becoming progressively worse as Miché joins in the laughter. Suddenly, Darri excuses himself and runs from the room before he is terribly disgraced, causing us to laugh uncontrollably, temporarily freeing us from grief.

Within the depths of grief, my natural inclination is to return to work and the next morning, Odo gives me that opportunity. With his brother's epic rise to King of England, Odo is titled the Earl of Kent and he regularly travels between England and France to conduct his business. The newly appointed Earl offers his condolences and quickly continues with the business at hand.

"We would like to commemorate the Battle at Hastings with a banner, or an illustration, that depicts the battle, scene by scene. We need an embroiderer who will oversee the project and will liaise between myself, who was at the battle, and the women who will be working on the tapestry, in Kent. With your knowledge of the craft and your connections to Guilliam, and Knights of the Inner Circle, we think you're just the person for this exercise, Ailie."

"Your Grace, you humble me. I would be honoured to work on this piece for you." "Bear in mind that this tapestry will be a grand and a permanent record for future humanity to understand the juxtaposition between the devastation and the supposed glory of war. *La Telle du Conquest*, will be hung in the Bayeux Cathedral at its dedication in 1077." Odo informs me. "And remember it has to be impressively large."

I am overwhelmed with the new role that I've been given, but also pleased with the distraction, given my new circumstances, I can't wait to begin.

"You'll sail for England and work with the weavers as soon as we can arrange your passage."

"Thank you Your Grace, I will do my best to honour those who have fallen and those who found Glory in battle."

Within a week, I sail for England where I'm to meet with the embroiderer's guild. I've requested that Osanna travel with me as she had been my mentor all those years ago and I would love her help on this project, she has such a good eye for detail. A messenger is sent to Breteuil to fetch her. However, on their return a week later, the messenger reports that Osanna has died.

"I'm sorry to say that she passed away from a strong fever Ma'am." The messenger looks mournfully down at his feet.

"Oh, dear." I am pained and saddened at another sudden loss. Osanna meant a great deal to me and I will miss her greatly. The messenger pauses for a moment to allow me to process the information, he shuffles his feet, then continues as he has other messages to pass on. Time is of the essence.

"In her place, Ottho will send Bertram. He has been learning weaving and embroidery under Marc."

"Oh, thank you. I look forward to seeing him." Before I had finished my sentence the messenger has bowed and fled the chateau.

When Bertram arrives, I barely recognise the young man who stands before me. I remember Bertie as a boy, who'd swept the workroom floor and quietly comforted me in times of stress. Now, he is a young man who has grown tall, his hair is still a dusty red colour, his facial features are sharper though, he has lost his boyish pudge. When he tells me about Osanna's death, he gently pats me on the back as he has always done and I immediately feel calmness wash through my grieving soul. I don't know what it is but he always has the magic touch just when I need it.

Bertram and I pass the evening catching up on old times, talking about workmates, family and friends from Breteuil. Eventually, I broach the prickly subject of Sarra.

"And how is your sister faring these days?" I ask tentatively.

"Oh Sarra, now where do I begin with her?" Bertram rolls his eyes and winks. We begin to laugh at the thought of Sarra who is all bluster and bluff on the outside, and a scared little girl on the inside.

"I do hope she's happy though."

"I think she is, but you can never be sure with Sarra, she's always complaining about something. Her husband is a solid man, but she bullies him terribly. You know, she has about a hundred children, well five robust mouths to feed at least." He continues with a smile.

"Well, we best turn in, we have a big day ahead of us tomorrow."

"Good night Ailie."

"Good night Bertram." As I climb the stairs to my chamber, I turn around. "It's so nice to see you again Bertram, thank you for travelling to Falaise to help me with this project." I continue up the stairs while Bertram simultaneously smiles, blushes and waves.

"You're welcome Ailie."

Odo makes the voyage with us to Kent. Our passage across the channel is a little rough, however Bertram and I have never seen such a large expanse of water before and we sit in wonder, marvelling at the view before us. We find joyous pleasure from the bow spray on our faces, while Odo huddles away from the damp, shielded by a large trunk. As we sail, I remember the dream that I'd had many years before, the one about this body of water and the battle that waged on the other side.

I realise now that the love that I'd been searching for was Leo and no matter how hard I look when we land, I'll never rediscover him in the flesh. Bertram sees my face slip into grief, he clasps my hand and holds it for some time while I search the horizon for a glimpse of peace.

When we reach land, a coach drives us to Odo's manor house in Kent where he is the Lord.

"Please consider this your home while you're working on the tapestry. I'll be here for a few days and then I'll return to Bayeux to consult with the builders of the new Cathedral."

"Thank you, Your Grace." Bertram and I chorus.

The servants have built us a lovely fire in the dining room and have prepared a hearty dinner which we enjoy by the fire.

"I hope you enjoy the wine, I bring new supplies from France every time we sail and I stock the cellar so that I don't have to drink the English fare." He turns his nose up in disgust and we politely laugh.

When dinner has ended, Odo produces a large piece of paper that would have cost a small fortune, but as he is the King's step brother, he can well afford it. With the table cleared of clutter, Odo begins to sketch out his ideas for the tapestry, providing a timeline of the battle, he wants immortalised in fabric and threads.

"Goodness! This will be an enormous project." I realise Odo wasn't joking when he said that the tapestry needs to be big.

"You can do this Ailie." Bertram assures me. "I'll help you and I know that the embroiderers here will also be of great assistance."

"Thank you Bertram, you always know how to make me feel better about myself." I return my attention to Odo's sketches and as I see the battle play out in front of me, I sense a pang of anxiety tug at my stomach.

The next morning, the senior embroiderer from the Kent Embroiderer's Guild arrives to meet with Odo, Bertram and myself. Odo shares his sketches and ideas with Hildred. As she assesses the sketches, she sees and hears of Odo's vision, a portrayal of the bloody battle fought by French knights and the Duke, against her countrymen. I see a harrowed look cross her face, a look I recognise as my own.

"Are you alright Hildred, you appear sickened."

"I'm sorry my face gives away my grief, but my husband was killed in this battle." I peer down at my dress for a moment and then at Hildred, I take her hand in mine.

"I'm so sorry for your loss, my husband also died in this battle."

We exchange the knowing glances of those who share the anguish of a similar trauma. It's going to be difficult working on such a significant and difficult piece, but we are hopeful that we can work through our pain and be healed by it. Hildred reaches into her pocket and retrieves a white hanky. She leans over to me, wipes the tears from my cheek and gives me a quick, self conscious hug. Despite having just met, our encounter feels like motherly love. I feel nurtured, loved and understood, I hope Hildred feels the same. Then I pull out my handkerchief and show her my embroidery work. We examine each others art and smile. Her handkerchief is almost the same as mine except for the different initials in the corners.

During our meeting, Hildred, Bertram and I, make notes of all the different materials we'll require to realise Odo's dream.

"We'll need many crewel cones, in various colours of course, different shades of greens, blues, gold, reds, yellows, oranges, russets would be good, and a lot of black to outline the pictures. Considering Odo's drawings, we'll need about 75 metres of linen, lots of needles, and some thimbles for all of the workers. What do you think?"

"That sounds fair." The senior embroiderer agrees. I give Hildred the list so that she can place the order as she knows the local merchants and more importantly, she speaks the language.

When the materials finally become available, the team of embroiderers begin the onerous task of carefully sewing the battle scenes onto the fabric using the coloured yarns. The sewers outline the illustration using stem stitch and fill in the outlines using couching stitches. Slowly but surely, I witness the battle scene come alive on the fabric. It's painful for me, and the other embroiderers, who have lost love ones on the battle field to see such a vivid depiction come alive, but I revel in the opportunity to use my skills, to make a piece of art which will adorn the new Cathedral in Bayeux. I bond with the women as we sew, they have been through this torment with me, even though they are supposedly from the other side, they are humans who have been through horrific circumstances as well. I will not separate myself from my humanity, just because it may have been one of their husbands who had killed mine. They have suffered just as much as me. Leo wouldn't want me to carry hatred in my heart, he never did. These women are my sisters, the sisters I'd never had, but now I do.

After months of painstaking work, pricked fingers, sore backs and weary eyes, the tapestry is completed on time. It is time for Bertram and me to return to Bayeux and present Odo with his commemoration piece. I'm disappointed that I can't make time to go to London, to see Matilda and Millie, but I have to return to France to meet with Odo and then return to Paris, news of my work has reached the Palace. Known as the amorous king, King Philip has requested that I work on some new tapestries for the royal house, he won't be outdone by Guilliam. I know that when things settle down I will return to London to visit Matilda and Millie.

Three Years Later: Ailie

"I can't believe it's taken you ten years to visit us." Matilda wraps her arms around me, hugging me tightly. Robert, and his two new siblings that I haven't met before, are playing in the garden while Matilda is glowing, her rotund belly heralds the imminent arrival of a fourth child.

"I know, it's been a lifetime, yet only a few years." I marvel at the English castle and the loving family it contains.

"We never really miss you, we see your work all over the place and think of you. Our messengers tell us that your pieces have been displayed in castles and cathedrals all over Europe. But we do wish that you could visit us more often."

"Well, I have a team of people to help me. Its not just my work you know."

"Still so humble, despite your success."

"By the way where is Millie? I wanted to offer my congratulations and give her a big hug."

"She'll be here soon. She's so excited that you will be here for the wedding."

"I'm looking forward to seeing the groom. How is Sir Miché?"

"He's okay, I think, he's a little sad that his best man won't be by his side."

"I can imagine." I look down at my dress, a wave of sadness washes over me again. I think of Leo. But I'm not sad for very long as Millie bounds into the room. I stand to greet her, I wipe my eyes as tears flow for a variety of reasons, then she grabs me with both arms.

"Oh my goodness, it has been a lifetime." She squeals and hugs me even harder.

"I just said that to Matilda."

During our embrace, a small and delicate spider inches its way towards the top of the woodpile which sits underneath the wedding tapestry that I helped to make all those years ago. The spider catches my attention, drawing me in. Breaking away from Millie's embrace, I inspect the spider and her web. In the threads I see a face, it's Leo's face and a thousand years wash over me in an instant. Then the spider returns to her web at the top of the woodpile, waiting patiently for her next adventure into the unknown.

Chapter 74 Allie

A gravel path wends through pretty garden beds lined with tulips, iris', freesias and daisies. Their fragrances waft skywards and mix with the heat of the sun while moisture, left from the rain, creates a heady scent. Honeyeaters and rainbow lorikeets chirp merrily from the tree-tops, rejoicing in the freshness. A spider web glistens in a tree and the strings of its home shine like tiny diamonds in the sun. Couples laugh and whisper to each other, aware that I walk towards them, black in my heart. They stare at me, following me with their eyes as I move along the twisting path. Butterflies flutter, in and out, around my head. A cool breeze teases the fine, wispy hair around my face, blowing it into my eyes and mouth. My feet crunch in time on the gravel beneath my shoes. But despite the beauty surrounding me, I can't appreciate it. My heart is empty and crushed, my stomach retches and is nauseous. It's too soon to feel. It's too soon to be.

I push my hands deeper into the pockets of my purple anorak and with the tips of my fingers, I touch security and reality. The poem I've clung onto for how many years is it now? I grasp it with the tips of my fingers and push it into the palm of my hand. I squeeze it tight extracting all of its strength. I've maintained the tension on the poem for quite a while, my hand is starting to ache. As I gently release my grip on the wad of paper, a hot tear rolls down my face. That's all that I will allow myself though, one solitary tear. I rummage through my handbag for the half empty bottle of Rescue Remedy, place the dropper under my tongue and squeeze the bulb gently three times. Almost immediately, I feel numbing relief.

With some renewed spirit and sense of purpose, I exit the lift on the second floor. I am trying. When I venture out into nature, even for a short period of time, as always, it makes me feel slightly better. I'm determined to show a brave face and cope. Aubrey the mail boy, delivers an enormous stack of mail, I roll up my sleeves and launch into my tasks. The radio on my desk is switched on for ambient noise and I mumble to myself tunelessly, in that barely audible, no one else needs to hear my singing voice. All of a sudden, while I'm opening envelopes, sound fails to leave my lips. A song wafts up from the radio, it's our song. The tune fills the empty spaces of the room and my mind. My head is fuzzy and loud. My trance is shattered by the ringing of the telephone.

I lift the receiver to my ear, half concentrating on the song playing on the radio. Even though I'm at work and this is my job, I'm a little annoyed to be distracted from my memories.

"Hello, Allie O'Neil, how can I help you?" I use my clipped work voice, then wait for a caller, but I can only hear our song playing at the other end. No one replies. "Hang on a second, I'll just turn down the radio." I reach over to turn down the radio and put the handset back to my ear. "Sorry about that. Now ......" All that emanates from the telephone receiver is our song, the song that has been playing on the radio. I can't believe what's happening. The radio is definitely off, I have switched it off at the wall. "Hello is anybody there? Hello?" I yelp with panic in my voice and heart. Nobody answers. The song eerily continues to play and when it ends, the line goes dead.

I let go of the receiver, letting it crash down onto my desk. In a silent daze, I walk numbly to the ladies, straight into a cubicle and throw up into the toilet. My empty stomach retches. Slouched over the bowl, I'm hot on the cold tiles, depleted. After cleaning myself up, I return to my desk confused and alone. Who can I confide in? I don't want to tell anyone, I feel like I'm going mad. People will tell me it's the overwhelming grief. Am I imagining the call to bring myself comfort? But it doesn't bring me comfort at all, it scares me.

After I leave the toilets, I call it quits on my work day as I know that I won't be able to focus on my tasks, I'm too rattled. Before I leave the building, I tell Marie at the next desk that I'm not feeling well and I go home. I catch the number five bus and when it stops, I continue home in a daze. With a puff of exhaust fumes, the metropolitan bus roars off into the distance and I soon find myself standing at our front door, keys in hand, ready to enter emptiness.

I switch off the alarm at the key-pad control, struggling to remember the combination of numbers I've recalled easily for over a year.

Entering the hallway, I glance at the pictures Leon had drawn and we had framed. I'd found them in his draw when we first moved in together, not long after we arrived home from France. At first, he was embarrassed by the drawing he'd done of me, from that first awkward encounter, but he had it framed for our first anniversary and now here we are, without him. I open the backdoor for Hugo, he sadly flops down onto Leon's side of the couch, he rests his head on his paws and snuffles. He's getting old, but he knows his friend and master hasn't returned, he mourns right alongside me.

I flick through the junk mail I've automatically collected from the letter box and let the glossy papers drop onto the coffee table as I do every evening. I'll go through them later, with a glass of wine, with the intention of giving them more attention. Looking across the room, I notice lights flickering violently on the CD player. I tentatively open the clear glass doors of the stereo cabinet, my heart thumps. Through the clear cover, I can see a CD whirring around at great speed. The volume control is wound down to zero so I twist it around to two so that I can just hear the music playing. Hugo hears it before I do, he cocks his head to one side. As I hear the first few notes, my hand slips and the dial winds around to ten, blasting the room with our song. "*And I will la la la la!*" The bass thumps in my head, my chest, my feet, my soul, my core. Hugo barks and jumps off the couch.

"It's alright boy. Shh. Where are you Leon?" Frustrated and scared, I direct my plea to the ceiling while I pat Hugo's back.

With my other hand, I reach for the volume control, turn the sound down and decide to turn the stereo off. To make doubly sure, I pull the plug out of the wall socket. I don't remember putting that CD on the stereo, in fact I've gone out of my way not to play it at all, it's too painful. Didn't I purposely put it at the back of my CD stack so that it wouldn't be played by our friends who fossick through our collection when they visit? But there's the cover, sitting open, on top of the CD player.

At first, the song was a bit of a joke. Someone gave it to us for a secret Santa present, one of our cheap friends, who took it from their mum's CD collection. We would fawn with surprise when it played in a pub, or club. The song reminded us of our first date in Barcelona and brought us fond memories. We'd smile secretly at each other and sing along, sometimes in an outrageous Spanish accent. Occasionally we'd sing along quietly and thoughtfully, at other times we'd sign loudly and wildly, enacting the lyrics to each other. It all depended on how we were feeling and how our relationship was at the time. The way we sang the song was litmus paper for our relationship, but it was also our private guilty pleasure. We thought that it was a bit of a cliché, to refer to it as our song, but after a while, it really did become our song.

I reach for the cordless phone, ignoring the flashing light signalling missed calls. The phone had sat on a small table next to a vase, exploding with delicate pink tulips, a gift from Aunty Diane. I key a pre-set number and bite at the cuticles on my left thumb.

"Can you meet me at the bar in half an hour?"

"See you there. I was just about to leave work anyway." Sara answers

The singer in the corner strums lightly on his guitar as the crowd settles in for after work drinks. Vince sings at the bar every Friday night, as professionals cleanse the stress and worry from their life, drinking the magic liquid that makes them fabulous and sexy, no matter how bad their lives are. He's used to, and expects people to stare at him as they drink suggestively through long black straws. Of course he'll smile at them, letting them think there's a chance, but he's always faithful to his one true love, himself. He'll only digress for a truly delicious and exceptional man. In his mind, the stranger has to be a true mirror of his own dark, mysterious, beauty, a vision that rarely crosses his path. However, many people try to tempt him, none are successful.

I'm alone at a small table in the back corner waiting for Sara to arrive. I order a dark and stormy, ironically his drink. When it arrives, I stir the ice, remove the straw and take a long gulp of the dark amber wonderful. I repeat the process and find there's no more numbing deliciousness to be had, only ice dregs. The waiter brushes past me, I embrace the opportunity to order another one. When the next drink arrives, I stir the ice with the straw before taking it out and balance it on the redundant ashtray. This time, I carefully sip my drink and enjoy the feeling of the cool liquid, trickling down my already semi numb throat.

Halfway through my second drink, Sara arrives shaking the rain from her hair and shoulders. Sara's hair is styled in a neat bob, her clothing is impeccable and in one beautiful movement, she removes her coat and silk scarf from around her neck, she thrusts out her cheek for me to plant a friendly kiss. Sara sits down, carefully surveying the room, regarding the regulars and the waiter. When her eyes finish scanning the room, they settle on me. Despite the humidity, her hair remains intact.

"Where did you get to yesterday? No one could find you." Sara's brow crinkles, I just shrug my shoulders.

"Oh, um, I walked around a park for a bit and then I had to get back to work, I don't know where the day went." I laugh nervously and take another sip of my drink.

"I switched off my phone and had my work phone diverted to my dormant mobile. I just didn't want to talk to anyone anymore. I was too overwhelmed at the wake and I needed to get out of there. Their family has a piece missing, I just couldn't." I feel as if I'm going to start crying again, I sniff back the tears and take another swig of my drink.

I decide not to tell Sara about the telephone calls and the music, just yet. I have to keep it to myself for a while because the pain and confusion won't allow me to verbalise what's happening. I'm spiralling with grief.

"Allie, the rest of the wake was actually really nice. I don't know how she did it, but Claire made such a lovely speech, thanking everyone for their support. I think the whisky was helping her though, Declan was really strong for everyone. But you weren't alone in your escape act. Archie went AWOL for a while. He's crushed, the stress of being the strong patriarch has obviously taken its toll. But then after a while, he came wandering back into the pub, he went straight for the duke box. He programmed the music he knew that Leon loved. They played a few retro songs and that song you two always sing. What's that song?"

I know straight away what the song is, but I don't have the energy to explain it, besides, Sara will remember it eventually, tomorrow perhaps. "Everyone asked where you'd gotten to. Cathy said she was really worried about you.....blah, blah, blah, blah."

I'd tuned out at the mention of his name. Sara suddenly stops mid-sentence, realising that I haven't listened to a word she's said. She sips her pinot noir and while she replaces her glass on the table, she quickly considers the room once more before waving her hand in front of my blank face. I snap back to attention, straighten myself while I flick my fringe with my fingers and place a section of hair behind my ear. The alcohol has kicked in, I sweep up my hair into a ponytail with my hands, my elbows held high in the air and then in one motion, I let my hair cascade down around my shoulders, releasing it all with a verbal sigh. I've started to loosen up a little bit and Sara senses it, she ceases talking about yesterday, and the days leading up to yesterday. We clink our glasses.

"*Sante*, here's to getting drunk!" We chorus, skulling the remaining contents of our glasses and immediately order more.

The room fills with revellers and the talk, laughter, and music, fight for supremacy. None of them win, but an overall hum fills the air. Sara and I gossip about the regular and new patrons, about work mates, and family. Not that either of us has much of the latter, but they enter into the conversation, every now and then. Sara knows instinctively not to broach the subject of Leon again, she waits for me to bring him up. She'll have to wait a long time though, something she already knows. I try hard not to allow sorrow to enter. I'm stubborn and I know that if I let it in, it will spin me out of control. But then I'll have to let him go eventually, it'll be too much one day, but I'm not prepared to do that yet. I can't let him go.

The next morning, feeling hung over and hungry. I don't think I ate anything the day before. I go to the kitchen to make my usual breakfast of toast, a smear of apricot jam, and a strong black coffee. I layer the toast with thick globs of sticky apricots which jut out all over the bread, slosh milk into my coffee, and plop in three teaspoons of sugar.

I deserve a bit of sweetness I think, as I unwrap a mini chocolate and plop it into the cup as well. Another steaming cup of coffee sits on the kitchen bench, forgotten, I always make two. Sickly sweet, milky coffee in one hand, I hate milky coffee. What am I thinking? Jammy toast clenched in my mouth, I retire to the lounge room. This is going to make me feel better, temporarily forgetting my hangover and milk aversion. I switch on the telly and turn the channels to the video music channel. This is a Saturday morning ritual of ours. Then I am supposed to be going to yoga, but I don't think I can go back there again. It's probably what I need to do, but no.

I'm alone, except for Hugo, he's sleeping at the end of our bed. Despite the music, the apartment is too quiet. Bored with the song playing on the television, I turn my attention to the flashing light on the telephone and press the key pad to retrieve my messages. A worried message from Dad escapes the receiver.

"Hi love, um, I hope you're okay, Give us a ring when you're up to it hey. Finn and I are here all day if you want to pop over. Flo came over the other day and asked after you as well. Oh well, I guess you'll call when you're ready, bye pet." A loud piercing beep heralds the next message.

"Hi beautiful, it's Mum, sorry I can't be there for you right now. I'm in Paris visiting Trudi. Hope you're okay." I hear a few more messages from concerned friends, Audra telling me not to rush back to yoga which makes me feel better about missing it today. Then some messages from family, even some from Leon's family, but Finn has been quiet, I haven't heard from him yet. Even though he reads a lot of words, I know he has trouble verbalising them. Mitch left quite a long rambling message too, then another beep.

There's silence for a few seconds, then flowing out of the receiver, our familiar song chimes in mono tone. "And I will la la la la la la." Part of the way through the song, a recorded message chimes in. The sound of the message fights against the noise of the television. When the message is finished, three loud beeps signal it's completion. There's a voice, a man's voice in the distance, his voice? Another beep, then a women's voice.

"To hear this message again press........" When the telecommunication woman finishes her spiel, the phone beeps again, then there's silence.

But what did he say? In the race to hit the mute button on the remote, I almost send my coffee flying across the room, but like a circus juggling clown, I manage to save it at the last moment. I follow the woman's instructions to replay the message, again and again, but the sound is too muffled to hear precisely what is said. I hold the phone tightly to my chest for a few moments. Staring blankly at the soundless television set, I absently lick a piece of apricot from my toast as Hugo wanders in. He'd heard it too.

I open the crumpled paper that I've been carrying around for the past year and slowly read his poem.

Forget the past
Open a window
Let me breathe you in
Slowly deeply
Catch my heart pounding
Stop the world
Let us begin
Start the world again
Race to know infinitely
Slowly, savouring,
Warm rain

Phase Four: Chapter 75 Allie

As I begin to heal, the songs and calls subside. I carry Leon closely in my heart, but I have to sell our apartment. It's too painful, living in the place where we'd shared so many great memories. Dad will take care of the sale, he suggests that I move my things back into my old bedroom and take off somewhere. I've outgrown my job as a receptionist and I'm not feeling the vibe of the college any longer. My role has become routine, too comfortable, too boring. I type my resignation letter on my new laptop at Dad's kitchen table, when I've finished the letter, I switch to a search engine and research travel sites.

Paris is our city, however I want to spread my wings and visit somewhere else. But try as I might, to discover South East Asia, or South America, I keep returning to the pages on France. Perhaps, I can fly into Paris and branch out from there, use the City of Lights as a stepping stone. Before I know it, I've grabbed my car keys, my sunglasses and handbag, I'm out the door. At the travel agents, I inform the smartly dressed lady that I'd like to fly into Paris, but I don't need accommodation because I'll be staying with my friend, Trudi. I'll make further arrangements once I arrive.

"When do you want to leave?"

"Is Sunday too soon? I have to tie up some loose ends and then I want to be out of here." It's Wednesday so I'll have to act fast. Luckily my passport is still valid.

"Yes there are seats available. Shall I book you in?"

"Yes lets do it."

Sara, Mitch, Declan, Dad and Leon's parents, all see me off at the airport and while we are saying our farewells, Cathy tearily hands me Leon's old blue day pack.

"He would've wanted you to have this love." She also gives me a beautiful silk scarf which has been wrapped in tissue paper. The white scarf has pretty blue, pink and violet flowers hand stitched in the corners. "Every young lady needs a silk scarf to wear in Paris."

"Thank you Cathy, it's really beautiful. Take good care of Hugo, he's getting old like the rest of us." I'm doing my best to suppress my emotions, I fear it's not working very well. I swipe a tear.

"Don't you worry about Hugo, he's my favourite grand-baby."

"Yeah, he'll be looked after better than she looks after me. Since all the kids have moved out...." Archie shuts up immediately and inspects his shoes while he thinks about his son who won't be visiting him ever again. We hug and shed more tears. Cathy kisses my forehead, we both sob. I wipe my runny nose and shove my handbag into the day pack, then drape the scarf around my neck as I say my goodbyes to everyone. My friends and family wave furiously as I disappear into the international departures area, suddenly I'm alone again.

My aircraft stops in Singapore, with a long wait until my next flight. Luckily there's a lot to explore in Changi Airport. Guiltily, I eat a fairly bland meal from a chain takeaway, I always experience a funny stomach when I fly, even though the temptation to try more adventurous cuisine beckons. To squander time, I mooch around luxury boutiques, recline in the waiting chairs while I observe weary travellers from all over the world, try to regain a sense of comfort within their various confines of arrival and departure. I watch mothers feed their small squirming babies on the vinyl seats, business men conduct meetings and process documents from the business class lounge, they are separated from the hoi poli, some of them are scattered at the general bar, backpackers call ahead to secure accommodation. Husbands and wives phone their partners and children at home, informing their families they'll be home soon. However, the hardest people to watch are the young couples heading to Europe. So in love, adventures to look forward to. And here I am, Allie Bell, starting all over again with few, if any ties to the world.

Out of curiosity, I reach into Leon's backpack and fossick around the pockets. Most of them are empty, but there is something smooth and cool in one of the side pockets. I pull out a crystal which I haven't seen before and wonder where Leon found it, or how he came to have it. There's a piece of paper at the bottom of the pocket and I read it carefully. It says that it's a moonstone, and apparently, it's helpful for new beginnings. Since I'm between worlds, in every aspect of my life,

I'm hopeful of a new beginning and I carefully re-wrap the crystal in the piece of paper and put it in the zipped pocket inside my handbag so it won't get lost. I walk to my departure gate.

As I leave the arrivals hall at Charles de Gaul Airport, I notice the crispness in the air as I roll my suitcase to the adjacent train station. I laugh out loud, remembering the first time I was here with Sara and how we'd stumbled with the different RER and Metro stations, our nervousness, our naiveté. Our first big journey jitters. I make connections without a hitch this time and stroll down Rue de Passay where Trudi is at home to greet me. The Frenchwoman appears older and a little tired, she must think the same about me. We embrace warmly and Trudi places my bag in the hall.

"Let's go out for breakfast, shall we? I have something to tell you."

We peruse the menus which are already on the table when we arrive.

"I'm so sorry about your loss Allie. I can't imagine how you must be feeling." I'd forgotten that Trudi knew about Leon. But of course she knew of him, she'd even met him at the very beginning, when we'd spent some time in Paris before travelling back to Australia. Naively, I thought that Paris would be a Leon free zone, but who am I kidding, it's the second place we'd spent time together. The whole city is a Leon zone. Trudi senses this and advances the conversation.

"So, your mother is here in France at the moment, she's been here for quite some time actually." Trudi bluntly announces.

"Yes, I know, she rang me last week after the funeral. I thought she might still be here."

"It's really not my place to say this, but your mother and I have been spending quite a lot of time together, we're very close. Isabelle returns from Normandy soon, she's been staying with my family there for a while. She thought she would let you land and have a bit of a break before you reconnect. She really wants to make amends with you, you know?"

"Wow! That's a lot to take in."

The waitress arrives to take our order and when she returns to the kitchen, I take a deep breath and continue.

"I know about you and Mum, Sara told me. She'd seen your photo albums and put two and two together. Mum comes here so often, we figured you must've been the reason." I pause to collect my thoughts. "I'm really angry at Mum, she abandoned us for long periods of my life, to do what ever she wanted to do, but if she needed to be with the person that she loves, over everyone else, then I understand that now more than most people my age. But at the same time, that doesn't discount the fact that I have massive abandonment issues. We were only little kids." My voice breaks, I feel the hot wave of my emotions flood throughout my body.

I hold in my sobs while we sit with our thoughts for a while. It's difficult to be angry and love someone at the same time.

"You know that your mother loves you very much Allie, but she's such a free spirit, no one can contain her. Not even me." Trudi pauses, then changes the subject, she senses my anxiety.

"Have you thought about what you're going to do when you get back to Australia?"

I take a sip of water to calm myself. I'm glad she's changed the subject. I don't want to discuss my mother at the moment. It's too confusing, processing two very different types of grief all at once is exhausting.

"I was thinking on the plane over here, that I might study textiles. I was remembering when I was little, has Mum mentioned Flo to you?

"Yes, once, or twice. I think she's a little jealous of the time that Flo's spent with you as a child." I ignore the comment about Mum's jealousy and continue with my train of thought.

"Well, Flo used to do cross stitch and she'd give me some fabric to sew and embroider, it seemed to come naturally to me. I've been making my own clothes, cushions, and soft furnishings, that sort of thing, my friends seem to want them as well." That felt good to say out loud. I haven't verbalised my feelings about my hobby to anyone, but it feels right and for a change, I'm excited about my future.

"What about your photography? You're so talented Allie."

"Thanks, but that's a hobby I keep for myself, my sewing is something that I really want to share with people."

Trudi and I spend the next couple of days wandering around Paris, eating and drinking our way through little side street restaurants, shopping on the wide boulevards, meandering through art galleries, taking photos of everything. My camera had been in storage for a long time, but Dad made sure that I had it with me on this trip.

"I think you'll need this Allie Peg." Dad smiled weakly when he handed me my beloved camera at the airport. I retrace my steps from the past and memories of time spent with my friends greet me around many of the city's corners. However, attempts to recapture these moments on my camera are futile. Even though the buildings are the same, it's different somehow, it isn't the same. My people aren't here.

On a day out by myself, I walk alone along the Seine, I stop at a book stall where the vendor, also an artist, is drawing portraits of tourists. While he's occupied with another customer, I scan the antique books, the vintage records, and the postcards, which are strung along the roof line of his little booth. I remember my to do list from all those years ago and a tug of war is staged in my mind. Will I have my picture drawn, or won't I? As the previous model departs with their drawing, I seize my chance to sit on the wooden stool in preparation of this stranger capturing my likeness.

"*Bonjour, mon nom est* Otto."

"*Parlez vous anglais*, I'm Allie. How long have you been drawing here?" I say before listening for his response. I'm nervous.

"Oh, *oui*, of course I speak English. And, I have been working here a long, long time, before you were a twinkle in your mother's eye, no."

"Do you know my mother?" I say, it could be possible. Otto laughs, but doesn't respond, he makes long sweeping strokes with his 6B pencil, occasionally glancing at his work, but mainly maintaining eye contact with me which I find a little unnerving. Though, his face is kind, he seems like a nice man.

"You are very sad, yes?" He says, eventually.

"How could anyone be sad on a day like today, and in Paris. No, I'm not sad." I attempt to brighten my voice while he frowns a little and continues drawing in silence. When he completes his drawing, he turns it around for me to inspect and immediately, I see what he's talking about. There it is, for all to see, my grief. I thought I was hiding it so well. In acknowledgement, I smile weakly at Otto and pay him while he rolls up my drawing, securing it with a wide rubber band. Then he kisses me on both cheeks.

"It will get better, I promise you."

"I hope so, *merci*, for my drawing. *Au revoir*. I walk away with my picture, not sure how I'm feeling, numb perhaps. Besides, I'm not used to people randomly kissing me.

Trudi's flat is tiny, I know that I'll have to leave soon, I probe my host for suggestions as to where I should head next, although I already have an inkling of where I want to go. When we'd talked, face to face, laying on our pillows in the dark of night, Leon told me about the time he'd caught the train to Le Havre, but disembarked at Rouen, the day he was reunited with Mitch and cemented their friendship. I think that I might visit Normandy for myself and jump right back to where life had changed for Leon.

When Trudi arrives home from work that evening, I find the courage to show her my drawing.

"Did Otto do this?"

"Yes, but how did you know that?"

"Oh, I'm familiar with his style. He's worked at the same kiosk since the dawn of time. He has captured your likeness, no?"

"I guess so, but don't you think it makes me look sad."

"Of course you are sad. You have just lost the love of your life and your life has been spun into the unknown. It's okay to be sad you know? Feel it in the depth of your soul. Cry, scream, get angry, buy something inappropriate, eat and drink too much, get a wonky tattoo, but remember to surface, because there are people here who love you very much." I don't have any words to respond to Trudy, but I hug her tight until I'm sure that I won't cry again. I want to do that in private. I take a deep breath and feel a bit better.

"By the way, did Mum know Otto?"

"*Tout le mond connaît Otto.*"

"Of course they do. Look, I think that I'll head off in a few days, do you have any recommendations as to where I might start. I've done Versailles with you, perhaps Bordeaux, or the Alps? I hear Alcace is pretty."

"They're all good options Allie, however I know this sounds strange and not at all popular, but you know my family is from Normandy, I'll be heading there on the weekend to see Isabelle. You're welcome to come with me, if you want to." I laugh to myself. If that isn't a sign, I don't know what is.

"Righto, we're off to Normandy."

The train is full of French nationals and foreign tourists of course, but there are also many chatty Irish people heading for Le Havre to board the ferry to Rosslare.

"Where does your family live Trudi?" I hadn't thought to ask her where we are headed after Rouen, I am happy to go with the flow.

"They live in a small village called Breteuil."

"Oh, I don't know where that is. Is it close to Rouen?"

"About one and a half hours drive away. We'll look around Rouen today and my nephew will collect us tomorrow, my father is too old to drive."

Trudi and I check into our moderately priced hotel, in the centre of the pedestrian quarter, near the cathedral and immediately I want to explore the city. I'm antsy, I want to head straight to the cathedral. I can see the spires from our room as I peruse the tourist information laid out on the coffee table, while I wait for Trudi to change. As we wander down a small lane, before confronting the large church, I can feel my pulse quicken and my heart tighten. A heavy lump forms in my throat, anxiety has grasped my body. And when we arrive in front of the cathedral, its gentle power, together with our shared history, washes over me. Finally the floodgates break.

Trudi wraps her arms around me and offers me a tissue from her handbag as we stand in awkward silence, my grief releasing in heavy sobs. After five minutes of solid crying, I blow my nose again, and sob.

"I just wish you were here with me right now. This is your special place." More tears start to flow and all poor Trudi can do, is to be with me and offer me comfort, which she does very well.

When most of my tears have subsided, I instinctively walk towards the bank of cafes on the other side of the small park. Trudi follows me and we find a table on the terrace, where Leon had sat with Mitch and Tom, all those years ago. We eat a beautiful meal from the *menu de jour* and enjoy a couple of glasses of red wine. My frazzled mind begins to relax and I smile when I think of Mitch bumping into Leon, in this exact spot. It's so like Mitch to appear from nowhere and make a life-long friend. I begin to regale stories of the pair to Trudi, but somehow my retelling of the past doesn't mesh with the present day. My story trails off, I'm drained.

Trudi suggests we find an ice-cream and go for a walk to stretch our legs. We stroll around the beautiful city and spend a great deal of time inspecting the Gros Horloge.

"This mechanism is one of the oldest in France you know." We marvel at the clock's beautiful features, the blue background and the golden sun. "Look, can you see that it shows us the phases of the moon, and the days of the week are at the bottom of the clock?" Trudi points out the time pieces' features to me.

"Oh my goodness, the more I look at it, the more I can see." I am fascinated with the wrought iron clock face, which hangs over a charming archway, beckoning us to inspect the medieval buildings on the other side. I stand under the archway and study the intricate carvings in the stone wall. I could have lingered here for ages, observing all of the nuances and fine details in the archway sculptures, but Trudi pulls me on wards.

"Come on, we have more to see and we're leaving in the morning."

Trudi and I continue to explore the city on foot, stopping in little shops where I purchase a small snow dome of the cathedral, to go with Leon's, and a postcard of the Gros Horloge. We regard the beautiful buildings, promenade along the river front and finally, at the end of the day, we find a bar to rest our hot, weary and puffy feet. Too tired to leave, we eat our dinner in the bistro before retiring to our hotel for an early night. I'm drained emotionally and physically. As we're about to leave the bistro, a local lady approaches us, speaking rapidly in French, she continuously points to my scarf. She strokes my hair as she talks to Trudi, which would normally make me feel very uncomfortable, but I'm not at all. It all seems perfectly natural, like a grandmother stroking a grandchild's hair. Trudi exchanges a few words with the lady before she leaves us.

"*Au revoir.*" Trudi waves.

"What did she say?"

"She was looking at your scarf and said that her great grandmother had a handkerchief with very similar flowers that had been handed down to her from her ancestors. She thought that you look like the women in her family and I told her that was impossible because you are from Australia. But perhaps, you never know do you, anything is possible. Most Anglo-Saxon Australians would have ancestors from Normandy."

"Huh, that's funny and a bit weird. But yes, you're right, Dad's sister had our family tree done and I think it went back as far as William the Conqueror." I hadn't thought much of the family tree that Aunty Diane had been working on years ago, but now I wonder if Dad still has a copy of it. I'm excited to explore more of Normandy and my connection to this land, not just Leon's. Perhaps looking back can help me understand more of who I am today. Then a few more tears trickle down my cheek.

"You know Trudi, Leon has lead me back to my own roots and he's not even here. How weird is that?"

"It's not weird at all, lets get you to bed."

After we eat breakfast, Trudi and I wait for her nephew to collect us in the hotel lobby. I know it's him as soon as he arrives. A tall red haired, French man saunters into the lobby and immediately makes eye contact with his aunty.

"*Tatie.*" He kisses her gently on both cheeks, then his attention turns to me.

"Bertram, this is Allie, Allie, Bertram." Bertram and I consider each other for a brief moment. Do I know him from somewhere, I think to myself? Bertram collects himself as he has a similar realisation.

"Have we met before?" He enquires, shaking his head as he tries to place me from his past. He then plunges towards me and kisses me gently on both cheeks.

"I don't think so." I say, but I can't be sure of anything anymore.

"Right, where's your luggage? We should make a move, we have a big day." Bertram grabs my wheelie bag from my hands and begins trundling the suitcase out of the hotel. We follow Bertram to his car, he heaves the luggage into the boot and we're on our way.

On the way out of town, he drives through a conservation park area and circles Caen.

"Where are we going, I thought you lived in Breteuil?" I'm confused, I'd perused the routes from Rouen to Breteuil in the tourist magazine in the hotel room and this doesn't appear to be the correct way.

"We're taking a bit of a detour. It's a surprise." While he's driving, Bertram asks about life in Australia and we spend most of the journey discussing New World wines, koala habits, and Australian musicians and singers, who are famous in Europe, but I forget to ask Bertram what he does for a living. I've been so overwhelmed by all the new experiences, I'm not thinking straight.

Bertram drives confidently into the small town of Bayeux which is bound by industrial estates, he turns from the main road onto a ring road, then down a series of smaller roads, until he reaches a narrow lane. He parks the car and we walk down a deserted alley. There is no one else around.

"Where are we going?" My nerves are already frazzled, I'm nervous. I look at Trudi who is trying to suppress anxious giggles.

"You're so impatient. Let's enjoy this little walk and I will show you something special." Trudi pats me on the shoulder to calm me.

We arrive at a stone building covered with a slate roof and access through a large set of arched crimson doors. Bertram leads us through the doors, through a courtyard, and into a museum foyer where Bertram addresses the staff by name, we wander through to a tunnel like room. A shiver runs over the top of my head and I instinctively know something is imminent. As I enter the room, my heart races and I struggle to breathe.

Encased in glass, the nearly seventy metre long embroidery illustrating the Battle of Hastings stretches along the wall of the curved room. Bertram gently guides me to the first position of the embroidery, Trudi follows us. Overwhelmed with the whole experience, I strain to see the finer details and try to understand the story from the embroidered depictions, but I can't see anything through my tears. My heart is going to burst, great heaving sobs flow from my soul. Trudi and Bertram stand sentinel, just like a thousand years ago, Bertram gently pats the middle of my back.

When my tears have subsided a little, I sense another presence behind me.

"Hello Allie." Mum tightly embraces me.

"Hello Mum." My anger towards my mother diminishes a little for now, we'll both have to work hard to mend many years of absences, my tears flow again.

"Surprise!" Trudi beams. "I hope it's a good surprise?" She tries to decipher my tears.

"When you said you wanted to work in textiles, I thought of Bertram straight away and he suggested that we come here, to see the tapestry. What do you think?" Trudi holds my hand as mum hugs my other side. I can't speak, I shrug and cry some more. How can I explain my connection to this tapestry, when I can't explain it to myself.

During our embrace, a small and delicate spider inches its way towards the top of the protective glass which surrounds the tapestry, it rests by a fallen knight. The spider catches my attention and draws me in. Breaking away from my mother's embrace, I inspect the spider's knight lying in a sea of blood. It's Leon. It's Leo. A thousand years wash over me in an instant. Then the spider returns to her web at the top of the tapestry case and waits patiently for her next adventure into the unknown.

"See how our threads span lifetimes Allie." Bertram says to me.

Amanda is a wanderer, a traveller and an observer. Her love of discovery of all things new, has led her to travel the world and to find deeper meaning in cultures similar, yet different from her own. In recent years she has followed in the footsteps of pilgrims of the Camino de Santiago de Compostela, in Spain and Portugal, four different ways, once solo. She draws inspiration from her experiences of travel and working abroad in a variety of different roles from administration, guiding, retail, volunteering and a life changing work experience placement in Kakadu National Park. Her sense of discovery, led her to learn more formally at Flinders University in Adelaide with Honours in Ecotourism and a Post graduate degree in Education. With these qualifications in hand she taught science and tourism. When teaching gave way to a slower pace of life, she combined her love of reading, research and writing.

www.ingramcontent.com/pod-product-compliance
Lightning Source LLC
Chambersburg PA
CBHW070203120726
47909CB00001B/225